Sophie had never been short of attention but the thought of falling in love with any of the local swains hadn't ever entered her head. She had never doubted that one day when she was ready her prince would come. And Lydia? Her thoughts were her own, her dreams were her own but she had no power to control them. The 'sisters' had never had secrets from each other, but now neither of them wanted to discuss Christian.

Even though jealousy wasn't part of Lydia's nature, she was constantly aware of just how pretty Sophie was, how young, how full of fun—everything that she could never be; time and again she reminded herself that Sophie was a darling, the same now as always.

On the surface she treated Christian as she might a brother. There was no doubt that he liked her, never had she felt so relaxed with anyone outside the family. But how would he feel if he could know the desires he had awakened in her, desires that thrilled her, frightened her, overwhelmed her?

A FAMILY DIVIDED

Connie Monk

First published in Great Britain 2005 by Judy Piatkus (Publishers) Ltd. Paperback edition 2006 by Harlequin Mills & Boon Limited, Eton House, 18-24 Paradise Road, Richmond, Surrey TW9 1SR

A FAMILY DIVIDED © Connie Monk 2005

ISBN 0 263 85103 6

169-0906

Printed and bound in Spain by Litografia Rosés S.A., Barcelona

A FAMILY
DIVIDED

CHAPTER ONE

1923

For the villagers of Kingshampton, the third Saturday afternoon in July was like no other in the year. Come rain or shine, everyone was intent on wringing every ounce of pleasure out of the few hours of the fête. Early in the week, two housewives waiting to be served in the butcher's shop had needed no interpreter to make sense of their brief exchange. 'Let's hope this sunshine lasts for us,' from one, and from the other: 'We'll be lucky this year. My bit of seaweed outside the back door is dry as a bone.'

And she was proved right. Under a clear sky, by three o'clock on the Saturday afternoon the large lawn of Shelton Manor was thronged with people. Sir Herbert Dinsdale, who annually allowed his garden to be used, had formally declared the fund-raising event open and was already setting a good example by spending at each stall.

On the stone-flagged terrace in front of the house, tables and chairs were set out in readiness for the strawberry tea and it was here that already Archibald and Adelaide Westlake were sitting, enjoying their vantage point. Not that they'd be afraid to spend; when they'd had their tea they would dig as deep into their pockets as anyone.

'Ask me what's best about this village, Addy, and I reckon I'd say it was out fête day.' Archibald viewed the scene, his expression spelling contentment in all he saw. Not that there was anything unusual in *that*, for Archibald was seldom less than content.

His wife looked at him with tolerant affection. 'None of it happens all by itself,' she reminded him. 'Think of the hours those roped in to help spend, begging around for prizes for the hoop-la and for that thing they call a tombola; persuading Ernie Waldeck to let them take the strawberries from his fields without paying—how they do it I can't think, so tight he squeaks, is Ernie; George Bryant from the farm, now he's a different matter, he gives the cream willingly and glad to do it; then between them they make all the scones and little fancies. Easy for us, all we have to do is come along and enjoy it all. Plenty of work for the lady helpers.' She said it with pride, for one of those ladies was their own daughter Lydia.

'Ah, she's a good lass, our Lyddy.' He followed her meaning.

Despite the mass of people milling around on the large lawn, stopping to view or to purchase at the fancywork stall, queuing to buy their children the ice-cream cones being served in the shade of the tall elm, or spending their pence trying their luck on the various games, there was an atmosphere of peace about the afternoon. Perhaps it had to do with the smell of the newly mown grass, the tinkle of crockery as the cups were set out on the trestle table for teas or with the fact that on the afternoon of the annual fête, superficially at any rate, the village knew no social barriers; from the squire to the most humble villager everyone joined in the fun as they raised money to pay for a day out for the children from Oaklands, the gaunt-looking home for orphaned girls situated in Brackleford some five miles away.

'Year on year, nothing changes here, even during the war no one thought of letting this slip. Well, I should think not! Some of those poor little 'uns wouldn't have been put in the home but for that dreadful carnage. How long is it we've been coming? Long before Sir Herbert inherited the place.' Archibald doffed his Panama to the local schoolmarm as he spoke. 'No, looking around us we might be back twenty years and more except that our gals ain't children any longer. But for that, we'd not be able to put a date to it.'

That he bracketed the two girls together in the description 'our gals' hardly registered with Adelaide. The fact that Lydia was their own daughter and Sophie his orphaned niece had made no difference; they'd been brought up as sisters, the daughters of the house. In fact, sometimes—although Adelaide was loath to admit it, even to herself—she believed he made more fuss of Sophie. She had understood it in the early days, for he had adored his young brother Vincent and it had been as if all that love had been given to the toddler he'd left behind to be cared for. And no one could have helped loving her, she'd been such a jolly, happy, affectionate, pretty child. Even so, Adelaide thought now as she mulled over what he'd just said, it was more than time the girl grew up and learned to take responsibility for something apart from enjoying herself.

'That's just it, Arch, they're neither of them children. It

really is time Sophie realised it and tried to follow Lyddy's example.'

'No harm in the gal, Addy my love. Just look at her, eh? Like bees round the honey pot, the young fellas are.' There was no doubting his pride in the lovely girl. What harm was she doing anyone if she egged the lads on a bit? Life was just a game to her. Time enough to shoulder responsibilities when she had to, but for the present it was more than enough to see her enjoying herself. 'Can't begrudge any of them their ha'-porth of fun.'

'She's twenty-one years old; I was expecting Lyddy when I was her age.' She wished she hadn't said it, it was a reminder that of the two girls Lyddy was seven years the elder, a reminder that she'd reached twenty-eight with no sign of a suitor.

Archie was sensitive to the way his wife's mind was turning, and quick to restore the delight in the afternoon that might easily have been lost.

'That you were, Addy m'dear. But then, look who it was who'd bowled you over,' he chuckled, reaching for her hand across the table. 'Let time take its course, my dear. The lasses are as they are, and when the good Lord sees fit he'll point the way to their futures.' By no means a religious man in the accepted sense, Archie saw no point in worrying about things that couldn't be altered. 'Just let's be grateful that we're all of us here together, the sun's shining and—ah yes, here comes our Lyddy with that great teapot. Same old pot, year on year. Look at her, Addy, pleased as Punch she is, to be doing her bit.' This time his pride was for Lydia. Adelaide's misgivings melted.

Affection and admiration mingled in her expression as

her gaze rested on her daughter. How many young women of her age would concern themselves with anything more than making sure they enjoyed the event? Lydia was a truly *good* girl, she always had been. Never a moment's trouble. Now that other flighty one… But the fête day was no time to waste on comparisons and even the word 'flighty' wasn't without the accompaniment of an indulgent smile.

'Like I say, Addy, it'd take more than time to change any of this. I wouldn't mind holding the hands of the clock still for all that, just keep things as they are.' Not a romantically inclined man, it was seldom he put his innermost feelings into words. 'What would you say to that, eh?' Then, without waiting for his wife's answer, 'But doesn't it do your eyes good just to watch them? See, young Sophie,' he chuckled indulgently, 'fancy a slip of a girl like that thinking she'll get a better score on the dart board than those fellows who spend their evenings swilling ale at the Dew Drop Inn.' He watched proudly as his young niece hurled a dart in the direction of the board.

Adelaide wished he hadn't said it, somehow it cast a shadow on what had gone before about holding time still.

'The trouble is, Archie, you've always spoiled that girl.' She heard the sharp note in her voice but she couldn't help herself. 'Of course you tried to make up to her for what she lost, of course we all tried, even though we knew she was too young to remember. Think how Lydia accepted her as a little sister, never a scrap of jealousy. She has you eating out of her hand, she's always known she could twist you around her little finger. It's not good for her.'

'What nonsense the woman talks,' Archibald laughed at his wife's words and her carping tone alike. 'Spoiled her, you say.

If a thing is spoiled, then it's marred. But not Sophie. Nothing wrong with the lassie.'

'I didn't say there was. You know that's not what I meant. But the truth is that even if there were, you'd not see it. Pretty as a picture, it's no wonder every young swain in the county has an eye to her. She's a dear girl and I'm not saying it's she who makes the running, but you can't tell me she doesn't like being the centre of attention. Plays up to their every move. I've tried to bring her up just the same as I did Lyddy, but would you ever see Lyddy behaving the way she does? Look at them jostling round her, one, two, three, and now the rector's son joining them, all cheering her on.'

'And why not, my dear? Where's the harm? They're just lads, of course they have an eye for a pretty piece like she is. All right, our young Sophie is a show-off, that I'll admit. But it's the sort of showing-off of a child, not a scheming thought in her pretty head.'

Adelaide turned her gaze from the excitement in front of the dart board to the trestle table where tea would be served. The difference in the two young women couldn't have been greater: the one exposing altogether too much leg for decorum, set on following this silly new mode as if she were one of those flapper girls as they were called in fashionable high society; high society indeed, this was Kingshampton, a Berkshire backwater. Then there was Lyddy, dear Lyddy. Such good upright deportment, Adelaide's maternal pride boasted silently. In her heart she probably knew that Lydia's straight bearing was emphasised by her figure, tall, as flat as the newly purchased ironing board Ethel Mullens, their living-in helper, was so proud of. No one looking at Lyddy would suspect the other thing Adelaide tried not to see: the shyness and lack of confidence hidden beneath the efficient front.

'Just because Lydia knows the meaning of service and likes to help, just because she acts with proper decorum, none of those young men will give her a second glance. No, not even Reverend Hatcher's son—and wouldn't you expect him to have been brought up to know gold from dross?'

Archibald let the insinuation pass. He was more sensitive than she gave him credit. Reaching across the bamboo table, he took her long capable hand into his own. My word, the thought sprang into his mind, you can feel the strength in her just by the touch. Now me…time was when these soft, flabby hands of mine had the strength of an ox, but look what idleness has done to me. Not good for a fit man to sit on his backside behind a desk; muscle turns to fat. The only exercise I get these days is going around picking up my rents, and more often than not even that's something Lyddy does for me. Even my waistcoat is bursting at the seams, damned if it isn't. But Adelaide, she goes from strength to strength. It's because of Lyddy, that's what makes her sound so edgy. Why, the lassie's knocking twenty-nine and never a sign of a suitor to reach her down from the shelf. Pity, for, like Addie says, she's a *good* girl, she'd make a splendid partner for a chap. Ah, but little Sophie, she could have any she wanted at the snap of her fingers; and the little monkey knows it, bless her. Time will bring the right one to partner our Lyddy, best we can do is not look for worries. The danger with being content, content like me and Addy, is it's too easy to take our blessings for granted and forget to be grateful. It's when you take your eyes off being grateful, just relax a mite and start to get used to things, then your happiness gets snatched. Me and Addy, we've had more than thirty good years—and plenty more to come if Him upstairs lets us. Archibald's mind jumped back twenty-one years, as clearly as if it had been yesterday in his mind's eye—or was it his mind's ear—he could hear Vincent's sobs, the news he'd brought almost impossible to understand. His beloved Trudie had died giving birth to a baby girl. Who would have thought then that in less than two years he would have followed her, killed in a rock-climbing accident?

'I don't believe you heard a word I said,' Adelaide's voice cut through his reverie.

'I'm sorry, my love.' He turned his good-humoured face to her with a smile, taking off his Panama hat and using it as a fan. 'What a scorcher, eh? No, the truth is I was back down the years. Silly thing to do on a day like this. But Addy, we ain't done so bad, what do you say?'

'I say you've worked hard and got your just desserts, Arch. Plenty of folk would like to be as content as us. Let's go and collect our tray of tea before the crush, let Lyddy pour it for us while it's nice and fresh.'

'I'll go, my dear, you stay here in the shade. My, but it's a scorcher,' he said again, blowing out his cheeks as if to emphasise the words. 'Wouldn't mind being a kid again with a cornet to lick.'

'A cup of tea will cool you down.'

Adelaide watched him make his way to the refreshment stall. A fine-built man, she thought with satisfaction. Even if his hair was getting a bit thin and his waistline not what it was, he was still a stalwart figure. She noticed he took out his wallet. Tea and two plates of strawberries with thick cream wouldn't come to more than a shilling and tuppence even taking into account that things were over-priced in the need to boost the fund, but she knew he wouldn't take any change from the ten-shilling note he passed to Lyddy. His words echoed in her mind, 'We ain't done so bad, eh?' This afternoon she tried not to let his grammatical lapse irritate her. Archie was the same dear man who had first learned to lay his bricks, unchanged by ambition and the rewards of hard work; his nature had a core of gold which hadn't altered as his bank balance had grown and they'd moved into a larger house and engaged Ethel, a living-in maid. No, she thought, you're right, Arch, indeed 'we ain't done so bad'. Then she turned her gaze back to Lydia, watching with maternal affection as her daughter wielded the heavy teapot, greet-ing each customer with a polite—but, it must be said, a reserved—smile. It just wasn't fair the way no young man ever gave her a second glance. She was always well turned out; just look at her this afternoon with her new straw toque bedecked with silk roses. She never slouched, stood straight as a ramrod, excellent deportment. She was tall—on the thin side, that had to be said, but wasn't that better at her age than being too well-rounded? Anyone meeting her might be forgiven for seeing her as efficient and confident. Efficient, yes. But confident? Adelaide wouldn't let herself admit to seeing behind the façade.

Excitement round the dart board took her attention back to Sophie who, more from luck than skill, must have acquit-ted herself well. Now, who was that she was talking to as she turned away from her retinue of admirers? A well set-up young man wearing a navy blue, green and white striped blazer, his fashionable boater hat set at a rakish angle. Very up to the minute, Adelaide decided, and unless she was much mistaken not someone from around these parts. Now just look at young Sophie, there she was chattering to him as though she'd known him for years, or at least as though she had had a formal introduction, which seemed most unlikely. Not such a boy as the rest of the circle of local admirers: there was something in his bearing the others still lacked.

'Here we are, m'dear. Lyddy found me a nice big tray. Strawberries smell a treat, you get the waft of them right across the grass. Now, while I think of it, let me tell you: she said not to expect her home for supper this evening.' His words were met with a look of immediate interest. 'She wants to stay and help with the clearing-up after they've got rid of all us riff-raff, pick up the bits and get the garden back to rights. Then she's been asked to join those going into the manor. It seems the organising committee always get the use of the breakfast room so that they can get their money counted and bagged—that and hold a post-mortem on the afternoon, I dare say. She whispered that she'd been told to expect a bite of food would be sent through to them from the house. Pleased as Punch, she is.'

'All the work she does for the cause, it's quite time they showed their appreciation,' came the tart reply, followed almost in the same breath with, 'But Arch, this might be the start of her getting dragged out of her shell.'

'There you go again,' he chuckled. 'There's plenty a girl like our Lyddy can do with her life apart from waiting on some man hand, foot and finger.'

'Of course there is. Hand, foot and finger, indeed—is that

what you expect of me?' There was even something bordering on the flirtatious in her glance and he didn't let her down.

'You and me, ah, we get along fine. Plenty we share and enjoy, daytime, ah that and night-time too—'

'Hush, Archie, not here with all these people about.' She looked at the empty tables as if they had ears.

'Be a rum thing if we didn't share the pleasure we find in each other. Bet those girls of ours would expect all that sort of thing to be over for us, eh? Kids…they don't know the half of it.'

'Drink your tea, Arch, here comes the man who does the milk round for Farmer Bryant, whatever would he think if he could hear you?'

Archibald's round face beamed with merriment. 'Lucky old bugger, that's what he'd think,' and he gave her a broad wink that added to her confusion.

'Ssshhh, watch your language.' Then, turning to Eddie Thorne, who only at the fête had she ever seen in anything but his old work suit and tweed cap and with a yoke across his shoulders bearing two pails of milk, 'Good afternoon, how lucky we are to have such a glorious day,' she said with a cordial smile supposed to emphasise that on this special day social barriers were discounted.

Archibald doffed his Panama to Mrs Thorne, lapping up the atmosphere of fraternity.

As if to prove Adelaide's view that Sophie was a hoodlum—a dear hoodlum—the girl had left her retinue of admirers and was approaching them at a speed quite inappropriate for a young lady.

'Mums, I've invited someone to eat with us this evening. That is all right, isn't it? I knew you wouldn't mind. And I couldn't say to him, "Wait there, I'll have to go and see," before I asked him, could I?'

Archibald chuckled.

'Which one is it to be, then? Bertie Howarth? I see he's hanging around again.'

'Bertie Howarth nothing! It's really so that he can meet *you* that I want him to come, Pops. His name is Christian Mellor, he's an architect. He has some plans he wants to show you.'

Archibald frowned.

'I'll look at his work, be glad to look at it,' Archibald told her. 'This evening I'll make an appointment so that we can meet in the office.'

'Home is home, and work is work.' Adelaide nodded her approval.

'He's awfully keen, Pops, I said you'd give him some time this evening. You could shut yourselves away in your study.' Then, sensing rather than seeing his weakening of resolve and Adelaide's strengthening of irritation, '*Please*, Pops. I shall look so stupid if I have to go back to him and say that he mustn't bring his work. Anyway,' she pulled what she considered the ace from the pack, 'don't you see, if you won't talk work at home he'll get the idea I'm setting my cap at him and that's why I've asked him for the meal.'

'The gal's right,' Archibald chuckled, addressing himself to his less than certain wife. 'Don't want the young hopeful running away with any ideas, do we, m'dear. Work and pleasure don't mix, that's always been my rule. But just this once. What do you say, Addy?'

'Better than giving him the impression you are throwing

yourself at him, I suppose. How did you meet him? Who introduced you?' As if she didn't know the answer!

'Oh, we didn't need an introduction. He's very friendly, you'll like him.'

Adelaide shook her head helplessly. What was the use of arguing? Try as she might she seemed to have instilled no sense of refined behaviour in the girl. Just imagine Lyddy asking a complete stranger to the house!

'Personally,' she answered Sophie, meaning to 'take her down a peg', 'I shouldn't for a moment think he would harbour the idea that you had an ulterior motive. If he's the one I saw you walk away from the others with, then I'd say he's too old to see you in that light, dear. Yes, of course ask him to share the meal, but remember it can't be at our usual hour—six o'clock is so much better for the digestion—but today has to be different. Ethel is here enjoying the afternoon like the rest of us, she can't have a meal ready for us before eight at the earliest. Tell him about a quarter to. That'll give you a chance to size him up, Arch.'

'It's his drawings I have to size up, my dear. But you're right, if I consider a man a bounder, I don't want to do business with him.'

'He's no bounder, Pops. You'll like him, both of you will. Older than me, you say? Yes, I suppose he must be or he couldn't be an architect. He's over there with Lyddy getting my strawberries, we're going to eat our tea on the grass under the trees. Are you having fun, Mums? There are lots of things to try your luck on.'

Despite all her misgivings, Addy looked on her with affection. Twenty-one she may be, but she neither looked nor acted like it.

Archibald dug in his pocket and pulled out some coins.

'Here, open up your purse,' he told her, to be rewarded by a kiss planted on his sunburnt forehead.

Standing behind the long trestle table, Lyddy poured tea for the handsome stranger, wanting to feast her eyes on him but determined to keep her gaze firmly on what she was doing. Who was he? She'd noticed him with Sophie, but he'd appeared not to be the guest of any of the familiar locals.

'Would you like scones? Or strawberries and cream?' Her voice was calm and grave.

'I'd like both,' he answered, smiling. What a prim young woman! 'Is that permitted?'

'But of course,' came the unruffled reply. 'I'll find you a larger tray. Is that two of everything? For Sophie too?' More than anything Lydia wanted to recall the words that betrayed that she'd been watching them together.

'You know her?'

'She's my sister.' Just that, as if being sisters explained her curiosity.

'Really? Yes, for us both.'

That 'Really?', as if he couldn't believe two people so un-alike could be connected, only added to Lydia's discomfort. She piled the plates on to her tray and held out her hand for the money, dropping it into a china 'money' bowl and turning to the next customer, his sign of dismissal.

'Times are changing too fast,' Adelaide said critically as she watched Sophie and Christian Mellor settle themselves on the grass in the shade. 'Girls are losing their femininity.'

'Times have always been changing too fast for the previous generation, m'dear. And you'll never push the gals back into the place their mothers occupied. The war put paid to all that.'

'But look at her, Arch! Why can't she sit properly at the table the same as everyone else?' He looked and saw nothing to complain about in the childlike position, ankles crossed, knees wide apart, back straight, as supple as though she were made of India rubber.

'Sniff hard,' Sophie said to her companion, her chin raised as if that way she could inhale more of that special summer fête day aroma. 'It's a mix of so many things that you can't be sure just what it is. Warm earth, newly cut grass, fir cones, flowers.' She took a great gulp of the pungent air. 'You know what, Christian?' Not answering, he watched her. There was no shyness in her, he had known that from the first moment he'd set eyes on her as she'd lapped up the admiration of the local hopefuls. 'You know what?' she repeated.

'If I don't, I soon shall,' he laughed.

'All this, shut your eyes and listen, a hum of voices, somewhere there's a bee too, the tinkling sound of crockery, strawberries and cream, and the smell, doesn't it make you understand why it is that an alcoholic can't stop drinking?'

'I can't say it does. Tell me.' There was a teasing note in his voice, but she didn't notice.

'If one could get drunk on all this, then I'd have no control, I'd just go on soaking it all up until I was—what is it they say?—legless.'

And that, he thought, would be a pity! While most of the young women at the fête wore skirts no more than six inches above their ankles, he recognised that Sophie was a girl of her time—in a country district like this, even forging ahead of her time. The hem of the pleated skirt of her yellow silk dress was scarcely below her knees, the waisline was low. Any suggestion of immodesty was dispelled by the effect of the puratanical large white Peter Pan collar. The outfit was delightful, bright and uncluttered, so different from most of the village girls, who, in Christian's opinion, were either dressed in their Sunday church clothes or bedecked with every bauble in sight. No wonder he looked at Sophie with such open admiration, even though all he could see protruding from the skirt she'd pulled over her knees was her ankles, slim, enticing. Legless, did she say? Yes, that would be a pity.

'It's good of Mr Westlake to agree to see my drawings this evening. The best I'd hoped for was an appointment for some later time.'

'After the excitement of the fête it will be nice to have some company.'

'The young lady serving tea tells me you and she are sisters.'

'That's Lyddy. You'll like her, she's,' she looked at him solemnly as she groped for the right words, 'she's—real gold. Does that sound affected? I don't mean it to, it's just the best I could think of. She's older than me, more like your age, I expect.'

Christian leaned back against the trunk of the elm and watched her. Never had he seen a more expressive face. Was she beautiful? Feature by feature, perhaps not: her eyebrows and lashes were darker than her golden brown hair, a purist would have considered her retroussé nose barred a claim to beauty, her mouth so ready to smile yet in repose the full bottom lip might even be seen as a pout. Did she know it was crying out to be kissed? Somehow he thought she probably did, despite her innocent chatter. She interested him, she would have interested him even if he hadn't heard of her as the gateway to Archibald Westlake and the rumoured development on the lower field of Highland Farm.

That evening he arrived promptly at a quarter to eight, his blazer and flannels replaced by a sober dark suit and striped silk tie, earning him a favourable point from Adelaide.

'I must be honest, sir,' he told Archibald. 'I'm not from around here, but I've been visiting friends in Brackleford. You may know the family, my friend's father is a councillor by the name of Enfield.'

'Housing committee man. Aye, lad, our paths have crossed. Fair-minded enough, but it irks me how some of these fellows who earn their livings in quite different fields can give the yea or nay to our work. So what did Councillor Enfield have to say about Westlakes?'

'Perhaps I shouldn't repeat it, after all he spoke to me as a friend. Is council business confidential?'

'I dare say it is until it's made public. He told you that I have had plans approved to build thirty houses on the lower field at Highland Farm. Is that it? Well, nothing confidential about that, it's all been published in the *Brackleford News*.'

'Yes, he told me you'd had outline approval. So you've not yet submitted detailed plans of what you intend to put up?'

'Ah,' Archibald nodded, openly sizing up the young man. 'That's not saying I haven't been talking to local architects, not saying I haven't and not saying I have either. So he told you how to corner me, is that it?'

'No, sir, talking to him just gave me the idea. I went to have a look at the field, then I called at the Dew Drop Inn.' Christian held Archibald's gaze. Adelaide thought his smile quite beguiling; what a personable young man he was. If only Lyddy hadn't been out to supper! Archibald was not a man to be easily swayed by charm, but he liked this young fellow's direct approach. 'If you want to learn local gossip the pub is the place for it. All the talk was about the summer fête, clearly an annual event not to be missed. I put out my feelers and I was rewarded.' Exactly what feelers he'd used he didn't elaborate as he turned to Sophie with a broad smile. 'I was led to believe that the prettiest girl there would be Sophie Westlake.'

Sophie laughed, enjoying the compliment despite the inference that Christian had attached himself to her for the furtherance of his own ends. Still, she preferred not to dwell on that. Pops wasn't stupid: if the drawings weren't suitable that would be the end of it, and if they were she was proud of her part in getting Christian the commission. In her usual fashion, she was prepared to find all the pleasure she could from the situation.

'Knock back that sherry, lad, and we'll clutter off to the study and have a look at what you've brought to show me. Now what I have in mind—always supposing your councillor friend and his lot feel disposed to be agreeable—is ten detached four-bedroomed properties with gardens big enough to be worth having, room for a game of tennis or croquet, you know the sort of thing; ten three-bedroomed semis, and I mean them to have space enough for the folk to grow their veg if they feel inclined or make a good garden; and then for the not so well-offs, the youngsters just starting out and wanting a place to call their own—not that all of them have the sort of wage whether to rent or buy, more's the pity, but for those who can, ten smaller properties in a terrace and sited down near the road. Prices to suit every pocket, or nearer the mark, every pocket with something in it. The four-bedroomed would have pride of place at the top of the slope so they'd get a pleasant view across the fields to the back. Let's go and have a look at what you've brought me, then. This way, across the hall.'

'A very personable young man,' Adelaide said approvingly as the study door closed. Sophie detected a trace of regret in her tone.

'If he's any good, Mums, he'll be around for some time.' Then, laughing, 'And if he's not any good, then that makes him less personable.'

'Mustn't let yourself be carried away by his good looks, dear.'

'Me? I was just his ticket to get in to see Pops. He's nice though, isn't he? He must be about Lyddy's age, wouldn't you think?'

For a moment Adelaide looked at her earnestly, weighing her words, wondering whether the girl was mature enough to talk woman to woman.

'I wish she was here for supper. No, that's not true. When I heard that they'd taken her into their magic circle and she was staying on with the organisers, you don't know how pleased I was. She has no chance of meeting *anyone*, anyone suitable, I mean.'

'To be good enough for Lyddy he's got to be really super. Just look at most of them we ever see in the village, certainly no Douglas Fairbanks amongst them.'

'Silly child, looks are only skin deep.'

'I know they are, but we don't want Lyddy to fall in love with an unappetising-looking saint do we!' She poured them each a second glass of sherry, making the most of this being no ordinary evening. Normally the family sat down to their meal at about six o'clock when Archibald and Lyddy came home from the office in the builder's yard, a meal such as many a household might refer to as high tea but to the Westlakes was simply 'the meal'. This evening, having been to the fête and, more particularly being joined by a visitor, a bottle of good sherry had been decanted and both Sophie and Adelaide had helped prepare something more than the makeshift meal that had been intended. Sophie had shelled peas, Adelaide had taken charge of finding something for a first course (another rare treat and one that had taxed her ingenuity as she'd hunted in the larder for inspiration). The end result was hard-boiled eggs on a bed of lettuce served with tinned salmon beaten into mayonnaise and piped round each half egg. Not exciting, but it was the best she could conjure up, and setting the tray on the sideboard in readiness she felt rather pleased with her efforts. It wasn't fair to expect Ethel to come home to prepare a special meal, not on fête day. That's why a chicken had been cooked in advance and the new potatoes scraped before they'd set out for Shelton Manor.

'I wish you'd invited him tomorrow instead, Sophie. This really isn't good enough for visitors.'

'Poppycock! Anyway, when I took the peas to the kitchen Ethel was bustling about like anything, almost as excited as we are at having an unexpected guest. And I bet I know why: because she'd seen me with Christian at the fête and fallen for his good looks just like everyone probably does. Now, if he'd been an unappetising saint we should have been served up cold chicken and cheese and biscuits to follow. As it is, the chicken is going back in the oven for an extra blast and a rhubarb tart was already well under way.'

Keeping business and home separate, Archibald said nothing about his impression of Christian's drawings when they emerged from the study, but there was an air of satisfaction about them that was a good omen for the meal set before them. The conversation flowed easily. Sophie was as natural with a stranger as with someone she'd known all her life; Adelaide was more than impressed with their visitor and pleased that, from the look of things, they could expect to see much more of him; Archibald beamed his pleasure on one and all. Only Lydia was missing. But Adelaide consoled herself that if, as looked more certain by the minute, Christian Mellor was to have business dealings with Archibald, perhaps it was as well that Lyddy's contacts with him would be in the environment of the works office where she was a self-appointed and most useful helper. At home she might have been gauche (even thinking it gave her mother a nudge of guilt), but there in the office she would be at her best.

Christian was being seen out as Lydia arrived home. The events of the evening were filling her mind, and she greeted him with a friendly handshake, keen for him to be gone so that she could tell the family about her evening. She had been given a place on the committee, and more than that, she had been made Treasurer; the other members had watched as she signed the necessary form authorising her signature at the bank. As the door closed on the visitor, she poured out the news.

'They couldn't have entrusted it to better hands, my dear,' Archibald congratulated her, while, with a rare outward show of pride, Adelaide kissed her.

'That's wonderful, Lyddy,' Sophie joined the chorus. 'Tell you what you ought to do, you ought to arrange an event here in the garden.'

Lydia laughed. 'The village wouldn't want two fêtes even if we had a big enough lawn.'

'Of course not,' Sophie agreed. 'But you could organise a cream tea or something, maybe those little Girl Guides of yours might sing or dance or do whatever they're good at. I'd help.' Whether or not she was sensitive to other people's feelings had never crossed her mind, but she was aware that something in her suggestion had taken that look of pride off Lydia's face. 'I don't mean I'd help on the day,' she added, 'but I could go round the area putting up notices. Anyway, that's not important, Lyddy, you could probably make quite a bit for your orphans.' Clearly that was the angle that might tip the scales, and while Lydia was turning the idea over in her mind Sophie's imagination had jumped ahead, envisaging a sunny day, their garden as full of people enjoying themselves as Sir Herbert's had been a few hours ago. 'And wouldn't it be fun!'

'I wish I'd thought of it,' Lydia said, 'this evening I mean, so that we could have started planning.'

'Better and better,' came the quick response from the originator of the idea. 'You could send a note to each of them inviting them here to discuss your plan. Don't you think that's a good idea, Mums? We'd keep out of the way, wouldn't we?'

There might be times when Adelaide found it hard not to resent Sophie's easy ride through life, but moments like this made them as nothing. That fund-raising committee would soon see their error in not including Lyddy long ago! Her glance met Archibald's, both of them well satisfied with the evening. His words came back to her, 'We ain't done so bad.' Oh no, they certainly hadn't. Things were good, the future bright with hope.

Another hour and Kingshampton's special day drew to a close.

'I reckon young Mellor has his eye on our little Sophie,' Archibald chuckled as he climbed into bed.

'Like the rest of them. And she soaks up flattery like a sponge. What did you make of his drawings, did you like them?'

'Ah, that I did. Good-looking elevations. He's put a lot of new thinking into the layout.' But he said no more. Home was home, work was work. Only with Lydia did he discuss the plans in any detail. Except concerning the business, he wasn't a deeply thinking man. He accepted people as he found them and, as far as the family went, he loved them all just as they were. But nudging at the back of his mind was that worry that Adelaide so often hinted at: Lydia needed a boost to her confidence. Funny, really, when you considered that she could take eighteen giggling and excited Girl Guides away to camp and never turn a hair, yet send her into a room full of strangers and she would be miserable as sin. That was why he liked to encourage her interest in the business. Easy enough to pay a girl to come and type his few letters and sort up the men's time-sheets, but it was good for Lyddy to feel he depended on her. And tell the truth, he enjoyed having her there, and her grasp of the business often surprised him. Then his thoughts jumped away from his dear, solemn daughter and alighted on that other image— Sophie. Not realising it, his mouth softened.

In a fortnight's time Lydia, or Captain, as her troop of Girl Guides respectfully called her, was taking her party of eighteen to the New Forest for their annual camp. Time after time she had tried to persuade Sophie to join, but the answer had always been the same. Group activities weren't for her even though of the two it was Lydia who found mixing difficult; perhaps children gave her the confidence she lacked.

'Now that Sophie's old enough she ought to start going to Guides,' Adelaide had said the day after Sophie's eleventh birthday. 'She'd soon get to enjoy it.'

But Archibald had known better. 'Can't push the lassie. If you'd known Vincent as a child you would see, she's inherited that streak in him that—oh, jiggered if I know what the devil he got out of it, but he was happiest when he was all alone pitting himself against some challenge that, to be honest, I could see no point in trying.'

'And if he hadn't he might still be with us. Where is the child today?' Only the previous day Sophie had been given a new bicycle for her birthday. 'Off by herself, if you please, with a pile of sandwiches and not a clue where it was she was heading.'

Archibald had laughed. 'I dare say she had some secret mission, Sophie never drifts with no direction. Give her her head, m'dear, she's wise enough to come to no harm.' This was *Vincent'*s daughter, loving, headstrong, courageous, full of fun, a constant reminder of her father. In the evening, Sophie had arrived home tired but triumphant, full of apologies that she was late for 'the meal'.

'It took longer to get home than I thought.' Contrite or not, she couldn't keep the beaming pride from her face. 'Guess where I've been? Well, you won't be able to, you'll *never* guess, so I'll tell you. I cycled all the way to Windsor.' As she'd eaten her solitary meal she'd talked incessantly of her adventure: she'd been into St George's Chapel, she'd watched the Guards, she'd eaten her sandwiches in the Great Park.

That had been her first long cycle ride—no wonder her legs had felt like jelly when she'd put her new bicycle away in the shed—but the day had been more than that. It had set her on a course that, better than any of them, Vincent would have understood. Always everyone's friend, yet solitude was important to her. When she persuaded Archie to buy her a canoe, she kept it in a boat house on the Loddon, which meant a four-mile ride to get to it but, once there, the boat and the river were the only companions she needed. Paddling with determination, her adrenalin would race as fast as any explorer's. On summer days she'd tie the boat while she swam. At other times she would travel the country lanes on her bicycle, always by herself with no one to tell her where to go or what to do. Yet although she'd never needed close friends, she'd been popular at school, where she'd worked as hard as she'd played; perhaps because of her unfailing enjoyment in all she did, it had been accepted without resentment that she'd been something of a show-off in physical training drill, invariably the fastest runner on the annual sports day and had suffered no stage fright in the annual drama production. All this had made her something of a heroine, something she appeared not to notice. Orphaned at less than two years old, yet she'd lacked nothing, she'd known herself loved and cherished just as if her Mums and Pops had been her true parents.

The night of fête day, buoyed up by the excitement of the evening, Lydia took longer than usual to get ready for bed. Letting her thoughts race where they would, backwards to the moment when Miss Harkness, the retiring Treasurer, had nominated her as successor, followed by the unanimous approval of the other members—even thinking about it made her heart race—then a leap forward to the moment Sophie had suggested the cream tea. Just imagine if they were all in agreement, the grass newly mown, the beds weeded, people coming *here* to her own home. One by one she peeled off her stockings, shaking each one and draping it carefully over the back of the chair; next came her petticoat and her thin, summer-weight vest. The long mirror showed the reflection of her folding first one garment, then the next, but seeming to have no interest in the gaunt body left exposed.

'Lyddy, are you awake still?' came Sophie's urgent whisper as she opened the door an inch or so. 'May I come in? Don't want to wake the others.'

'Of course you may. I'm not even in bed yet.'

'Get your nightie on. I've been thinking. We ought to talk and I expect you'll be off to the office with Pops in the morning.'

Turning her scrawny back on her young visitor Lydia slipped her nightgown over her head.

'There! Ready! Do you want to hop in too? There's enough room.'

'No, you get in. I'll sit the foot end, that way we can see each other. Listen, Lyddy, I've had an idea about your Guides. What if we wrote some sort of a sketch to be put on at the cream tea, would they act it, do you think? It could be a Guides' sort of thing, some sort of adventure at camp, or— oh, I don't know, but we'll think of *something*. That might encourage new recruits and your lot might like to rehearse it round the camp fire while you're away. What do you say?'

'The idea's lovely. But write it, you say? Sophie, I don't think I'd be any good at writing.'

Sophie chuckled. 'Nor me. But nothing's impossible. We can't know if we don't try. If you like I'll see if I can pull something out of the air, then you can make improvements.

I don't know anything about the mysteries of what you lot get up to, so you may find lots to alter, but it'll be a start. How much do you think you could make—if the weather's good, of course? I thought cream tea at sixpence, tuppence extra for a second cup or a second scone, with perhaps forty or maybe fifty people. We could ask to borrow the crockery from the church hall; the rector couldn't refuse if he was told it's for your orphans. If we do notices and put them all round the village we may get lots more; people are always nosy when it comes to having a look at other people's gardens. If you pop round and see each member of the committee you could arrange a meeting quickly.'

'Call on them! Oh Sophie, I couldn't do that. I can't look as though I'm pushing, they'll wish they'd left me where I was as just a voluntary helper.'

'Faint heart never won fair… But if you won't do that, what about if you type a nice polite letter to each of them tomorrow, then the next day I'll pedal around and push them through their letterboxes.' Secretly, she thought she might have an opportunity to speak to one or two, then she'd tell them that Lyddy had had this brilliant idea but felt it wasn't her place to sound pushy. She knew just the way to say it— with slight variation of expression according to whom she was approaching. The idea of serving on the committee, or even tying herself to helping regularly at fund-raising events, didn't appeal to her at all, but this evening with the idea at the front of her mind she looked forward to the challenge. Once the date was fixed she could really get to grips with things.

'Sophie, thank you. You really ought to get more involved, you'd be such an asset.' Lydia turned solemnly to the girl she looked on as her sister.

'I wouldn't, you know,' Sophie chuckled. 'Most of the time I'd be more of a liability. But this sounds like being fun, doesn't it?' How pretty she was, Lydia thought, with no trace of jealousy. Eyes the blue of cornflowers, light brown hair with a sheen of gold cut short and with a fringe in that modern way, hair that sprang into waves until it grew just long enough to curl, each cheek home to a dimple so exactly like those in the picture of her father. 'Write your letters tomorrow, Lyddy'.

'What if they don't think it's a good idea?'

'Oh *Lyddy*, if you can't see trouble you go out and hunt for it. If they're so stupid that they don't want anything to do with it, then we'll get along without them. It's not up to any silly old committee to tell Pops whether he can let his garden be used to raise money.' Then, seeing her threat had only added to Lydia's uncertainty, 'Of course they'll be thrilled to bits, anyone with half a brain would be. And they won't have to do anything, only pay their sixpences and have their tea. Mums will be able to get lots of offerings of jam and scones from her Mothers' Union friends, I bet. It'll be wonderful, you just see!' Then crawling up the bed she planted a kiss on Lydia's forehead. 'I'm off. By the way, what did you think of our visitor? Quite the handsomest man at the fête, I bet you noticed him when he collected our tea, didn't you.'

'I wondered who it was you were with,' was as far as Lydia would go.

'It looks as though Pops will use him for the new development. He didn't actually tell us so, but he was all smiles and you could tell he was deep down excited by what Christian had shown him. So you'll have to get used to seeing him in and out of the office, I expect. Night night, sleep tight.' And she was gone.

But for both of them sleep was elusive, their minds were racing, filled with images of the day that had gone and dreams of the days ahead.

Two days later, just as Sophie was getting her bicycle out of the shed, a motor cycle drew up at the gate.

'I came early; something told me that you weren't a girl to waste time. Hop on the back of the bike, it'll save you pedalling,' was Christian's cheery greeting. 'Lyddy showed me her letters yesterday and said you were going to deliver them to save time.'

'I know if she'd put them in the post yesterday they would have arrived this morning, but don't you think a hand delivery shouts "Urgent"? I do. I was planning to cycle, but I'd love a ride on the motor bike.' She'd been looking forward to her delivery round, imagining what her approach would be if she were able to pass any of the letters over by hand. But riding for the first time on a motor bike was too tempting to refuse: it presented a new situation and there was nothing she liked more.

'You called her "Lyddy",' she shouted as, with a roar, they set off, 'you've soon got to know each other. It was Miss Westlake when you were introduced the night before last.'

'I, like you, my pretty maid, don't waste time,' he yelled back. 'You're very different, you and Lyddy. You get on well?'

'Of course we do. I told you, no one could *not* love Lyddy, she's pure gold.'

'How's the play coming along?'

'She told you about that, too?' How unlike Lyddy to be so free with a stranger.

'You sound surprised,' he said, slowing to a gentler pace

that saved them having to shout quite as loudly. 'We got along splendidly. Which is as well, because we shall see plenty of each other once the plans have approval. Seeing your designs take shape, isn't that how a composer must feel when he first hears his work played by an orchestra?'

She had to strain her ears to hear him even though he repeatedly turned his head in her direction.

'A bit different,' she laughed as she shouted her reply, 'he could hear a whole symphony in about forty minutes. You'll have to wait months, brick by brick, it'll take ages.'

'I'll stick around. Now, which way do we go?'

They delivered the letters. The one or two committee members with the luxury of a telephone in the house took the lead and contacted the others, all of them congratulating themselves and each other on the wisdom of involving young Miss Westlake and deciding on a date convenient to them all to accept her invitation to meet at her home. By nightfall it was all arranged and the date fixed.

'Any replies?' Christian asked Lydia the next morning.

'Better even than that,' she smiled. 'They're all thrilled with the idea and today Sophie is finishing the draft of a sketch for the Guides to do. If she sets her mind on getting something done, nothing stops her. I shall type out each part and take it all to camp for rehearsal.'

'You'll need notices. I'd like to do them for you if you'll let me?'

'She didn't push it on you, did she?'

'Sophie? No of course not. This is *your* event. If I can do the notices for you I'd like to feel involved.'

'I'd be grateful,' she made herself say it calmly; she even turned her back on him as she moved to open the window wider, frightened that her cheeks might have the sort of tell-tale flush that would let him guess her strange and unfamiliar excitement. 'If you're interested I'll bring the draft sketch in for you to read through—just if you'd like to, I mean. She says it's just bare bones, but to be honest I don't think I'd be much good at putting flesh on them.' Then, as another thought struck her, 'But I don't want Sophie to feel I'm taking it away from her. I tell you what, why don't you come to the house this evening? Let's all of us go over it together.' Then, surprised that she could have been so bold, 'If you are free this evening, I mean. Of course, you probably already have arrangements made for something else.'

What a funny, prim old stock she was! Old? Probably no older than he was himself but, pure gold or not, youth seemed to have passed her by.

'Nothing better than a lonely evening in my bedsit, or a solitary drink in the Dew Drop Inn,' he assured her. 'I'd be delighted to join you for the reading.'

That's how it was that for the second time in the space of three days he found himself invited to share 'the meal' at Drydens. Adelaide was overjoyed when at lunchtime Lydia told her that he was coming to the house in the evening to read through the sketch.

'We shall expect him to the meal, dear. I hope you invited him.'

'I—I—well, I thought he might think…' She didn't finish the sentence, didn't want to give a hint of what was stirring into life in her mind. 'But he's coming in this afternoon, Mum, so I'll give him your invitation. Or Dad can, that might be better.'

Sophie knew no such reticence. 'That's great, Lyddy. He's nice, isn't he, and isn't he the most handsome creature!'

'Beauty is only skin-deep, I'm always telling you,' Adelaide admonished.

'Course it is, Mums. But he's nice too, he must be or he wouldn't want to help.'

That was the beginning of Christian's easy acceptance into the household.

CHAPTER TWO

Before Lydia went off to camp with her troop of Girl Guides, Christian showed her the first of the notices he was preparing. Throughout the week she was living under canvas, teaching the girls self-reliance and rehearsing them in their roles, her mind was racing ahead, eager to be home as it never had in previous years. She made sure the girls were word perfect not only in the sketch but in the campfire songs which, at Christian's suggestion, were to follow it. His idea was that while the uniformed Guides led the singing of well-known songs the 'comfortably cream-tead' audience would join in to the accompaniment of his piano accordion.

By the time she arrived home she found that he was a regularly accepted visitor at Drydens. Her joy ought to have been complete; indeed she told herself constantly that it was.

Sophie had never been short of attention but the thought of falling in love with any of the local swains hadn't ever entered her head. She had never doubted that one day when she was ready her prince would come; she had assumed it as her natural right. And Lydia? Her thoughts were her own, her dreams were her own but she had no power to control them. The 'sisters' had never had secrets from each other, but now by common unspoken consent neither of them wanted to discuss Christian. Even though jealousy wasn't part of Lydia's nature, she was constantly aware of just how pretty Sophie was, how young, how full of fun—everything that she, herself, could never be; time and again she pulled her thoughts into line and reminded herself that Sophie was a darling, the same now as always. On the surface she treated Christian as she might a brother, a cousin, a family friend; what lay beneath the surface, only she knew. There was no doubt that he liked her, never had she felt so relaxed with anyone outside the family. But how would he feel if he could know the desires he had awakened in her, desires that thrilled her, frightened her, overwhelmed her?

And Sophie, who had taken adulation as her natural right, what had those weeks done to her? Always admiration had been part of a game she enjoyed. Now, for the first time, she was frightened that it wasn't she who was in control of the situation. Patience had never been part of her make-up. And hadn't Christian said to her, 'Like you, my pretty maid, I don't waste time'?

But summer passed, the cream tea became a memory—one that exceeded Lydia's dreams—with the money paid into the orphanage coffers; autumn turned to winter. If Christian wasn't a man to waste time, why was he letting the weeks and then the months drift by? Surely he must see that Sophie was in love with him? Inexperienced and naive as she was, in her view it all could have been so simple.

As the seasons went by, Christian spent a good deal of his time with the Westlakes, either in the office 'hindering' Lyddy, on the site where the building work was progressing or at Drydens. For Liddy those months had about them an aura of wonder. Everyone respected her; those who came near enough to start to know her—and that included the fund-raising committee—liked her. Had she been more confident, more able to make the overtures, friends would have been there for her, but something always held her back. A psychiatrist might have found her an interesting case, the outcome of being a gawky nine-year-old who had suddenly found herself elder sister to the irresistible Sophie, everyone's darling. Rather than being jealous of the toddler she had almost burst with childlike pride to be included under the same umbrella of admiration; when the young Sophie had lapped up attention, soon learning to take it as her due, Lydia had looked on with adoration. As she'd gone from childhood to adolescence, that she'd been too tall and with no sign of the feminine curves of other girls of her age, that her features were angular and her complexion pale, even sallow, she'd accepted in the same way as she did Sophie's loveliness. In her secret heart she might wish she could have been different, but that was something she wouldn't allow herself to consider. That same psychiatrist might also have recognised that her acceptance was to a large extent based on the unchanging certainty of her parents' love, that and the bond that held the two girls ever closer.

'Pity our Lyddy can't let herself go a bit, Addy m'dear. That's what holds her back from joining in the fun like Sophie always manages. Keeps herself too buttoned up for her own good.' That was Archie's opinion, said with affection not criticism.

'Sophie's idea of fun wouldn't be hers. Wait a while, Arch, just you see which one of them wears better with the years.' Addy was quick to come to their daughter's defence. But in her heart she knew that what he said was true.

So why had it been so different when Lyddy had met Christian? Why, on that first morning in the little office on the building site had she been utterly relaxed in his company? Here again the psychiatrist might have had views: only the previous day Sophie and Christian had been together at the fête; it had been as Sophie's guest he had been invited to Drydens for the meal, so as Sophie's sister she had offered him her friendship and, hardly realising it, talked of Sophie's idea of the cream tea to boost orphanage funds. The ice had been broken before it had had time to set.

As his plans were adopted for the new Westlake development, he spent a good deal of time at the office. In fact, Lydia knew he came far more often than necessary and even though she was frightened to let herself admit to it, she believed that as the warmth between them grew he took pleasure in being with her. Even so, his own work wasn't suffering: through the intervening months he had been given plenty of commissions, individual houses or extensions, a village hall, but nothing else on the scale of the Westlake housing development, which incorporated many different designs, no two houses being identical. He always showed her his plans, he talked about his hopes and ambitions. She knew their friendship was as important to him as it was to her. Friendship? She tried to tell herself that that was what she felt for him. She wasn't blind to her mother's anxiety that, like so many women in those years after the carnage of the Great War, she would go through life a spinster. The idea hadn't worried her, not until now.

He had become a familiar figure in Kingshampton, where he had been accepted like a local at the Dew Drop Inn, and having an outgoing charm had been entertained at most of the

more well-to-do houses. He seldom walked the length of the
High Street without someone stopping to speak.

In the beginning he didn't suspect the pleasure it gave her
parents to find her so relaxed—and indeed blossoming—in
his company. But he had no doubt that beneath her companionable manner she harboured feelings quite out of keeping
with the well-ordered, prim young woman known by the
community. Enjoying the humour of the situation, he gave no
sign that he noticed, instinct telling him how quickly she
would learn to hide the emotion he was sure was new to her.
As for Sophie (and, like everyone else, he felt himself wanting to smile at the thought of her), he recognised the open invitation in her glances and wasn't surprised. Hadn't he seen
how she'd behaved towards the young hopefuls on the day
of the fête? So he had no qualms in leading her on, just far
enough to keep her guessing. To him it was a game at which
he excelled and one for which Sophie had a natural flair. All
in all, during the time the development took shape, Christian
found life very sweet. No mother in a Jane Austen novel
could have been more anxious to see the family married off
than Adelaide, first the elder and then the younger. Christian
read her thoughts and played along, finding the same enjoyment in the situation as an angler when he is playing a fish
he knows will end safely in his keepnet to be released when
he decides. There was something about the atmosphere of
Drydens he found irresistible: it was as if the four of them
had been in a perfect circle, complete in themselves, and yet
were prepared to draw him in. He enjoyed the evidence of
their interest; he enjoyed knowing he had Archibald's respect; he enjoyed the sport of 'playing' the sisters; but perhaps most of all he enjoyed the freedom of bachelorhood.

Work progressed at Meadowlands, as the housing development was called. The original outline permission had been granted for ten detached houses, ten semi-detached houses and a terrace of ten more. In fact when the detailed plan was submitted it was for ten five-bedroomed detached properties, each standing in its own spacious garden just as Archibald had envisaged and, to complete the development, just ten more also detached but with four bedrooms and, here again, standing in sizeable ground. As far as the construction business went, it wasn't often Archibald was open to advice, but on this occasion he had listened to Christian and seen the wisdom of what he said. Twenty residences of the standard these would be would bring him in as much rent—or capital repayment if any were sold rather than rented—as the thirty previously envisaged. When people in unchanging Kingshampton had objected to a development of houses on the perimeter of the village Christian had pointed out, 'Make each house a gem—and they will be—no two alike, each in a good-sized garden, then they will enhance the village.' What he'd sensed better not put into words to this one-time bricklayer was his opinion that anyone interested in moving into high-priced homes such as these would think again if they had to approach through a complex of terraced houses with rows of washing hung out to dry and children playing in the street. Already, even before building was completed, he was being proved correct: there was no shortage of tenants, the sort of tenants who would have no trouble in having the rent when either Archibald or Lydia called to collect it on the first day of each month.

Month followed month, another fête day came and went. On a morning in late September, as Christian came out of Mrs

Triggs' general store-cum-post office, Lydia appeared along the road on her bicycle.

'Hello, friend Lyddy.' He doffed his soft felt hat, returning it to his head at his usual jaunty angle. 'Where are you off to on this lovely morning?' And indeed it was a lovely morning; the summer that had shown every sign of being over had suddenly returned, giving them what looked like being the warmest day of the year.

'I'm on my way to see the furniture into the show house.'

'I'll help, I'd like to. Have you time to walk?'

Immediately she slipped from the saddle; with one hand she straightened her straw hat and with the other she held the handlebars as she started forward.

'Here, let me push that. Off we go then. We'll turn the show house into a home fit for a king. Seeing the place with furniture will be the icing on the cake. You know, Lyddy, I've never watched my work take shape like I have here. And it's not just that. All of you, you and your family, have made me feel that this is where I belong. I've had more than enough of being in digs, I've a good mind to look for somewhere to rent in the village and make a permanent base. Perhaps one of these houses. What would you think?'

Calm, unemotional Lydia was frightened to trust her voice. It took all her willpower to keep her tone level, not to let him know what his words were doing to her. The way he said it, the way his free hand brushed against hers as he walked pushing her bicycle (was it intentional? She didn't know. She was frightened to ask herself). One of these houses…what did she think?…what was he hinting? She mustn't let him guess how every nerve in her seemed to be tingling at the very thought. If he guessed *that*, then that might lead him to knowing all those other fantasies, fantasies that threatened to bring the colour to her cheeks as she imagined them.

'Stay permanently in Kingshampton? You could do a lot worse, Christian.' Thus might a maiden aunt have answered. 'It's a good location. Did Dad tell you that someone moving his family into one of the top houses is coming from London? He means to travel there each day but wants his family to have a country life. The service from Brackleford is excellent. That advertisement we put in a national newspaper proved to be money well spent, it's awakened a good deal of interest.' How could he not know how hard her heart was hammering? 'If your commissions come from anywhere in the home counties—and from what you tell us, they do—you've already found that you can easily work from Kingshampton.' She knew she ought to have left it at that, but she couldn't. 'Dad would be delighted, he enjoys having you come in and out at home. I've never known him take to a young man like he has to you. If only he'd had a son—for the business, I mean.'

'Indeed, yes. Still, if it wasn't to be, perhaps there's a good reason.'

She laughed. 'What a comforting approach to life when things don't go the way you want. Look, the furniture van has arrived. And that must be Sophie's bike, she said she'd probably come over. She'll enjoy deciding how the things should go.'

'Don't you mind? You work with your father every day, don't you want to be the one to arrange the furniture?'

'Oh, we'll all have our say, I expect. It's nice when she shows an interest, I know Dad is always pleased.'

Seeing them coming, Sophie ran to meet them. Just like the unseasonal change in the weather from the previous week's autumnal storms, she seemed to believe it was still the height of summer. Wearing a white pleated skirt and sailor blouse she could have passed for fourteen instead of twenty-two. 'Good, now all three of us are here. We've put the big rugs down, me and the furniture men. Isn't this fun! The kitchen is really smart, glass-fronted cabinet with a let-down flap for a sort of work-bench. That's what Arnold—he's the one in charge—that's what he called it. If Ethel sees it, she'll be green with envy having to put up with the old dresser and wooden table.'

'A good deal more space to work, I expect,' Lydia the practical answered, trying not to notice how Christian's eyes devoured Sophie.

'We live in changing times,' he laughed.

A shiver of apprehension ran down Lydia's spine. Did she only imagine that his whole demeanour brightened at the sight of Sophie? His voice echoed in her mind. 'Perhaps one of these houses…what would you think?' But she pulled her thoughts back to the work they'd come to do and, not even conscious that she did it, held her tall, straight figure even more erect.

'Where shall we start?' she asked, 'Upstairs or down? I want to be back at the office by half past eleven, that's why I brought my bike. Dad has an outside appointment.'

'Let's just see how it goes. The office won't run away if you're not there.' To Sophie it all seemed so simple. But Lydia's sense of responsibility was strong enough for the two of them.

'I'll start upstairs,' she said. 'You can do the downstairs.

You two have more idea on arranging things than I have.' As if to punish herself for letting her wild dreams get out of hand she threw the two of them together, belittling her own ability at the same time. She mustn't build her hope on dreams—and yet, '… perhaps one of these houses…what would you think?' Fearful they might read her thoughts, she said, 'People's interest in bedrooms doesn't go much further than size, there's not much scope for choice of arrangement. And I can hang the curtains while I'm here, Sophie, I'm taller than you are.'

Sophie beamed on them both, indeed on the world at large. 'Good idea, Lyddy. The chaps are still up there, ask them nicely and they'll put the beds up.'

At the idea of asking the delivery men nicely to do something outside their remit, anything that remained of Lydia's self-confidence evaporated. 'I can manage, I've brought spanners and things.'

'Give me a shout and I'll give you a hand if you like,' Christian offered. His words were willing enough, so how was it she knew he said it only because in the circumstances he could do no less? Mounting the stairs, she was determined she would erect the three beds unaided. In fact, the fat and jolly driver from the furniture van was already organising his team, one bed was erected, one well on the way and the third stacked against the wall of the third bedroom waiting. The amount of tip she had intended to give them took a leap upwards, even while she seemed to stand outside herself considering what great importance she put on independence, while to Sophie it seemed to mean nothing. But then, why should it? Looking as enchanting as she did, Sophie would never have to ask for assistance, instead she would seem to bestow a favour on whichever of her willing helpers she chose. And today she'd chosen Christian.

From downstairs came the sound of their voices. To Lydia's ears they were happy voices, laughing, teasing, turning the chore into the sort of fun that Lydia never felt able to be part of. She set about hanging the bedroom curtains while the delivery men erected the final bed, then came to tell her, 'We're off now, missus. Reckon we've done all the heavy, you'll be all right from here.' The hint wasn't necessary, a more than generous tip was waiting on the dressing-table.

'I really am grateful, now we'll have everything done in no time.' She smiled. A minute later they were clattering down the stairs, well pleased with her appreciation of their morning's work.

'And right nice it's going to look. Lucky families who can find the cash to live in one of these and no mistake,' the foreman said as he pocketed the tip and followed his helper out of the house. Once they got back into the truck he'd see to giving the fellow a share. It was a pity Lydia couldn't hear what he said as they shut the front door behind them. 'A real nice lady, that one. I dare say you fancied that other little madam, all legs and smiles. A pretty smile don't pay the bills, my lad. Here, put these sponduliks in your pocket, it'll pay for your pint and a bite of cheese before we go off back to town.'

The van disappeared from sight and Lydia concentrated on getting the curtains hung, bedrooms, bathroom, then the downstairs rooms too before she went back to look after the office. By twenty to twelve she viewed their work with satisfaction. Was it Sophie or Christian who had such a good eye for effect? The sitting room looked delightful; it wouldn't be long before someone would want to buy or rent it just as it was. She forced herself to imagine the people who would live here, probably a husband and wife and two children, the man cycling each day to work in Brackleford and glad to do it, knowing his family was out of the bustle of a growing town. Lydia sighed, her gaze going involuntarily to Christian before she could pull it back in check. Fortunately, he was busy admiring the end result of their labours.

'I'm not coming home at midday, Lyddy,' Sophie was saying. 'We're doing awfully well, but the dining room will take a while. I want to get it all perfect before we leave. Christian says he's in no hurry today so he'll stay and help.'

After Lydia had gone, the other two kept up their pace of work and soon the whole of the ground floor looked good enough to tempt the most critical would-be resident.

'Lyddy's done the upstairs curtains, but there's this box of ornaments and bits for the bedrooms,' she said.

'I'll carry it, it's heavier than it looks.'

So work went on for another half-hour or so, setting chests of drawers and dressing-tables in the most advantageous positions. Sophie made up the beds in the three double bedrooms while Christian, with an eye for effect, hung pictures and arranged ornaments. Every few minutes they stood back to admire their handiwork. Then all that remained to be done was the smallest bedroom.

'Let's stop for five minutes.' Christian held his hand out to her and drew her towards him. 'We've earned a break.' As openly friendly as a child, that's how Archie and Addy saw Sophie; but, holding her at arms' length as he looked at her, Christian would have had to be blind not to read the message in her eyes, a message he'd seen for months but never been

more aware of than this morning, a message he saw as a reflection of the way his own thoughts had continually turned.
Only a man made of stone could fail to respond and this
morning there was nothing stone-like in the racing of his
blood. 'It's been a good morning.' Still he held her at bay—
but only just. 'My fair maiden is more than a pretty girl,
she's a great worker. We did well, pretty Sophie. You liked
our morning?'

Sophie's eyes shone as she turned to him, nodding.
'Magic,' she whispered. She felt that the one word said it all.
Arranging furniture, choosing how they wanted the room to
look, making a home… None of the local 'eligibles' had ever
made her feel like this, as if a million butterflies were flut-
tering in her arteries—or was it her veins, she didn't know,
didn't care, didn't care about anything except something she
believed as last she could read in his eyes.

'Sophie,' he whispered, drawing her close against him. In
an age of innocence, Sophie was anything but ignorant. Pressing herself to him she thrilled to feel the proof that he felt the
same as she did. As if to let him know it hadn't gone unnoticed, she moved her hips. Pulling her blouse from where it
was anchored under the waistband of her skirt, his hands
moved on her naked back. Pressing against him she could feel
the beating of his heart; the butterflies grew stronger, wilder.
It wasn't the first time she'd felt this deep ache of longing, but
never had it been to the accompaniment of excitement so great
that she felt she could scarcely breathe. 'You know what you
do to me?' She heard the urgency in his whisper. Yes, oh yes,
she knew and with all her heart she rejoiced in it. He was telling
her that he had this same hungry, empty, dreadful and yet
wonderful feeling; he was telling her he was in love with her.

When he steered her backwards towards the unmade-up bed, willingly she moved with him, dropping first to sit and then to lie back on the mattress. What was he doing? Although she asked herself, she knew exactly what he was doing and, as his hand moved beneath the folds of her pleated skirt she altered her position so that he could reach his goal. She wanted him to touch her. His fingers caressed, delved, explored. All reason was lost to her.

'I want you, you don't know how much I want you,' he whispered urgently.

'And me.'

'Yes, and you. You want it too. I know you do. Say yes, Sophie, tell me you do.'

'Yes, yes, yes.' Whether she expected more than the glorious wonder of knowing he wanted her, the thrill of his touch on her body, she didn't question. She felt she was sinking into a great abyss; she had no power to resist, she wanted no power to resist. With eyes closed, she spoke through clenched teeth, rejoicing in the unknown bliss of the moment, rushing blindly into what she only half understood. This was love, *love*. It was what she'd imagined and longed for, Christian loved her too. Opening her eyelids just far enough to find out why he'd taken his hand away, she saw that he was releasing his shoulders from his braces. 'Yes, yes,' she whispered again. Eagerly she opened her arms to him, raising her body as he pushed her skirt high and her knickers low as if in one movement. Now there was nothing between them, nothing. Never had she experienced such exquisite anticipation.

'I've wanted you, wanted this, ever since I've known you. And you have, too, you know you have.'

'Yes,' she breathed. 'Yes, Christian…yes.' Surely even her

voice was different, breathless, frightened of breaking the spell.

Again his hand was working its spell. He would teach, she would learn. He loved her, he wanted her to be his, *his, his*... He was heavy, she felt as though she were being torn apart, he was thundering into her, pounding into her, crushing the breath out of her. She hadn't expected it would be like this. Was it seconds, minutes? Long enough to bring her out of the realms of glorious fantasy. She turned her head to one side, gasping for breath; she opened her eyes and saw the unfamiliar room, the bare mattress that would soon belong to some stranger; she longed for it to be over and yet longed even more to recall those moments when she'd willingly hurtled into this. He loved her, he wanted her, that's what she must just keep remembering. He seemed oblivious of everything but what drove him as he moved faster, harder. Involuntarily she thought of a train racing towards its destination, juddering and shuddering as it braked too quickly coming into the terminus; then like a ton weight he collapsed on top of her, crushing out of her what little breath she had left.

'God...wonderful, wasn't it wonderful...' Not quite a question, she could hear the satisfaction in his words. How could he call it wonderful? She tried to wriggle from under him but he made no effort to move. 'All morning I've been thinking of nothing else—and you—we knew it had to happen—'

'Yes,' she managed to gasp as her lungs became her own again, trying to instil the right note. 'Get up, we mustn't spoil the new mattress,' she heard herself say, wanting to be able to tell him it had been wonderful for her too, but frightened to speak the words lest he recognised the lie in her voice. If only it could have been true.

'Cruel maiden,' he laughed softly, still gasping for breath as he rolled off her, 'asking a poor broken man to get up. But you're right, as practical as you are pretty,' he panted, 'we mustn't soil the mattress.'

She wished they hadn't said the word 'soil'; it seemed to underline how she felt and take away her hope of recapturing that elusive magic. It was gone beyond recall, even when he pushed her blouse out of the way and bent to kiss her.

'Sweet Sophie, did I hurt you? I ought to have realised. My pretty maiden was a virgin.' He was recovering, his jaunty smile was back in place. 'But no longer. I've deflowered you for ever, sweet Sophie. I'm truly sorry it had to hurt you. Next time it'll be better for you.'

She nodded, partially restored.

'We ought to get up.' Yet still he lay there. 'Christ, I feel weak as a kitten—'

'Sshh, listen. There's someone coming.' In a second she was sitting up, pulling her skirt into place. But weak-as-a-kitten Christian's reactions were slower.

'What the *hell* do you think you're up to!' Reaching the open doorway, Archibald had no doubt what they were up to, or had been. Sophie had never heard him shout like that. His face was flushed with rage, his eyes standing out like organ stops.

'It's all right, Pops.' She tumbled off the bed and ran towards him, instinct guiding her and, even then, confident that she could make him see things her way. 'It's not a bit like you think. We love each other.'

'How long's this been going on?' Ignoring her, Archibald turned on Christian, his cold anger even harder to face than his initial roar.

'It was the first time.' While Christian was still collecting his wits it was Sophie who answered. 'Pops, you mustn't be angry. Can't you be happy that we love each other? You know you've grown fond of Christian. Just be glad we want to be together always.'

Christian's brain was once again functioning, although in his present state he wished himself anywhere but where he was. Putting his feet to the ground he hoisted his trousers and slipped his arms through his braces, better able to face the on-slaught he knew was ahead.

Archibald looked from one of them to the other, shock and anger being overtaken by concern. Again he spoke to Christian, ignoring Sophie's pleas.

'You ought to be ashamed. She wouldn't lie to me, and if this is the first time then let it be the last. Not a word to any-one. What's been going on goes no further than this room. Am I understood?'

'Yes, sir,' from Christian, his spirits rising at the thought that the matter looked like coming to a conclusion. He'd blotted his copybook fair and square, he couldn't see himself settling in the village now.

'Yes, Pops,' from Sophie. 'There's no need to tell anyone anything. Mums and Lyddy won't be a bit surprised when they're told we want to get married—'

Married! It was Christian's turn to look helplessly from one to the other. He'd bedded girls before this and, damn it all, she'd been as ready for it as he had.

'And that's *all* you are to tell them. As for you, young man, I'd like to take a whip to your back. You say you love her and you put her in a position like this!'

'I shouldn't have let it happen.'

'Damned right you shouldn't.' There was no forgiveness in Archibald's tone. Then suddenly the wind seemed to go from his sails, and he dropped to sit on the edge of the bed. There wasn't even the ticking of a clock to break the silence in the room. To varying degrees the next step was unclear to all of them. Christian couldn't keep the focus of his mind on any one thing: his choice was to walk away from all of them, to disappear where they couldn't trace him, or to marry Sophie. And would that be so disastrous? She was a lovely girl, she was fun in a childlike way, she was good company, she was eager enough in bed, she didn't hide the fact that she idolised him, she was the apple of the old man's eye even though she was the younger daughter—so wouldn't he be wise to make the best of things? Sophie wished Pops hadn't arrived when he had; desperately, she wanted to make herself think of what had happened as beautiful, just as she'd believed it would be. But Pops made them feel like culprits, as if they should be ashamed, as if they'd done something sordid. She wouldn't give an inch to the memory of her own feeling of distaste, her longing just for it to be over. Of the three it was Archibald who forced himself to find the straightest path to what he saw as inevitable. Sophie had said this was the first time, so it was unlikely the young fool would have made the child pregnant. Please God he hadn't, please, please dear God he hadn't. Ask and then trust, that's what he had to do. Don't let the young devil have given her a child. My poor Addy, she doesn't deserve this. We were married more than three years before Lyddy was expected, so surely no God would let that happen to little Sophie. But once having tasted forbidden fruit they weren't likely not to have another bite. So the thing to do was to get them married as quickly as possible. He didn't want Addy worried—he *wouldn't have* Addy worried—so there must be no gossip and talk of shotgun weddings. He had to think of a way to get them wed without some tomfool engagement holding things up.

'There's plenty I'd like to say, but what's the use?' It was as if his initial anger had crushed his spirit. He looked defeated.

'Don't let's quarrel, Pops,' Sophie knelt in front of him. As Addy had so often said, she'd always been able to wind him round her little finger; but now all she felt was tenderness. 'Pops, it will be all right. We ought not to have let it happen, but somehow…' She hesitated; she couldn't try and explain to Pops what had led up to it, and even if she'd been able to she wouldn't have let herself. Those moments belonged just to Christian and her. 'The way it's all worked out is what I've wanted more than all the world.' Her blue eyes gazed at him earnestly; surely if he knew that marrying Christian was all that mattered to her then he would accept without being cross and disappointed. She felt his hand on her head, gently rumpling her hair.

Looking at a still dishevelled Christian, Archie told him, 'This time yesterday I would have said you were the man for one of my girls, the son I wished had been my own. I feel let down, damned if I don't.'

'For that I'm truly sorry, sir. Give us your blessing and I promise you won't regret having me in the family.'

'Umph,' was as near as Archie would come to giving his blessing. Instead, after a long silence that none of them seemed able to break and seemingly apropos of nothing, he asked them, 'This house, all the things you've been putting about in it this morning, what do you think of it? Make a good home for some young family?'

'We did it really well, Pops.' Sophie was regaining her usual cheerfulness; in fact when she saw the slight movement of Christian's foot as he kicked her knickers out of sight under the bed, a laugh wasn't far beneath the surface. 'Christian hung the pictures and decided where the stuff ought to go, I just did as I was told. Oh, and Lyddy hung all the curtains. Looks lovely, doesn't it?' He heard her pride in the morning's work. 'You think so too, don't you?'

'Never mind what I think about the place. More important is deciding a plausible reason for getting you married without some damn fool engagement while you get a bottom drawer together or whatever young girls are supposed to do. Whatever we hit on, there's to be no confiding what's really gone on, not to Addy and—and you mark this, Sophie—not to Lyddy either. I know what you two girls are, you never could keep a secret from each other. Now listen to me: this is *our* story and I defy you to breathe a word. I've been up to the big houses, taken someone to see No.8, that's how it is I'm over here on site. All that's true, Lyddy knew that's where I was going, and she knew too that I told her I'd look in here and see how you'd been doing with the furnishings. Now, here come the lies. Dear God, what a way to start a marriage! When I got here *you*,' looking at Christian, 'you told me that you'd asked Sophie to marry you. And *you*,' this time he spoke to Sophie, 'begged me to let you have this house. Soft old fool that I am, when have I ever been able to refuse you?' Then looking at Sophie in concern, 'But what is it child? You're crying.'

'I feel so mean, so rotten.'

'Here, here, duckie, dry your eyes. No one's going to believe our yarn if you go home sore-eyed. This house and the bits in it will be your wedding present.'

Sophie dried her face against his trouser leg as she knelt in front of him. She ought to be over the moon with excitement: how many brides started married life with a home like this? So why did she feel so low? As long as she could remember Pops had been there for her; he'd trusted her just as wholeheartedly as he'd loved her. What a moment to call to mind that her beloved Pops was really Uncle Archie, not even her real father, and yet no father could have been closer, dearer. Speaking her mind had always been part of her character, and it had never been more sincere than now.

'So ashamed,' she sniffed, wiping the heel of her thumbs across nose and eyes. 'I've always loved you as if you were my proper father. You know that, don't you, Pops? I expect you've thought I've taken it all for granted, but I haven't— not when I've stopped and thought about it.'

'Then, my dear, you should have taken it for granted. You're as dear to me as if you were my own daughter— extra dear, because of what Vincent meant to me. As for a lot of nonsense about it being wrong to take Addy and me for granted—ah, and our Lyddy too—ask any of us and we'd all say the same. We all take each other for granted, that's what families are for. So enough of that silly talk. Off your knees now, girl, blow your nose and run a comb through your hair. As for you, young man, I'll talk to you downstairs while Sophie makes up this bed.'

Christian meekly followed him down the stairs, leaving Sophie alone in the room where the last half-hour had changed the course of their lives. The last exchange between Archibald and Sophie echoed in his mind. '…as if you were my own daughter…' So he wasn't really her father. Pops…

Mums… how the hell was he to have guessed she wasn't theirs?

Sitting on the edge of the bed just as Archibald had, Sophie tried to overcome her feeling of shame. What she had done this morning had shattered the very core of the principles on which she'd been brought up. That was only part of the reason for the confusion of her sentiments: if she could have said, as Christian had, 'That was wonderful,' wouldn't she simply have been looking forward to their future together? And oughtn't she to have been thrilled that this house they'd furnished together was to be their home? It would be a constant reminder to her just how much she'd let Pops down. There was one other fact she overlooked completely and that was that Christian hadn't actually proposed to her, not in so many words. She didn't doubt that he was in love with her and had intented them to be married, her naive faith had no limits, for if it weren't the case then he wouldn't have wanted them to make love. The idea of living in this house ought to make her dream of their future perfect, yet looking around the room it was impossible to forget her disillusionment that what in her half-understood imaginings had been a glorious moment of love beyond words had proved to be without tenderness, painful and uncomfortable. Next time it would be different, next time her body would be ready. She was a woman now, *his* woman. Already her spirits were reviving. She wouldn't let herself think of Archie's 'I feel let down, damned if I don't.' She and Christian would come here again, they would want to see everything was right for *them*, not just for a house to show off to prospective residents. Next time it would all be different; there wouldn't be that mad scramble that almost crushed the life out of her, next time they would already know they belonged to each other, love-making would be slow and tender, she would feel like a goddess.

'Buck up, Sophie,' Archie called up the stairs. 'Time I was back in the office.'

'You go on, Pops, I've not quite done,' she answered as, hurriedly and none too neatly, she tucked in the bottom sheet. What did it matter how she made the bed as long as the counterpane was smooth? All this was to be hers.

'We'll all walk to the village together,' he answered. 'Just get a move on.'

Two minutes later, when he locked the front door he put the key in his pocket. They'd already sipped the forbidden cup, he was jiggered if he was going to give them the chance to go back for another swig.

Addy listened to their story with mixed feelings. She was genuinely delighted that Christian was to become part of the family and even though her secret hope had been that he would fall in love with her dear Lyddy, the engagement didn't come as a surprise. She'd been all too aware of the way he'd watched Sophie. But what was the hurry?

'Wait until spring; let's have the winter making preparations. You'll need to have a trousseau made—'

'Oh Mums, these days I can get lovely things ready-made. You and Lyddy and I could have a day in London; think what fun we'd have. The house is all ready, just crying out to be lived in. We could go shopping next week—or this week even. If you like more than a day's notice, what about the day after tomorrow?'

'Nonsense. We can't rush into things like that.' Adelaide was never as easy to win over as Archie.

'Well, while you ladies mull it over, I have a business to run,' Archie said. 'Can't leave Lyddy holding the fort on her own all afternoon.'

'I dare say Christian will have gone in to take her the news,' his wife said. But, for some reason he couldn't quite explain, Archie thought he probably hadn't.

'Let me be the one to tell her, Pops,' a thoroughly recovered Sophie pleaded. 'You come on in a few minutes; let Lyddy and me do some girlie planning first.'

To be honest he was glad to have a few mintues of sanity with Addy. If only he could tell her the truth. A trouble shared is a trouble halved, came the words of the old adage; but this was something he could share with no one.

Bent forward as if to gain extra speed, Sophie pedalled to the office in the village.

'Lyddy, listen! Just listen to this!' she cried as she threw open the door.

'Are you all alone?' Lydia greeted her. 'Is Dad still with that family?'

'No. Lyddy, Lyddy, I wanted to come and tell you all by myself. Lyddy, Christian and I are going to be married.'

Lyddy's pen dropped—accidentally? Purposely?—to the floor and she stooped to pick it up as she answered.

'I wondered when.' She managed to force a smile into her voice. Then, getting up, she came towards Sophie and hugged her. 'We've all seen it coming, so I know just how happy you are both going to be.'

'Course we are. But Lyddy, I want you to help me.'

'How can you possibly want help?' She was proud that she

managed to laugh as she asked, 'Christian loves you, isn't that everything? What more do you want?'

'Course that's all that really matters. But, well listen while I tell you about the house and everything.' Hardly 'everything', for she kept strictly to the story Archie had laid out. 'Mums says we ought to wait until the spring. But that's silly. *You* can see it's silly, can't you? Mums always listens to *you*. The house is there, we know what we want. So what's the point of waiting? Pops understands, but Mums says we ought to wait and take our time with stupid arrangements. She'll listen to *you*, Lyddy. That's why I wanted to come and tell you myself, to get you on my side.'

For about two seconds Lydia was silent. Then she had herself firmly in hand again. 'Trust me,' Lyddy said. 'Don't say you've asked me, just that you've told me you and Christian are engaged. Leave the rest to me.'

'I knew that's what you'd say. I'd do the same for you, honestly I would. I'd better dash off home. Christian is getting his motor bike and then we're going in to Brackleford,' she chuckled. 'A little matter of an engagement ring. Who would have thought this morning the day would have turned out like this?' And without waiting for an answer she was gone.

Lyddy pushed her chair back from the desk. Alone, she felt like a rubber band that had been stretched until it snapped. Hunched almost double, she leaned forward. Back came the echo of his words 'perhaps one of these houses…what do you think?' It was years since Lyddy had cried, she kept her emotions much too tightly controlled for tears. Now she wanted to cry, not to weep quietly, but to howl, to beat her flat chest in her anguish and misery. But she didn't. Instead she sat hunched, still as a statue, frightened to move, frightened even to breathe deeply in case the sob that threatened couldn't be held back. I'm glad for her, yes I am, I have to be glad for her. How could I have been fool enough to believe— no, not believe, in my heart I never believed—to imagine it was *me* he cared for? Of course he fell in love with Sophie, they all fall in love with her. She's lovely, she's loveable, she's—she's *Sophie*. Help me never to let anyone guess how I've let myself dream, help me to be happy for them, help me, help me, can't talk to anyone, only to You. Look at me, just look at me, I have a life too. A life that will go on like this, day after day, months, years, me and millions of other women. Why couldn't Sophie have fallen in love with one of the young men in the village? They were all keen enough. Why did Christian have to come here at all? Until I knew him I was content…the orphanage, the Guides, the business. I used to think my life was useful—didn't I? Or didn't I think at all? Did I just accept? Please, it's all I can ask, beg, help me to feel like that again, make me strong so that I can truly *truly* be happy for her. And all those wicked fantasies I've let myself have, please, dear God, help me not to give way to temptation—temptation that's a mockery, a sneering mockery.

Footsteps that she recognised. 'Well, Lyddy m'dear, here's a turn-up for the books, eh!'

Instinct—or was it that her plea had been heard?—made her sit straight as Archie opened the office door.

'Don't pretend you're surprised, Dad.' Could he guess the pain in her heart, a pain that ached in every limb, as she turned to him with a smile?

It was Archie's idea that she should 'Go home and have a talk to your mother' for he, like Sophie, knew if Addy listened to anyone it would be to her. She had never let Sophie down, and this time was no exception.

So it was that by four o'clock on that same day Sophie and Christian set off to Brackleford to buy her engagement ring. First they went to the newspaper office to arrange the wording of the announcement that 'Mr and Mrs Archibald Westlake have great pleasure in announcing the engagement of their dear Sophie to Mr Christian Mellor, to be followed by a wedding in St Luke's Church, Kingshampton, in December', than on to Morris & Milsteads to buy the ring. Of the four jewellers in Brackleford, that was the best and most expensive, so that's where she led him. She didn't even consider any of the others.

'Shall we talk for a while? Shall we start making some plans?' How she wished Pops hadn't made her promise not to say a word about what had happened at the show house. The sight of Lyddy, clad in her cotton nightgown, standing gazing out into the starless night, seemed to Sophie to underline the wonder of her own day. Not just what had happened before Pops had walked in on them, that was someting she meant to keep right at the back of her mind until she was ready to make herself believe it had been all she'd expected. But all the rest, the excitement of planning a wedding, the pleasure of knowing the house was to be hers and Christian's, her pride in hearing Christian telling that oh-so-grovelling sales assistant that he wanted to see a selection of engagement rings, she could share all those things with Lyddy, along with the fun it had been during the evening talking about getting a wedding dress made and what Lyddy ought to wear as a bridesmaid. Yet her first glance at the back view of the tall, lonely figure crushed some of her exuberance.

At the sound of her voice, Lydia turned, one arm outstretched to welcome her in.

'Hop into bed, we can talk there,' she said. Always she'd been there for Sophie, taken for granted as much as the light of each new day and just as necessary.

'Isn't it wonderful?' Sophie said, snuggling into the comfort of the feather bed. 'Who would have thought when I went off to the show house this morning that the day would have turned out like this? Had he said anything to you—about *me*, I mean? About being in love with me?'

'Not in words.' Lyddy pulled the covers around their shoulders, taking Sophie's hand in hers. 'But I could tell. You'll make a splendid couple.'

'Shall I tell you a secret? Promise not to say a word. Go on, promise.'

'I promise. But if it's something between you and him you ought not to tell me.'

Sophie giggled, sounding just as she might have ten years or more ago. 'He'd be the last person I'd tell. Do you believe in old wives' tales? I've always scoffed. But Lyddy, when Ethel was skinning that rabbit for tonight's pie I stole the foot and put it in my pocket for luck. Who'd have thought it would have worked so quickly?' Joy, anticipation, satisfaction, the combination was almost too much to contain, a spasm of excitement tugged at every nerve in her body. Lyddy felt the movement and gripped her hand tighter.

'This wasn't anything to do with a lucky rabbit's foot, we all knew he has been watching you for months. You knew it too, you must have.' She was proud of the up-beat tone of her reply. But if she had feared Sophie might suspect the emptiness in her heart she need not have worried.

'I know he's been watching me,' she chuckled, 'but you can look at things in shop windows then decide you'd rather save your money than spend out on them. And talking of spending, isn't my ring just the most beautiful!' She freed her hand and waved it so that the light shining on the diamond sent shimmering shafts of colour. Unable to contain herself, she leaned over and planted a kiss on Lyddy's cheek. 'If I were a cat I'd purr, I'd purr and purr.'

Lydia had been fighting her own private battle but it was overwhelmed by affection for her 'sister', so full of naive trust.

The village turned out in full force to see the wedding of the local beauty and the smart young architect who had settled amongst them. Anyone able to get to St Luke's church by noon on the second Saturday in that December of 1924 was guaranteed to be there. Their Sunday best was given a week-day airing and those who couldn't find a seat in the small church contented themselves outside.

'See that child over there? She belongs to that painted tart who's taken that hovel at the end of Tanners' Alley,' one tenant from Wykeham Street whispered to another, nodding her head in the direction of a ragged urchin standing near the church door. 'Sybella, if you please, that's what my Bess says her name is. What a name to give a scarecrow like she is!'

'Bert tells me that her mother's already getting a name for herself round about. Down at the Dew Drop they know her as the "threepenny bit". Get my meaning?'

'Bess said there's a hole right through the sole of the girl's shoe. Tried to keep her skirt over it in prayers, she did, but Bess—and the others—they all saw. But look, the doors are opening, yes, yes, here she comes. Did you ever see such a pretty bride?'

No wonder they caught their breath in pleasure at the sight of Sophie as, while the eight-bell peal rang out, she emerged on her husband's arm. The sight brought back memories of photographs they had seen the previous year of the Duke and Duchess of York after their marriage ceremony, and surely Sophie Westlake's gown must have been copied from that worn by the royal bride. She looked exquisite. Behind them walked Lyddy, a less that comfortable bridesmaid, her deep gold gown looking opulent and out of keeping with her thin lanky figure. Such a nice young lady too, those who knew her thought with one accord. Of the two it was Lyddy who was known in the village where the long terraces in Wykeham Street and Mulberry Street had all been built by Westlakes for letting. More often than not it was Lydia Westlake who tapped on the doors on Friday mornings to collect the rents. 'A real lady' was how she was described, never one to gossip from one house to another and yet always interested in the families, always caring if a person was under the weather or if one of the children had chickenpox or mumps, always remembering and enquiring next time she called. Yes, a real nice young lady. There was more to a person than a pretty face. But what a picture that little one looked, and was there ever a happier-looking bride?

'Stand back,' the photographer ordered the crowd before he ducked beneath the black velvet focusing cloth and peered through his view-finder. 'First just bride and groom.' He waved the rest of the party back into the gloom of the porch. 'That's lovely, lovely, smile now…' and like a conjurer performing his magic he slotted the dark slide into the back of the camera, opened the sheath, squeezed the rubber bulb, then closed the sheath. 'There, that's one. Now the rest of the bridal party…' And a repeat of the same performance. The day would be recorded for ever.

Photographs done, the bridal party moved forward to the waiting cars and carriages. Amidst the excitement it was only Lydia who saw the waif-like child who had recently come to the village, saw her and felt a tug of sympathy.

For Sophie, those hours were everything she'd dreamed. Never had she been the centre of such attention as she was when the guests returned to the house for the wedding breakfast. Silly to want to cry when, in his speech, Pops told them all that he knew she would bring joy into Christian's life just as she had into his and Mums'. Then, dressed in quite the smartest outfit she'd ever possessed, how grand she felt as Christian ostentatiously held out his arm for her to take, then amidst applause and cries of 'Good luck', 'God bless you' and from Pops 'See you take care of her now', led her out to the awaiting motor bike and sidecar. She hung on to the glory of the day as they roared and jolted all the way to Southsea.

Arriving at Melrose Hotel, she was determined not to show her disappointment that it wasn't on the seafront; instead she told herself that such a little thing wasn't important. Nothing must cast a shadow on this, her perfect day. Tonight she would go to sleep held in his embrace; she would wake to the first day of the rest of their lives. By the time they arrived the evening meal was over, but the proprietress, a Mrs

Higgins, had kept something for them—ham with tinned peas and mashed potatoes which had been kept warm since the other guests had eaten, followed by jelly and custard. Not a promising outlook, and what a moment for Sophie to remember that first evening when she'd invited Christian home for the meal. By home standards Mrs Higgins' spread was below par even for fête day fare. Sophie brought her thoughts up short, aware that Christian was as disappointed in what they'd found as she was herself.

'Doesn't matter,' she said, her smile telling him more than her words.

'No. We won't go out tonight, what's the point? We ought to have waited until spring like Mrs Westlake said. I doubt if there is even a show to go to this time of year.'

'Doesn't matter,' she said again.

'You're right.' He pulled his spirits up by their boot strings, reminding himself of all the good things in the situation. No wonder he'd felt proud of her today: she was more than pretty, she was exquisite. Poor Lyddy, he told himself as if to set his thoughts firmly on the track where they belonged, being dressed up in finery doesn't suit her. Pure gold, that's what Sophie had called her. But put her in a gold dress like she'd worn today and she looked more like someone's sallow maiden aunt. Pleased with himself, one hurdle overcome, he was keen to race on.

'So, Mrs Mellor, this evening we stay in.' The invitation in his tone was lost on her. The dingy hotel seemed a very dull place to spend their first evening.

'We could always just walk down and listen to the waves.'

'Not yet. We have our bags to unpack. All that finery you bought will get creased. Let's go upstairs and sort our things.'

Disappointment vanished. His reference to 'our' things was all it took. Yet once upstairs, she'd hardly started to hang her new clothes in the wardrobe when she discovered his real reason for deciding they'd stay.

'No, Christian. Let's wait. Let's wait until we're in bed and can just stay curled up together after.'

But Christian had other ideas. It wasn't quite a repetition of that other time, for now he peeled off most of his clothes; he undid the long row of buttons on the back of her dress and slipped it from her shoulders. She gave herself over to his ministrations as he undressed her. If this was what he wanted, wasn't it simply because he loved her so much? Of course it was. So, willingly, she let him undress her. It surprised her that she felt no shred of embarrassment to stand naked in front of him, instead she was proud in the certainty that her body was beautiful, proud that the sight of her so affected him.

From downstairs came the sound of a clock chiming the half hour, half past nine. This time it would be all she dreamed, today they had made those solemn promises…with my body I thee worship…to have and to hold…love, honour and obey…

With willing obedience she lay on the bed holding her arms to him. He'd told her it would be different this time. Surely the miracle of love would unite them body and soul. But the fading memory of that other time was nothing compared with what she felt only seconds later, her face crushed against him; she couldn't turn her head, she felt she was being smothered, crushed, battered.

'Can't breathe,' she managed to gasp. But he seemed not to hear, not to care. Then it was over, the act that destroyed all the joy of her day. She felt too numb to speak, she felt unclean.

'Well, wife?' He panted in satisfaction when at last he rolled off her. 'How was that?'

It was as if something in her snapped as her dreams toppled around her. How *could* he talk like that, sounding so sure, so pleased with himself, as if he'd performed some wonderful feat? Was this what he'd meant by 'with my body I thee worship'. Worship? Use! Make filthy!

'How was it?' Her voice was shrill, unnatural to her own ears. 'It was beastly, no it was *bestial*, that's how it was. Not that you'd care just as long as you can pound away like—like the bull sent to serve the cows at Highland Farm.' She heard the croak in her voice and was lost. Her face contorted like a child's as the hot tears rolled down her cheeks. As she screeched at him she climbed off the bed and gathered up her clothes, holding them in front of her to protect her nakedness from his sight. 'Didn't care when I said I couldn't breathe.' She heard herself, she was ashamed and yet she gloried in the release of her near-hysteria tears.

'God's truth!' he exclaimed, coming to stand in front of her.

'Isn't God's anything. Nothing holy about it, nothing like the things we said in church.' She was behaving disgracefully, she knew she was. All she cared about was hurting him as he'd hurt her.

'Oh for heaven's sake, what have I done wrong now? You'll be telling me I raped you next.'

'Didn't say that. But all *that*,' she nodded her head towards the rumpled counterpane, 'I thought being married would make it different.' She'd stopped crying, but she couldn't breathe steadily, her whole body trembled.

He stood there watching her, his expression telling her nothing.

All her life Sophie had loved solitude, but never before had she felt so utterly alone. 'Wish I wasn't here,' she mumbled.

'Too late for either of us to wish that. And whose idea was it that we rushed into marriage? Was it mine?'

'It was yours that we went to bed that other time.'

'God Almighty! You'd been begging for it for months. Who was it who told your father—uncle or whatever he is—that when he caught us red-handed it was because we wanted to spend the rest of our lives together? Was it me?'

'I thought—' But she couldn't finish the sentence; tears were still too near the surface.

'Whatever either of us thought, we have to make the best of things.'

'I thought it would be—be—a sort of—of—'

His anger seemed to have turned to humour but all she saw was mockery. '… sort of?' he prompted.

'Benediction. That's what I thought it would be after the things we promised. And it will, won't it, Christian?' She pleaded for his understanding.

He said nothing. It seemed his pretty maiden was also his ice maiden.

'Went off a treat, Addy,' Archie said with satisfaction as he got into bed and watched her sitting on the edge and pulling on her bed socks. 'She looked a real picture—and so did our Lyddy in her posh gold frock.' Then, as Adelaide took up her hairbrush and started her nightly hundred strokes, 'I'm getting your side warm, buck up and get in. Real proud of the pair of them I was, we both were, eh? And you, Addy m'love, don't often say it to you, not much of a one for fine words.'

'Never did trust too much grand talk, Arch. You did well

with your speech,' she added as she climbed in by his side. He noticed that tonight her hair had had short shrift, only twenty-two strokes before she put the brush down.

'I don't envy them, being young and unsure of themselves,' she said as she wriggled close to him.

'Thirty-three years, Addy. Let's hope they get on like we have.'

Later—how much later? Five minutes? Ten? More?—he whispered, 'Please God they'll find what we always have.'

'Umph,' she agreed, holding him close.

'Young and full of hope…' For a moment she thought he was drifting into sleep as she settled comfortably for the night. 'You know what I read somewhere, years ago but I've never forgotten?'

'You? Read? Never thought of you as a reader, Arch.'

'This was different, it sort of jumped out of the page and hit me. Something to the effect that the bedroom is a couple's private place, and in a family that's true enough. About the only place you can shut the door and know it's your own.'

'I could have told you that, silly. No need to read it.'

'Ah but here's the bit that hit me. The chap who wrote it called the bedroom their own country and the capital city of that country the marriage bed.'

Addy gave a most un-Addyish chuckle. 'I'd never thought of myself as a city girl.'

In her room at the other end of the landing, Lydia stared at the dark ceiling. The bed was cold, her stone hot-water bottle brought her no comfort. If Christian had married anyone but Sophie she could have found an outlet for her misery in jealousy and resentment. But it was Sophie he'd fallen in love with, innocent, fun-loving, open-hearted Sophie. Schooled to kneel by her bed for her nightly prayers for the family, for the poor, for those little girls in the orphanage, for the hungry and lonely but never for herself, yet surely no plea had ever been more heart-felt than the one that filled her mind as a single hot tear escaped. 'Help me to accept…wanting his love is a sin, I know it is…a sin against You and a sin against darling Sophie…forgive me…help me…give me the courage and strength to face each day seeing them together, watching the happiness they give each other…help me…forgive me.'

CHAPTER THREE

'I worry about that child, Addy, jigged if I don't,' Archie said, putting his unfolded copy of the newspaper down and reaching to put another knob or two of coal on the fire.

'So you always would, Arch, come what may. But to be honest, I don't like the look of things either. A bride of three months—especially one with that nice home—ought to be more full of the joy of life than our Sophie. Does the blame lie at *my* doorstep for not making sure she was better equipped to run a home? Is that what worries her, do you think?'

'Rubbish, m'dear. She knows she only has to come to you for a bit of help and you'd be glad to give it—more than glad. But then, perhaps that's just the way she is, she's always been a gal to want to find her own way. What does Lyddy make of things, does she say?'

'When have you ever known either of those two talk about the other? If Lyddy has opinions of her own, that's the way she'll keep them. You see more of Christian than I do. He's as bright as usual, is he?'

'Oh ah, no change in Christian. Reckon I'd worry less if there was. Can't he see that something isn't as it should be with Sophie? A young bride, and one in a smart home like she's starting off with, ought to be as bright as a button.'

'Perhaps it wasn't a wise move making them the gift of the house but putting it just in *her* name. You know I said at the time I didn't like it. Perhaps the root of her trouble is that she feels we're only pretending to accept him as one of us. A man should be master in his own home, that's what I say. Oh, I know all about those suffragettes, marching about and creating a disturbance—and I'm not saying their thinking has ever been wrong, as far as having a say in putting in the government we want, I think a woman has a mind every bit as good as a man's, often enough better, and those of us who've got the right they fought for have reason to be grateful to them—but in the home, the man has to be seen as captain of the ship. Putting the house in Sophie's name, and her so inexperienced too, belittles him. There isn't a woman born who doesn't like to feel her man is looked up to and respected. And when the bill for the rates comes in, the envelope should be addressed to *him* not her.'

Never had Archie been more tempted to tell her why he had done what he had. In truth he avoided thinking about it too deeply. Christian had taken advantage of the child's innocence, he told himself—repeatedly. For an honest streak in him couldn't ignore Sophie's never-failing ability to get what she wanted. Had she been the one to lead the way? But if she had, she'd been too naive to realise; she would simply have been following her heart. Now that it was all over, would there be any harm in telling Addy the whole truth? No, he couldn't do it. It would cast a shadow. It was best forgotten. So his moment of weakness passed.

'I dare say we're worrying for nothing,' he said, making

sure his voice was cheerful. 'He's chipper enough, just what you would expect of a healthy young man with a wife at home ready to make a fuss of him. If there's a change in him at all, it's that he seems keener than ever to be part of everything in the business. Still kept busy with his own work, mind you, but keen to be part of our show. Cupid's a funny fellow, where he chooses to aim his arrows. As long as he—Christian I mean, not Cupid—as long as he's good to young Sophie, and she's happy, then I've no argument with things as they are. But, just between ourselves, it would have been ideal if she could have lost her heart to someone else and he could have set his sights on Lyddy. I wish you could hear them there in the office: her grasp of what has to be done there is as good as any man's, Addy, you'd be right proud just like I am of the way she handles things. And there's no disputing what an asset young Christian is. Get along together sweet as anything.'

'That was always *my* hope, you know that. But he had his eye on Sophie from the word go, just like a good many more from round these parts. Lyddy's going to get wet walking back from the church hall after Guides, just listen to that rain on the window. Why don't you take the motor over and pick her up, Arch?'

He laughed. 'Why? Because we both know our Lyddy, that's why. Can you see her getting into a nice dry motor car and swanning off, leaving the girls to trudge home through the rain?'

Addy knew he was right.

At number fourteen Meadowlands, too, the westerly wind was driving the rain to beat against the dining-room window.

'Your skills are improving,' Christian said, his voice teasing, 'that shepherd's pie was nice. And to follow?'

Sophie's spirits rose.

'Apple Charlotte.' Then, cheered by his praise, she laughed. 'But don't expect two miracles in one meal. I did what Mrs Beeton told me, but my things never look like hers do in the book.'

This evening, though, Mrs Beeton ought to have been proud of her.

'Too wet to go out for a pint at the Dew Drop. Leave the dishes in the sink, do them in the morning. Let's wind up the gramophone and dance.'

Willingly, she did as he suggested, putting off the thought of morning and trying not to hear the echo of Ethel's view on left dishes: 'Leave them till morning and they have pups in the night.'

With the gramophone wound to its fullest, a new needle screwed in, the sound of ragtime filled the room. What fun this was! Sophie wouldn't think of anything but the moment. No, that was only half the truth; but she pushed the things she hated to the back of her mind, and into these moments she crammed all the excitement of being in love with him. Of course she was in love with him. If she weren't she couldn't possibly have felt that surge of joy when he looked at her as he had this evening with a teasing, affectionate light in his eyes—or when he'd told her how well she'd done with their meal tonight, for certainly she'd found no pleasure at all in following those boring instructions to make it. Twirling around the room with the rug rolled up and the furniture pushed back to make some space, she felt she would burst with happiness. If only it could go on like this for ever.

One of the first things Christian had noticed about her was that her face was a window to her emotions. If he'd thought it added to her attraction at the fête nearly two years before, he certainly felt filled with optimism on that March night. Perhaps tonight she'd not lie there like some stone image, cold, unyielding, enduring what she couldn't avoid. Why the hell couldn't she 'give' like she did when she danced? His confidence would have been boosted if he could have known how even after more than three months of marriage, she could still be stirred to hope for some half-understood miracle.

'No more,' he said at last, closing the lid of the gramophone, 'time for bed.'

'Just five more minutes…'

But already he was putting the guard in front of the dying fire.

'We're not tired,' she argued, finding another record. '*Please…*' She would her arms around his neck, her bottom lip pouting provocatively, her eyes shining with hope, a tactic that was second nature to her and one she expected to get what she wanted. Now what it got her was his mouth on hers, his hands pressing her close.

'You've had your fun,' he mumbled, his lips so close that she could feel the movement as he spoke, 'now it's my turn.' She could feel a sudden change in him: his hands moved to grip her shoulder, he moved back just far enough for him to look at her. There was no escape. 'Damn it, damn it, Sophie, why can't you unbend, relax? What sort of pleasure do you think you give *me*, lying there with no more life in you than a dead fish on a marble slab?'

'Stop it, Christian. Don't spoil everything. It's been a lovely evening—'

'So could the rest of it be. Does what I do to you hurt? Actually hurt?'

She shook her head. 'Don't you see? What you do to me, that's what you said. You just *use* me.'

'And whose fault is that? Mine? Would you rather I went to someone else? Would you rather I went outside for my entertainment?'

'Stop it.' Sophie felt the sting of tears; she was past caring as she felt them wet on her cheeks.

'For Christ's sake, don't start that. I'm sorry, Sophie, dear Sophie, I shouldn't have said it. But I'm no different from any other man. Do you think all of them are made to feel like filthy letchers because they want to make love to their wives?'

'I'm sorry, Christian, it's my fault.' And again her arms were around his neck, her tear-reddened eyes pleading.

'It's all right, darling,' he rocked her gently, his hands caressed her back, 'it'll get better for us, for both of us.' She wondered what he could mean by 'both of us'; it seemed to her his pleasure lacked for nothing. But tonight would be different, tonight he would be tender, he would be gentle, whatever he found so wonderful would be the same for her; then hard on the heels came another thought: tonight would indeed be different, after seeing her crying he'd not expect *that*, he'd be satisfied just to cuddle her. Almost eagerly she went to bed.

But she was wrong on both counts. Nothing was different and nothing could have destroyed the pleasure of the evening more completely. A dead fish on a slab, his words echoed as she suffered him. And next morning as she looked at the pile of waiting crockery and cooking pots, even the success of her cooking did nothing to raise her spirits. After the rain, the world smelled fresh and clean, the sky was the clear blue of winter. She'd do the dishes, no one else would, so she had no choice. She'd make the bed and she wouldn't let herself remember how, even after her tears, he had climbed on top of her with his customary gusto, knowing she wanted it just to be over and not even caring how she felt. That was yesterday; today was her own. She would cut some sandwiches for her lunch, she would leave him some cold meat and pickles and bread, then, on her bicycle, she would find freedom in clear, cold air. Damn the housework, damn the pile of ironing that waited in a basket in the cupboard, she would be alone and free.

'I'll do the Friday rent collections, Dad, shall I?' She always asked him even though it was ages since he'd done the weekly round. 'I've bought some toffees to take to little Ernie Prescott in Mulberry Street; he's home from school with chicken-pox.'

'Right you are, Lyddy m'dear, if that's the way you want it. Is there enough change in the bag for you to take?'

So Lydia set off, a leather bag of small change around her neck in the fashion of a bus conductor and a pen in her pocket to sign the rent books. Ill at ease on many a social occasion, yet talking to the tenants as she collected the rents presented no such problem. All went well as she progressed up the left-hand side of Mulberry Street, then started back down the right. It was when she got to number eight that she was kept waiting on the doorstep so long that she was about to turn away when the door opened.

'Thought it must be you, Miss Westlake,' old Mr Fulbrook greeted her. Usually Dulcie, his daughter, was ready with the rent so Lydia was unprepared to be faced with the tenant himself. 'Dulcie left the book all ready for you, she said the money was right. Count it out to make sure, but she said it comes to five shillings.' There was something pathetic about the pile of small change.

'Not often I find you at home, Mr Fulbrook,' she said, doing as he said and counting the pile of copper, threepenny pieces and sixpences into her bag.

'Often? Never, more like it, not till now. Never get old, Miss Westlake, that's the best advice I can give you. Got stood off at the gardens. To be fair, I can't blame them. What sort of use did I think I was being?'

So he'd lost his job. Seeing him standing bent over his two sticks, Lydia couldn't find it in her heart to blame the council, but her heart went out to him all the same. As long as she could remember, she'd thought of him as old, getting slower and more bent with each year as his arthritis took hold; but perhaps appearances were against him for his daughter Dulcie couldn't have been more than her mid-twenties.

'Young Dulcie's out now,' he explained, 'going around trying to pick up a bit of work.' He shook his head helplessly. 'She'd be better off if I was gone. Where's the sense in any of it, eh? Her mother, my Alice, you remember her, she was taken in the prime of life. Married her when she was just a girl, I'd no business to do it. Now look at me, nothing but a drain on our Dulcie. No chance for the poor girl with me to hold her back. Was different for Donald, that bit older and a boy, so off he went to earn a living in Bristol.'

'I remember him. How's he getting on?' She wanted to steer the poor sorry-for-himself man to a cheerier channel.

'In the docks, earns good wages, I dare say. Married back last year, but I didn't feel up to the journey. Our Dulcie went on the train. Just once he brought his young lady to see us.' His lined face broke into an unexpected and not altogether cheerful smirk. 'Braver than I gave him credit for, I tell you. Hard-faced female, looked as though her corsets were too tight. Never came this way again; not that I'm sorry. Missed the boy, though, when he upped and went.'

'Yes, of course you must have.'

'Now poor young Dulcie's got me under foot all day, more hindrance than help.'

'I'm sure that's not the way Dulcie sees it, Mr Fulbrook. I really am sorry about your job. Gardening must have been hard for you, though. We'll have to all put our heads together to see if we can't think of something else.'

'Too old to be useful, my dear. What I did was selfish, me all those years older than my Alice. Now there's Dulcie with me on her hands, younger than you are yourself, I dare say, and me well past my three score years and ten. Wonder they put up with me in the gardens as long as they did, if I'm truthful.'

'You feel down in the dumps this morning. I know how hard men find it when they see a woman as the bread-winner. But times are changing.'

'Not in my book, they're not. Now you, it's different for you, giving your father a hand. I tell you, Miss, I feel nothing but a burden. And why I'm talking to you like this the dear Lord alone knows.'

'I'm glad you have,' she told him. 'Sometimes it's easier to talk to someone you don't know too well than it is to the family.'

'Ah, I can't let Dulcie know how useless I feel. Go to peel the spuds now, for our dinner. About all I'm fit for.'

'That's only fair,' Lyddy said briskly. 'If you and Dulcie change roles you have to pull your weight.' She had no time for self-pity, her own or anyone else's either. 'You never thought of her as being useless when she kept the home going smoothly for you. Now it's your turn. If she's to be out working, then your side of the bargain won't leave you that much time for idleness.'

'You're a straight talker, that's for sure.' Then, leaning on his sticks, he stood taller. 'About time someone set the score straight for me. Well, there we are then. I've let off steam, you've listened, you've set things out for me and, bugger me—pardon my French—you've made me feel I might have a bit of use left in me yet.'

Lydia laughed, instinctively reaching out to cover the old man's hand with hers and surprising herself that she should.

'I'll see you next week,' she told him. 'A lot can happen in a week.'

She meant, of course, that by the end of the following week Dulcie could be bringing home a wage. Even so, as she went on her way the Fulbrooks' plight was on her mind. As honest a man as one could meet, she thought, how he'd hate it if they couldn't scrape together their five shillings. Well, if things are hard somehow I'll see to it they aren't made to feel bad about it. Then, almost at the end of Mulberry Street, she knocked on the door of the Prescotts' cottage and felt in her pocket for the bag of toffees she'd brought for Ernie.

Rent-collecting came as high on Lydia's list of pleasures as her evening with the Guides or her meetings with the fundraising committee. It really stemmed from the fact that their perfect family circle had been broken when Sophie had left home. Not that she and Christian didn't come frequently to visit, but *her* Sophie had been replaced by Christian's wife.

Would it have been like this if she'd married someone else? Lydia didn't delve into the question, she stamped on it as firmly as she did on every wayward dream that haunted her. She loved Sophie as dearly as she always had, she told herself, but no longer could they share confidences. Sophie was a married woman whilst she had nothing beyond dreams, dreams to which she had no right, dreams that filled her with shame that she couldn't find the strength to overcome the part played in them by her sister's husband. How they'd both mock her if they knew! In an attempt to give her own life more purpose Lydia had offered to spend her Saturdays at the orphanage, where, without the opportunity of wearing Girl Guide uniform, or making the solemn Guiding vows and becoming part of the world-wide movement, the eleven- to fourteen-year-olds would be given over to her care. She would teach them the same skills as she did the children of Kingshampton.

Her rents collected, Lydia strode back through the village to the yard, the Fulbrooks' plight pushed to the back of her mind. The day followed its usual Friday pattern. While she set about bringing the rents ledger up to date, Archie ate a hurried sandwich lunch at his desk then drove off towards Brackleford and the bank. It was early in the afternoon when she looked up as Christian came in, clearly wanting to talk.

'Are you all alone? Tell me if I'm disturbing you—if you're too busy?'

'Of course I'm not. Dad's gone to Brackleford to pay in the rent money and draw out the wages, his usual Friday jaunt. He doesn't like me doing that on my bicycle.'

But Christian wasn't paying attention. 'Do you know what I had for my lunch?'

Immediately she was on the defensive, believing Sophie's attempts had met with failure.

'Be patient with her, Christian. It's easy for you, someone else has always prepared your food and put it in front of you—and that's how it had been for her until she married.'

'What? No, you don't understand what I'm telling you. Sophie's morning wasn't spent trying to conjure up some culinary delight, Christ no. Just read that.' He threw a note on to her desk. '"Such a glorious day, too good to be indoors. I have taken some sandwiches and have gone for a ride. Your meal is under the plate. You know where to find pickle and bread."'

'Under the plate?' she prompted.

'Between two plates—a couple of slices of overcooked leather-like cold beef.' He looked like a child who'd been punished for something he hadn't done. Like everyone else—or everyone except, very occasionally, Adelaide—Lydia always made excuses for what her mother called Sophie's selfishness. Now, though, she was angry. But she mustn't let Christian see it for, if he recognised *that*, he might be aware of the other emotion that gripped her.

'She'll make up for it tonight, Christian. I bet while she's out she's planning a special treat to make up for your having no proper lunch.'

'Make up for it tonight,' he scoffed. 'Christ, Lyddy, you don't know the half of it.'

'I don't understand. Be patient with her, Christian. I expect it's our fault at home, we've always loved to spoil her—no, not spoil, nothing has spoiled her—but we've loved her just as she is. We ought to have seen she was better prepared for running a home.'

'Damn the home. A home doesn't make a marriage.'

'Of course it doesn't.' By the way she said it, he knew she was putting an end to confidences she didn't want to hear. This was Sophie's marriage, she wouldn't let herself listen to its secrets. 'I'm glad you've come in, Christian. While I put the kettle on the gas ring, can you glance through these delivery notes and check the bags of cement that came in this morning? I'll make us a drink.'

'Umph.' He stretched his arms high, as if in the physical act he was putting a line under what had gone before. 'Yes, of course I will. You do me good, Lyddy, do you know that?' Of course it must have been just in her imagination that there was an underlying message, and Lydia wasn't going to give way to imagination. Much later, she recalled the conversation, resolved to find a way of helping Sophie. If what irked Christian went beyond the way Sophie looked after their home, then it must be her need to escape on her own. But there was nothing new in that, she'd done it since she was a child. Yes, but she was an adult now, she had responsibilities. So Lydia set about looking for a way of taking some of those responsibilities from her freedom-loving sister. To Sophie freedom and fun went hand in hand. That's how she used to be—and how she would be again.

'I thought I'd neglect everything and ride over,' was her greeting as Sophie opened the front door to her knock the next day. 'We never seem to see each other these days, properly see each other, I mean.' Yet, even putting it into words seemed to widen the gap that had grown between them.

'You have a busy life. Not like me,' came Sophie's disgruntled reply.

'I fill my time as best I can,' Lyddy answered honestly.

'But what you do is much more important. Listen, Sophie, I have a purpose in coming to talk to you.'

'You're going to nag me because I deserted my post and had some fun yesterday,' Sophie pouted. 'I suppose Christian ran tittle-tattling to you.'

'Nothing to do with yesterday, at least nothing to do with what you were up to.'

'No?' Sophie immediately brightened up.

'Yesterday I did the rent-collecting…' and she told the story of Samuel Fulbrook losing his job and his daughter having to earn their living.

'That's rotten,' Sophie said. 'Although she can't possibly want to spend her life stuck at home in Mulberry Street. Where's the future in that? You were keen enough to escape to help Dad in the business.'

'Of course I was. And I was lucky that there was a place for me there. Sophie, what if I suggested to Dulcie Fulbrook that you might have a job for her, just a morning a week or something? If it's the money that stops you, I'd give you the wage to pay her. I don't want to push in, but Dad insists he pays me for the time I spend in the office and—well, I really don't have many expenses. I'd like to help her, but I can't see how else to do it.'

'What's she like? Being sorry for her doesn't necessarily make me keen to have her poking around here if she's— well, you know—frowsty or unwholesome.'

Lyddy laughed, giving her a spontaneous hug. Dear little Sophie, nothing would ever change her. Then she turned the question over in her mind. What was Dulcie like? She hardly knew her, she was one of the less talkative tenants, so she could go no further than her appearance.

'She's as clean as a new pin.'

'Lots of women are clean. Is she young? Old? Jolly? Prim? Will I like having her around? I'm sorry she needs to work but that doesn't mean I want to have her under foot if I shan't get along with her.'

'You'll have to meet her first anyway, so it's up to you whether you give her a job. But, yes, I should think you'd like having her here. It's a funny expression, but I think the best way of describing her is that she's comely. About my age— no, younger, somewhere between me and you—she's quite pretty, you can tell as soon as you see her that she's a nice person, kind, gentle, caring. A very ready smile, a bit on the plump side—no, that's not the way to describe her, that makes her sound fat and she isn't, she's sort of soft and rounded.' Then, with a laugh, 'Not a bean pole like me, nor yet slim and just right like you. With an invalid mother to care for until she died, then an ageing father, poor Dulcie has had a narrow life. I don't really know her very well.'

'Give me a loophole, so that if I don't like the look of her I don't have to take her on. Tell her it's just your idea that she might like to call and ask me if I needed help—me being more or less newly married, you know the way to put it to her. Then I'll look surprised when I open the door to her.' Sophie's girlish giggle reassured Lydia that nothing about her had changed. 'If she looks like an over-wholesome kill-joy I'll tell her I just love doing my own housework, I'll lie like a trooper. Do troopers lie or do they just swear?'

Lie or swear, Sophie did neither when she opened the front door to Dulcie Fulbrook's knock. She almost forgot her planned look of surprise.

'It may be that you aren't looking for anyone,' Dulcie made it easy for her to send her away, 'but your sister suggested it might be worth my while just asking you. I couldn't not come, you understand, she's been so kind in trying to help me. But I don't expect—'

'Come in, Miss…I don't know your name,' Sophie lied.

'Dulcie Fulbrook. My father and I are tenants in Mulberry Street. I do need to find work, but *please* don't try and find something for me to do just because I'm asking. I'm sure that if I got a bicycle I could find a full-time job in Brackleford,' she added, her burst of independence endearing her to Sophie.

There was something innocent and untouched in Dulcie's expression. The clothes she wore were far from new, but despite being what Sophie saw as old-fashioned there was something appealing in her appearance. An unexpected thought came into her mind as she opened the door wide to invite her caller in: Dulcie Fulbrook was 'fragrant', a fragrance that had nothing to do with perfume but rather with the certainty that, stripped of her outer garments, her underwear would be as well cared for, the crocheted edge of her petticoat as carefully pressed, as anything visible to the eye. Sophie was beginning to enjoy her visitor.

At Drydens most of the gardening was done by Eddie Tidman, who spent three half-days a week on keeping it weeded and the lawn mown. Archie enjoyed planting his vegetable plot ('About the only bit of man's work I do these days,' he maintained), while Addy made the tubs of annual flowers her responsibility. Gardening had never appealed to Lydia and, although Sophie loved the countryside, she didn't acquaint that with planting and hoeing. But with a newly built house, the large garden was as empty as an unfurnished room, something had to be done about it and Christian showed no sign of being the one to do it. Taking it for granted that Eddie would be glad to do as she wanted, she asked him to plant a lawn. Of course, he agreed; it didn't even enter his head not to for, like everyone else, he had delighted in giving her pleasure since she'd been no more than a toddler, following him around as he worked. So he dug, he raked, he sieved and he rolled the one-time farm land and only when he was satisfied did he scatter the grass seed and cover the area with string and bird scarers. That had been early in March, a week or two before Dulcie came on to the scene. By the end of April the garden was beginning to take shape, the young grass giving a fragile impression of a lawn even though no one could walk on it, and the surrounding borders already dug not by Eddie but, this time, by Dulcie. Christian had no leaning towards spade or fork, but the promise of what could be done with the space inspired him to draw out a plan for the workers to follow.

'She's something of a Trojan, this woman you've found,' he said conversationally to Sophie as they sat down to share the excellent lamb casserole and extra-early new potatoes brought over by Archie, together with the asparagus. All of it had been prepared by Dulcie, with written instructions how long each should cook. 'I say, this is good. You and Mrs Beeton seemed to have formed a bond.'

She saw no reason to disillusion him.

'A Trojan?'

'I see the border is taking shape,' he explained. 'Housework, gardening, is there no end to her talents?'

'Oh, we're doing the garden together. We worked out there

all the morning. I never knew I enjoyed gardening, Christian. We had such fun. You know what I think? I think it's extra fun just to see how much she enjoys it. I've never thought about that with anyone else.'

'We'll turn you into a philanthropist yet, like your sister— cousin or whatever she is.'

'*Sister*,' came Sophie's sharp reply, 'we've always been sisters. And she's not a philanthropist, in that condescending voice, she's just a really good person.' She wasn't sure why it was she felt irritated. She didn't want his praise for Dulcie or for Lyddy either. They belonged to *her*, not to him.

'I remember you said that to me the day we met. Lyddy's pure gold, you said. And of course so she is.'

Her momentary—and, she admitted, unwarranted—anger melted. Watching her across the table, his eyes smiled. That his benign expression was brought about in part by the quality of the lamb casserole didn't diminish her own rare contentment.

'Christian,' she said, instinct telling her this might be a good moment to broach the subject, 'Dulcie comes here on Mondays and Thursdays. That's not really enough work for her, I know that. I'm scared that someone else will want her every day and I shall lose her altogether. Do you think we can afford to ask her to come in more? Or, if you say we can't, I'm sure Lyddy would like to help with her wage. I know how worried she was for them when old Mr Fulbrook lost his job doing the garden for the council.'

'You think I'd let your family pay my bills? I have no shortage of commissions, I'm certainly not dependent on charity, however kindly meant. I'll give you an extra ten shillings a week on your housekeeping money. What you do with it is your own affair.'

Getting up from the table she came round to stand behind him, bending down, her arms around him as she rubbed her cheek against the side of his head.

'Thank you, thank you, darling Christian. Except for Lyddy, do you know, I've never had a real friend before. I've known lots of people, at school and all that, but a friend, someone you feel in tune with…'

'You have a husband. Or don't husbands count?'

'Silly,' she laughed. 'Husbands are different, you don't marry your friends.'

'You mean we're not friends?' Putting down his knife and fork he turned in his chair so that he could look at her. 'Not friends. So are we lovers?'

'Of course we are, we fell in love, that's why we got married. And if you mean—all that—if that's what you mean, I've never once stopped you when you've wanted to make love.' Even if he hadn't been able to see her expression, he would have heard the pout in her voice.

'Make love, is that what you call it?'

'Don't spoil things, the evening was so nice.'

'Friends, lovers, forget it. Go and eat your food. Then leave the dishes till morning and we'll go in the garden and see what you've been up to.'

Partially restored, she went back to her seat, aware that some of the magic she'd tried to clutch at had gone beyond reach. She hated the beastliness of washing up, scraping dirty dishes, plunging her hands into that bowl of hot water and soda, scrubbing the casserole with her disgusting saucepan cleaner, a casserole that would be determined to hang on to the gravy that was burnt on to it. If she and Christian were real partners they could have done it together, it could even have been fun. Fun! What fun was there in any of it? Not like this morning when she and Dulcie had been kneeling by the newly dug border, digging their fingers into the dirt and planting the seedlings brought on for her in the greenhouse at Drydens.

And if that was the way her mind was working, Christian's was going off in another direction. Friend…husband… lover…shouldn't a man be all those things and isn't that how she should think of him? And he, how did he honestly see his pretty, childlike Sophie? Friend? Surely a friend was a person you could relax with, be honest with? A person who shared your interests? A person who found her greatest pleasure in your being together, not just together at the meal table or presenting a united front to the outside world, but together in the way that really counted when the rest of the world was forgotten? A bachelor of thirty, he'd bedded women enough before he got ensnared by Sophie and they'd seemed to enjoy it. What was it she'd said to him just as he was drifting into sleep the other night? That she wouldn't mind his love-making if it could only make her pregnant. Wouldn't mind it! Why couldn't she grow up and understand what it was like for a man to make love to a body so utterly unresponsive. Yet, partly that was what aroused him, it was the challenge, the hope, surely the confidence that one day, like a butterfly emerging from a chrysalis, she would become a woman with a woman's sexuality. If underlying that thought was another, that his pride in his own manhood was slighted by her passive submission, he wouldn't admit to it. And what of her? Did she not think of herself as his friend? Did she hold him in pride of place, caring for him above all else? The silent answer came back immediately: above all else what Sophie cared for was herself. When did she ever look outside herself? Even now that she wanted Dulcie to come in each day instead of twice of week, was it because of the woman's need to earn extra money or was it because she was frightened of being thrown back on her own resources?

'Let's hurry up and stack the dishes,' Sophie's voice cut through his thoughts—seemingly already she had bounced back to her cheerful self, 'then we can go in the garden and I'll show you what we've done. I wish we had some trees, Christian, I used to love the hammock in the garden at home.' Wherever her thoughts had been as they finished their meal, they'd obviously not travelled on the same lines as his.

As spring rolled on into summer the only outward change in the daily pattern was that Dulcie came each morning to the house in Meadowlands and often in the afternoon too. Further along the long terrace in Mulberry Street lived Jack and Tilly James, Jack, who had lost both his legs, and his interest in living too, in the trenches of Flanders, and Tilly, who took in washing so that she wouldn't have to leave him alone while she was out trying to earn enough to supplement his meagre war pension. Her constant and unspoken fear was that if she left him too long by himself he would find a way of escaping the misery of his life. Some afternoons she pushed him out in his wheelchair and it was on one of those occasions that they stopped to speak to Samuel Fulbrook, who'd brought a wooden chair outside to the narrow pavement so that he could sit in the sunshine. With his old felt hat pulled low over his closed eyes, he seemed to be asleep.

'Mr Fulbrook,' Tilly whispered, to be answered by a gentle snore.

'No good whispering like that. Give him a prod. What the hell's the old fool doing blocking the path?' She was too used to Jack sounding tetchy to be surprised by his tone.

'Sshh!' Tilly held a finger to her lips. 'Don't talk like that, he might hear you.'

'Better hear one of us unless we're to be here all day. Give him a prod, can't you.'

With a snort, Samuel woke.

'Oh my dear, I'm sorry.' He grasped one stick and with the movement knocked the other to the ground.

'Don't worry, I'll get it. Haven't seen you for a long time, Mr Fulbrook, Someone said you'd given up your job.'

'Thanks, m'dear.' He took the stick she retrieved for him and struggled to his feet. 'If I'd had a ha'porth of pride I'd have gone before I got pushed. Getting the sack when you have a chance to look for something else, that a man can take. But I don't have to tell you these things, young Jack,' (young Jack being not much older than Dulcie, like so many more whose lives had been thrown off course by war) 'what the deuce do I have to complain about, a man with a good life behind me.'

Rarely did Tilly see Jack smile, but that's what he did now as he looked at Samuel.

'Is Dulcie at home with you these days, or has she found herself something now that you've packed it in?' he wanted to know.

'Dulcie goes over to one of those new places they've been building, Meadowlands. She's working for Mr Westlake's girl→the pretty one, the young one. Got married back in the winter.'

'Yes, I heard,' Tilly chimed in. 'With a lovely home like

that to start their married life in, fancy her wanting someone to come and help with the chores. Most of us would give our eye teeth for the chance to keep a home like that up to scratch. How does Dulcie get on with her? Pretty as a picture, she always was. But looks can deceive.'

'Never known Dulcie so chipper. Better cleaning away someone else's dirt than your own, it seems. Any road, off she goes each morning like a dog with two tails, on a bicycle, if you please. Miss Westlake that was has given it to her so that she can get along quicker.'

'So you get left with the chores at home?' While Tilly talked she moved the chair on to the road so that she could pass with Jack. It wasn't so much that she was interested in the arrangements in the Fulbrook house as she felt that as long as they talked it seemed less obvious that the old man had been in the way. Over these past few years she'd become adept at sparing sensitive feelings.

'I do what I can. Shopping and the like. Well, most of everything I have to leave to young Dulcie, if I tell the truth. You ladies, you know how to set about things. Isn't a man's place to be pootling about in a house. While we're sizing up how to set about a job you ladies get it done.'

'Excuses…excuses,' Tilly laughed.

She wished she hadn't said it, she wished she hadn't seen that momentary naked misery in the old man's expression. 'Ah, that's about the truth of it. Excuses!' He nodded. But he had himself well in control again; he would admit to resentment towards his ageing and failing body, but not to the anguish of his soul. 'To be honest, m'dear, giving up that job was the worst thing happened to me. When your bones get seized up like mine, the less you move, the less you can move. As long as I had to keep going then I felt I was keeping pace with the battle. But now…set solid as a rock. Took me best part of the morning to make my way up the street to buy a couple of chops.' Then, his face creasing in a proud grin, 'But I did it. Got them sizzling in the pan and yesterday's tatties fried crisp and golden pretty as you please ready for when she came home. But it's a struggle that seems to get worse by the day.'

'She's out shopping now, I suppose?' It seemed the old man wanted to talk and, if Tilly were honest with herself, she was glad to have someone to talk to. For Jack got more and more morose, never considered that his tragedy was hers too, never wondered what sort of a life she had, working from morning till night so that they could pay the rent and put food on the table. Even as she thought it, she pulled her mind back on track, resting a hand on Jack's shoulder even though he didn't seem to notice.

By the time Samuel answered her question she had forgotten she asked it.

'No, she bolted her food, then off she went back to her work. Five mornings, that's what it was supposed to be, but lately she and the pretty little girl she works for, they've been busying themselves in the garden. Getting it real nice, so she says. Comes to me for tips of course, but wouldn't I just like the use of my legs so that I could get over there and have a look at what they've done. Sorry, old son, me saying a thing like that to you. I tell you, it ain't till your body lets you down that you even begin to understand.'

Jack remembered him when he'd been upright, browned by working in the the open air all day long, full of vigour. That had been back in the sunshine of his own youth, a time he tried not to think of.

'Tell you what, Mr Fulbrook,' he found himself saying. 'Most afternoons Tilly is busy with her ironing, no chance of me getting out. Why don't you send Dulcie along sometimes to see whether the chair's going to be used? She could push you up to those smart new houses and I bet she'd be real cocky to show off what they're making of the new garden.' This time he felt the pressure of Tilly's hand on his shoulder. There's no sense in it, he told himself, but damned if I don't feel better for doing something for the poor old bugger. A minute before, he hadn't even been conscious that she'd touched him but now he knew and understood the wordless message. The sun seemed a little brighter, his desolation a little lighter.

That's how it was that two days later Dulcie pushed her father through the village and beyond to where Sophie was waiting.

The garden was already looking what he liked to think of as 'furnished', thanks largely to Drydens, where Eddie had done more than bring on seedlings in the greenhouse; he'd divided plants from the established herbaceous borders, and with Archie's approval he'd even dug up one or two of the younger bushes from the rose garden.

'I'll make the tea, shall I, Sophie?' Dulcie said, embarrassing her father by her familiarity. It wasn't right. On the way home he'd speak to her about it.

'Lovely. I'll chat with your father, I'd like that.'

My, but what a pretty little thing she was, he thought as she sat on the new garden bench by the side of the wheelchair, not a bit like the mistress of the house talking to the father of her daily cleaner. And that's what his Dulcie was, and best she remembered it.

'I don't like it,' he said, as much to himself as to Sophie when they were left alone.

'The garden? But we've done ever so well, Mr Fulbrook. Eddie—he looks after the garden at home, at my old home, I mean—he says we're doing really well. What don't you like about it?'

'The garden's pretty enough, does you credit Mrs…um Mrs…'

'Sophie. Never mind the Mrs bit.'

'No, Miss, Ma'am, that's just not good enough. And I shall speak to Dulcie, you just see if I don't. Familiarity doesn't sit comfortably between mistress and maid, never has and never will.'

'That's stupid!' Sweet, pretty Sophie had a streak of steel and he knew he'd just kicked against it.

'It's not my place to tell *you* how to carry on, if I tried to do that I'd be behaving no better than she is, acting as though she's your equal. Makes me angry. Worse, it makes me ashamed and embarrassed.'

'You know what I think? I think you're being old-fashioned and stupid. And *wicked*. It's like saying that a good person is one with lots of money and a bad one is someone without.'

'Good and bad don't come into it.' After weeks at home with no one to challenge him, no one to discuss anything with except for how many potatoes to peel for dinner, Samuel was coming into his own. Anyway, he told himself, he was *right*. To step out of your own circle meant that you didn't fit anywhere. 'I apologise for her, I dare say she's showing off a bit because I'm here.'

'Mr Fulbrook, Dulcie is my friend, I've never had a friend so dear.'

'What would your family think? And your husband?'

'They can think what they like. Here she comes. Don't say anything, let's just have our tea. She made a cake this morning especially.'

Watching his careful manner of drinking his tea and eating his cake—a cake such as Dulcie must often have made for him at home where, surely, he wouldn't have attacked it so delicately?—Sophie gave no sign of the inexplicable fear she felt. She wished he hadn't come; his beastly mean attitude had soiled something that had been perfect. Still, he had let the subject drop, so perhaps that would be the end of his stupid servile attitude. But she was wrong.

'Leave the cups. I'll wash them when you've gone,' she told Dulcie.

'No, I'll see to them, I've got the water hot already. I won't be many minutes.' And picking up the laden tray, 'Just open the door for me, can you.' It was said so naturally, just as naturally as Sophie's, 'Right you are,' and the way she jumped up to do as Dulcie asked.

'It's got to stop,' Samuel said as soon as he and Sophie were alone again. 'And if you care two hoots about her, you'll see to it that it does. She's had no life, a mother who was a dependent invalid, and now me just an old crock. Friends, you say. And for you I dare say that's a nice comfortable way of looking at it. But for her…If only she came home from working here and had a nice young man courting her. She's not like you, Mrs Sophie, you with a new husband and a lovely home. You're doing her no kindness letting her feel you are her friend. Find her a nice young man if you want to do something to help her.'

'Rubbish,' Sophie pouted, annoyed at his interference.

'Well, I'm telling you here and now, it's not right. And I won't have her behaving like it.'

'Like what?'

'Don't like it, don't like it. And I'll see to it there's a stop put to it.'

Sophie said nothing; there was no need, for at that moment Dulcie reappeared. It was only after they'd gone she thought of his anxiety. It was ridiculous, she couldn't bear to have to look after this place without Dulcie and she wouldn't let him spoil things for them with his Victorian views. The image of her friend was clear. She shut her eyes, almost hearing Dulcie's voice, hearing her laugh, knowing the *completeness* of being with her. How could that be wrong? What if the old man's hopes were fulfilled and that nice young man came courting Dulcie? Dear, gentle Dulcie, with her slightly plump figure, her round face and that deep dimple in her chin. Think of her hands, soft despite the way she worked. Dulcie, who never probed or questioned and yet she was sure understood her every thought. How dare he say their friendship was wrong? It was the most *right* thing she'd ever known. But what about Lyddy? She and Lyddy had always been close; surely they still were, even though these days she felt Lyddy avoided being alone with her. But that was silly, of course she didn't. Why should she? In any case, Lyddy was family, so that was quite different from her friendship with Dulcie.

A few months ago, if she'd been honest she would have said she regretted getting married. Even now, just as she had in the beginning, she trusted with a blind faith that some sort of miracle would make things better and would bring the romance she'd dreamed of into her life. Given the opportunity of putting the clock back, she wouldn't want to be the girl she'd been when, single, she'd lived at Drydens. Now each morning she woke looking forward to the day. She knew it had to do with Dulcie, to the friendship which grew stronger, would continue to grow stronger, a friendship that was becoming the most important thing in her life.

Next morning Dulcie was quiet; she seemed ill at ease.

'Dad talked to you yesterday, didn't he, about us, I mean? He told me. We had a row. Sophie, I felt awful, poor old Dad, I know he only wants things to be good for me.'

'You're not going to listen to him. Promise me, Dulcie. You won't leave me.'

Dulcie shook her head.

'Never had a row like it with Dad. He's written off to Donald, that's my brother. I saw the envelope, but he didn't tell me what it was he'd said. I know Donald had offered him a home when Mum died, him and me too.'

'You won't go, Dulcie? Promise me you won't go.' Sophie could feel the pounding of her heart; she didn't even realise how hard she gripped Dulcie's arm.

'Couldn't go, Sophie. Never known such happiness as I have these months. But like Dad says, it's not right. Frightens me.'

Sophie took hold of both her hands. 'I hate the weekends when you don't come. You're sort of like my second self. Of course it's right, Dulcie, nothing has ever been so right.'

'Just came here to work,' Dulcie croaked, upset by the quarrel with her father, upset by the rush of affection she felt for Sophie, 'I never meant things to rush away with us.'

Rush away with us; in her mind Sophie repeated the expression, knowing the truth of it. 'We won't let them inter-

fere with us,' she said, wiping her hands across Dulcie's wet
cheeks. 'We don't live in the days of Queen Victoria, why
shouldn't we be friends? Please don't cry, Dulcie. Wipe your
face, then I'll tell you what we'll do. We'll put some food
ready for Christian, then we'll cycle to the boat house. On
the way I'll call at the office and ask Lyddy to tell Mr Fulbrook that you're staying on to do extra hours and not to expect you until late. It's her rent day today so she'll be calling
there. I've been wanting to take you on the river, it's one of
my favourite things. I've always been on my own until now,
that's what I wanted. But now I want you to come too. We'll
have such fun, you'll love it, I promise.'

Dulcie ought to have refused; she didn't want to deceive
her father. But he'd left her no choice.

CHAPTER FOUR

As villages went, in those days Kingshampton would have ranked as medium or large. The high street was home to the usual assortment of shops, three butchers, two bakers, two general shops, one of which doubled as a post office, three public houses (the Dew Drop Inn, the Queen's Head and the Plough), Alfred Hicks' men's wear shop, proclaiming itself 'A. Hicks, Gentleman's Outfitter' in gold lettering on the side wall of the building, a ladies' wear shop with no such pretensions and with stock which made no pretence of keeping up with changing fashion, a cobbler, a fish and chip café, a greengrocery, a haberdashery and an ironmongery. The locals prided themselves on being self-sufficient. Of course it wasn't strictly true, but a trip down the High Street for day-to-day necessities ensured that most people found what they wanted with the added bonus of always meeting someone to speak to.

Even so, there were those who were made to feel invisible, and Norah Knight knew that she and her daughter Sybella would fall into that category. Since they'd moved into their squalid accommodation at the end of Tanners' Lane the hostile glances thrown in her direction from the local women had left her in no doubt. Now the men, they were a different matter. Not that any of them in the village had gone further than a knowing wink or a cheery smile—that, and a whisper between themselves. She wasn't born yesterday, she knew the score well enough, she'd had years enough to learn it in. Anyway, she thought as she paid her penny-ha'penny for the potatoes she'd come out to buy, a few days and she'd move on.

'See who's coming, out spending her ill-gotten gains,' one woman said, nudging her companion as Norah came towards them carrying her shopping. 'My Jim says she's the talk of the Dew Drop, well known in Brackleford where she picks up her trade. Threepenny bit, that's what they call her down in the alehouse.' She made no attempt to lower her voice. If the newcomer heard, so much the better. Kingshampton was a good-living, God-fearing village—people like they were could do without her sort. Wouldn't you think that, after the cold shoulder they'd been shown, she and her child would have got the message and moved away? Her sort of trade could be picked up as well in one place as another.

'Meaning me?' Norah moved close, blocking their path and holding her painted face close to theirs.

'Don't know what you're talking about. I was speaking to my friend. Just let us pass, if you please.'

'Why would I want to hinder you? You live your life and I'll live mine. And shall I tell you the difference?' The other two looked at each other for support, neither answering. 'The difference is that you seem to find mine interesting. Good luck to you if your own is so bloody boring you've nothing better to do than mind other people's business.' Then she stood to one side and with an exaggerated bow of her head let them pass. Seeing the way they looked back at her, the way their heads wagged as they talked and imagining just what they were saying, Norah laughed loudly, the sound a mockery. Anyone watching might have believed she saw herself as having scored a point; they wouldn't have suspected that her aggressive attitude was as unnatural as the cheap powder and paint she plastered on her face.

As she resumed her walk back to Tanners' Alley, she saw Lydia coming, her rent bag slung in its customary way. Still stinging from the encounter, she wanted to hit out, to hurt someone in retaliation. She knew exactly who this tall, gaunt-looking woman with the leather money-pouch hung round her neck must be. When she'd broken with local convention and gone into the Dew Drop for half a pint, one or two of the male drinkers had clearly enjoyed chatting, she'd even been bought a top-up. Given half a chance they'd like to be paid 'in kind' too, she could read it in their eyes. Poor sods, if they had to go home to those narrow-minded miseries. That's how it was that two evenings ago, quite by chance, she'd heard what had set her on a trail that had eluded her for years. A bit of flattery and she'd managed to pick up a good deal of what she needed to know and that's how she recognised the spinster daughter of the Westlakes, the one who collected the rents on Friday mornings.

'Good morning, *Madam*, oh no, I beg your pardon, of course it's *Miss*—the maiden lady with her bag of rent money.' And just as she had with the other two, she blocked Lydia's path. It was a long time since she'd had such a satisfactory time as she had these last twenty-four hours.

'I'm sorry, I don't think I know you,' Lydia answered her.

Norah knew how to handle women like the two she'd just

left, but Lydia spoke as respectfully as she would to any new neighbour.

'No, not yet you don't. But I knew you. I may be looked on as an outsider in this miserable village, but I know more than you think.'

In truth Lydia had no doubt who the woman was; on her rent rounds she'd heard about the mother and daughter who rented the tumbledown shack at the end of Tanners' Lane. 'Can do without her sort here,' 'Could tell you a thing or two about her. Got a name for herself in Brackleford, so I hear. That's where she was till she planted herself on us,' 'Kingshampton doesn't need her sort, hers or the child's either. Sybella, did you ever hear such a name, and for an urchin like my Daisy said she is. Poor Daisy, had to sit next to her in class yesterday. Hardly a rag to her back. It's not right. And the mother—soon run up debts for their rent, I dare say, then they'll do a moonlight flit and the sooner the better. Wouldn't mind betting that's why she moved on here from Brackleford.'

'In a village like this most people know each other.' Lydia made sure she held on to the pleasant tone, sensitive to the cold-shouldering the mother and daughter endured. 'I've been collecting rents in Mulberry Street. Someone said you had a daughter at school with theirs. Is she settling?'

'Would you, in that lot? Have the devil's job to push her off; given half a chance she'd never go near the place, that one or any other. But unless she bolts off on the way—and if I hear she does, then she'll get the beating she asks for—then she's there today and every day. You be thankful you haven't got the troubles kids bring with them.'

'I'm sure you don't mean that.'

'I've never had the chance to find out,' Norah Knight answered, surprising herself. 'Got lumbered when I was too young to have got a taste of what a proper life could be.' She pushed her face closer, so close that Lydia could smell the stale tobacco. But thinking of the poor child and the unfriendliness she was facing at the village school, she steeled herself not to pull back.

'Never had a life to call my own.' Norah asked herself what she was doing unburdening herself to 'this starchy old maid'. 'Got kicked out at home when my people found I was up the spout. And what did *he* do, the bastard? Disappeared like a snowman in a heat wave, that's what. And my people, just like these folk about the village here, good-living, that's how they saw themselves with their best clothes and chapel every Sunday. But me, I'd brought shame on them, nothing for me but hell fire. Good-living, my arse, easy enough for anyone not to slip up when the path's level and smooth. Good-living, what does it mean? To you? You with your good works and home? Didn't I tell you I knew more about you than you thought? I'll tell you what it means, same to you as it does to all the God-fearing miseries who get their pleasure in looking down their long noses on me, it means you're all, the lot of you, like the Pharisee: cross the road rather than help the poor bugger who'd got beaten up. Easy enough to show kindness to those like yourselves, but get someone who doesn't come out of the same mould and you turn a blind eye. Not that a blind eye means a silent tongue. Still, if lives are so dull and empty that keeping an eye on me gives it a fillip, then I can't begrudge any of you your two pen'orth of pleasure.' What was the matter with her this morning? Why was she taking such pleasure in trying to shock Miss Prim and Proper? Give the poor dried-up stick something to think about. A smile twitched the corners of Norah's painted mouth as she imagined the impression her words were making.

'It can't be easy for you,' Lydia tried to show understanding. 'But to have a daughter surely makes every hardship worthwhile.'

'And doesn't a damn fool thing like that just go to show how little you know about life, about *real* life, when you don't get a ha'porth of anything you can't pay for. So I earn a living, enough to put a roof over our heads. Not that that little bitch appreciates the drain she is on me. Every time I look at her I see her father.'

'Can't you find him, can't you make him help you?'

'And did I say I haven't found him? Finding him's one thing, holding the slippery devil down is another. His sort don't give up easily.' Then, with a sudden grin (for it couldn't be called a smile) and something akin to a wink, 'But wait long enough and things turn your way, you ask any fisherman. First time you get a bite, the catch might fall off the hook. But you learn. He's done the dirty on me once, twice: once when he left me in the cart, once when I found him and thought I'd got him in my net then he vanished clean away. He'll not do it again, buggered if he will.'

There was something in her expression that made Lydia uneasy; it was as if she knew she had the trump card hidden in the pocket of her too-tight skirt.

'I really am sorry,' Lydia answered. 'Have you managed to find work in Kingshampton, is that why you've come here?'

The question was answered by a raucous and mocking

laugh. 'Work, you call it! Don't sit in an office every day or go out rent collecting, if that's what you mean. No, miss, and I don't envy those who do, either. Been on the game for years.'

'Pardon?'

'The game, girl, the oldest game in the world. In posh society I'd be living in the lap of luxury—even though there'd still be plenty who'd think themselves too good to give me the time of day. But hanging round the public houses in Brackleford's never going to buy me a silk gown. Still, it won't be for ever. There's light at the end of the tunnel.' And she gave a chuckle that held more malice than humour.

Then, going off at a tangent, she again forced her face nearer to Lydia's and said, 'Hey, take a look at me. Go on, a good look. How old do you reckon I am?'

Lydia didn't want to give offence but in truth there was nothing girlish about the made-up face and certainly not about the expression in her pale blue eyes. Fortunately she'd been told her daughter sat next to Daisy at school and she knew Daisy to be thirteen. Based on that and on the fact the girl with the unsuitable name of Sybella had been the product of Norah Knight's youthful misadventure she calculated her to be about her own age. Despite her instinctive dislike for the woman, Lydia felt an urge to answer her kindly. Surely kindness was a rare commodity in her life.

'Somewhere near my age, probably younger. Say twenty-seven, twenty-eight.'

Her companion seemed well pleased with the reply. 'Thirty-one, that's what I am. Looks were always on *my* side.'

Lydia found something touching in the way it was said; it

seemed to tell her that no matter what the local gossips said, this 'lady of the night' looked back with nostalgia to a time when things might have been different. Or was sympathy making her over-sensitive? In that moment she wanted just to bolster Norah's self-esteem.

'So I'm two years behind you—but then I was never near the front row when looks were handed out,' she smiled.

'I was rude—the way I've been speaking to you. Purposely I was rude. I'm sorry. When I got shown the door at home, there were one or two people—the sort my family wouldn't have given the time of day to—who tried to talk me into taking what wasn't my own. Easy enough, they said, just slip something in your pocket when the chap behind the counter is busy with his back turned. I was tempted, I tell you. Don't know why the hell I didn't do it. I'd have got caught and put inside. When the kid was born it would have been taken off to the orphanage. Better for her and better for me. I could have got a proper job, might even have made something of my life. And the kid, she'd have been better off than she is living like we do. But I couldn't do it.' Again that unpleasant, mockery of a laugh, 'All that chapel training must have made its mark.'

'I'm so sorry.'

'I don't want your sympathy. Don't know what the hell I'm talking to you for. A fat lot you'd understand in your ivory tower, same as all the others—what is it they like to call themselves?—God-fearing Christians. Some of the men, they give me the time of day; like to give me plenty more, I know that from the look in their eyes. You'd be surprised. I could open your eyes to plenty and I tell you one thing for sure— the more buttoned-up the women, the more their men's eyes, and fancies, roam. Bear that in mind, Miss Westlake, if ever one of them looks like taking you down from the shelf.'

'I'm not looking to be taken down. And you talk of my living in an ivory tower: yes, I dare say you're right. I know how lucky I am. I suppose we have to take what life gives us and do what we can with it. You have a daughter, so you see it's for *me* to envy *you* in that. She must be thirteen, from what you say. Did you know I run the Guides? We meet at seven each Wednesday evening in St Luke's Hall. Why don't you persuade her to come along? If it's the uniform that's holding her back, tell her I have one at home that would fit her.'

'And turn her into one of those oh-so-good prigs? Bad enough for her having to go to school where they look on her as an outcast, I'm damned if I'm going to chuck her into a double dose.'

'She get a tough time?'

'Never tells me. Just creeps further into her shell. It shows how little you know about anything to say you envy me her. Envy me a daughter who is ashamed of how I earn our keep? Little bitch ought to be grateful. It's me who puts the food on the table. Make the best use of what life hands out, isn't that what you said? Well, I make use of it right enough, every chance I get—and get a bit of pleasure in doing it.' Again, she leaned towards Lydia, leering, trying to shock and humiliate. 'Better pleasure than teaching these good girls of yours to think themselves better than the next.'

Ignoring the jibe, Lydia urged, 'Have a word with your daughter. I promise she'd not regret it, I'd be there for her.'

'Don't want your charity, not yours or any of these other "holier that thou" prigs who look down their noses. I've never grovelled and I'll see to it that she doesn't. If I earn my living on my back that's my affair, at least I do *earn* it.' Then without another word she turned away, hurrying towards Tanner's Alley, her head high, while Lydia went on her way, hurrying to make up for lost time.

Today was no ordinary day. Today was her mother's birthday. It was a rare occasion for Archie to take Adelaide out to lunch, but by way of celebration he'd booked them a table at the White Hart in Brackleford. Festivities would continue into the evening, when Sophie and Christian were joining them for 'the meal'; it was to be an evening for donning their best, something Sophie would enjoy. She had seemed much more cheerful these last months; Lydia supposed she was settling down to married life and looking after a home. Having some help had been a really good idea, for Dulcie had experience enough to teach poor Sophie so much. Lydia blamed all of them not to have seen to it that she'd been more prepared; why, before she was married she had never had to so much as boil the kettle to make a pot of tea. It wasn't their fault that she'd not been interested to learn, but it was certainly their fault not to have foreseen how unhappy she must have been when one failure followed another.

Arriving back at the office, she found Christian sitting on the high stool he'd brought in months ago, staring at his drawing board. She was sure she didn't imagine the sudden tensing in his shoulders as she opened the door, yet he didn't look round.

'I'm glad you're here,' she greeted him. 'I got waylaid.'

At the sound of her voice he turned round, greeting her with his usual smile. 'No trouble, was there?'

'Everyone seemed in a chatty mood,' she laughed, already forgetting that fleeting moment of tension. 'What possible trouble could there be? What are you doing?'

She went to stand behind him, looking over his shoulder at his work. Anyone seeing them together, listening to their easy manner, might have taken them for brother and sister sharing their interest in the business, always relaxed in each other's company. And that's what they were, of course—brother and sister. Didn't she remind herself so a dozen times a day as she watched his look of concentration when he drew, as she gloried in the sound of his beautiful speaking voice or admired his never less than perfectly turned-out appearance? Those things were no more than the threshold that would carry her to fantasies she wouldn't give space to in her mind and yet which could never be banished. Sophie's husband...last night Sophie would have slept in his arms...this morning they would have shared the companionship of the breakfast table, probably talked about what was in the newspaper that had just come through their letterbox, best friends, lovers and friends...and this evening when he went home she would be dressing ready to come to Drydens for Mum's celebrations...he would help her dress...he would hold her...he would—Lydia felt the warmth of embarrassment, she was frightened to speak in case her voice might carry a hint of where her wayward imagination had been taking her. Sophie's husband, dear, blessed Sophie, more to her than any sister, her own very best friend. What was wrong with her that she couldn't overcome this stupid, *yes*, *stupid*, girlish infatuation? That's what it was, time and again she told herself so. What was it the woman who'd waylaid her had said about if ever she was taken down from the shelf? Supposing, just supposing, she had been—not by *him* of course, being loved by him belonged to a world of fantasy—would she still be consumed by this aching need? Did other women feel like it? Those whose paltry rents she collected each week? Those who never looked outside the rut of marriage? That painted creature who used the gift she'd been given and enjoyed the using of it? Sophie? No! Don't think, don't imagine…She bit her lip so hard that it hurt, she wanted it to hurt. I'm a fool, worse, I'm a frustrated spinster envying my darling sister a love that I know nothing about. Nothing? That's right, *nothing*. Shame flooded through her as she thought of how night after night she had no power, and finally no will either, to overcome the desire that consumed her. Always it was *his* voice she heard whispering to her, always it was *his* hands that moved on her thin, bony form. Yet, too soon would come stark reality that was all the harder to face because of the heights from which she fell. In the isolation of her dark bedroom there would be no way of escaping the shame of where her mind had carried her. If what she'd done had been a solitary thing, purely a physical way of satisfying a natural need, afterwards she might have known some sort of tranquility just as she would had her 'dream lover' been no more than a figment of her imagination. But how could it ever be a solitary, purely physical, quest? Surely it should be part of loving, of sharing.

'I'll see to the rent ledger, then get on with the time sheets.' She made sure her tone gave no hint of where her thoughts had been. 'So when Dad gets back all I have to do is take the wage envelopes round. He went into the bank yesterday so that the money was here ready. I told Ethel I wouldn't go home at midday. She is making great preparations for this evening, she won't want to worry about lunch just for me. I'll go along to the Green Lantern presently.'

'Better than that, come home with me. The culinary standards have improved tenfold since the advent of Dulcie Fulbrook. Whether she's been teaching Sophie or preparing the meals herself, I don't enquire.' Then with a laugh that, despite Lydia's reminder that it was she who was the outsider to the intimate jokes he and Sophie shared, sent a rush of joy coursing through her veins, 'You know me, Lyddy, always the height of tact.'

'She won't be expecting me, she might not have enough for an extra.'

'Always enough for you, you know that.'

Much of the joy stayed with her as she locked her rent money in the safe and pulled on her straw hat.

'All set?' He smiled, holding the door for her to precede him into the yard. Behind her, he glanced to left and right, frightened of where his thoughts wanted to take him. It was then that Constable Rickett, the village policeman and known by the local children as Bluebag, pedalled through the open gate of the yard. Christian swallowed an Adam's apple that was too large for this throat; his heart raced. But where was the logic? Be calm, he told himself, be calm.

'Been to the house first,' Constable Rickett panted, speaking to Lydia, 'got here as quick as I could, Miss Westlake. Word's come through to the station, a message about your parents.'

'Tell me,' she heard herself speak, the words steady, giving no hint of the sickly premonition of disaster.

'Your people,' he hesitated. 'Mr and Mrs Westlake,' another pause. There were times when he would rather have had anyone's job than his own.

'Yes? Go on,' Lydia prompted impatiently. 'What's happened to them? Did they ask you to bring a message?'

'On the way to town, they must have been. You know the level crossing…' Again his voice petered into silence.

'But there's a signal on the road, warning when there's a train coming. Dad would never have taken a risk at the crossing.'

'As steady a man as ever you'd find, that was Mr Westlake.'

She seemed to hear just the one word—'was'.

'Go on.' This time it was Christian who did the prompting, his own problems temporarily forgotten. 'You're saying the train hit the car, is that it?'

'Never had a worse job put on me than this.' The constable nodded. 'Seems, sir, the signal must have failed and you know how that bend in the rail track is no distance from the road crossing. The driver must have braked the second he saw trouble ahead, but there couldn't have been a hope of stopping. Hit the motor car square on, so they told me when they put their telephone call through to my station. Off side, I think that was the expression they used. Driver's side.'

'Dad's been killed…' Lyddy heard herself say it, the constable's words, 'that *was* Mr Westlake', echoing and re-echoing, making no sense and yet inescapable.

'I'm that sorry, Miss Westlake. They say he wouldn't have known, that's what I've been told. Your mother, Mrs

Westlake, she's been taken along to the hospital in Brackleford. Now that I've had a chance to speak to you, would it be kinder if I left it to you to break the news to poor little Miss Sophie?' Then to Christian, 'Miss Sophie that was, I mean. Poor little soul, she might take it easier coming from you, sir.' Like so many more in the village, P.C. Rickett had had a soft spot for Sophie since the pretty toddler had come to make her home at Drydens.

'Thank you, Constable,' Lydia said. She heard her tone as dismissive, cold, showing no more emotion than the grimace that passed as a smile. 'We'll collect Sophie and go straight to the hospital.'

'Wait here, Lyddy,' Christian said, 'while I go and get the bike. One of you can ride pillion and the other in the sidecar.'

'Christian, I won't wait. I'll start walking. I'd rather,' she told him, locking the door of the office building as she spoke, then she started in the direction of Meadowlands. 'Be as quick as you can,' she called back to him; but it was unlikely that he heard, he hurrying in one direction and she breaking into an undignified run in the other. At least in hurrying on her own feet to Sophie she felt was *doing* something, even though she'd get there no sooner than waiting for a ride on the motor bike. One or two people noticed her, it might even have entered their heads to reflect what a gawky inelegant figure she made in her haste; but she saw no one.

From where she sat eating her midday slab of bread and scraping of butter, Sybella Knight noticed her coming. She hated school, this one and every other she'd been to in her nomadic existence. But she'd given up playing truant, what she'd faced at home had been worse than the misery of the classroom. 'You go to school whether you like it or not,' her mother had told her that morning, just as she had plenty of times previously. 'You understand? Not much longer and you can pack it in, you'll be old enough. Then you can go out and earn a bob or two, and thank God when you do. In the meantime you have to put up with those mean-minded little bitches in the classroom, same as I do with their rotten mothers. Bugger the lot of them, that's what I say. And if you've got anything about you, that's what you'll learn to say too.' As clearly as she remembered the words, she also remembered the rush of mixed emotions she had felt: a rare burst of affection for her mother, but more than that, a suspicion that her rough, uncouth way of talking was no more than the armour she wore against an unkind world.

As Lydia came closer, Sybella sat tense, waiting to be questioned. What was she doing, sitting there on her own? She ought to be in the playground with the others who ate their sandwiches at school, or else at home having a cooked dinner. Over the years she'd had enough brushes with the beadle to feel permanently under threat. But Lydia didn't even notice her. Puffing from her exertion, surely more than puffing, for Sybella seemed to fancy she heard a sound like an animal whimpering, Lydia lolloped by, unaware that she was watched and, believing herself alone, making no attempt to hide her misery. Sybella watched her pound inelegantly on, the sound of her heavy tread growing fainter. Then she climbed off the stile, what she'd witnessed somehow making her more able to retrace her steps along the path that skirted Oakley Copse and brought her to the national school. But the image of Lydia stayed with her, the strange, frightened expression. She'd gone out of earshot when the motor cycle passed the empty stile so she didn't see Lydia hoist her skirt and clamber on to the pillion seat.

Sophie was in the kitchen with Dulcie when she heard the sound of the motor cycle.

'You go and say hello to him, I'll get it dished up,' the domestic treasure told her. 'Oh, look, he's brought Miss Westlake with him. Well, don't worry, I've done plenty, it'll stretch for an extra.'

Sophie glanced through the window, laughing to see the cumbersome way Lydia climbed off the motor cycle, then hurried to open the front door.

'Lovely surprise. Dulcie says there's plenty of lunch for us all. I forgot, Dad's taken Mum to town, hasn't he?'

It seemed to Lydia that the horror of the news must be printed all over them, yet clearly it wasn't.

'We can't wait to eat, none of us can,' Christian called, still sitting astride the motor cycle.

'You mean we're joining them in town? I wish I'd known, I'd have been ready. I won't be two ticks changing.'

Her childlike pleasure at the thought of an unexpected treat was in such contrast to the reality of their mission that it pierced Lydia's protective armour of control; instinctively she reached out and took Sophie's hand.

'Just get your hat and coat, Sophie. We have to go to the hospital. There's been an accident.'

'Accident? Not Pops, not Mums? They're not hurt?' Those expressive blue eyes were wide with fright. Like everyone else she had been aware of tragedies, other people's tragedies…but Mums and Pops… 'Who told you? What happened?'

'Constable Rickett came to the office. They had an accident on their way to Brackleford. Get your things, Dulcie
will lock up for you.'

'Won't be a jiff,' and already she was on her way up the
stairs to get her hat and coat. It was Lydia who told Dulcie
where they were going, and a good thing she did, for Sophie
forgot even to say goodbye to her.

Watching them go, Sophie in the sidecar, Lydia again on
the pillion seat, Dulcie thought only of Sophie. Please, she
asked silently, help poor darling Sophie, she's not ready for
grief, she doesn't deserve this. I'm there for her, she knows
that. But she's not prepared for tragedy, help me to give her
the strength she'll need. Me! I ought not to be asking it for
me, it ought to be *him*. So how is it I'm so sure it's *me* she's
going to need? What little I've ever seen of him, he
always—hardly seen him at all, to be honest—seems a nice
enough young man. I must imagine there's something not
quite right between them, I must imagine that poor sweet
little Sophie is—is what? Unfulfilled? Hunting for something and not finding it? You know your trouble, Dulcie
Fulbrook, you live in a romantic dream. And that's all
romance is. Look round you, up and down the roads in the
village. Romance! Hard graft more likely, no knights in
shining armour, that's for sure. But has that anything to do
with love, proper love that binds you to a person? That must
be what Sophie has with her Mr Mellor. Mr Mellor, that's
how I still think and it can't be just because I don't know
him; I don't know her Mums either and I've only met her
Pops a few times when he used to be the one to fetch the
rent. So, is that a clue to how I know there's something
amiss? She talks easy as anything about her Pops and

Mums, about Lyddy; chatters about them free as a bird. But not about him. Perhaps that's because what she feels for him is too personal, too private. But I know that's not the reason, I know it with my heart. My poor Sophie is eaten up with the sort of misery she can't talk about, perhaps she doesn't even know what's amiss. I don't know the man, of course. No getting away from the fact, he's handsome enough to turn any girl's head. But think about today, think about what Miss Westlake just told me. It'll knock Sophie sideways, she'll need all the love we can give the poor little soul.

Then her thoughts took a leap in another direction, home to the little house in Mulberry Street and the letter her father had had from Arnold, her brother in Bristol. What had happened this morning decided her: let him say what he would, she wasn't going to let the family dictate her life to her; Sophie was going to need her love and support. She wasn't blind, she knew very well the sort of letter her father must have sent to Arnold and Bertha after he'd been to see the garden here at Meadowlands and after they'd gone home and had the quarrel she hated even to remember. Since then he'd said no more, but she'd been conscious of his displeasure that she spent so much time with Sophie. Such old-fashioned, servile, narrow-minded bigotry! If Sophie looked on her as good enough to make a friend of, then it was no one else's business. And now, this morning, when her father had given her the letter to read she had felt they all saw her as a child with no right to think for herself. The last thing I want is to fall out with Dad, bless his heart, her thoughts raced on, he just wants what he sees as right for me. But I won't go, I *won't* let Sophie down. I've never had a friend so dear, don't I say thank You each night for letting me be here with her? If Dad goes to live with Arnold like he says, I'll be able to afford the rent to stay in the house, and if he says he's taking the furniture then I'll find a room in the village. I won't go. I don't want to hurt him—please don't let him think it's because I don't want to be with him—it's just that I must have my own life. Then, pulling her thoughts away from herself and her own problems, she imagined the three hurrying towards Brackleford. No good asking You to make everything all right, too late for that. But please help them, make them strong. I'll do what I can for Sophie, but it's nothing compared with the strength that only You can give. Poor little Sophie was crying, I could see she was, and she didn't even know the half of it. Miss Westlake, well she's never one to show her feelings, but Mr Mellor, handsome he may be but worried to death, I could see it as he sat there on his motor cycle waiting, jumpy he was, impatient to be off. Must have grown very fond of the family, I dare say.

By common unspoken consent, the full impact of the accident had been kept from Sophie in those first moments; even Lydia foolishly believed that by breaking the news gently it would hurt less.

When they reached the level crossing a policeman from Brackleford was there, his duty to watch from the bend in the track for approaching trains and to hold back what few motor cars there might be until he assured them it was safe.

'Just wait while I check, sir,' he told Christian. 'Signal's not in use, you see, and there's a train due along almost any minute. Wicked bad accident there was this morning. Poor devil didn't stand a chance. Not the train driver's fault, but I tell you it turned my stomach to see. Just hold on where you are, sir, while I make sure there's no sign of it coming.'

'What did he say?' Sophie, enclosed in the sidecar, wouldn't let herself believe she'd heard correctly. 'Lyddy, did he say something about not standing a chance? Lyddy— Pops—it wasn't him? It couldn't have been Pops.' It wasn't so much that she'd only half heard as the expression on Lyddy's face frightened her. Now, as she spoke and the motor cycle waited for clearance to move forward, she opened the door of the sidecar and started to climb out. 'Lyddy, what did Constable Rickett tell you? It was another accident, wasn't it? Not Pops? Not Pops hit by a train?'

'Don't move away,' Lydia hissed at Christian. 'I'll squeeze in with Sophie.' Already she was clambering off the pillion seat.

'Stay where you are, there's not room for two there. Get back in, Sophie, I'll pull up when we get to the other side.' Christian was watching the policeman, ready to get across the track if he had a sign the train wasn't in view. But neither Lydia nor Sophie listened to him any more than either of them noticed the sign that they had to wait where they were until the approaching train had gone through.

To Lydia, caring for Sophie was second nature.

'Hop out a second and let me get in first, then you can sit on my knee,' she told her 'little sister'. The years seemed to have rolled away, even Christian didn't exist for either of them as Sophie did as she was told. Both inside and the door closed, there was no one but the two of them in their small, enclosed world.

'It was there on the railway line.' Lyddy spoke softly, aware of the closeness that held them, held them as it hadn't for months. 'Sophie, we have to be brave. For them, for Mum, we have to be strong. It's what Dad would want.'

'What do you mean?' Pale with fright, Sophie drew away and sat bolt upright, her head pressing against the roof of the sidecar. 'You know things you won't tell me. How badly are they hurt? I've got as much right to know as you have. They're mine too. They're *mine* too, mine as much as yours. For Mum—Dad would want—what do you mean?' She heard the high-pitched screech in her voice. And why did being frightened of what she would hear make her ache, her arms, her legs, her stomach? She felt as though something was crushing the strength out of her and she had no power to stop it. Neither did she have any power to stop the way her clenched fists beat Lyddy's shoulders, knocking her unflattering hat awry.

'Of course they're yours. I promise I'll tell you everything, I should have done right from the beginning. I was trying to make it easier for you. But it can't be made easy.' It wasn't just the words, mostly it was the way Lyddy's hold on her tightened that prepared Sophie for what she was told.

She listened without a word as Lydia told her faithfully all that she knew. 'They might be wrong, Lyddy.' They *had* to be wrong. Pops couldn't be gone, it was impossible to imagine…dead…Pops dead…she'd never even known him to be ill…his life couldn't be snuffed out like some old flickering candle. 'He might have been unconscious, they couldn't be sure he was dead, how could they be sure till they got him to hospital?' The shrill defiance in her tone had gone, now she spoke quietly, it was as if she was pleading for Lydia to agree. 'They wouldn't have been proper doctors. Pops—I don't believe it—we mustn't believe it, Lyddy—if he's lying there in-

jured, don't you see we have to believe he's still alive.' She
looked wild, like a rabbit trapped in the beam of a torch, turning this way and that, looking for escape.

'No, Sophie.' Lydia drew her closer in her arms, she held
her close as though she were a troubled child. 'They say he
couldn't have known a thing about it, he would have been
killed in an instant with the impact.' No saying now that they
must be brave; instead she rocked Sophie gently, hearing the
rasping sobs tear through her, feeling them moist on her own
neck.

The noise of the train rushing past broke through Sophie's
helpless misery. She turned her head to see it just as, with a
jolt, the motor cycle started forward at a signal from the policeman. They bumped across the track and it was then that
they saw the tangled metal of the car they knew so well.

'Stop a minute,' Lydia yelled to Christian, aware that it
would take a miracle for him to hear her above the roar of
the engine. Perhaps it was a miracle, but more likely it was
that Christian's thoughts were in accord with hers, for he
pulled up about ten yards beyond the wrecked vehicle and
climbed from his saddle.

'Come on, Sophie,' Lydia's whisper was firm. 'We have
to see it, we have to go with Dad right to the very end.'

Sophie didn't argue; with the acceptance of what had happened the spirit had gone from her. The wreckage told its own
story: the driver's side had been crushed and the passenger
side was in only a slightly better state.

'Christ!' Christian muttered. 'God, it makes you feel ill to
imagine.'

'Pops,' Sophie wept as she dropped to her knees, reaching into the wreckage to grip the steering wheel, as if putting

her hands where his had been would somehow reach out to him. In such a distorted pile of metal by some stroke of fate the steering wheel remained intact. 'Silly to hope... Pops...Lyddy, he can't be alive, can he? Just hoped...'

'If there's a merciful God he went without knowing. Poor Mum... Come on Sophie, Mum will be wanting us.'

'This was her birthday treat,' Sophie gulped as, like an obedient child, she got to her feet and let Lyddy take her hand to lead her back to the motor cycle where Christian was waiting.

'I think we know now what we must expect,' he said as he opened the door of the sidecar and, without question, Lydia and Sophie both got in. Being together was their strength, it had to be.

Even then they expected to find Adelaide had been taken into a ward at the hospital but, instead, they were told she was still in the theatre.

'Pops had ordered a huge bunch of flowers to be delivered, I was with him when he paid for them at Finden's yesterday.' Sophie might have been talking to herself. 'Let them be taken to the house late in the afternoon, that's what he told Mrs Finden.' No longer was she crying, yet her voice was full of misery as the two of them sat at the back of a waiting room full of uncomfortable wooden benches. After a whispered word to Christian from a man in a white coat, Christian had followed him out. He'd not explained where he was going and the incident hadn't pierced their anxiety enough for them to be curious. 'They'll have brought them when you get home.'

'I know. Dad told me. She'll be kept in, Sophie, she must be. They won't let her home if she's being attended to now in the theatre. I wish they could tell us more, tell us what they think is happening. Do you think they thought it better to talk to Christian—because he's a man?'

'Her birthday…her birthday flowers. He chose roses, he said he didn't mind what colour as long as they had a good scent.'

'I know. Dad told me,' Lydia said, just as she had before. 'When Mum was busy upstairs I got the silver rose bowl from the top of the cupboard and gave it a good polish, then put it away again. And now…' Lydia's strong teeth clamped the corners of her mouth. She had to be strong, she had just to think of the moment, not to imagine, not to look ahead and think of the office with no Dad…home with no Dad. She didn't realise just how tightly she was gripping Sophie's hand.

'All that whispering to Christian. Where do you think he went with them? Will he know where to find us if they let us see her before he gets back?' His departure had suddenly registered with Sophie.

'If he doesn't, he'll soon find out. I think he went…' But she didn't finish the sentence and, as at that moment a young nurse was bustling towards them, Christian's mission was forgotten.

They were taken to a small room containing just one bed. And there lay Adelaide. Not that much of her face was visible for her head was heavily bandaged. Her closed eyes may have been uncovered but they made a stranger of her for she was swollen, cut and bruised beyond recognition.

'Her face will mend,' the sister who was waiting by the bedside told them. 'Mr Sargent has attended to the fractures, her right leg and left arm; they will mend. Her head took the worst blow, a fractured skull. Ribs—well, from the bruising they may well be broken, they have been strapped to prevent any movement as far as possible but really, for ribs, time is the only healer.'

'But she'll be all right?' Sophie begged the nurse to give the answer she wanted, she begged it with her voice and with her eyes. 'It's her birthday, they were out for her treat.'

There were times when the sister, even after years of experience, wished she'd chosen a different profession. 'I wish I could give you the assurance you want.' She looked directly at Sophie. 'But that isn't to say that she won't recover. These are crucial hours. So far she hasn't regained consciousness since the accident. Everything possible has been done, now we must trust and wait. Her birthday, you say. My dear, I am so sorry.' It was seldom a case moved her as this one did and she was honest enough to know it wasn't the patient, it was the young daughter, in years a woman but with a face that held the trusting innocence of a child, a child for whom birthdays still held the magic of childhood, who moved her so. Just for a fleeting moment she rested her hand on Sophie's then, holding herself a little more erect as if to prove to them and to herself too that she was all professional, she glanced back at the dormant figure on the bed.

'There is a cord by the bedside, it rings the bell in my office. If there is any movement, any slight movement, pull it and I will come immediately. She may sleep for hours, she may...' Her voice trailed into silence.

'My sister's husband brought us,' Lydia told her while Sophie bent over the bed, oblivious of the others as she talked to Adelaide's unknowing form. 'He was taken away when we arrived. I think perhaps they wanted one of us to identify—'

'Ah yes,' the sister nodded. 'When he comes back, I'll see he knows where to find you both. Ring the moment you need me.' And off she went to her next errand of mercy.

Adelaide didn't regain consciousness. It was a sudden trembling sigh that sent Lydia's hand to reach for the cord. It was over. Half past six, the hour when they would have been raising their sherry glasses to drink her birthday health; instead they stood by helplessly while the sister confirmed to them what in their hearts they already knew.

During the next hours and days Christian was grateful for tasks to give him an excuse to be away from the village. Thankful to leave the essential arrangements in his hands, Lydia tried to immerse herself in the work of the business, feeling Archie's presence as she talked to the men who came to find her in the office, to try and put into words sympathy and sadness they hadn't the skill to write. Such an accident at a level crossing is rare; even though the victims were known no further than their own county, the very next day most national newspapers carried a report. Three postal deliveries a day and each of them brought letters of condolence, some from people Lydia knew, some from business acquaintances of her father's she'd never met, and all of them had to be acknowledged. Anything was better than idleness, empty time to look into a future which had no shape. She felt that Sophie was avoiding coming both to Drydens and to the office in the builders' yard, but she didn't blame her for it. She knew that poor little Sophie was running away from what she didn't want to face. But things couldn't be allowed to drift; soon the two of them would have to make a decision, for a business couldn't run itself and Lydia was honest enough to admit that her knowledge of the building trade was minimal. In her heart was something that brought with it a feeling of disloyalty: life should be more than this, more than trying to tread in the footprints made by her beloved father. But through those first days she was scarcely aware of anything except the numb sensation of loss as with determination she filled her hours with work. In her gratitude for the immediate responsibility Christian was shouldering, she saw him as a rock they could depend on. When they'd first met him he had worked at his drawing board in the bedsitting room he rented in the village; it was when work started on Meadowlands that he had moved his draughtsman's table and tall stool to the office, spending several hours of each day working there. But he had his own career, he was an architect, and a good one; Lydia was determined not to take advantage of his willingness to support her.

So in the wake of the accident she lived day by day, almost hour by hour, not letting herself see beyond. For the moment there was building work on hand but time didn't stand still, neither did it make allowances for shock or grief, and certainly not for ignorance. For all her brave determination, she longed just for Christian to come, she longed for the comfort of his presence. Yet no sooner did her mind stray in that direction than she would pull it back into line, concentrating on the future of the business her father, with his knowledge and experience of the trade, had built. She excused her wayward thoughts with the reminder that no decision could be hers alone. The future of Westlake Builders would depend on Sophie's wishes (which meant Christian's) as much as her own. He registered the deaths, organised the arrangements for the joint funeral, then brought her copies of the certificates.

'I stopped off at your father's solicitor's office, and gave him a copy of the certificates. I thought that would be one letter I could save you.' Usually so bright, yet since the accident he had looked terrible. Death was a stranger to all of them, and what she read in his eyes touched a chord in her.

'Christian, if Dad knows—and I'm sure he does—he must be so thankful to know you are here. How's Sophie? She's frightened to come here, Dad's place, or to come home, isn't she? Poor Sophie.'

'Yes. I won't stay, Lyddy,' he answered. He was as jumpy as a cat and gaunt as if he'd not slept properly since the day of the accident. Lydia had an overwhelming desire to comfort him, to weep with him, to share the loss that seemed to have knocked the ground from under them. But he didn't let himself relax; she felt it was as if he was frightened to let down his guard, his eyes darting from one thing to another in the familiar room. 'I'd best get home. Nothing else I can do?'

She watched him go, the emptiness of the room closing around her.

That was on the Monday, three days after the accident. After that she saw nothing of him. And why should she? At the sound of each step in the yard she'd look towards the door in hope, even though she reminded herself that his place was with Sophie. If they wanted her they knew where to find her, either at home or in the office. And because she heard nothing from them she turned the knife in the wound of her own misery, imagining them together, imagining him comforting Sophie, imagining them being drawn closer in their grief.

It was late that same afternoon when she heard someone coming towards the office. Hurrying to open the door in greeting, she came face to face not with Christian but with Sophie.

'When I came in I saw the notice on the gate,' she said. 'Closed on Friday for…oh, Lyddy, it's all so horrid. Not just for *you*. Mums' and Pops' funeral, even people walking by the gate will know when it is and all about it; it's only *me* you didn't think important enough to tell what you'd arranged.'

'Christian saw the undertaker and the vicar this morning, I've only just written the notice. Sophie, if he didn't tell you it's because he didn't think the moment was right.'

'You haven't even been to see me,' Sophie's voice croaked a warning. 'All the weekend and you haven't been. Mums and Pops weren't just *yours*, they were *mine* too,' she rasped just as she had on the way to the hospital, anger and hurt behind the tears that threatened. 'They never pushed me outside like you are.'

'Oh, Sophie, you know that's not true. I could tell how upset Christian is too, I was frightened of being in the way. I thought you'd want just to help each other.'

'Christian? Upset? You ought to know better than me, I've hardly seen him.' She climbed on to his draughtsman's stool, hugging her arms around herself, her lovely face a mask of tragedy. 'If I hadn't got Dulcie I'd have no one. Now her father's trying to take her away, he's going to live with her brother in Bristol. He's being horrid to her because she cares about me and doesn't want to leave me.'

'He's giving up the house in Mulberry Street? He hadn't told me.'

'He says she and I are too friendly. He's a hateful old man! Anyway, what's it got to do with him? She's miserable because she hates to quarrel with him. If she hadn't met me

I expect she would have gone with him as he wants. Well, if she hadn't met me, he would have stayed where they are.'

'Doesn't he like her working? But he needed her to find a job, he told me so.'

'He doesn't like it because—because—oh Lyddy, I'm so miserable. If she goes away I'll have no one.'

'That's not why you're miserable, Sophie, you're miserable the same as I am, because of Mum and Dad. If Dulcie goes we'll soon find someone else. And until you get someone I shouldn't wonder if Ethel would agree to come over for a morning or perhaps two each week.'

'It's not the work. I don't care about the work. Don't care about the house. It can be a mess, the meals can be rotten just like mine always are, I don't care. If she goes—I can't explain.' These days, tears came easily to Sophie. Lydia envied her the relief of them. Poor little Sophie, life had always been such a happy thing for her; now she seemed to be grasping in any direction to find something, anything but the real tragedy, to explain her misery.

'Perhaps Christian can persuade her to stay. You've got plenty of space, why don't you suggest she has your little room? Or the proper guest room and make it a bedsitting room for her if you're so keen on keeping her. Talk to Christian, see if he agrees.'

'Nothing to do with him! It's *my* house.'

Lydia looked at her in disbelief.

'Don't, Sophie! Being unhappy doesn't give you the right to behave like that! Mum believed it was wrong to put the house just in your name, it belongs to both of you and it's only the misery in you makes you say such a beastly thing.' Then, torn with compassion and love, 'Don't cry so, Sophie love.'

She pulled the trembling form into her arms, taken completely off-guard when Sophie threw her off, her loud sobs growing wilder.

'You always think he's so perfect. Pity it's not you who's married to him instead of me. I hate being married, it's disgusting,' she snorted. Rubbing the palms of her hands across her face, she looked at Lydia, her expression hard to read. Then, making a sudden decision, 'I'll tell you, Pops always said we must pretend his story was the truth—but it can't hurt now, so I'll tell you.'

'I don't want to hear. If Dad said—'

'It's *my* life and I want you to know. It can't matter now anyway, I know he concocted the story so that Mums wouldn't be worried. Even then I was stupid enough to have agreed to telling any lie just so that Christian and I could be married. I believed it would all be as I'd dreamed.' So, her words almost lost in gulps and sobs, she told Lydia the truth. 'Making love, that's what they call it; that's what I supposed it would be. I don't think Pops ever really trusted Christian after that, that's why the house is *mine*, Pops really loved me. I never meant to let him down. I was crazy, I thought making love would be sort of holy, even when I hated it that first time I truly believed it would be different once we were married. But Lyddy, oh Lyddy, you don't know…' Her voice trailed into silence, a silence that hung in the air between them. 'Say something,' she gripped Lydia's hand. 'Say you understand. I thought I was in love with him. Perhaps I was, when he's nice I expect I still am in a romantic, unreal sort of way. But there's nothing romantic in—in—so horrid. He says—don't know if I can even say it—he says I'm like a dead fish on the fishmonger's slab. Just because I can't pretend to get excited with all the beastliness. Romance! I hate being married.'

'He's never given any hint…until these last few days, until the accident, he'd always seemed so happy, so content…'

'Well, he would, wouldn't he?' Sophie sneered. 'I made vows, I'm his wife. And that seems to be what wives are for. I don't know why I'm telling you all this, you can't possibly understand. You're lucky, your body's your own. I haven't even got that. I haven't got anything and now they're trying to take Dulcie away from me.'

'I'm glad you've talked about it, sharing always helps. I'll keep Dad's promise, I won't say a word. But Sophie, I'm sure, absolutely sure, Christian loves you. Perhaps because of the way Dad found the two of you, and because he must have known that was the reason for the house being in your name, that has made things hard for him. Try and see it from his angle. If he wants to make love to you, it's because you're *you*, try and forget everything but that next time. There'll be joy for you too.'

'You don't know anything about it,' Sophie scoffed. 'How can you? You live in a dream world like I did until he came along and wrecked it for me. Dulcie understands.'

Lydia's shock was genuine, she didn't attempt to hide it. 'You've told all this to Dulcie?'

'Not the first bit, not about Pops making us get married. She's my friend. Being married doesn't take away my right to have a friend,' Sophie mumbled, not meeting Lydia's gaze. Where was the sunny girl of less than a year ago, where was the trusting, beautiful bride?

CHAPTER FIVE

It was soon after nine o'clock the following morning when the shrill bell of the telephone brought Lydia in from the yard where she had been signing for the delivery of a load of sand.

'Miss Westlake? Ah yes, good morning, Miss Westlake. I did put a telephone call through to your home, but your maid told me where to find you. This is Hardy and Giles, Thomas Hardy speaking.' Hardy and Giles, her father's solicitors.

'I believe my brother-in-law called on you yesterday—'

'Yes, indeed. May I express my condolences. A dreadful tragedy.' But clearly he'd not telephoned simply to express sympathy.

'I expect you'd like my sister and I to come to see you,' Lydia prompted.

'No, indeed no, my dear lady. I wouldn't ask it of you at such a time, especially when I dare say so much has fallen on your shoulders. May I suggest that I motor over to Kings-hampton, perhaps this morning if that's convenient to you.'

'That's kind of you. I shall be here in the office, and I'll cycle along to ask my sister to come in too.'

'Did I understand you to say "sister"? I don't know what

had given me the idea, I thought you were the only issue of the marriage.'

'Sophie is strictly my cousin, but she's been with us nearly all her life; my parents looked on her as a daughter.'

'I see.' But did he? Lydia heard the hesitancy in his voice. 'That would be Mrs Mellor of number four Meadowlands, I assume? She will have received a letter from me this morning, so it won't be necessary for her to be present. I anticipate being with you within half an hour. Until then, my dear Miss Westlake…'

Lydia considered herself intelligent, quick to understand, yet she wasn't prepared for what Thomas Hardy had to tell her.

The clock on the tower of St Luke's church struck midday as if it had been stage-managed to emphasise the change in Lydia's world. Her visitor turned the starting handle of his motor car, satisfied when the engine roared, then he held out his hand to her in respectful farewell. She watched him turn out of the gate and start back to Brackleford, but still she stood there, surrounded by materials that made a familiar backdrop to the building trade. Familiar and yet suddenly, in the light of the last half-hour, filling her with foreboding. She had never felt so utterly alone.

Squaring her shoulders, she went back into the office. She seemed to hear her father's never failing 'Hello, Lyddy m'dear', to see Christian's smile. But there was no one. It was unlike Lyddy to flop into a chair, but that's what she did, her thoughts rushing one after another into the confusion of her mind. She was the owner of Westlake Builders, she was the owner of Drydens and when probate was finalised it would be into *her* bank account that, with the exception of personal legacies, all her father's assets would be transferred. Hers, just hers. But this couldn't be the way he'd want it. Closing her eyes as if better to reach into the spirit of the parents she loved, she tried to think clearly, to do what he would have wanted.

He can't want it to be like this…neither of them can…help me, help me make Sophie understand. She will have had her letter this morning…I must go and see her…I'll go now…I'll lock up and go…lock up even though it's the middle of the day and there's no one to look after any-thing…just me, every day, always, just me…I can't do that…Dad wouldn't even expect me to…would he?…don't think about it, not now. Now I'll just think of Sophie. She'll be hurt, remember what she said the other day that her Pops and Mums had never made her feel she didn't belong—and now *this*.

Twenty-four hours ago, Lydia had expected that she'd get through this day just as she had the others since the accident, answering letters of sympathy, doing her usual tasks in the office, trying to see through the mists to the future. But what-ever shape she'd expected, it hadn't been this. She must make Sophie and Christian see that if only her father had brought his will up to date the share would have been equal. Three hundred pounds 'to my brother Vincent, or in the event of his pre-deceasing me, to his heirs'. Three hundred pounds must have sounded like a lot of money thirty-three years ago; it would have been a lot of money to her father in those days when his business was in its infancy. Between them, she and Sophie would agree what had to be done. Nothing could alter Archibald Westlake's last will and testament, but once everything was finalised, once everything had passed into her hands, then they would go back to Mr Hardy and arrange for a half share of the business to be made over to Sophie. And then what? Before her was an empty canvas and she vowed that what she painted on it *wouldn't, couldn't* be a shadowy copy of her father's ambitions, and neither would it rely on the friendship of someone else's husband.

She locked the office door and wheeled her bicycle out of the yard. Christian hadn't been to the office, so he must be at home with Sophie. She needed to talk to both of them, to make sure they understood the decision she was making. Even though her future had no shape, her decision was made; she couldn't go on as she had been, her days revolving around the hours she shared with Christian; she'd make something of her own life; she'd learn to look on him as a brother. But what was ahead for her, stripped even of the day-to-day tasks that had become her own? Don't think, don't try and picture it, not now, not yet.

Opening the door to her, Sophie's expression showed neither pleasure nor resentment; it showed no emotion.

'I have to talk to you, Sophie, to both of you.'

'Christian's not here. He said he had a lot to do in town— Brackleford? Reading? London? Where have you sent him? There's just Dulcie and me here. We're going to eat in the garden.' Her voice was expressionless, her eyelids pink and swollen.

'He must have thought of something we'd overlooked. I wonder where he went. I'm sorry he's out, I wanted to talk to both of you together. It's about Dad's will.'

'You don't need to tell me about that. I had a letter from the solicitor.'

Lydia began to understand her cold, withdrawn manner. Poor Sophie, she must feel so hurt.

'We have to sort it out ourselves. Dad made his will ages ago, before either of us was even born. Mr Hardy came to see me to tell me about it. I came straight over here when he left. He said he'd written to you about that legacy that should have gone to your father.'

Sophie shrugged her shoulders, angry defiance in her sulky expression.

'Christian went off in quite a huff. I expect he thought he'd married an heiress. Dulcie says three hundred pounds is a fortune, and it sounds like it to me. Anyway, if Pops had wanted anything different, he would have written a new will when he went to instruct the solicitor about this house being in my name. I don't want to talk about it. Like Dulcie says, haggling over money is—is—oh, it's hateful.'

'I know. So don't let's. The will has to go through probate, but once it's all settled I mean for us to share it equally. We both know that's what Dad would want, too. I'm going to sell the business—'

At last there was something that pierced Sophie's unnatural reserve.

'Sell Pops' business! He didn't leave it to you so that you could get rid of it! You can't do that! He built it up from nothing, it meant the world to him. It's *Pops*. And you want to throw it back at him, change it for money. Lyddy, that's *hateful*. Don't you care how he would have felt? Well, if you sell it, don't come to me with a handful of silver.' Her voice had being rising hysterically, bringing Dulcie in from the garden where she'd been setting their table in the late summer sunshine.

'Whatever is it?' Then to Lydia, 'Don't you see how upset she is? We've had a good talk this morning, she was just calmed down and now you've come along and upset things. Come on, Sophie pet, your Mums and Pops can't be happy in their better world if they know how miserable you are.'

'I don't expect they care. No one cares, only you. Thought they did…' She was a picture of misery as she made no effort to wipe away her tears.

'Leave us, Dulcie.' Lydia spoke with quiet authority, annoyed at what she saw as an intrusion. 'We have things we have to discuss.' If only Christian were here, at least he would listen to reason.

'Leave her? Upset like she is? Not likely, I won't leave her like this. Hush now, hunney.' Dulcie wrapped her comfortably plump arms around Sophie, drawing her close and rocking her gently backwards and forwards while to Lydia she said, 'As for him, what sort of man would clear off running errands for his sister-in-law when his poor wife is so miserable? It breaks my heart.'

Ignoring her, Lydia addressed herself just to Sophie.

'For goodness sake, Sophie, stop wallowing in self-pity.'

'You don't even care,' Sophie snorted, rubbing her tear-damp face against Dulcie's shoulder. 'I don't want to hear about your beastly money. Just want Pops and Mums. He knew I loved him just for himself, him and Mums.' Then spitefully, 'Expect he left it to you because he knew how important money is to you.'

'Pull yourself together and try and think like a grown-up. I told you, Dad made his will thirty-four years ago; when he said "issue of his marriage" he probably thought he'd have a brood of sons to carry on the business it was his ambition to build. Well he didn't. He had just me.'

'And you won't do it. You just want to let him down, all you want is the money you can get by selling the things he cared about. Well, go and sell it then. Say goodbye to how things used to be. But never, never think you can clear your conscience by paying me off.'

'Stop it, Sophie. I was wrong to come so soon, I can see that. But we must have a proper talk, not a hysterical slanging match in front of an outsider.' Lydia seemed to stand outside herself, ashamed for what she heard herself say and yet having no power to curb her tongue.

'You just say goodbye nicely,' Dulcie said gently to Sophie. Ignoring the jibe, she might have been talking to an unhappy child. 'Isn't there unhappiness enough without saying hurtful things to each other?' Then, when her words brought no response, 'Well, never mind. Today's no ordinary day, next time things will be different. I'll see you out, shall I?'

Cycling away, Lydia's disquiet went further than Sophia's hysterical outburst. She had been made to feel an outsider, treated like a visitor. And Dulcie? They'd known for weeks that she had become indispensable to the running of the home; at Drydens, Adelaide had congratulated Lydia on having the idea of introducing her to the job. Ethel was indispensable to the running of Drydens, but even after all the years she'd been there, there was a difference between her behaviour and Dulcie's. Perhaps I'm being old-fashioned, Lydia chided herself as she pedalled back to the builder's yard, Ethel's been with us since before the war, when things were different. And there's no doubt that Dulcie cares about Sophie, isn't that the thing that matters? Anyway, what I think about Dulcie Fulbrook isn't important; the thing that matters is what Sophie said about Dad and the business, about it being wrong and disloyal to sell it. If I didn't, if I carried on, perhaps took a manager, perhaps muddled along with Christian to help me—no, that's not possible. Be honest, look at the truth of your reason for wanting to sell. I have a life ahead of me, that's the honest truth, and somehow—please, God, show me how—I have to do something worthwhile with it. I must not, I *will not* let time drift by with the highlight of each day being the hours Christian spends in the office. Oh Dad, you understand, I know you do. If you were alive and waiting for me at the yard—if only you were, if only you'd look up just as you have a thousand times with 'Hello, Lyddy, m'dear', oh Dad, why did it have to happen? Sophie thinks I don't care, I care so much I'm frightened to let myself think— but if you were still here with us, then you might have thought I was running out on you, wanting to make a life of my own. So, is Sophie right? Is it just shock, that and fear that I might fail the business, is that why I have this feeling that beyond these next days and weeks there is a place for me somewhere in the great unknown? Am I being fanciful and cowardly? Ought I to do what Sophie believes, take the responsibility you have given me and make it the purpose of my life? When you went into business on your own and built the first of those houses in Mulberry Street, you couldn't have felt like this. You must have been fired with ambition and excitement. Christian was too, when he was on hand to watch his plans becoming houses. But me…I haven't a goal, a dream to strive to make reality. And yet, somewhere out there, I know, I just *know* something is waiting if only I have the vision to recognise it.

Arriving at the yard, she hopped off her bicycle and unlocked the heavy wooden double gates, the notice pinned there telling every passer-by why no one would be working the following Friday and what time the service was to be. Then, before she pinned the gates wide open, she reached into the post box and collected the letters brought by the second post. Her afternoon began to take shape; she'd concentrate on answering her letters, she'd not give space in her thoughts for anything else. Hanging her tall, crowned—and totally inappropriate for cycling—hat on its customary peg, she sat down and proceeded to slit open the seven envelopes brought by the midday delivery. Those who addressed their letters to the house were personal friends, members of the Mothers' Union, of Archie's masonic lodge, some of them so much part of the village that she'd known them all her life. Letters that came to the office were from tradespeople, suppliers of sand, cement, bricks, suppliers of tools, glass and even turf. It was these that brought the spirit of her father close.

The letters read, she took her writing pad from the drawer and dipped her pen in the ink. In her usual bold hand she started to write the date, the 6th August 1925, when she straightened in her seat. Each time she heard a step outside, she listened, hoping it was him, yet now it wasn't a case of waiting and hoping. She recognised his tread, Christian had come. Perhaps Sophie had told him what she meant to do, perhaps he too saw it as disloyal.

'Sophie told you?' she greeted him. 'Christian, it's not like she thinks.'

'Yes, Sophie showed me the letter from the solicitor.'

'No, not that. That's only part of what I want to talk about. In fact, that doesn't really come into it. Christian, she's so hurt. But it's not a bit as she sees it. Dad's will was written thirty-four years ago. He ought to have brought it up to date, we can say that now. But we all expected he'd be alive for years, and Mum too.'

'Thirty-four years. Was that before he was married?'

'No, it was at the time of their wedding. He worded it so that Mum would inherit for her lifetime and after that everything would pass to what was termed "issue of their marriage". But that's not how he would want things now. Sophie and I are like sisters, that's how Dad and Mum saw us. She's so hurt, that's what makes her angry.'

He frowned, not understanding.

'I had to go to Reading, I've been out all the morning. Tell me.'

So she did, right up to the moment where Dulcie had intervened. Instinct told her that was better not mentioned.

'Am I disloyal? Christian, I cannot spend my life trying to fill Dad's place. But does that mean I don't care? I do, I do.' She bit hard on to the corners of her mouth, she mustn't cry, not here with Christian. He'd be kind to her, he'd be sorry for her. She couldn't bear it.

'Do you think you have to tell me that? Caring has nothing to do with kicking up a scene, Lyddy. Your father knew he could always depend on you—and so he can now.'

For a moment she was frightened by his words, 'So he can now.' Was he telling her he agreed with Sophie and believed she was abusing her father's trust? She felt hopeless.

'None of you understand,' she whispered. 'I can't make this my life. I wish I could, I wish I was fired with ambition just like he must have been. But I feel imprisoned by the thought of the years ahead.'

'It may be shock, Lyddy.'

She shook her head. 'No. I've looked at where I am—and

I'm frightened. I'm thirty years old. I can't be idle, but there must be something, *something*, there must be something that will give me a purpose—one that's *me*, not me trying to mould myself on someone else, not even someone as dear as Dad.'

'Of course, you're right,' he agreed. So why was it she felt she only had half his attention.

'I shall put it on the market now, while it's a thriving business. We have plenty of work on our books. I told Sophie that whatever we sell for must be half hers. This morning she was difficult about it, but that's because she's hurt. It's easy for me, being his own daughter, but poor Sophie feels she's been brushed aside. You can see it's not like that, Christian?'

'Yes, yes, of course.' His attention focused on her now. 'That's a generous thing to suggest, Lyddy. But I can see it's what he would have wanted.'

'I knew you'd understand. Next week I'll—' But what she would do next week didn't get said, for at that second they heard the outside gate, the gate that normally stood open during working hours, being closed and then footsteps approaching on the gravel. Perhaps Sophie had come, perhaps now they could all talk together, this morning's scene could be forgotten. But even as she thought it, Christian was on his feet, a quick glance through the window sending him towards the little anteroom where they hung their coats and boiled the occasional kettle on a gas ring.

'I'm not here,' he hissed at Lydia, 'you've not seen me. Reading, say you think I'm in Reading—no, say in London. Not expected back tonight.' The door clicked shut behind him. Still Lydia expected Sophie, even though she had a sense of foreboding that he could be planning to spend a night away from home and expecting her to back his lies. In an attempt to clutch at her own control of the situation rather than to support his alibi, she reached for her pen. I can't tell Sophie the truth, today has hurt her too much already. Perhaps it's not about him that she's come, perhaps it's just to say she understands why I'm selling up, perhaps it's to tell me she agrees that Dad would have wanted us to share, perhaps—

The door was flung open and she found herself face to face with Norah Knight, the blowsy, painted woman who'd waylaid her in the village in what seemed a lifetime ago. Last Friday...the day that had changed their lives...Could this creature have come to her as so many villagers had over the last few days to express sympathy?

As the thought was born, so it died.

'Where is the cheating bugger? Got away last time, but I'm damned if he'll do it again.' Norah's gaze flitted round the room as if she expected the person she was looking for to be hiding in the filing cabinet or behind the dark green, hard-wearing curtains. (Christian? But she can't be looking for Christian...why is he hiding?... cheating bugger she called him. How dare she!)

'I don't understand. Who are you looking for? One of my building gang? You can see, I'm on my own.'

'So he isn't here. Never kept his promise to bring me what I asked. His last chance, I told him that. Blacken his name, I will, him with his airs and graces. If he doesn't turn up by this evening I shall go to his house; you can tell him that, if you see him. And that'll only be the beginning. No one wants to do business with a man with the reputation he'll have by the time I've put my notice in the papers.' There was no humour in her laugh. 'I told you, didn't I, I said I'd traced the bugger. Didn't guess who it was, did you? Well, now you know. And that pretty little sister of yours, by tonight she'll know what sort of a man she's tied herself up to. But you, Miss Westlake, I'm sorry I've had to barge in on you when you've got troubles enough. No time to waste, though, I know him of old. Slippery as an eel.'

'You can see for yourself, he's not here.'

'I see the notice on your gate about the funeral. He'll be here until after that, poncing round like God Almighty What A Good Chap Am I. But come Saturday morning and you won't see him for dust unless he's managed to come up with the goods. But like I say, I'm sorry to come troubling you, you're about the only one in this miserable hole of a place who's bothered to give me the time of day. Just tell him when he turns up. If I don't see him by this evening I'll set about writing out my notice for the papers. And I won't stop at the locals either. If it costs my last ha'penny, I'll bring the swine a cropper like he deserves.'

And with that she turned and left. Lydia went to the window to watch her as without a backward glance she crossed the yard, opened the heavy outer gate and disappeared, but not before closing it carefully behind her. The action seemed to emphasise the reason for her visit and her satisfaction in its effect.

'You can come out,' Lydia called knowing that Christian must have listened to every word. Normally she faced any problem head on, but now she couldn't look him in the eye, frightened of the furtive expression she didn't want to see.

'She's gone? Lyddy, oh God, Lyddy, what the hell am I going to do? You heard what she just said—she'll ruin me.'

Still Lydia avoided meeting his eyes, but that didn't prevent her recognising what lay behind his next words, surely said as an afterthought. 'I can't bring that sort of shame on Sophie. Lyddy, I can't even tell her.'

'Isn't it better for her to hear it from you than from that woman? And that's what she'll do. This evening, she said.' But she couldn't hold herself away from him any longer. Her hand moved to rest on his arm and she had no power to stop it. 'Christian, I knew something was wrong, I knew your thoughts were only half on what we were talking about. If it helps to talk, I'm here to listen. But I know, at least I think I know, what she is holding against you. And, from what I've heard of her poor illegitimate child, she is entitled to hold it against the man who deserted her.'

'How do you know—?'

'I knew there was someone, I met her the other day and she told me a lot about herself. God knows how much was true and how much was an elaboration of the truth. But I think I understand now why she stopped me, why it was me she told her story to. Can't you tell me the proper truth? The whole story—why you ran out on her, what it is she wants of you? She knows you're married so it can't be *that*.' Then, voicing a hope she was frightened to let take hold, 'Or is she accusing you without grounds?'

'Oh Christ.'

'Why don't you talk to Sophie?' Lydia asked gently. 'It's not me who should be asking you these things.' And yet, as a physical ache in her thin body, she felt her need to help him. Slippery eel, the woman had called him; that had been one of her more kindly descriptions and Lydia had no doubt that it held more than a grain of truth. Yet, for her, none of that counted.

'You're my only friend,' he said helplessly, dropping into the chair facing her across her desk and gripping her hands tightly in his. 'If I don't tell someone I shall go mad with worry and, Lyddy, you're the only one I can trust.'

'Wait,' she said, standing up. 'I'll lock the outside gate. Then, between us Christian, we'll find a way—to help you, to help her and perhaps most of all to help that poor child she calls Sybella.'

'God, what a name! Typical!'

Without answering she hurried out to the yard, then drew the bolt across the heavy double gates. Now no one could disturb them, if anyone called on business they'd read the notice and understand why there was no one there.

'I was seventeen,' he started as she came back into the room. 'I made a bloody mess, Lyddy, but it wasn't all my fault. You were brought up in a happy home, a home where your parents had a natural love—for each other, for you girls, for life. I felt that mine were full of hate, yet my father was some sort of a cranky evangelist, he used to spend his days on street corners, outside public houses, on the beach, where he saw the joy of holiday-making as a sin. I can still see the banner he used to keep in the passage by the front door, "Harken not to the Devil". He'd rant on about the sins of drink, of lust, of fornication, he'd threaten eternal hellfire to anyone who put a toe off the straight and narrow. My mother? God knows, I certainly don't. She prepared the food—plain and unseasoned; she polished away every speck of dust as if the house had to be as free of dirt as the people in it had to be free of the joy of living. I never really knew either of them any more than they knew me. I suppose I was the same as any adolescent lad. No, that's probably not true. Every adolescent urge was exaggerated because of them. When Norah Knight—that's her name—picked me up one winter evening on the seafront—I remember to this day even though now I'm sickened by the thought of her—I was more than ready. She was probably no older than me, but for her there was no hell fire waiting to punish her for enjoying her body. Lust—that became my guiding star and she led me to it.' It seemed that once started, he couldn't stop the flow of words. With his eyes closed he might have been no more than thinking aloud; Lydia suspected he'd forgotten her presence. 'There were other men. Men? I was no man, I was a boy, a sex-starved, unloved boy. But for me during those weeks a new world was born. Love? Being in love? That didn't come into it, not for me and not for her. I couldn't go on living in that house of repressed desire, of spite and hatred, for that's what it was. I wrote to a firm in London, in front of me was a new life, unfettered. Something must have told me I mustn't share my plans with Norah, we were at the end of the road. Ahead of me was freedom, freedom to do the work I wanted to do, freedom to follow the desires of my body. Then she told me she was pregnant, she said the child was mine.' His eyes shot open, perhaps he had been aware of Lydia all the time. 'Perhaps it was. But there had been others before me and I knew that when I'd gone there would be plenty more. You know, I'd not even thought about any of this for years.'

'I thought she said she'd traced you before this?' As slippery as an eel, well he won't get away a second time, Norah's words seemed to stand between them. Was he being honest, wholly honest?

'She did. About five years ago. Doesn't it show how thoroughly I'd forgotten her? God knows why I even went back to Brighton for my father's funeral, I suppose I thought my mother might have wanted me there. It was a waste of time; as long as she had a roof over her head and a tin of polish even his death didn't seem to touch her, so I'm sure my turning up from out of the blue didn't. But that's when Norah waylaid me. She didn't know where I was working, though. Now it's different. Lyddy, I haven't the sort of money she wants. Brought my child up for thirteen years, that's what she says; lost her own youth and any chance of a proper life; been deserted by her family. Money, with money she could make a new start. But with a wife to keep—and that woman she insists on having there every day—Lyddy . . .' He bent forward on to the desk, his head buried in his hands.

He'd opened his heart to her, he'd told her that she was the only one he could talk to. Was it so wrong of her to have this wild feeling of joy? Joy that he'd chosen *her* to share his confidence, joy that she had the power to help him. Reason told her that he had behaved disgracefully, but love is stronger than reason. Love? She told herself it was love for Sophie too, for scandal about him would rebound on her. Nudging at the back of her mind was Sophie's tearful confession about her marriage, 'hateful', 'disgusting'. But things would get better for them, Lydia told herself firmly, things had to get better. And she must do the only thing in her power to help.

'Christian, I have enough money. I don't mean Dad's will, I had a legacy a few years ago from my godmother. Drive me into Brackleford to the bank. Come on, buck up, we have to get there before they shut the door at three o'clock and it's a quarter past two already.' Practical help needed practical action and they were both glad of it.

'I'll pay you back,' he told her as a minute or two later he wheeled his motor cycle out of the shed where he'd purposely hidden it, feeling that Norah's eyes were everywhere. 'As soon as your father's affairs are settled and you make arrangements for the proceeds of the business to be shared with Sophie, I'll pay you every penny.' She wished he hadn't said it.

They reached Brackleford just in time for her to make her withdrawal, one that entailed having a word with the manager.

'Miss Westlake,' he said in an understanding, fatherly way, 'you must have in mind the expenses in the immediate future,' and having written his letter of condolence he didn't actually mention the death of her parents. 'It is quite customary for all that to be taken care of by the officiating solicitor. And I do believe you are being over cautious in the amount you believe may be necessary. Are you quite certain you want your cheque cashed?' Then he said in an embarrassed tone of voice, 'Such a figure will leave your account extremely low.'

'It's the way I want to do it, Mr Easton. But thank you for troubling to reassure me.' If he thought she wanted ready money for the immediate expenses then she was glad.

It was next morning when she arrived at the yard to find a very different Christian already at his drawing board.

'I saw her, Lyddy,' he greeted her, smiling broadly, clearly pleased with where life had brought him. 'Feel ten years younger, I can tell you. Yesterday I made a bit of a fool of myself, I'm sorry. There's nothing like a shortage of cash to frighten a man. But I'll put it straight, just as soon as I can, I promise you.'

'You don't have to. Look on it as a gift to the two of you, you and Sophie, even though she won't know anything about it. So Norah Knight has gone.'

'I wrote something for her to sign, a receipt for the money and saying that it cleared me of all responsibility towards her child and promising that she would leave Kingshampton this morning and had no further claim on me. Signed it like a lamb,' he laughed. 'You don't know, I can't even begin to tell you, what it's done for me to know I'm free of her. I said yesterday I'd not given any of it a thought, but I believe that it was always there at the back of my mind.'

'So now we must hope she finds a new life, makes a proper home for the poor child. Dreadful to think of them living in that hovel in Tanners' Lane.'

And so a line was drawn under Norah Knight. Lydia hardly realised how seeing Christian's anxiety, being able to help him, had helped her through the last twenty-four hours. Now there was nothing but the stark truth of what had knocked the foundation from their lives as she concentrated on preparing for the arrival of seldom seen relatives for the funeral on Friday. And when the day came, in true Lydia fashion she hid her grief and, as convention demanded, played host to everyone who flocked back to Drydens after the service.

'Poor little Sophie, not like the merry child she was when we last saw her,' one cousin of Adelaide's whispered to another, both of them enjoying the rare chance of meeting and catching up with news and gossip, wishing there was no need to hide their enjoyment of such a gathering. The last time they'd seen each other had been at Sophie's wedding, such a happy occasion. Now they kept their voices low, they wore their best black clothes. It wasn't that they weren't very sorry for what had happened, of course they were.

'What a happy day that was, who'd think it wasn't a year ago. It's only at times like that—or this—that we have a chance to all be together. And goodness knows when the next will be.'

They both looked at Lydia, silently sizing up the possibilities.

'Too late for romance in that direction,' cousin No.1 spoke for them both.

'Late or early, she's an old maid if ever I saw one. Not a tear. Mother and father gone and she shows no more sorrow than she showed joy at little Sophie's marriage.'

'Perhaps we shouldn't judge. She's always been a good girl, and she's Addy's daughter, we ought not to find fault.'

Even so, as Lydia got through the day of the funeral, those two cousins simply spoke the thoughts in many of the minds. She was an enigma to them. Now Sophie, whose loveliness seemed not at all diminished by her pale face and pink eyelids that reminded them all of how she'd cried as they'd stood by the graveside, she they could understand. Not even a real daughter…but it was cruel even to think of that, Archie and Addy had loved her like one of their own.

There could be no slipping back into the rut of life before the accident. Lydia's mind was made up: the business would go on the market as soon as it legally passed into her hands. Mr Hardy assured her that her father's affairs were very straightforward and things would soon be finalised, all debts paid— and as the bank manager had suggested, that would include expenses incurred for the funeral.

As good as his word, summer had hardly been chased away by the first northerly gales of autumn when she found herself the owner of all that had been Archie's, with the exception of Sophie's legacy. If only he'd written a more recent will, Lydia knew not only Sophie would have been treated as he would have wanted, but Ethel would have had a recognition for her years of faithful service. On the morning she received Mr Hardy's final letter she sat alone at the breakfast table reading it, mentally making a timetable for the day ahead. First she must talk to Ethel.

'I had to wait until now, Ethel, the solicitor had to sort everything out,' she said when she carried her dirty dishes to the kitchen.

'Till now, Miss Lyddy? What have you got in mind then?' But this morning, even Ethel seemed ill at ease. And when Lydia explained how long ago it was that her father had written his will and how differently she was sure he would have done it now, Ethel's mind was clearly only half on what she was being told.

'There's Sophie and, Ethel, there's you. The first cheque I've written drawn on my new account, Ethel, I want you to have it and put into your post office savings.'

'No, *no*, Miss Lyddy. Don't say any more. And don't give me that bit of paper. Been turning over in my mind how to tell you ever since the post came this morning—and before that if I'm truthful.'

'Tell me what?' Lydia put the cheque down on the wooden table.

'My sister, Hilda, you've heard me speak of Hilda—'

'Of course I have. Her husband, Dougie you called him, he died early in the summer.'

Ethel bit her lip, how could she tell dear Miss Lyddy? Who else would bother enough to even remember Dougie's name? Well, perhaps the missus would, she was pure gold, same as Miss Lyddy.

'Oh dear Lord, I feel like I'm being torn in two,' she mumbled, shaking her head miserably.

'Sit down, Ethel,' Lyddy said, dragging a chair to the table and setting an example for Ethel to follow. 'Something's worrying you. If it's because of Mum and Dad, you know it won't alter—'

'Oh dear, Miss Lyddy, that makes me feel—oh dear—like a rat deserting a sinking ship, that's how I feel.'

'Deserting?'

'It's Hilda, you see. They say blood's thicker than water, and come right down to it I suppose that's about the truth of it. She lost her only child—'

'Sylvia, I remember.'

'Yes, Sylvia,' and how many young women would remember a thing like that? 'That was nearly two years ago and now Dougie's gone. She's gone right to pieces, I've known it for weeks. I've tried to cheer her up when I write, tried to help her see there's still a life in front of her. Easy for me, I dare say. Anyway, I suggested that she might find somewhere to live nearer to me. Now this morning I get this letter, much more cheery, I will say that, but pinning all her hopes on us setting up home together. I tell you, Miss Lyddy, I've been that worried about her. Right since she was a girl, poor Hilda's never been strong, not with the sort of strength tragedy demands. Tough as an old boot physically, but in a way that seems to make it harder, more's expected of a person.' In Ethel's book, nothing was worse than letting down someone who depended on her. Now she was pulled both ways: by a dear and distraught sister and by her loyalty to Lyddy. There were moments when her worried thoughts would stumble on the image of herself and Hilda, a little home of their own, perhaps having time to join the Mothers' Union and make friends with local people, take a book from the public lending library, no longer planning each day round someone else's comfort. Immediately, she would stamp on the thought, filled with shame at her disloyalty. Now she gazed at Lydia, good, kind Lydia, surprised at a new idea. Perhaps Miss Lyddy would suggest Hilda coming to Drydens, they could share the work, then everyone would be suited.

Whatever Ethel's problems might have been, Lydia hadn't expected to hear anything like this. She was surprised, too, at the way her own imagination carried her.

'Of course you have to do all you can for your sister, Ethel. Isn't that what families are all about? I'll come to that in a moment. First, I want you to promise to do as I said with this cheque.'

'How can I, Miss Lyddy, when here I am talking about letting you down just when you've taken the knock you have?'

'You *must* take it, Ethel, for Mum and Dad's sake. It's really from them. None of us thought this would happen to them, we expected them to have years more.' Then, squaring her shoulders, 'Now that's settled. Next what I'm going to suggest may not appeal to you at all, you may want to get right away and have a new beginning for both of you. But one of our tenants, Mr Fulbrook, from a house in Mulberry Street, is leaving at the end of the week. He's going to make his home with his son in Bristol.'

'Fulbrook? But isn't that the girl who works for our Miss Sophie? You want Hilda to take over from her, is that it?'

'I thought you and your sister might like Mr Fulbrook's house. Dulcie, that's his daughter, is staying behind; she's moving in to Meadowlands. Much better for Sophie, she and housework don't have much appeal for each other.' Lydia laughed. 'Dulcie has always taken good care of the house, it's spotlessly clean. The present rent for it is five shillings a week. I shan't charge you rent, you know that. But now we come to something else. For all of us what has happened has brought us to a time for change.'

No wonder Ethel's own uncertainties were pushed to the back of her mind as she listened to what Lydia told her. Sell the master's business! But how could she sit there and calmly talk about handing everything to some stranger, the ladder the master had climbed so proudly since he'd been no more than a young man learning his craft? Miss Lyddy of all people, behaving like that! And her parents hardly had time to settle in their grave!

'It may take me some while to sell—'

'A good business like your father built, a reputation like it has—and you say it might take time.'

'It's because of Dad that it may. You don't imagine I'd let it go to just anyone? Ethel, it needs a man at the helm who knows the trade like he did. I'll not see it run downhill.'

'And you, Miss Lyddy? Have you considered the emptiness in your own life without having that office to go to every day? Why, that and your Guides and such have been your life. Surely Miss Sophie's husband would be there to back you? Here all day long by yourself, me gone, Miss Sophie soon, I dare say, busy with a family of their own.'

Hit on a raw spot, Lydia's moment of sharing her confidences vanished.

'I have other things in mind to be doing,' she lied, her tone putting a firm full stop. 'If you like the idea of the house in Mulberry Street, write to your sister and suggest it. This is a time for change, Ethel.'

'Oh, she'll jump at it, she always has envied me being here in Kingshampton. She had to stay in Bristol because of Dougie's work. Funny old world, Miss Lyddy, her coming here and Mr Fulbrook going there.' Not the most adventurous exchange in the world, but from the way she said it Lydia knew Ethel's worries had diminished and she was already looking ahead with hope.

Sitting with her back to him, Lydia had no idea how closely Christian was watching her as she worked at her ledgers. She interested him, she always had. Even in the beginning when he'd let himself indulge in the game of playing along with both of them, Sophie so obvious in her adoration (adoration? Now he tossed the description aside, seeing it for what it must have been), and Lyddy his faithful friend. Well, nothing had changed there, but hadn't he recognised something deeper than that, some dormant passion waiting to be aroused? Perhaps he had been as wrong about her as he had about Sophie. And yet…and yet… He let his imagination go where it would, driven by a combination of curiosity and frustration. There had been plenty of willing women in his life, from when Norah had shown him the pleasures waiting to be enjoyed right through to Sophie. He wouldn't have to cast his net far to find others; that was something experience had taught him. But Lyddy was different. Lyddy, he mused, his drawing pencil idle in his hand, as mentally he stripped her of her sober, rather old-fashioned attire, I doubt if there's a curve in her body. Has she got breasts? No sign of them under the loose bodices she always hides behind. Firm, white flesh, oh yes, it'd be firm all right, smooth, untouched. Cool as a cucumber—but is she? Seducing a woman like Lyddy wouldn't be the push-over it was with Sophie the day Archie caught us with our pants down. What if it had been Lyddy he'd caught me with? Remember that morning on the way to see the furniture in, I reckon if I'd said the word she would have jumped at what I had to offer. So what stopped me? Certainly not the idea of marrying Sophie, not the idea of marrying anyone. I couldn't have done that to Lyddy. Oh, I could take her to bed all right—then or now—but is that how you treat 'pure gold'? She's the best friend I've ever had. She'll be part of my ongoing life, she's almost a sister to me. And here I am mentally stripping her, mentally feeling her thin, bony body. Nearer the bone, the sweeter the meat. I could make earth move for her, poor Lyddy, poor pure Lyddy.

'When you can give me a minute.' Her voice cut into his thoughts as she swung round towards him from where she sat on Archie's swivel chair. 'I don't want to disturb what you're doing.'

A minute to give her, oh, he'd got that all right, that and more. Mustn't stand up, even poor old Lyddy might be knowing enough to notice where his thoughts had brought him.

'Let me just finish this, two minutes and I'll be there.' Two minutes' concentration of the elevation of a detached house to be erected on the outskirts of Reading and he was once more in control.

'I think everything is in order to show to Mr Chivers tomorrow,' she said. 'See the list I've drawn up. Can you see anything I've overlooked?'

'You know what I really think?' He smiled at her, having looked through all she'd done. 'I think you are as efficient and capable as any man who might buy this business.'

'You mean, you think I ought to carry on? Not you too, Christian? My mind's made up. I mean Sophie—and you— to share whatever it fetches, but this mustn't be my life, I won't let it.' Like a trapped animal, she looked at him.

'Of course I don't think you're wrong, Lyddy. And Sophie has no right to make you feel that you are. But afterwards? What are your plans?'

She shook her head, his words underlining the emptiness of her future. Then, just as she had when Ethel had said more or less the same thing, she straightened her shoulders, her head high.

'Until the sale is through I can't look to a future, I'm not free to start to think.' How could she tell him how night after night she prayed for guidance? 'For Dad this was the ladder he had to climb; there are other ladders. I'm not a complete fool, I must be free to find my own destiny.'

'And that is an ambition in itself. I'm always there for you, Lyddy, you know that.'

How cool and unmoved she looked as, almost royally, she bowed her head to him in answer to his pledge of support.

'Now that Ethel's gone, I hate to think of you going home to get your own meal in that empty house. Why don't you come home with me this evening? I wish you would. I think perhaps it's because Sophie is making herself so difficult to you that she's—oh, dammit, I can't explain. It's like living with a polite stranger. Come home and see if you can break the ice.'

'I can't, I have Guides this evening. It'll be nine o'clock

by the time I close up the hall. In any case, Christian, if Sophie surrounds herself in ice, there's only one person who can melt it. And that has to be you.'

For a moment he didn't answer; she felt the silence hanging between them. Remembering Sophie's hysterical outburst soon after the accident, Lydia waited, dreading the confidences she ought not to hear. When he spoke there was none of the confused and frightened emotion in his voice that she'd heard in Sophie's.

'I'm the last one. I remember when you and Sophie had no secrets; now she seems to have gone out of reach of all of us and furthest of all from me. She shies like a frightened horse if I touch her. If only she'd talk to you.'

'Don't you see, that's something she won't talk to me about. How could she? I know nothing of—of marriage—of the things she's running away from.' Wasn't that what Sophie had told her herself? 'She's hurt, she's angry. In everything else Dad was so efficient; now nothing any of us can say can take away from her the feeling that all these years she's been looked on as different. And it just isn't true.'

'I know that—and so does she, only she chooses not to see it. Dear God, I heard him tell her so himself. It was the day we furnished the house, the house he gave her—*gave her*, not both of us; I wonder that didn't make you wonder what it was he held against me. Lyddy, I've got to tell you. On that day—'

'I know what happened, Sophie told me.'

'And you're still my friend. I'm glad you know.'

'Of course I'm your friend, we were friends from before that day. We all knew she was in love with you. She'd had lots of admirers but they'd been a game. With you it was different. Be patient, things will get right. When Ethel was try-ing to look into the future, she said soon, probably, Sophie would have a family. Once that happens everything will fall into place.'

'Small chance of that. She's moved into the small spare room—the scene of the crime,' he said bitterly.

Dressed in her navy blue uniform of Guide Captain, complete with lanyard, neckerchief, toggle and whistle, the whole en-semble topped off with the wide-brimmed soft felt hat which did nothing for her aquiline features, Lydia saw the last of her troop out of the church hall. In her naturally methodical way, she glanced round the room, making sure everything was left as they'd found it, then she put on her navy blue gabar-dine coat, took the door key from its hook and turned off the gas, throwing the room into darkness. Outside, the evening was cold, and since she'd arrived a fine rain had started. It was out of her way to take the hall key back and put it through the letterbox of the churchwarden's house, but she almost welcomed the detour. These days, home held no welcome; it would be in darkness, the fire unlit and she certainly wouldn't bother to light it. Ethel used to keep the kitchen range per-manently stoked, but now she had gone it was much better for Lydia to prepare her meals on the gas cooker—and this evening put a match to the oven and leave the door open to warm the room. The contrast between the home she'd been used to and what Drydens had become was never more ap-parent than on returning to it after an evening out. So easily she could have given way to depression, but she saw that as self-pity and not to be given an inch. So she pedalled hard, head down against the fine, driving rain.

She might have kept self-pity at bay, but what she couldn't drive from her mind was what Christian had told her that afternoon: Sophie had moved into the small spare room. What had gone wrong for them? Please make things right again, they must have loved each other when they married...he shouldn't have told me...Sophie shouldn't have said those dreadful things either, about being married being disgusting...they had a bad start...but what would I know about it, wasn't that what Sophie said? That I couldn't know what I was talking about...but I *do* know, I *do*—I must be right—if you love each other then nothing, absolutely nothing could be disgusting, whatever it was he wanted from her, surely that's what real, complete loving is about. But I don't know, I'm a silly, dreaming spinster, I don't even know whether reality is anything like I imagine. But I mustn't keep thinking about them, Sophie and Christian, I must think about *me*, about what I mean to do with all the years ahead of me. Am I a fool to sell the business when at least that would have given me something to battle with? No, I'm right, I must be right. Life is God-given, it's not just something to be lived through. Dad climbed his own ladder—and so will I. Help me find my ladder, please help me, show me a vision at the top of it so that, whatever the struggle, I can see a goal.

The wind gusted and brought down a shower of dead leaves, cutting against her face and seeming to mock her.

Her bicycle in the shed, she walked to the front of the house and in the darkness felt for the lock.

'Lyddy, I was waiting.'

At the sound of that familiar voice, familiar even though it was hardly louder than a stage whisper, everything else was driven from her mind.

CHAPTER SIX

When Archie had had electricity brought to Drydens soon after the end of the war, he had seen it as another step up the ladder of ambition. The family, and in particular Sophie, had spent an excited first evening going from room to room, switching on, switching off, all of them feeling themselves part of changing society. Now, more than six years on, as she pushed open the front door, Lydia's hand reached automatically to the dome-like switch in the dark hall then, suddenly and with startling clarity, she and Christian came face to face.

'What's wrong?' She was almost frightened to ask it. 'Is it Sophie? Or is it about tomorrow?'

'Yes, yes on both counts,' he answered.

'Come into the kitchen and take off your wet coat. It's cold, everywhere's cold. I'll light all the cooker burners and the oven, that'll take the chill off.'

'Lyddy, you can't live like this. You must find someone to replace Ethel.'

'Don't tell me what I must or mustn't do, Christian,' she said firmly but with no anger. 'Soon I shall have more time on my hands than I'll know what to do with. It's *that* that I dread, not coming home to an empty house.'

He took off his wet raincoat, shook it and draped it over the back of a chair, then did the same with hers.

'What's wrong, you ask,' he said, going back to the reason for his coming. 'God, Lyddy, I don't know how to tell you. Will you understand? Will you even know what I'm talking about?'

Remembering Sophie's burst of miserable confidence, she believed she knew what was on his mind.

'Sophie will change.' She tried to sound reassuring, glad to keep her back to him as she crouched to light the burners in the oven. 'She may be twenty-three years old but she's always been protected. She didn't know enough about life when she got married.'

'And you do? I'd have thought she probably had more idea than you.'

Lydia kept her back to him, warming her hands over the flames from the gas rings on the cooker, purposely leaning close to the stove in the hope that he might think that was what made her face and neck feel so uncomfortably warm. Just like everyone else, he saw her as a confirmed spinster, dull, hard-working, doing good works, knowing nothing!

'I know Sophie married you because that's what she wanted more than anything else. Don't talk to me about things that are just between the two of you, it's not fair to her. Christian, be patient with her, treat her gently. Perhaps it's our fault—I don't mean yours, I mean ours at home.'

'You say don't tell you, but Lyddy, you've got to listen. Come here and sit down.' He pulled two chairs close together in front of the open door of the oven. 'You're the only one I can talk to. Christ, it's such a mess. I knew it was, even before today, I knew there was no future for us. I was such a bloody fool, Lyddy. That afternoon at the show house, I should never have let it happen. Easy to say now, oh hell, how can I start to expect you to understand? She knew where the way she behaved was heading—I knew it too. And I'm not blaming just Sophie. Now look at me and tell me I'm still your friend.'

'Of course you are. Go on. I told you I know all about that afternoon.'

'Do you remember the morning, Lyddy? We walked together to Meadowlands, I talked to you about wanting to settle in Kingshampton, I asked you what you thought. Remember?'

She nodded, frightened to trust her voice in case he would hear a hint of how her hopes had sprung to life, how she had mistaken the meaning behind his question.

'My friend, Lyddy, always practical. You recommended the village for all the sensible reasons, not a word of what I wanted to hear: that it was for myself that you liked the idea of my staying. I was a fool, I'd thought you cared—not as Sophie did, with stars in your eyes and your thoughts full of romance. I thought—but what does it matter what I thought? I knew that morning that I'd been wrong; you saw me as a friend, a brother perhaps.'

'Of course I see you as my brother. That's what you are, Christian.'

'No, Lyddy, no.'

Her heart felt as though it were beating right into her throat.

'Christian, this isn't what you wanted to talk to me about. We were together this afternoon, has something happened since then?'

He shook his head helplessly, the movement making her reach to touch his hand before she could stop herself.

'I came near to saying a lot of this this afternoon, but I couldn't, not when you tried so hard to make me believe things would change for Sophie and me. You know what I did? I went home determined to talk to her, to beg her to let us try and have a fresh start.'

'And?'

'I thought the house was empty, but I couldn't understand why the doors were unlocked. I expect I should have shouted to her, and yet you know I'm almost thankful I didn't. That would have given her warning that I was home, given her time to answer. Can't you just hear it: "I'm nearly ready, you pour our sherry and I'll be down." Often that's what happens, she'd still be upstairs changing when I got home, and I can see now how pouring the sherry—a recently acquired habit—gives her time to cover her tracks.'

'I don't understand. If she'd been shopping or something, it's not unreasonable to expect she might not be prettied up when you get home. As for the new habit of sherry,' and this time Lydia's laugh held all the affection she felt for Sophie, 'it's not that she particularly likes it as a drink, I don't think, it's more that having an early evening sherry set the scene with Mum and Dad that the evening was to be something special.'

Her hand was still on his and now he gripped it hard. Yet she could see from his expression that she might just as well not have spoken.

'I went up the stairs, I don't know why I did it, what made me so sure that something was wrong.'

'With Sophie?' She was filled with such dread that every-

thing else was pushed out of her mind, everything but the
memory of Sophie's hysterical crying, her abhorrence of
what she called disgusting. What had she done? Surely, oh
please God no, don't let her have…but even in her silent plea
she couldn't bring herself to let the words form.

'Wrong, dear God, but it's—even if she weren't my wife—
perhaps it's because I'm a man—'

'What? Christian, is she all right? I can't keep up with
what you're telling me. Something wrong, you said?'

'I meant to go to her room—remember I told you she has
moved out of our bedroom—I meant to talk to her, to make
her see that we can't go on living like that.'

'And she wouldn't listen?'

'She wasn't there. I thought I'd ask Dulcie if she knew
where she'd gone, so I went across the passage and before I
got to the door of Dulcie's room I heard—I heard—how can
I make you understand? I knew and yet I couldn't believe what
I was hearing. There are locks on the bedroom doors, but there
was no key in that one. I expect she never locks it, why would
she? Sophie hated even to be touched, used to grit her teeth
and bear it. Lyddy, I looked through the keyhole. What sort
of a man would do that? What I saw disgusted me and yet I
felt released, free. She's your sister, had you never guessed?'

Whatever Lydia had expected to hear it certainly wasn't
what he was implying. 'What I saw disgusted me and yet I felt
released, free…' his words echoed but she wouldn't listen.

'Sophie and Dulcie…but Christian, it must be that she was
miserable, perhaps Dulcie had been trying to comfort her. I
know she's been unhappy, I know marriage wasn't the sort
of thing she'd made of it in her romantic dreams. She was just
a child.'

'There was nothing of the child in what I saw. I shouldn't be talking to you like this—not because, like you said this afternoon, some things are just between Sophie and me—but because I want to keep everything about you just as it is, I don't want any of this to cloud your *goodness*, like lifting the lid on Pandora's box.'

'I'm not even sure what you are saying. No, that's not true. I am sure, but I don't believe it. I know her so well. Ever since she was tiny, if things upset her she used to bring her troubles to me. Over the years it never changed. Anything to talk about, good and bad alike, she used to curl up in bed with me. And Christian, what you are saying is *wrong*, do you think I wouldn't have known?'

'I don't know what I think. God, but I was such a blithering idiot. Remember that morning when we walked together to the show house, remember how I talked to you about finding somewhere permanent to live in Kingshampton? I knew Sophie thought she was in love with me but, like you say, she was just a child playing at love. I believed, though, that you cared. You never guessed that morning how I was waiting for you to let me see—'

'Stop it, Christian. Don't spoil what we have.'

'What we have is nothing compared with what we ought to have, you and me, Lyddy. I believed—I still do believe—we could be so much more than friends. Friends, yes, I knew we were that, but partners, companions and lovers too. That's what I should have said to you that morning, but I was too damned sure of myself, I thought time was on my side. And so it would have been if I'd not been such a fool. Was I wrong, Lyddy—about you—about us?'

'It's Sophie we're talking about.' She heard her voice as

prim; she who never slouched felt herself sit even a little straighter. 'You're letting yourself imagine things because you feel miserable and rejected. But you shouldn't, Christian. I *know* your relationship has been difficult. Does she feel that you love her, love her for herself? Perhaps because of Dad finding you together that day she needs more reassurance. You say you went home intending to talk to her, to make a new start. Don't give up. You've got years of marriage ahead of you.'

'You think I want her, after what I saw? Lyddy, she was practically naked.'

'Both of them?

'No, Dulcie I hardly noticed, I think she was wearing her clothes, I would have noticed if they'd both been like Sophie. Just her dressing gown and that wide open, and there she lay—' He turned his face away. 'And you never knew? You never had any suspicion? Tell me the honest truth, Lyddy.'

'Of course I didn't suspect. And I'm sure even now there's some explanation. Perhaps she wasn't feeling well, Dulcie is kind and caring. You must have let your imagination run away with you.' It couldn't be true. Sophie, little Sophie, sunny, happy, fun-loving Sophie. Involuntarily she shivered. 'Anyway,' she went on, remembering what he'd said and feeling a rush of anger, '"felt released, felt free," you said. If that's how you feel, do you imagine she doesn't know it?' Then, lest he thought she had changed her view and was beginning to give credence to what he'd told her, 'Anyway, there's no tale you can tell me that will make me believe what you say about her. I don't mean I don't believe what you saw, it's just that I know, positively *know*, it has an explanation. Let's try and forget it, let's just pray that when you get home you'll find that I'm right.'

'Accuse her, you mean? If I'd been going to do that I would have opened the door on them this afternoon, caught her red-handed. Second time, for her to be caught,' he added bitterly. 'I don't want to talk about it to her. Have you anything in the house to drink, Lyddy, anything better than something from a kettle of hot water? We both got soaking wet on the way, a drop of malt whisky wouldn't come amiss.'

'Yes, I'm sure there is. Dad always kept a supply in the alcove cupboard in the drawing room.'

'I'll get it, you wait in the warm. Do you want anything in it? Water? Soda water?'

'Should I? I don't think I've ever drunk it before. I seem to think Dad had it neat.'

'Wise man. So do I.'

She heard him moving about, the clatter of glasses. There was a feeling of unreality about the evening, two people huddled close to the warmth of the gas oven discussing something as impossible as the reason that had brought him to her.

'Here we are,' he said as with his foot he closed the door behind him then came back to his chair in that patch of warmth. 'One for you and one for me,' he said, passing her a glass of the amber-coloured potion. 'Your very good health, Lyddy my friend. And more than that, tonight we should drink to the future of Westlake Builders. Only a fool would fail to see what a good business it is. So let's hope the sale goes through smoothly and quickly. You haven't changed your mind about the letting properties in the village? You still mean to hang on to them?'

A fiendish devil whispered into her mind: if she were to sell the properties with the business it would mean an extra share for Sophie and so for him. Immediately she stamped on the thought, ashamed.

'I must, Christian, at least for the time being. If I let the houses go with the business—always supposing a purchaser wanted them—how could I be certain that the rents wouldn't be increased, or the new owners might decide they wanted to sell them on? The people living in Mulberry Street and Wykeham Street are all good tenants, I've known them since I was a child and used to go with Dad on his collecting round. As long as I live in Kingshampton I shall keep the houses. Of course I shan't have our own workers to fall back on when there are jobs to be done in any of them, but the rents will more than cover any outlay.' As she'd talked she'd been conscious that he was watching her, his expression hard to read.

'As long as you're in Kingshampton, that's what you said. Lyddy, you can't go. You can't mean—'

'I don't know, Christian. I have to make something of my life, I've told you that before. We don't get a second chance, I can't just drift along without a goal. That would be worse than trying to carry on Dad's business. You know why I put it on the market, because I can't make my own way treading in someone else's footsteps, not even Dad's. Neither can I make a life out of fund-raising for the orphanage, looking after a troop of Guides, collecting rents and talking to the same tenants at the same time each week. Miss Westlake,' she heard the bitterness in her voice, 'such a *good* woman.' As if to emphasise her point she took a long swig of the fiery drink, catching her breath as she swallowed it. 'And I'm tired of being "a good woman", I can't go on like that, there must be more…'

'Don't go, Lyddy. I beg you, don't go.' Leaning back he put his glass on the table, then took her free hand in his. 'Stay here, be here for me.'

He held her hand to his cheek, then turned it palm upwards and pressed it to his mouth. She could feel his teeth lightly nibbling, she could feel her heart thumping. Yearning…such a powerful word, she thought, but now I know what it means. I yearn, I'm yearning, my whole body aches with yearning, I can feel it in my arm, in my legs, in my stomach, in my groin. I want to sink into it, surrender all that I am. Instead she took refuge in the comfort of the whisky, draining the glass as if it were water and choking as she swallowed.

About these moments was a quality half real and half dream; she let herself sink into it. His hold on her hand didn't slacken, the warmth from the flaming jets in the oven seeped into her very being.

'Take off this ugly hat.' Christian took if off her head as he spoke, throwing it on to the table. 'That's better. Now the pins.'

The feeling of abandonment that came over her was out of keeping with the plain navy blue uniform of Guide Captain; it belonged to the creature who'd lived imprisoned by her daily round of good works, who longed for the cage door to be opened so that she could fly free. She kept her eyes closed, subconsciously she avoided being brought down to earth by the familiarity of her surroundings. Perhaps it was the effect of the whisky that gave her the muzzy, deliriously exalted sensation that had connection with neither yesterday nor tomorrow. *Now* was all there was. Even when she felt the warmth of his breath she didn't open her eyes, she mustn't break the spell. And as his mouth covered hers she had no power over her arms, they held him close; instinct, desire, a wild joy that was beyond anything she'd believed possible drove her as she parted her lips, moving them against his, the glass she still held forgotten. His hand moved over her navy blue uniform, it came to rest on her breast. All her adult life she'd been ashamed and humiliated by her thin, shapeless body but this evening she knew nothing but wonder, wonder, joy, desire. If she'd been like a caged bird longing for the door to be opened, now it wasn't freedom she sought. It was as if she'd been lost and had been found. His thumb was moving on her hardened nipple, neither the closely woven material of her uniform nor the soft wool of the vest she wore under it could diminish the sensual excitement. Again his hand moved, to her knee, then beneath her skirt beyond the tops of her black stockings until he found his goal.

'I knew,' he whispered, 'I knew you'd be like this. You want me just as much as I want you. Tell me, darling Lyddy, tell me.'

She had no power: love, years of empty dreams, whisky, they combined to take away all the control she always fought so hard to maintain. He felt the movement of her head against his as she nodded.

That was when her empty glass slipped from her hand and shattered on the stone-flagged floor. As if she was waking from a dream, the sound brought her back to earth from the paradise where she'd seemed to float. Even now the room wasn't quite steady; she knew she must sit still.

'No, Christian, *no*, we can't do this.'

'Yes, Lyddy, *yes*,' he mimicked her voice 'for us this can't be wrong. You and I were meant to be together. I was a blind fool, that day when I let us all spoil the rest of our lives. That morning, why couldn't I have told you what I felt? Instead I was so sure of myself, I thought I could take my time. Then, like a weak fool, I let myself get carried away by the heat of the moment—and look where it's brought us. You and I are right for each other, we're friends, partners (that's what I've always felt in the yard), companions, and lovers (I know and you know that's what we both want).'

But her moment was gone. Yes, it was what she wanted, if only he were free, if only he hadn't made vows of faithfulness to Sophie. She'd made no vows, but her own loyalty and love for her 'sister' gave her no choice but to pull away from him. She did. She sat bolt upright on the wooden chair (something that wasn't easy in a room that seemed to be behaving like a ship on the ocean). In those next seconds she made herself remember the things she knew of him: he'd walked out on Norah when he knew she was pregnant; making love to Sophie had led to their marriage; and now he was prepared to forget his vows of loyalty. She had no illusions about him, she knew his weaknesses. But nothing clouded her love for him. She, the 'such a good woman' Lydia Westlake, wanted to abandon all she'd been brought up to revere and to follow her heart. Her heart? Was it just her heart? She didn't want to listen to the question her conscience silently whispered. Was it her heart or her frustrated body? How cruel a conscience can be, in that moment when heaven seemed within her grasp, how cruel to scream at her that she was plain, hard-working, 'good Miss Westlake', born to be a spinster. Tonight she could grasp her moment of physical wonder; tomorrow he'd be gone just like he had from Norah and plenty of others between her and Sophie.

Yet it wasn't fear of tomorrow that prompted her as she pushed him away and got to her feet, standing upright and stiff, frightened to relax lest the room would spin again.

'If you're desperate for a lover, then find one somewhere

else. Sophie is my sister. Do you honestly think I could let you and me be lovers?' If she sounded angry it was no more than a shield to hide behind, for even now her battle wasn't won.

He gripped her shoulders, the pressure of his hands giving her the extra stability she needed.

'Lyddy, dear, dear Lyddy, can you tell me honestly that you don't know what I say is the truth?'

'That we're friends? Yes, of course we are.' She was pleased with that, she sounded like a sister-in-law should.

'You know that's not what I mean. Lovers,' he pulled her close, holding her against him, 'lovers, Lyddy, giving to each other all that we are. Tell me the truth.'

'Yes, it's what I want,' she buried her face against his neck, she could smell the faint perfume of lavender from the dressing on his hair, she felt the burning sting of tears she couldn't hold back, 'yes, yes, *yes*, I want us to make love. I'm thirty years old,' she sobbed, 'a starchy spinster, a virgin. I've imagined, I've pretended. Some faceless lover—until I met you. Now you're the only one I want.' Surely the cage door must have been left open, never in all her thirty years had Lyddy behaved like this. She seemed to stand outside herself, having no power to stop the flow of words, finding comfort in her outburst. What would come next? Where was she heading? Again her conscience must have prodded. 'It's no use, Christian. Go home to Sophie. Talk to her, say to her what you did to me—'

'Say that she and I are right for each other? You know it's not true.'

'About this afternoon. That's why you came here. She'll be able to explain, she'll make you see that you'd got the

wrong impression. Sophie is as normal as any girl, I promise you that's true. She has always had lots of young men
vying for her favours and she's loved every moment of it.
Probably she thought you were taking her for granted, expecting her to be there for you every time you wanted to make
love. Treat her like you did before you were married, don't
push her. She's in love with you, Christian, I'm sure she is.'

'Damn Sophie, it's you who matters.'

'Go home.' She was standing tall again, her large and sensible handkerchief mopping her tear-stained and blotchy face.
'I've behaved abominably, must be the drink,' she sniffed, determined to make the laugh she forced sound natural. 'The
occasional glass of sherry hadn't prepared me.'

'Lyddy—'

'*No*! Just go, Christian. I'll see you tomorrow. Tonight
mustn't spoil our sharing what we have in the business. Be
there with me to show Mr Chivers around, promise me.'

'You think I wouldn't? I'm going to make sure he doesn't
try and pull a fast one on you. Some men – most men—think
a woman can't hold her own in the business world. If he sees
he has two of us to reckon with he won't offer below the value
and expect you to clutch at it.'

'Whatever I am, I'm certainly not a pushover.' She was recovering, she was even twisting her long hair into a coil and
starting to pin it back into austere place.

'If you were, my darling Lyddy, we'd not be standing
here. Even the cold of your bedroom wouldn't have—'

'Go home, Christian. Talk to Sophie. If thoughts—and
prayers too—will help, mine will be with you.' Thus spoke
Captain Westlake of Kingshampton Guide Troop, that oh-so-
good woman, back in her cage with the door shut and bolted.

* * *

Next morning when they met in the office neither of them mentioned the evening; it was as if it had been as much a dream as those other dozens of times she had reached out to him in the isolation of her bed. When Mr Chivers came it was Lydia who received him, she was Archibald Westlake's daughter, it was she who set the pace of the interview. Aware of how closely Christian watched her, pride gave her the mettle she needed. Only after Albert Chivers had left, saying that he would contact Haig and Digby, the agents, confirming the price he had agreed with her, did she let down her guard.

'It'll be all right, won't it, Christian? Dad would have approved?'

'There are moments when I marvel at my dear friend Lyddy. I came thinking you might need support. I should have known better. If your father is able to know what's happening, he'll be proud of the daughter he has reared. I was proud of you, darling Lyddy.' Then, his eyes shining with laughter, 'The whisky must have done you good.'

'What nonsense you talk. It did me no good at all. I had a shoe factory full of cobblers all hammering in my head, I even got up at half past three to take aspirin. Did you get a chance to talk to Sophie or had she gone to bed?' She said the first thing that came into her head, anything to steer them from where they'd been heading. 'No, don't tell me. It's not my business.'

'It's very much your business. Left to myself I wouldn't have gone home with the good intentions you planted. Good intentions? God alone knows! I certainly don't. She was in bed; they were both in bed. Separately or together? I dare say God knows that too and He's not likely to tell me. This morning Dulcie carried her breakfast up on a tray. "Sophie's idea of heaven" she told me when I saw her come out of the kitchen with it. Not what I had in mind last night as *my* idea of heaven, nor yours either.'

'We've moved on from last night,' came the prim answer. 'Now, about Mr Chivers…'

He followed her lead as the conversation went back to the prospective purchaser, but she didn't miss the teasing laughter in his eyes. They discussed the financial aspect of dividing the sale price, after all hadn't he said that they worked together as perfect partners?

'I shan't be in this afternoon,' he told her as she pulled her cloche hat well down and none too attractively on her head to withstand the wind as she cycled home. Often she went into the village and had lunch at Miss Parker's Tearooms, but lying in bed the previous night, her head throbbing, her mind restless, she had resolved that in future she would bring comfort and warmth to the house. If she were destined to be a solitary old maid, then at least she'd keep up her standards. She would light two fires, one in the kitchen range and one in the drawing room, then bank them up to burn slowly until evening. That done she would call at the office to check the midday post, then cycle over to Meadowlands and talk to Sophie. It wasn't something she looked forward to, but she wanted to reassure her that Dad would surely have approved of Mr Chivers—and somehow she wanted to find the words to make her believe Christian was jealous of her friendship with Dulcie. To tell her what he suspected would only drive the wedge between them deeper, for Sophie would be hurt and angry that he could have brought his misgivings to someone else, an outsider to their marriage. By the light of day and with her headache still slumbering, waiting to thump back into life when the effect of her midday aspirins wore off, she found masochistic pleasure in punishing herself for so nearly following the devices of her own heart with no thought for the hurt she was doing Sophie. Anyway—and here that same masochistic pleasure really came into its own—last night he wanted sexual satisfaction, he felt deprived because Sophie needed more patience than he was prepared to find, that's all it was. I happened to be there, she told herself firmly, the only available woman. By this morning he'd recovered, he'd been almost laughing about last night. Well, let him laugh. See if I care. What did I say to him last night? There's so much I half remember, yet I can't be sure. He must have given me all that whisky so that I'd let him do what he wanted. Dad only ever had about an inch up the glass; what he gave me was much more. Now I can't remember. I think I cried, I remember wanting to scream—but did I actually do it? I've got to put things right between him and Sophie, then he'll know that last night was just because I'd drunk too much.

As she propped her bicycle against the side of the house, Sophie opened the front door.

'I saw you coming. I haven't seen you for days.'

'I know. I hoped you'd come to the office,' Lydia answered, stopping to kiss the upturned face. 'We've been busy. Christian will have told you that Mr Chivers was coming this morning. And you'll know how it all went.'

'How would I know? Christian hasn't been home. Anyway, who's Mr Chivers?' Clearly she was on her guard, not a promising start to the visit.

'He's meeting the price, Sophie. By the time expenses are paid, this is a rough estimate I've made of our shares. Christian has seen it and he thinks it looks about what we might expect.'

Sophie took the piece of paper then, holding Lydia's gaze as if defying her to look away, she tore it down the middle without so much as glancing at it.

'I told you, I'm not some Judas to be paid off with pieces of silver. I expect Pops knew what would happen if ever you got your hands on it. That's why he left something especially just for me. You might think it's a pittance, but to me it's a lot of money. And the house is mine. It's not Christian's so if I sell it he can't stop me.'

Lydia dropped to sit on the arm of a chair, concern written on her face. Since the wedding she'd been to the house many times, yet on that day it was as if she was back in time to the day the show house was furnished, this three-piece suite delivered from McBrady's Emporium in Brackleford as an enticement to would-be purchasers. She'd hung the curtains, she'd watched Sophie and Christian together, she'd known herself to be an outsider. And where was the difference now? Those things he'd said to her last night, hazy as the words were, she knew they were what she'd longed to hear and yet now she must make herself believe—and surely it was the truth?—they had been no more than the voice of momentary desire, probably not for *her* so much as for a willing woman to give him what Sophie refused. But this was no time to think of herself: Lydia pulled her thoughts back where she intended to keep them, determined somehow to make Sophie understand his hurt. Whatever had gone wrong *had* somehow to be put right.

'Oh Sophie, don't let anger and hurt come between you. Never mind about the business, we can talk about that any time. What I really wanted to say is, please, darling Sophie, sink your pride, talk to him. He's as miserable as sin, I know he is and so are you.'

'Is he? If he is, then it's not what I intended.'

'Then you'll talk to him? I know I'm an outsider, you and Christian are a couple, bound by vows that both of you never doubted. But I do feel responsible. It was through me that Dulcie came to you—'

As nimble as a cat, with one swift and graceful movement, Sophie was across the room and on her knees, her blue eyes wide with…with what? Anguish? Shame? No, there was something in her expression that sent a shiver of fear through Lydia.

'I told you, Lyddy. When I was afraid she was going away, I told you.'

'She's your friend. You were angry that Mr Fulbrook disapproved, and I can understand that. But this is Christian we're talking about. Surely you're not trying to make him jealous?'

'I'm sorry, I'm sorry,' and those lovely eyes filled with tears that she made no attempt to hide. 'I don't understand it either, but I can't help it, Lyddy. And *no*, I'm *not* sorry, I never felt so free, so *right about myself*. I told you being married is disgusting.'

'No, Sophie. If you love each other nothing can be disgusting.'

'Oh, *you*! You with your high-flown ideals, and what do you know about the beastliness of it? Nothing. Lyddy, I'm going to tell you. You may not love me anymore when you know but I can't help that. Don't blame me, blame God. If He's so clever and makes us what we are, and if He is love like we've always been taught, then I am like I am because it's the way He wanted it.' Lydia sat as still as a statue; she felt frightened to breathe, unable to reach out and touch poor distraught Sophie. 'Say something, can't you! Lyddy, when I got married I imagined I'd find what I was looking for, what I'd dreamed about. I knew—I knew—well—I'd thought about it and—all right, I'll tell you. Before I was married, before I knew Christian, I'd found out for myself the sort of miracle that happens when you make love. I expect there are proper words, but I don't know what the thing that happens is called. Anyway, I don't expect you to understand. I thought it would be like that with a husband, a wonderful sort of exalted feeling. But it was beastly, I felt dirty, used, soiled. Love isn't like that, that's not love, the sort of love God gives us.'

'Don't bring God into it. You made sacred vows, vows to Him.'

Turning away, Sophie sniffed loudly, snorted, gasped for breath, and finally, in a voice devoid of all feeling, she said, 'I knew you wouldn't understand. But I'm glad I've told you. I don't expect you knew that a woman could feel like this for one of her own kind any more than I did. Not just being friends, but—everything. So now you know.' She stood up, her head held high. 'You try to tell me that Christian's jealous. I don't believe it. Ask him whether things are better here now than before Dulcie came, and I know what he'd say. He gets well fed, well housed. We're invited out as husband and wife and I know I'm a credit to him. I don't carry a banner saying I find his habits distasteful.'

Lydia stood up. She felt she was looking at a stranger. Whether for her own sake, for Sophie's, Christian's or because something in her refused to accept what she'd been told, she made one last effort. Poor Sophie had been thrown from carefree childhood (childhood that had stretched well beyond its years) into a life for which she'd been unprepared. The things she'd just said, surely they were a way of escaping what frightened her.

'Sophie, in the beginning it was a shock to you, you weren't ready—'

'Stop it! You stupid thing, blithering on as if you know it all! I'm not one of your oh-so-good Girl Guides. But I'm not wicked either. Can't you understand? I am as I am. And if I don't slot into the place you think I should fill, then that's your worry not mine. Go away, Lyddy. You don't see anything immoral in what you're doing to what had been Pops' life's work, oh no, that's fine. Because he's *dead*' (and even though she kept her back to Lydia, there was no disguising the hysterical rise in her voice) 'you think none of it matters. You think you can ease your conscience by giving me my Judas money—or it is because of Christian? Is that why you want to share it? Yes, that's what it is, isn't it? What do you hope to get from it? Even before I married him, do you think I didn't see the way you used to look at him? Bet he saw it too. If you pay him enough I expect you think he'll use you like he did me.' She had lost control, the words spilled from her with venom, out of character with the 'sister' who had always been so dear.

'Stop it! Be still!' Lydia was on her feet, pulling Sophie round so that they were face to face. 'What sort of devil has got hold of you?' She tried to pull the girl to her, but instead Sophie wrenched herself free. 'Get rid of Dulcie, forget all this. If you and Christian had a baby—'

'Go home! Leave me alone. You don't care about me, it doesn't matter to you that I've found real, complete happiness with someone. No, all you want is for me to live the same as every other woman. Well, I won't. I can't. This is *me*, this is what I am. And if you try to talk to Dulcie, try to take away what I have, I'll—I'll…You won't change anything, you can't. Go away, Lyddy, don't interfere with my life. I know just what I'm doing, and it's none of your business.'

'You can't pretend you're happy, just listen to yourself.'

'I was until you came interfering and I shall be again when you've gone.'

The drawing-room door opened and Dulcie appeared, her kindly face rosy from cooking.

'Whatever is it, love?' Ignoring Lydia, she took Sophie in her arms. 'You mustn't let her upset you, hush, love.' Then to Lydia, 'Do as she says. I heard her tell you to go home. She's all right, you mustn't worry about her. I'm taking care of her.'

'She has a perfectly good husband—'

'You really don't understand. Miss Westlake, give her freedom to be herself. Leave her alone.'

Without a word, Lydia left. To say that the visit had been unsuccessful was to say but half the truth. Christian had been right: Sophie and Dulcie were lovers. Hardly aware of where she was going, Lydia pedalled back to the office, a place that had been the foundation stone of adult life. Yet now all she was aware of was that already Mr Chivers would have set the wheels in motion, taking all this away. The morning's headache was back, hammering her brain, a reminder of yesterday evening, a reminder of Sophie's mocking words that Christian had always known she was his for the asking. She pulled off the cloche hat that gripped her forehead like a vice. Her empty stomach rumbled loudly, reminding her that she'd spent all her time at home lighting the fires and hadn't stopped to eat. Yet at the thought of food she felt horribly sick. Her mind raced, from Sophie to Christian, from Christian to those wonderful moments last night, back to Sophie and her taunts, on to Dulcie, to Dulcie and Sophie, to a past that in memory held no clouds, to the mockery of the many, many times she had hidden beneath her bedcovers, her hands guiding her imagination to bring Christian to her in that supreme moment. Had he known how she felt? Last night when he'd said the things she'd longed to hear, had he known that, no doubt like thousands of other spinsters, she had another world beside that of prim Miss Westlake? Last night when finally she'd got between the cold sheets she had tried to relive those moments, to feel his touch, but she'd not been able to find what she'd sought, she'd not been able to pass the barrier of her thumping head.

And still it thumped. Surely two inches of whisky couldn't have such a lasting effect? Again her empty stomach rolled loudly. Her hands were clammy and shaking, her mouth dry as sawdust, her throat tight. He'd said he wouldn't be back this afternoon, that's why she'd expected to find him at home so that she could talk to the two of them together. So where was he? Perhaps he would come in after all. At the same second that the thought came to her, so her body convulsed as she retched. She couldn't let him see her like this. Somehow she managed to get across the room and lock the outer door, but there was no way she could hold back the loud and threatening retch as she blundered towards that back room where Christian had hidden the day Norah had come looking for him, and from there to the small closet where she dropped to her knees in front of the lavatory without stopping to shut the door behind her.

Five minutes later, spent, limp and shaking, she was back at her desk, the door once more unlocked. Always determined and ready to overcome any obstacle, yet thinking of her visit to Sophie, Lydia knew herself to be utterly helpless. However, there were two things her bout of sickness had done: one was to clear her head of its hammers, the second was to take away her dread that Christian might come. A quick glance in the mirror from her handbag showed her that some of her colour had returned and she knew that with it had come something like a return of her natural resolve. If he came—when he came—ought she to tell him about her visit? No. To do that would be to accept. Little Sophie, who'd been her shadow as a child…Sophie, the prettiest girl in the district and with every young gallant vying for her favours…Sophie, the beautiful bride looking at Christian with such open pride…and now Sophie, saying she is as God made her, saying she has found the real truth of love. Mum…Dad…Lydia closed her eyes as if that way she could hold the image of them, bring them closer as in her heart she spoke to them, you must know what's happening. You love her, you love me, but is there a right and a wrong? I feel sick at the thought of what she is doing—but I can't pretend, not to you. From where you are, can you read our hearts? If you can, you must know that deep in my soul there is a sort of joy too: Sophie doesn't want him, if what she says is true (but how can it be? Not Sophie…) but if it is, then I'm free. If I'd known this last night I would have—have—lived the miracle of giving myself to him. Giving? That sounds passive, as if it would have been a duty. I know so little, isn't that what Sophie told me? Don't know what I'm talking about, that's what she said. But I do. I know with every fibre of my body. Is that a sin? Good-living Miss Westlake, pillar of the community, and what would the community think if they knew what goes on inside my head and my heart?

What was left of the afternoon ticked away. As the short hours of daylight faded she heard the familiar clatter of hobnailed boots on the cobble-stoned yard, telling her the men's working day was over. She heard the rumble of wheels of their handcart and the clatter of tools, all sounds so much part of her life that normally she was hardly aware of them. But this day had been like no other. Listening, she felt removed, looking back on a past that today had taken beyond recall, looking forward into an unknown abyss.

There was no logic in the hope that Christian might appear, after all he'd told her he wouldn't be there, and yet she waited. With the departure of the men there was nothing but silence. At last she had to face the fact he wouldn't come—and after the way she'd sent him away the previous night he certainly wouldn't arrive on her doorstep at Drydens. Without so much as glancing in the mirror, she pulled on that functionally unattractive cloche hat, then closed the office. Cycling home, she was facing the wind, wind that was whipping itself into the frenzied force of a storm. At least this evening there was no rain; she arrived at Drydens dry and cold. Silence. At home…in the office…silence, emptiness.

Somehow, the evening dragged by. She cooked her solitary meal and, just as she'd resolved, instead of taking the easy way and eating it in the kitchen, she spread a cloth on the gate-leg table in the drawing room and made herself uphold the standards Adelaide had set. There was a limit how long she could take to eat a fried pork chop and fried mashed left-over potatoes. By nine o'clock she had washed up, banked up the kitchen range to last the night. For weeks she'd lived there on her own, so why was it that on that evening every sound seemed to echo, emphasising the emptiness— of the house? Of her life?

I'm cold, she told herself, cold and tired. Neither was true, but she needed to find an excusable reason for this feeling of dread. A hot bath, that's the answer. So with true Lydia-like determination she mounted the stairs. But thoughts caught up with her, thoughts she couldn't escape. Sophie…why did I mind so much what she told me? Oughtn't I to be glad for her that she has found a way to be happy? Just for a minute, forget Christian, forget the humiliation for him that she rejects him and finds all she wants with Dulcie. We are as we are, she says that's the way God made her. Is that true, or is she running away from a mistaken marriage? It's not my business; she made that plain. It that what hurt? Sophie told me to keep out of it, to go away, to leave her alone. Sophie, who's always shared every thought with me. But had she? What was it she said about knowing her own body, knowing what she expected to find with Christian? Did she ever share that with me? Or I with her? No, of course not. Keep out of it, keep away—that's what she wants of me. If she could have seen me with my head over the lavatory, if she could have known that it was shock and misery that made me so sick—because it *was*, shock, misery that she could cast me off like last week's washing. Is that honest? Is that the whole truth? That alone wouldn't have made me feel ill, sad yes, but ill no. Even stronger than being upset by Sophie was that other feeling, one I was ashamed of and yet gloried in. She had turned against Christian and me too, so surely now I was free. No wonder my insides churned so disgustingly. But he hasn't come. Why am I such a fool, don't I know he's unreliable? He found he couldn't get what he wanted from me, so where is he now? Casting his net somewhere else. Didn't Norah tell me exactly what he was like? Sophie says what she is doing is the way God made her. Did He make me to spend all my life an old maid, filling my empty hours with good works, helping other people who more often than not have a bloody—yes, *bloody*—sight more in their lives than I have myself? If that's all there is to be, then help me, I beseech You, help me to see it as all I need. Take away from me this aching, empty hunger; take away from me this stupid—yes, *stupid*—feeling that I was put on this earth for Christian. Partners, friends, companions, lovers. Help me to be strong, I can't see ahead. Show me the path, give me courage to carve something out of my future. Only You can can show me the way and give me the courage to follow it.

Tomorrow was another day, tomorrow she would be one step nearer to finding her goal. It was while she was lying immersed in the comforting hot water, half awake and half asleep, that an idea came to her.

CHAPTER SEVEN

The next morning Lydia had to collect her rents. She knew it would take longer than usual, for the tenants had to be reassured before rumour spread about the sale of the business, as it undoubtedly would now that the men knew. Over the years they had taken it for granted that their tenancies were inextricably linked with Westlake Builders, so now at each house she meant to give time explaining the situation and restoring any slipped confidence.

All her dreams that yesterday evening Christian would have come to her had been overtaken by reality. And why should that surprise her? She'd made herself abundantly clear to him: yes, she cared about him; yes, she was his friend, but no, she couldn't and she wouldn't let herself come between him and Sophie. He must have accepted easily enough: yesterday morning he had behaved as if the previous evening had never happened. If she hadn't been to see Sophie yesterday, she would have imagined that his suspicions had been unfounded and that he was determined that they should make a new beginning to their marriage. So there was no ducking from the truth: on Wednesday evening when he'd come to her he had believed she would be putty in his hands, and finding he was wrong, he'd gone elsewhere for amusement.

By ten o'clock on that Friday morning it was apparent that he wasn't coming to the yard. There was no alternative but for her to leave the office unattended. No one looking at her as she rammed her cloche hat on, then slung her rent bag over her head to hang round one shoulder, would have seen anything to hint at the misery of her soul. 'Back about midday' she wrote on a card in her firm, bold hand, then pinned it to the outside of the door to the office before locking up. If there was anything remotely different about her on that particular Friday morning, it was in the way she walked—nearer the truth to say, the way she marched. Left right, left right, head high, there was nothing downtrodden in the familiar sight of Miss Westlake as she went about her business. No time this morning to dwell on the aching loneliness that threatened to overtake her if she let down her guard. Her loneliness went deeper than what had happened between Christian and her, the glorious height she'd let herself soar, only to be plunged into depths darker and gloomier than ever they had been when she'd tried to accept that all they could ever share was friendship; it was loneliness far deeper too than the emptiness of the house, the loss of the parents who'd been so dear emphasised by memories of them in everything around her; the loneliness that was still raw and new was one from which there could be no escaping, for nothing between Sophie and her could ever be the same.

Wherever her mind went, it came back to that same inescapable truth: the most important person in Sophie's life wasn't Christian, wasn't even *her*, but hard-working, gentle, caring Dulcie Fulbrook.

Her thoughts were brought up short as she reached No. 1 Wyckham Street and came face to face with old Mrs Durrant, who'd been a tenant there since the houses were first built. Now she had the task of telling everyone that she was selling the business and reassuring them that she had no intention of getting rid of the houses; their tenancies were secure. Usually the tenants had their five shillings ready, the job was smooth and straightforward. On this Friday it all took much longer, not that they had anything to fear from what she told them, but given the opportunity most of them enjoyed a chat. At last Wyckham Street was done and she started on Mulberry Street. There was no need to call at No. 7, for Ethel and her sister lived rent free. However, with her collecting finished, she never went back to the office without knocking on Ethel's door, knowing that she would be expected to go in for a few minutes. Ethel liked to know she was managing all right at Drydens and to hear news of Sophie.

The door was opened even before she reached for the knocker.

'There are you then, I've been watching out for you. I saw you coming along the street with your money bag. In you come. Hilda's kept the kettle singing ready to make us a drink. We'll go and wait in the parlour. Now, just you sit down and tell me your side of things.' Having known Lydia all her life, bandaged her grazed knees, listened to her reciting her 'times tables', taught her almost all she knew of cooking and shared the family's pride when she was made a Guide Captain, Ethel saw no need to mince her words.

'My side of what story?' Lydia made herself laugh as she asked it, even though she could feel the sudden tightening of the muscles in her chest.

'Selling up. That's what Sophie tells me. I went along to see her earlier this morning; I haven't been home above half an hour. I took her a jar of her favourite chutney I'd been making. Oh Lyddy, my dear, she'd been looking so much better of late, brighter you might say. For there's no disguising how worried we all were when first she was married. But all that seemed to be over, or so I thought. But this morning she was in a right state. That Dulcic Fulbrook, kind as kind can be, she is to her. But an outsider like that, what can she do to cheer the poor little soul? First she told me about the business, that's rock bottom of what's upset things for her. But who would have thought it could lead to *this*. You've heard what's happened? Well, of course you have, you'll have been the first one she'll have come running to. If I could get my hands on him I'd give him the hiding he deserves, treating our Sophie like that.'

'Like what, Ethel? I went there yesterday to talk to Sophie, I wanted to explain to her exactly what's happening with the business.'

'Selling it, that's what she tells me. Selling your Dad's business. If that Christian Mellor was worth his salt, instead of ganging up with you and not listening to her, he would have buckled to and helped you look after things there so that you could keep it going.'

'So he has, Ethel. The decision to sell was *mine*.'

'Oh dear, oh dear. You always were headstrong, Lyddy. We were all proud of you for the way you tackled things; try and bend your way of thinking and we never got anywhere. And that's what poor little Sophie has found. Loved your Dad, she did, loved him, I reckon, above all else. Anyway, I've learned better than to ask you to change your way of thinking, so I won't waste my breath. But what are we going to do about that young man? Cluttering off like he has! Ought to be ashamed of himself. Did she come to you last night—or was she standing there at the window watching, waiting for him to cool down and change his mind about walking out on her? Like I say, he ought to be downright ashamed.'

'I've not seen Sophie since I called there during the day yesterday. I had hoped to talk to her with Christian there; I knew how she felt about my selling up and I wanted his support.'

'Oh, he'd give you that all right. Knows which side his bread's buttered, if you ask me. She told me, bless her heart, how she had refused to take a penny from the sale. But it's not for me to talk about what's between the two of you. So you're telling me you hadn't heard that he'd left her? You know what I think? I think—no, more than think, I'm sure as I am that today's Friday—that if she'd held out her hand to you, ready to take her half share of whatever you get for your father's business, then he would have stood by her. And you had no inkling that he was going to clutter off like he has? No, of course you can't have. It came as a bolt from the blue to her, so it's hardly likely that you could have known.'

'Christian gone? You say he left yesterday? Ethel, no one walks out on a good marriage. Did she tell you why he's gone?'

'Poor child, seemed at a loss. Is there some other woman? If you ask me—and I've heard a whisper or two, now that this has happened I don't mind saying so—he's a bit of a goer. If only your dear father had made them wait instead of rushing headlong into marriage, we would all have had that much more chance to size the rascal up. What with that, and now

the business going too, what your poor dear parents would
say now I'm frightened to think.'

'As far as selling the business goes, Dad would be the one
person in favour; he would know that a successful building
business has to be run by someone who knows the trade—
not just as I do, keeping the books, collecting the rents, paying the bills, anyone with half a brain can learn to do those
things. But the one in charge has to understand the trade—
like Dad did, and like Mr Chivers does. He's the man who is
buying me out.'

'Oh dear, oh dear. Look back just a few months and who
would have believed things could have come to such a pass.
And you say that handsome fop poor little Sophie is tied up
to egged you on?' Then as Hilda came in carrying a tea tray,
'Hilda knows all about it, she was with me at Sophie's when
we heard what the young rascal had done.'

'Morning, Miss Lyddy,' Hilda said, putting the tray down
and starting to pour their cups of tea. (Like Ethel, she was
happy to drink tea at any hour of the day and it didn't occur
to either of them that Lydia might have a different opinion.)
'Yes, I was there, and like I'm sure Ethel has told you, poor
Miss Sophie was knocked for six. That other one, Dulcie, she
whispered to me that the upset really started when you visited her around about this time yesterday, in fact Dulcie
seemed to think more of her tears were on account of the sale
of the business than they were about him clearing off like he
has. Between ourselves, I didn't think it was her place to
speak in the way she did.'

'Rubbish.' Ethel swept the criticism aside. 'We've seen
for months it's not the usual servant–mistress relationship;
those two do everything together: gardening, outings on

their cycles around the lanes, even on the river—and that's somewhere I've never known our Sophie take a living soul until Dulcie came on to the scene. I grant you it's not the usual way folk carry on, but there's no doubting the comfort the child finds in her, so let us not criticise Dulcie for voicing an opinion. What do you say, Lyddy my dear?'

'It was I who sent Dulcie Fulbrook to ask Sophie if she needed any help, so that answers your question. I believe she is a woman of exemplary character.'

'So she may be.' Once Hilda formed an opinion, argument only made it more firmly entrenched. 'But what's between your Sophie and her husband isn't her business, so what's she doing airing her views?'

'Over that I think she wants simply to cheer Sophie up,' Ethel said. 'Anyway, be all that as it may, what you won't have heard then, Lyddy, is that Mr Mellor didn't show up at the house during the afternoon, didn't put in an appearance until halfway through the evening. I can't give you a real account of what happened, and to tell the truth I felt certain it would be you telling me, for I felt sure Sophie would have come straight to you with her troubles. It seems they had words. I suppose it went against his plans that she insisted on turning down what could have given him a soft living. Anyway, he packed his things, threw his cases in the sidecar of that noisy contraption of his and that was the last they'd seen of him. Where he spent the night, whether he was alone or with some floozy, I don't want to think. What your poor Mum and Dad must be feeling I don't know. How can they rest easy in heaven or anywhere else when they've left such chaos behind them?'

'But Ethel, Christian has commissions from this area, he can't just disappear. He was in the office yesterday morning, he was with me when Mr Chivers came. He hasn't been in this morning, but his drawing board is there, his drawer is full of his things. It was probably no more than a tiff, Ethel, the kindest thing we can do is ignore it. When the dust settles he'll go home. And she'll have had a chance to think things over and to cool off.' Lydia tried to sound reassuring, but at the back of her mind was the fear that he meant to come back to the office after she'd locked up for the night, use his own key and clear his things away. And there was no way she could avoid the suspicion that his final decision to leave Sophie had been sealed by the things he'd said at Drydens on Wednesday evening. He'd married Sophie because the situation had forced him; now, because of Dulcie, he knew his marriage had no future, so the last thing he would want was to be trapped into another commitment, especially one with such close connections to Sophie. Above all else, Christian wanted freedom, wasn't that why he had run away from Norah? She tried not to listen to the silent voice that whispered: 'What if Sophie had agreed to share the proceeds from the sale of the business? Would he have been content to stay on at Meadowlands, her husband in the eyes of the world?' That was Ethel's opinion but then Ethel didn't know the way he'd talked on Wednesday, sitting huddled close to the open door of the oven.

There was only one thing that helped Lydia salvage a modicum of pride: Thursday morning she had made no reference to the previous evening; she had been determined not to let him believe it had mattered to her any more than it had to him—and clearly, that was not at all!

'It is to be hoped it's no more than a lovers' tiff,' Hilda said.

'It is to be hoped you're right,' Ethel agreed. 'It's one bit of trouble after another for that poor child. I dare say you'll ride over and see her, Lyddy m'dear. She needs someone, blessed if she doesn't, until that fly-by-night comes roaring back on that machine of his. Someone must have put him up for the night.' It was said with a sniff that spoke as clearly as any words just the sort of person Ethel had in mind.

'He has plenty of friends.' Lydia found herself defending him. 'I believe you misjudge him, Ethel. Working in the office, we all got along so well, Dad, Christian and me. We can't know what triggered this off, but to my way of thinking Sophie is being pig-headed over refusing anything from the business. Don't you think Dad would have wanted it that way?'

'Not for me to say. Asked what he wanted, I believe the same as Sophie does, that he would have wanted it to remain Westlakes. Poor dear soul, all those years he worked to build his empire. It's a shame, a real shame. And what about all the men who worked for him, what's to become of them and their families? And the tenants, will the new man, Mr Chivers, did you call him? Will he want to let things stand as they are?'

'You're making mountains where there aren't even molehills. I am not selling the houses, so the tenants won't be affected. As for the men, their jobs are quite safe. I've discussed all that with Mr Chivers. He's taking over all our existing work and there is plenty on our books. So don't look so worried, Ethel, honestly, there's no need.'

'Just as you say.' Archie and Addy's loyal retainer didn't disguise her doubt. 'It's a sad day, for all that. And thinking of it from your point of view, how do you think you'll manage? Getting up each morning in an empty house, no work to go to, no responsibilities…it bothers me, fair and square it bothers me.'

'I have plans. And Ethel, they're not based on trying to fit into Dad's shoes. He wouldn't expect it of me.'

'Well, my dear, all I can say is that I hope you're right. But one thing that would bother him above all else, is to see Sophie so upset. She looks on it as a betrayal of his trust. She feels you are letting him down.'

'Then she has no business to form her opinions without looking at it from any angle but her own,' Lydia answered crossly. 'We have one life to live—and not to make something of it is a sin. And now I must get back. I left a note on the door saying I'd be there about noon and it's more than that already.'

'You'll miss Mr Mellor waiting there while you're out. Well, I suppose he can see that our little Sophie means what she says, so there'll be nothing in it for him wasting his time there in the yard that's soon to belong to someone else. For all that, it wouldn't have hurt him to give you a bit of support up to the time you turn your back on it.'

'I always thought you regarded Sophie's husband highly,' was Lydia's reply. 'He hasn't changed, Ethel. You mustn't hold it against him because you think I'm making a wrong move.' While she spoke she was putting the strap of her money bag first over her head and then around her shoulder before straightening her hat.

'As long as things moved along gently, and your parents clearly thought a good deal of him, it wasn't for me to have opinions. Well, have them perhaps, but not to air them. One thing I believe in, Lyddy, is loyalty, loyalty to the dead as much as to the living. You're a good woman, a good woman grown from a good child. I've known you all your days and you've never been anything of a fly-away. Don't rush into doing something you'll regret. I know the home can't be like it was, nor that office either. Full of ghosts, I dare say. But you won't find life any rosier by not facing up to things. I shouldn't have left you there alone at Drydens, no wonder you want to make a break with the past. Nearer the truth, it's the past that's made a break with you.'

In a movement that was out of character, Lydia bent forward and kissed Ethel's cheek. 'You're right, Ethel,' she said. 'If Mum and Dad were still here, if everything was like it used to be, I expect time would have just gone on drifting by. But I can't let it do that. If I'm to make a new start I can't keep waiting for tomorrow and tomorrow and tomorrow.'

Ethel saw her out of the front door that opened straight on to the narrow pavement, then watched as she strode back down the road.

'Don't like the sound of things at all,' she said as she came back to the seldom-used parlour which Hilda always considered the correct place to bring the pot of tea for Miss Lyddy, such an upright, good-living woman, one with no frills and fancies about her.

'Difficult time for the poor woman,' Hilda said. 'That pretty little sister of hers, if she gets knocked for six she'll soon find a way of picking herself up. A pretty face, a ready smile, and the world is a kinder place. Here, pass me your empty cup and let me pour you a refill.'

No one watching Lydia striding back to the yard would have guessed at her racing thoughts. Christian had gone…he had left Sophie…did that mean he had walked out on all their lives just like years ago he had walked out on Norah's? The answer was plain. If he'd wanted to he could have contacted her, there was a telephone in the office and, another step up her father's ladder of ambition, there was even one at Drydens. She found satisfaction in inflicting pain, telling herself that when he'd said those things she'd so longed to hear, he had believed she was willing to be swept overboard and ready to leap into bed with him. All the time when she'd believed she had hidden her secret longing, what she felt about him must have been obvious to everyone, even to *him*. Secretly, how he must have laughed when she lapped up those things he told her—partners, companions, yes and lovers too. That was all he was aiming for.

Her mind raced. And if I'm honest, she acknowledged silently, weighed down with hurt and humiliation, wasn't it what I was aiming for too? Friends, partners, lovers—and I believed he meant what he said. Doesn't it show just what a daydreaming fool I am, wouldn't any woman with a modicum of intelligence have realised that a man like Christian could never seriously look at a frumpish old maid like me? As if to prove the truth of the thought, she caught sight of her reflection in the window of Miss Woodward's haberdashery shop, the image doing nothing to boost her confidence. How can I imagine any man—*any man*—and certainly not one with all the charm of Christian, could really fall in love with me? What am I? That's right, tell yourself, make yourself face the truth: I'm plain, I'm dull, my clothes have no style—and think how stupid I'd look if I wore dresses to my knees like Sophie does, showing her pretty legs. I haven't even a proper woman's shape, I'm flat as a board. What must he have thought the other night when he touched me? How he must have laughed—silently, so that I wouldn't know and be rebuffed enough to turn him away, for even skin and bone like I am would have been better than the frustration he must have felt knowing that lovely Sophie spurned him for Dulcie.

Memories of those few glorious moments haunted her, yet now there could be no joy in them. As long as she lived she would remember the aching yearning he had aroused with the touch of his hand, of that she was sure even though an inner voice mocked her that there had been nothing sincere in the way he'd behaved or the things he'd said. That it was so important to her simply emphasised the hopelessness of her future. Striding purposefully on, she nodded her head in greeting to the vicar's wife, the front she presented to the world a far cry from the anguish in her heart.

No one, her thoughts raced on, not even Sophie, had ever been given a hint of how—how—hungry, yes, *starved* for love I am. Yes, and so I always will be. I mustn't run away from it; if a thing has to be faced then I must face it. Remember how, ages ago when I first started working for Dad, I heard the men in the yard joking about Miss Armitage, the headmistress at the village school: 'a dried-up old maid', that's what they called her. Is that how they speak about me? And why not? It must be how they see me. But it's not true, *it's not true*. Perhaps it wasn't true with her either, skinny, prim little Miss Armitage…did she ache for love, did she know just like I do that nameless longing that night after night ends in such lonely mockery?

But her misery came from something more than her own disappointment and humiliation. There was the problem of

Sophie, always so lovely that every young man who met her must have half fallen in love with her. Marriage and all its beastliness, that's what she thought of it. I didn't believe her, I thought it was just that she hadn't been prepared. Now, though, there is no doubt. And that's why Christian has gone. How could he stay there, living in the house with his wife and her lover? Dulcie her lover? When he told me, if only I'd known then that it wasn't just in his imagination, if only I'd been freed of shame that I could feel like I do about Sophie's husband. Out of loyalty to her I sent him away, and yet she is outside it all; nothing we could have done would have hurt her. At least, then, I would have had one night. For the rest of my life I would have known the difference between make-believe dreams and the reality of lying with Christian, one body, one soul. Oh no, not that. One body, yes; one soul? That can only come with a true union, a bonding of minds…friends, companions, partners, lovers, came the echo of his words. But how much could she believe?

Left right, left right, planting her long slender feet firmly, on she marched.

The office looked just as she'd left it; there were no notes pushed through the door and clearly she hadn't been missed. So once again she locked the door and cycled home to make a sandwich and a cup of strong coffee, to stoke the kitchen range and light the fire in the drawing room, this time keeping her thoughts well in check and planning her afternoon. Then, back to the yard to get out the time-sheets and make up the wage packets. It was when she wheeled her bicycle to the back of the building that she saw the motor bike and side-car.

'You've heard?' Christian greeted her even before she had

time to close the office door behind her. 'Now can you believe what I told you? Sophie tells me you've seen her.'

'Yesterday, I went to tell her about Mr Chivers. I thought you'd be there, I thought you might help me persuade her about her share of the business.' She knew she was playing for time, fighting to keep her voice steady. Her visit to Sophie stood between them, yet it was impossible for her to be the one to say, 'I know about how she is, she is as God made her.'

'I couldn't go on living there. I can't live like a lodger in the home she shares with Dulcie. Lyddy, I can't understand it—I don't mean about Sophie, I don't think that surprised me. I thought she was frigid, I even tried to think that it was simply that she was immature and one day things would be different. I think—no, I don't think, I am *sure*—it was only in marriage that she came to understand herself.'

'What will she do? She's adamant she won't take a penny from the business; she can't forgive me for selling up. But what Dad left her can't last her if you leave her—'

'I told you I've talked to her. Surprisingly, she has no misgivings about taking money from me to keep the house going. I am her husband, she sees it as perfectly acceptable for the bills to be in my name.'

'Christian, I don't know much about the law. Do you mean to divorce her?'

'For the way things are? How can I? I don't know how the law stands; is it the same for physical love between women as it is between men? For men it's a prison sentence. Do you imagine I'd risk that for her?' He crossed the room to where Lyddy stood just inside the closed door. 'Take that monstrosity off your head,' he said easing off the unflattering felt hat. 'That's better. What have I to offer you, Lyddy my friend? I want to be your constant companion, your partner, your— mate. Such a maligned word, for what truer partner can there be than a mate? I want to be your lover, you know that.' She closed her eyes, she held her bottom lip between her strong white teeth, but somehow a hot tear managed to escape. He wiped it away, not with the silk handkerchief he wore in his breast pocket, but with the front of his fingers. 'Have I the right to ask you to throw in your lot with mine? I can give you love, I believe I can give you happiness, but I can't give you marriage.' As he stopped speaking the room was full of silence; she felt he must hear the heavy beating of her heart.

'Say something, Lyddy. Tell me the truth, can what I can give you ever be enough?'

She nodded, knowing her voice would be no more than a croak. But even a croak was unnecessary as his mouth covered hers, his arms held her so close that she felt the breath was being crushed out of her.

'What are you thinking?' he murmured, moving his mouth only just far enough from hers to whisper the question.

'Frightened to think,' she whispered back, 'frightened to move in case it's a dream.' But she did move, she pulled her head back so that she could look at him and will him to meet her eyes. 'It's a moment so perfect that I just want to hold on to it; nothing can ever be so perfect.'

This time he laughed, kissing her forehead. 'The best is still to come. What is there about you that does this to me?' He held her at arm's length, then let his hands run down her body from beneath her arms to her hips.

'I wish I was different. Not much like a woman at all.'

He laughed, pulling her back into his arms with one swift

movement. 'Not like any woman I've ever had, yet Lyddy, the thought of you haunts me.' Then, with a change of tone, 'We have things to do, my friend. Sort that money into the wage envelopes and I'll go and pay the men for you. I took the liberty of bringing a suitcase in the sidecar. Was that wrong of me? Are you imagining I took it for granted you would jump at the offer of giving me a bed—or half a bed?'

She laughed, little guessing how little she resembled that oh-so-highly-respected Miss Westlake known to the village. 'I'm glad. If you took it for granted, I'm glad I mean. Companions, partners, mates—surely they don't have secrets.'

'Let's get the wages done and shut shop for the day, eh? While I pay the men you can cycle home and see if you can find anything to feed us on. If not, we'll have to go to the Lion in Brackleford. Would you prefer that?'

She shook her head. 'I'd rather we stayed at home. You've just turned my simple world upside down, it's like an engagement and a marriage all in one. Today I don't want anyone but us.'

Never had she locked the office so early, never had she pedalled home feeling as though she were riding on cloud nine, never had she unpinned her long hair and brushed it with such vigour when it wasn't even bedtime, never had she gone into the room that used to be Sophie's and rummaged through her never quite emptied dressing-table drawers to find a lipstick. On Sophie it looked lovely; on her it seemed to stand out garishly, making her complexion even more sallow than nature intended. So taking an old handkerchief, she rubbed it hard, whether her action or the remains of the lipstick leaving her generous lips healthily rosy.

Watching from her bedroom window, listening for the first sound of his motor cycle, she pictured the selection of clothes in her wardrobe, desperately trying to think of something feminine and attractive. But all her clothes were on the same lines, made for service. Anyway, she mustn't waste time or he would be here before she'd coaxed any welcoming flames into the sitting-room fire she'd banked up when she'd come home earlier.

Downstairs, she added slivers of wood and within minutes flames licked round the 'sulky-looking' coals, their brightness surely an omen of the evening that stretched before them. She lifted the small gate-leg table on to the hearthrug, then covered it with Adelaide's favourite lace-edged cloth. There was nothing better to eat than the lamb chops she'd bought the previous day in the hope that he might be there to share them with her. Ethel had always dried their home-grown herbs and hung them in the pantry for winter, so she could at least make mint sauce. Potatoes…she had absolutely no other vegetable. But Lydia's Girl Guide training was ready and waiting to come to her rescue. She peeled them, then cut them into small cubes, tossed them in melted butter and put them in the oven. Next she laid the table in front of the fire, which by that time had responded to her ministrations; she filled the claret jug and put out two glasses from Adelaide's best set. Nothing left now but to fry the chops and open a jar of plums—not without a silent thank-you to Ethel.

The time had flown; she hadn't expected Christian to be so far behind her. Every few seconds she glanced towards the window, frightened to admit even in her thoughts that these magic moments could disappear just as they always did in her daydreams. Then she heard the roar of his motor cycle.

In her eagerness, she hurried to open the front door even before he reached it. But what a moment to glance at her reflection in the long mirror by the hall stand, a mirror put there at Sophie's suggestion. Some of her joy evaporated.

'It took me longer than usual,' he said as he left the bike standing in the gravel drive. 'They all needed reassuring that the work would go on just the same.' He followed her inside and shut the door. 'I told them nothing would change—but it will, Lyddy, darling Lyddy, for you and me it will change. Go and put on whatever it is you wear for festive occasions. This evening I shall take you to Brackleford. We'll dine in style at the Lion and drink a toast to our future in sparkling champagne. How would that be?'

'It would be lovely, except that I've tried to make something out of nothing for us here, the table's all ready. Which would you rather?'

'I thought women always wanted to don their finery and be taken out to eat. But then, my Lyddy isn't like the rest. Which would I prefer?' Through the open doorway of the sitting room he could see the fire, the table set ready, the claret jug with its silver top gleaming in the firelight. 'I'd prefer to stay here, just the two of us. We have a whole future to talk about…' By the shoulders, he held her at arms' length. 'Say something, Lyddy.' But her throat was dry and tight; she seemed to have lost the power of speech. This was no dream, this was reality.

And so began the hours that were to change the course of her life. At the Lion they would have eaten four courses, they would have drunk white wine with their fish and red with the beef that followed, and finally would have come the champagne. But the Lion had nothing to compare with the intimacy of their own hearth, the glow from good claret, and the inner warmth that came from the certain anticipation of where they were heading.

Summer or winter, Lydia would never have got into bed without first opening the window wide. So it was that Christian was able to lean out into the chill night air to light his cigarette. Behind him Lydia slept, perhaps exhausted as surely he ought to be. Yet his mind raced. He'd always suspected that hidden deep behind her outward semblance of restraint, kept well under control, was passion waiting an opportunity to find freedom. And tonight had been her opportunity—hers and his too. Through his mind rushed a pageant of women he'd known—his lips quivered into a smile as the word 'known' formed, known in the biblical sense. Of them all, none had been as lovely as Sophie, frigid, mixed-up Sophie. Yet never, *never* had love-making been as abandoned as with Lyddy, once her gates of captivity had been thrown open.

Stubbing out his cigarette against the brickwork of the house, he threw it into the garden, then turned back to the bed. His eyes were attuned to the darkness; in the shaft of moonlight that fell across the bed he could see her clearly. Her lips were slightly parted; she breathed quietly. His mind leaped back to when he'd pushed the straps of her undergarments from her shoulders, running his hands down her naked flesh as he stripped her of them, dropping to his knees as his hands continued their journey, easing her out of everything, even her stockings. Naked, she'd stood before him, something strangely touching in the way she had looked at him. He had sensed her shame. What woman wouldn't have felt shame at being so utterly without the soft feminine curves attributed to beauty? Reading her mind, how had he felt? He asked himself the question honestly. His paramount thought had been sympathy, sympathy even stronger than desire. As his fingers had touched her, explored, caressed, his own passion had been aroused. In not more than seconds he too had been naked, proud of his manly physique, glad of the proof of his own desire that must have been an education to her innocent mind. Taking the restraining pins from her hair he had let it fall around her shoulders. Painfully flat though her chest was, when first his fingers and then his mouth had tugged at her hardened nipples, a stifled moan had caught in her throat. Remembering, his mind raced on. Who would have thought that beneath that puritanical, spinsterish exterior such turbulent passion could live? How soundly was she asleep? How easily could he wake her?

Cold from the night air, he eased himself back into bed and moved closer to her. Turning towards him, her eyes still closed, she murmured something. Did she know or was she dreaming? He smiled. There was something satisfying in giving such pleasure.

In the morning, he woke to find himself alone. From downstairs came the sound of ashes being raked, then the clatter of cooking pots. Stretching, he smiled. Breakfast with Lyddy, now that would be a new experience. He imagined her downstairs, starry-eyed after her joyous night; he imagined the warmth of her welcome. He had no choice but to present himself unshaven, but probably she would be glad to see his dark shadow of stubble, evidence of the hours between evening and morning. The new abandoned Lyddy would probably be wearing a dressing gown, her dark hair hanging loose.

'You should have woken me,' he called as, washed, dressed and at least with his hair dampened and groomed, he came down the stairs. 'Or better, you should have kept me company.'

So sure that the Lyddy of morning would be the same as the Lyddy he'd discovered in the hours of night, he was unprepared to find her looking exactly as she did each day when she arrived in the yard: her hair brushed and pinned securely in a bun; her suit following neither today's fashion nor that of any other period, simply a functional skirt and jacket; her well-brushed leather shoes on her long, slender feet in keeping with the rest of her attire, low-heeled, designed to tread firmly and in comfort.

'This can't be the same Lyddy who travelled with me to such exquisite heights.' She could hear the smile in his voice, even though she had her back to him as she dished his breakfast on to a warmed plate. Yet when he lifted her tightly knotted bun and kissed the nape of her neck, he sensed a tremor pass through her. Despite her sensible shoes, her feet weren't yet firmly on the ground.

'You're in luck,' she told him, 'young Eddie Marcham lives in one of the tied cottages on Pinkley Farm, his father works there. He just left a basketful of mushrooms as he went by on his way to the yard, just picked this morning. I wonder you didn't hear him.'

'He'll have seen my motor bike. Do you reckon they'll guess I was here all night? No, more likely they'll think I've looked in with a message from Sophie. We mustn't let your reputation get tarnished.'

'Damn my reputation. I want to shout from the rooftops. Are you ashamed? I'm certainly not. Anyway, what we do is no one's business.'

'I do declare, the oh-so-good Miss Westlake is a changed woman. I say, Lyddy, this looks a breakfast fit for a king. Aren't you eating?'

'No. I had a slice of bread and marmalade while I was cooking. I'm going to leave you to lock up when you're ready. I shall just look in at the yard and make sure everything's all right, then I'm cycling into Brackleford to the orphanage. I said I'd be there at eleven.'

'Let me swallow this, then I'll run you in. You don't usually have your committee meetings actually at the orphanage, do you?'

'This is something separate. Christian, I have to do something useful with my days. Once the business is sold, I have to have something to fill its place. So, for a start, I'm going to spend my Saturdays with the orphans, girls the same sort of age as my Guides but with no chance of joining anything like other children.'

'I could fill your time—'

'My spare time. I have to do something productive, you should know me well enough to realise that.'

'Thus speaks my daytime Lyddy, my workmate. It's my after dark one that fills my mind this morning, despite this plate of appetising food. Don't pretend you've put it out of your mind already.'

She shook her head, her eyes inexplicably swimming with unshed tears. 'I didn't say that.' Then, not quite bringing herself to look at him, 'I'll never put it out of my mind. Christian, I never knew there could be such wonder, such joy. For me it was like a miracle. Nothing like that had ever happened to me before, I believed it never would. Now, this morning, here I am—just *me* again. And yet I'm different from what I was before, I'll never be the same.'

He wished he could have told her that he loved her, that for him there could never be anyone else. But Lyddy respected honesty too much for that.

'How long will you be playing games with your orphans?'

'I'll be out most of the day.' She rammed her hat on, taking no satisfaction from the reflection. For a moment she thought of Sophie, confident in her loveliness. And yet Sophie had talked of the beastliness of marriage. Turning from the mirror she rested her hand on his shoulder, longing to beg him to be there when she got home and yet unable to say the words.

'And tonight?' he asked with a half-smile that conveyed far more than the question itself, a smile that attempted to leapfrog them back to where they'd been before she forced her mind away from the night that was gone.

The attempt must have worked, for she felt her face must have flooded with give-away colour as, before she could hold them back, the words rushed out. 'Tonight—always—any night.' Then she pulled herself very straight as if she were reining in her wayward spirit.

'Now there's an open invitation,' he laughed. 'I have an appointment with the headmaster of Plympton Court School this afternoon to discuss the extension. I don't know how long that will take. And Lyddy, now that I've found a place in Brackleford I ought to shift my things across from the house and tell Sophie where I shall be living. And from the yard too, now that I have somewhere to work. It's no use leaving everything until the last moment, and from the way Chivers spoke he's keen to take over as soon as the legal side can be tied up. However, if things go smoothly I might manage to ride back to the village when I've got myself sorted out in Brackleford.'

'You know you'd be welcome to work from Drydens.'

'Yes, I know that—I appreciate it, honestly. But things being as they are with Sophie, it's much better if I keep my own establishment—humble though it is—over the iron-mongery in Butchers' Row.'

She nodded, giving no sign of what she read into his reply. She had believed nothing could take from her the wonder of the night, but in that moment she was frightened to remember.

'I've banked the fires up and put the guard in place in the sitting room. There's nothing for you to do except lock the door. You can take this key,' she added, taking one off the hook on the dresser. 'It was Dad's.'

He felt uncomfortably low as he put the key in his pocket then, touched by something in her appearance, stood up and kissed her forehead, or what forehead was visible beneath the firmly pulled on hat.

Since the middle of the previous century the orphanage had stood in Brackleford High Street, its iron gates backed with wood so that no curious eye could look in and no child longing for escape could look out. On the brick wall was painted an elaborate if faded sign: 'Brackleford and District Home for Orphaned Girls, Foundlings and Waifs'. Lydia had called there on one previous occasion when she had taken the proceeds from the season's fund-raising in Kingshampton. That she was expected today transpired from a letter she had written to the Matron, who had welcomed her offer of keeping the older girls occupied. Idleness wasn't good for young people and although she delegated cleaning work to them, once that was done it worried her to see the way some of them huddled together in groups, chattering, giggling and generally 'up to no good', or so she feared. She'd made enquiries about Miss Westlake (you couldn't be too careful who was given the chance to influence growing girls soon to be set loose into the working world) and had heard nothing but good spoken of her.

'Empty your pails, shake out your mops and dusters and go and scrub your hands,' she called in a loud voice, clapping her hands to attract attention. 'At eleven o'clock there is a lady coming to give you instruction, a Miss Westlake. I want all of you to present yourselves with tidy appearance, so once you've taken your tools back to the store—wet mops well rinsed and standing head upwards—just scrub your hands then come and line up in the hall. And don't waste time chattering; see to it that you're ready and waiting for her, show a little respect that a lady is willing to give up her time to you.'

There was never any warmth in Matron's voice, but those who had grown up in the orphanage knew her to be kinder than she liked to appear. From her they learned that your thoughts were your own and had little to do with the front you presented to the outside world.

Lydia had been told to come to a small door leading from the side alley, and it was here that Matron ushered her in.

'You're well used to girls of their age, so you don't need

me to tell you that some are eager to learn, some think they know more than we can tell them—and some do their best, but everything falls apart in their hands. It's good of you to want to help them, Miss Westlake. We do our best—but there's precious little time with the number we have here.'

'I'm sure we shall get along fine.' Lydia forced herself to sound confident. She'd never been nervous about facing a group of girls, but then she'd never had to face them bereft of her Guide Captain's uniform.

There were fifteen of them standing in a moderately straight row in the stone-flagged hall, fifteen pairs of eyes looking at her. In that moment, the wonder of her night might never have been; she was plain, gawky, scraggy Miss West-lake, spinster of the parish of Kingshampton.

'First, we must get to know each other.' She tried to speak brightly but from the unchanging expressions on the faces of the girls she knew she had overacted the part. Anything rather than standing facing them, instinct made her pull off the of-fending hat. Next came her coat. But the hall was empty of furniture, there wasn't so much as a chair to lay them on.

'I'll take them, Miss,' a more than well-built girl offered. 'There's some hooks in the passage.'

'Thanks so much.' Lydia smiled. 'Then when you come back I want you all to tell me your names. Mine is Miss Westlake—Lydia Westlake. I teach the Girl Guides in Kings-hampton and I thought you might enjoy learning some of the same skills. That makes it sound rather dull—skills. I think everyone enjoys what we do. So I hope you will too.' The buxom lass back from the passage, Lydia took the list of names Matron had given her. 'I have all your names on a list here, but it's asking a lot that I shall remember so many all in one go. So I've brought some slips of paper and safety pins and a fountain pen. One by one, when I call your name can you come forward and write it on a slip so that you can wear it. That way I shall soon get to know you all.'

'No table to write on, Miss,' from a thin ginger-haired girl.

'The window-sill will do. We'll manage. Now the first name on the list is Linda Burrell…' As she called each name a girl stepped forward. Lydia forced herself to concentrate on each one, trying to attach a name to a face, even though her eyes scanned the line still waiting to be called. Which one? Surely there could be no doubt, any more now than there could be any doubt of Norah Knight's claim on Christian. She knew, she absolutely knew, which girl would step forward when she called the name Sybella Knight.

There were nine down and six to go when Sybella's turn came. Only now did Lydia realise how, deep in her heart, she had wanted to deny Norah's story. Now any doubt died: there was no denying that this was Christian's daughter. Looking at Sybella, she felt a tug of love. But that was crazy, she told herself. Sybella was no more than evidence of the sort of life he'd led, his lack of responsibility, his lack of affection for anyone except himself and his own enjoyment. That's what she told herself; it was what her head wanted to believe. But her heart had a will of its own. This was Christian's daughter, unloved, unwanted. It took all her willpower to concentrate on what she was doing: her mind was racing with unanswered questions, with doubts. The money she'd given Christian to pass to Norah, that had been to buy his freedom, but more than that it had been to ensure the child's future. So what had happened? He must have paid her off. He *must* have paid her off…mustn't he? She hated herself for the suspicion that crept in with no help or encouragement. Yes, of course he must, otherwise Norah would still be a threat to him and clearly she wasn't. So what tragedy had brought Sybella here just when she had the promise of a better life?

CHAPTER EIGHT

If Lydia were in the midst of a group who were self-possessed and successful, she could feel gauche and tongue-tied. But with these children she was at her best. She tried to bring them out to talk about themselves and their hopes for the time which would soon be on them, when they would leave the orphanage and be part of a world which undoubtedly would be full of hurdles.

Domestic service lay ahead for some—and at least that would give them a roof over their heads. But what a lonely life for a girl who had no family. At the orphanage they'd formed something akin to one big family, did any of them realise how much they would miss the close-knit community? They would learn that deprivation was easier to bear than loneliness.

Of the others there were some who dreamed of finding shop work and earning enough money to pay rent on a room, one whose dream was to train to be a hairdresser and learn to Marcel-wave her customers' hair (and no doubt her own too), and another whose Shangri-La would be to work with animals. Lydia thought of her pack of Guides, all from loving homes, and she longed to help these unfortunate children who because they had so little had learned the value of dreams.

'And you, Muriel?' she asked the buxom thirteen-year-old who had taken her hat and coat. 'Have you decided what you mean to aim for? That's the important thing, you see. We all have to have a goal, something to set our sights on even when things seem against us.'

'What was yours, Miss?' asked a cheeky-looking blonde, whose pretty face and curly hair contributed to giving her more than her share of confidence, and whose eyes shone with mischief as she asked the question. 'Your goal couldn't have been to spend your Saturdays coming to a place like this. All any of us want to do is get out of it.'

Lydia made sure her laugh sounded natural. 'Mine? I didn't say we all achieve our goal,' she said. 'I said we all have to have one.' But what was hers? What had it been when she was the age of these girls? 'I was lucky, I had parents and a sister. Somehow that made it easy just to let time slip by.' Then, surprising herself that she could say it with such easy confidence, 'That's the trouble, if the rut is too comfortable we get stuck in it—and now look at me! So, I want to help each one of you to find out what you want so that at least you set out on the right track. Then it'll be up to you to give of your best and not be satisfied with taking the easy road.'

'You mean, Miss, we have to look at you and be warned, so that we go after what we want to make of our lives.'

'Yes, perhaps that's what I do mean.' Lydia's calm tone took the wind out of the cheeky little blonde's sails.

'Sorry, Miss,' she mumbled, 'didn't mean to be rude.' Of course they all knew that that was actually what she had meant to be. Then, her face breaking into a smile that sent a deep dimple into her left cheek, 'Jolly exciting, isn't it?'

'Yes, certainly it is jolly exciting.' Yesterday Lydia couldn't have accepted the dullness of her life so casually, not even to a group of girls she was determined to help. But today she had a new confidence. These children saw her as boringly middle-aged for, from the viewpoint of a thirteen year old, thirty is ancient. But no one knew, no one could suspect, the joy that pulsed through her veins. The wonder of the night inspired her.

'Muriel?' She turned back to her overweight and willing young friend. 'Have you any ideas?'

'Only just that I suppose I want to be married.' Then at the general snigger from the others, 'Don't really want a husband, not for himself I mean, but more than anything, Miss, I want to have babies.'

One thing the Guides had always liked about Lydia was that she never talked down to them; she listened to their opinions and encouraged them to voice their thoughts. Perhaps that stemmed from the way her own parents had treated her. Had she but realised it, that same manner was already earning her the respect of her new acquaintances.

'It'll be a long time before you're old enough to think of marrying, Muriel. But if you're fond of children why don't you make it your goal to get a job as a nursemaid? In the first instance I expect you'd have to be under a trained nursery nurse, but that's the way you'd learn and you'd probably love the work. The only heartbreaking thing must be when the time comes to move on from a job like that.'

'Cor, Miss, I wish I could do that. Don't know anything about looking after babies, but I'd learn.'

'Well done. And one of the things I thought we might all do together is work along those lines. I train the Girl Guides, you know, and childcare is one of the things they work at. How many of you would be interested in doing that?' Eight hands went up. 'Another thing we do is cooking and that's what I've come prepared for today— not this morning, Cook can't let us have the kitchen until dinner is cleared away. Whatever any of us do with our lives, to know the rudiments of cooking is a real boon. You know I told you I have a sister. She's a lot younger than me, and I think the prettiest person I've ever seen.' Even to the Guides she'd never talked so naturally; perhaps it was because these girls were apart from the village where she was known. 'When she got married she had no idea about cooking and she found life awfully difficult. It must be so depressing when you try hard to do something, especially if you want to impress a new husband, and it turns out to be an unappetising disaster. So who's for learning to cook?' Another array of hands answered the call.

'And you, Sybella? Any ideas about what you want to do when you leave here?' For so far Sybella's arm had stayed rigidly at her side and her face shown no interest.

'Something'll turn up. The main thing is to get out of here.'

'How long before you will be fourteen?'

'Too long.'

Lydia could feel the animosity between Sybella Knight and the other girls. The rest of them had been glad that this Saturday had been different from normal; even the one Lydia thought of as the 'pretty imp', who seemed keen to see how

far her cheekiness could go unchecked, had clearly been glad
to have her there. Sybella was more difficult. Not pointedly
rude and yet she showed no hint of cooperation.

'And then?' Lydia enquired, ignoring the lack of response
to her interest.

'Something'll turn up,' Sybella repeated, her voice void of
either hope or fear. 'A girl can always earn her keep. I don't
want favours.'

There was nothing forced about Lydia's smile. Here was
a sentiment akin to her own.

'I know. And that's important. Being independent, I mean.'

Sybella said nothing. Lydia felt a little progress had been
made, and yet where was the evidence of it? The girl looked
just as sulky; that 'touch me not' aura was as firmly around
her.

'Matron has asked me to eat with her at one o'clock. Is
that when you have your dinner?' The general assent gave her
her answer. 'So let's say we start at two o'clock; by then we
should all be fed. I've brought various ingredients with me
so that we can do some cooking. While they're clearing dinner away in the kitchen we'll talk about what we have and
what we can make of it. Then Cook says we can have the use
of the kitchen. How's that?'

'What have you got in your bags, Miss?' 'What are we
going to make?' The questions came from all areas, but from
Sybella only morose silence.

'We'll get down to writing recipes after dinner.' Lydia
smiled, her tone friendly but final. 'If any of you don't want
to cook, then you don't have to join in. Perhaps next week
we'll do something you like the sound of better. But, honestly,
learning the basics of cooking can never be a waste of time.'

No one suspected that her remarks were aimed at Sybella. She heard herself talking and felt they must look on her as a frumpish schoolmarm. None of them would guess at the excitement, the eager anticipation she felt at the discovery that here amongst these poor children was Christian's daughter. Tonight she would tell him. Just to look at the child was all she needed to know that he was her natural father. Ahead of her the afternoon stretched, but this evening he would come, she would tell him, they would be drawn close in their natural anxiety for the child he'd never even seen.

'We do what we can for the girls,' Matron said as they ate their stewed lamb and carrots. 'Some have been here since they were but weeks old. But there's one in your class—I did wonder if she might have struck you as familiar.'

'No. You mean I ought to know one of them? Which one was that? Not that I can hope to remember all their names.' Lydia tried to instil just the right amount of interest into her voice.

'The one called Sybella Knight. The vicar of Kingshampton brought her to us a month or two ago. Walking his dog in the woods there, that's when he found her. She'd erected some sort of a shelter with branches she'd broken from the trees, that and a bed of last year's leaves. He said she fought with all her might, anything rather than be brought here. But her might wasn't strong enough to hold out against him. Poor little soul, looked as though she hadn't had a decent meal for years. Can't get a word out of her, her name and nothing more. Your vicar made enquiries at the school in the village, one thing led to another, one person to the next. So it was that he gleaned something of the sort of life she'd had. Her mother was no better than a street woman. Then suddenly—leaving her rent unpaid, from what I've been told—she upped and went.'

'Perhaps she intended to take Sybella with her wherever she's gone; perhaps the child escaped and ran away.'

'Not very likely. Putting two and two together, the woman had no more maternal instinct than my old tom cat.'

'How did Reverend Mullins get her to you? I wonder she didn't manage to run away before she got handed over if she fought him as you say.'

'I think the last of her strength must have gone in her initial resistance. You didn't recognise her?'

'I don't think I'd seen any of them before.'

'Sybella—dear God in heaven, what a name to give a poor wretch like she is—Sybella Knight. Where she comes from, who her parents are, heaven alone knows. My job is to see that neglected children are fed and nurtured. But I'll be honest with you, Miss Westlake, when you wrote to me about coming here, it was partly on account of Sybella Knight that I welcomed the idea. I felt perhaps that if there was a link with your village you might be able to throw a little light on things she refuses to talk about. Even her age I've only guessed at.'

Lydia was tempted. If she told Matron all she knew about Sybella's parentage, would they allow her to take her home and unite her with Christian? But how could she do that without Christian being in agreement? She ought to put the child's welfare first—but she couldn't. This evening she would talk to Christian; she would offer to give a home to Sybella until he made better arrangements for the two of them together. Two of them? Her imagination leaped ahead, carrying her with it: she saw a home with the three of them, Christian and her and the child. She even saw Sybella being happy and smiling, wanting to be with them, eager for the future they would share.

She wasn't surprised to find that when the would-be cooks gathered ready to make their first scones, Sybella wasn't with them. The kitchen buzzed with activity; ingredients provided by Lydia were measured, mixed, rolled, cut into shapes and put into the large ovens. By the time the cooking utensils were washed and the kitchen brought back to the state they'd found it in, the scones were risen, light and golden. Then, gathered around the table, each girl took the two she'd made (some looking more appetising than others) while Lydia produced a jar of Ethel's last year's plum jam and a slab of butter. Her own pleasure came from watching them. Into the hour and a half of that Saturday afternoon they had made a giant stride into a world of independence.

'Can we cook again next Saturday, Miss? What will you bring for us to make?'

'I'll find something. Perhaps biscuits, something you could share with the younger ones.'

'Cor, they'll think we're the cat's whiskers.' And that in itself made the whole project worthwhile.

It was while Lydia was walking to the main gate on to the High Street that she saw Sybella sitting by herself under a sycamore tree that looked out of place in its barren surroundings.

'I wish you had come, Sybella. They made really good scones. But you prefer drawing? Not much use asking me to teach anything about drawing. I'm useless.'

Sybella shrugged her thin shoulders.

'May I see?' Lydia felt gauche and ill at ease, all the confidence of the afternoon fading and leaving her aware of her own inadequacy.

'You wouldn't be interested,' Sybella answered, avoiding looking directly at her. 'It's clothes.'

'Something else I'm not good at. You like fashion? I expect everyone does really, but…but…'

'You mean if you bought something stylish you'd feel uncomfortable and embarrassed in it? Yes, I expect you would.' Not a promising beginning.

'It must be so much easier to feel right in stylish clothes if you have the right build to wear them.'

Her honesty seemed to cut through Sybella's armour of rudeness; there was a change in her manner.

'You know what I think?' she asked.

'What's that?'

'Well, about having to be the right sort of build, or have a pretty face, all that sort of thing. Of course people like that are easy. But if people were honest with themselves, there aren't many like that. If I were a designer it's not the easy ones I'd want to make clothes for, they'd look good in *anything*. Any old fool could design styles for them! It's the others—'

'Like me, too tall, too thin—at the back of the room when looks were handed out.' Intentionally, Lydia belittled herself, in an attempt to prove that having a comfortable home and loving family still left room for failure. And perhaps it worked. For the first time Sybella came near to smiling.

'I reckon you wouldn't look so bad if you wore the right things. I don't mean shorten your skirts or wear things skin tight like some of the tarts do.' It was spoken with real venom and recalled to Lydia the image of Norah. 'I bet if I had the chance I could make some really attractive things for ordinary people to wear—instead of having to go around looking drab and dull, wearing clothes that shout as clearly as any banner "Here is a good woman, one who has a mind above how she looks."'

Lydia's laugh was spontaneous. 'Do I really look that gruesome?'

'I didn't say that. Anyway, I suppose that's what you are— a good woman. Otherwise you wouldn't give up the only time in the week that's your own to come and try to make things easier for us lot.'

From the reference to Saturday being Lydia's only free time, she knew Sybella must have known she worked in the office at the yard.

'You know about me? You come from Kingshampton, Matron told me. She thought I might have known you.'

'Nosy bat. Suppose that's what I am too—a nosy bat, watching other people. I used to see you around in the village, I often saw you. Don't expect you would have noticed me.'

'I thought perhaps your mother had told you who I was. I met her, you know.'

'You didn't go and blab about her to Matron? Not her business about how we lived. Anyway, Norah—that's what I had to call her, not Mum like other kids called their mothers— Norah never wanted kids, she said, and buggered if she was going to be Mum to anyone. Anyway, I was saying—she's cleared off. Suddenly seemed in a strange mood, excited. There was nothing unusual in her not being there when I got home from that hellhole of a school—hateful lot, they were there, I expect they were your oh-so-good Girl Guides. Well, if that's the way you teach them to be, then you can put it where the monkey puts his nuts. Guides and your classes here too.'

'You were saying, did I tell Matron about having met your mother. No, of course I didn't. If you'd wanted her to know about you, you would have told her yourself.' Lydia chose to ignore the rest of Sybella's remarks. This poor, hurt, muddled child was Christian's daughter, his own flesh and blood.

'Why didn't you go with Norah? Why did you run away.'

'You're putting the cart before the horse. Like I said, she was all sort of keyed up with excitement. It must have been a man. With her it was always a man. Someone with a bob or two to spend on her—a tanner for me sometimes if I promised to stay out of the way for a couple of hours. Some had miserable wives not giving them much fun at home (or that's what she always said), some I never saw and as I got bigger some I tried to keep out of the way of. Dirty old buggers. Anyway, she cleared off without inviting me along, and a bloody good job too. Left me a note, she did, well to tell the truth she left me three notes: one she wrote, "Won't hurt you to give up school, you'll be old enough in a few months anyway. Don't stay here, I promised Chapman he'd get what we owe for rent if he called this evening, so push off out. Get a job. Good luck. Try not to take the easy road, it'll only lead you into the ditch." She never signed it, just wrote that.'

'But you said she left three notes?'

'So she did. That was one, the others were money, one a pound and one ten bob. I did what she said, I cleared out straightaway, just put my things in a pillow case and pushed off. She'd been giving Mr Chapman the slip pretty well ever since we moved in. I suppose he couldn't have had a miserable wife like some of them; for him it was either pay up the cash or he'd take us to court. I heard the row last time he came and I heard her tell him that she had money coming to her and promising to pay off the lot. He's hard as nails, with him she couldn't get away with paying a bit in advance—or paying in kind, that's the way she always put it and some of them liked that better than with a few bob rent. I wasn't going to be caught hanging around when he knocked on the door that evening or he'd have had my thirty bob before I could say knife. There was no food in the house, I knew that because before I went off to school that morning I'd looked to see if there was any loaf left or a bit of cheese and there wasn't.'

'You'd had nothing all day?'

'Didn't often happen as bad as that, but I think she must have known what she meant to do because things had been getting shorter for days even though, like I said, she was sort of bubbling over about something. In the village everywhere was closed. Anyway, I reckon if they'd seen me trying to change a ten-bob note they would have said I'd pinched it. So I made a sort of shelter in the wood and made plans for what I would do. Next day I was going to walk to Brackleford. I knew I couldn't change a note for the fare and anyway it would have attracted attention. Once I'd had a bun or something to eat I was going to go to the baths, not to swim I don't mean, but to have a tub. Then, clean and brushed up, I would find myself a job. Got it all planned, I had. And then when it was not much more than getting light, along comes that interfering bugger of a priest with his silly dog sniffing around.'

At some stage as she talked she'd moved along the wooden seat to make room for Lydia. Now she seemed to realise where she was heading: talking to this do-gooder, throwing herself wide open for sympathy! In a flash her mood changed, her expression became hostile. 'Well, if you came here to poke your nose and find out, now you know.'

'Actually, I didn't, Sybella. I came over to talk to you because you'd so plainly been hostile to what I was doing and I don't think that's fair.'

'That's not fair either, saying that to me. Just 'cos I didn't gush over you like some of them did!' But her cheeks looked unnaturally bright and she glared into the mid-distance, not letting herself meet Lydia's gaze.

'If I'm seen as some sort of busybody getting my own enjoyment out of other people's bad luck—and it *is* bad luck, for you and for all of them, having no loving family like I had—but if that's how you all see me, I'm truly sorry. In a way I think you're all lucky; you're right at the beginning, whatever you make of your lives this is the outset. You know what?' Sybella's only answer was a shrug of her thin shoulders. 'I know how exciting an unknown future is, for at the moment mine is the same. You say you've seen me in Kingshampton, so you probably know about the business my father built up, Westlake Builders. I've worked there since I wasn't much older than you are now.'

'I heard about what happened to them at the level crossing, everyone knew about it. Must have been horrid for you, Miss.'

'For both of us, my sister and me. Of course it means that I have to be practical and think of the firm's future. If I didn't I'd be letting Dad down. So I'm selling it to a man who knows the trade just like he did himself. And that leaves me looking ahead and not knowing what I see. And it is exciting, it's challenging.'

'You told us lot that we had to have a goal. Easy to talk, though, isn't it? When it comes down to it, you haven't even got a goal yourself and you know a lot more about what's out there than they do. Me? I'm different. I've been around.'

And remembering Norah, Lydia thought there was truth in what she said.

'The truth is, I've lived more than twice as long as you have, but I've certainly not seen much beyond the way we live in the village. But I'll learn. It's like being given an open ticket—for both of us it's like that. But you seem to know what you want to do much more clearly than I do. One day perhaps you'll be a top designer, or even have your own fashion house. No goal is too high to aim for.'

'Some hope! I draw clothes because I like nice things to wear. Always looked more like a scarecrow.'

'A very pretty scarecrow.' Lydia laughed.

'Don't! Please, Miss, don't say things like that. Just now we were talking properly, like two people both the same. I don't want a lot of mealy-mouthed compliments. It's rotten.'

'I never pay mealy-mouthed compliments, Sybella. I said you were pretty because it's the simple truth. If you didn't scowl so much you'd be even prettier.' She spoke solemnly, her words being met with an even deeper frown. 'I like what you said, two people both the same. But I wouldn't want you to let the years slip past and end up thirty years old and still not sure where you're heading.'

'I'll tell you one thing for free, Miss. I'm not going down the road Norah went. Not really her fault, she used to say. I suppose it was mine. Her with no husband and lumbered with me, she had to earn money the best way she could. She wasn't wicked, if that's that you think about her. She just liked having what she thought was a good time, she liked compliments,' then, her dark eyes suddenly lighting with humour, 'even mealy-mouthed ones, I expect. Being tied to a kid must have been…well, she used to say it was a bugger.'

'I still think she ought to have taken you with her when she left Kingshampton.' After all, hadn't that been the main reason for giving Christian the money he needed?

'No fear! The best thing she ever did for me was giving me that thirty bob and setting me free. You know what, Miss? I hope this chap, whoever it is she's miked off with, treats her right. I'm glad she's gone off without me, but I hope things turn out right for her. And for me, I'll jolly well see to it that they do for me. But now I've got myself stuck here till I'm fourteen and can be let loose. I expect you reckon it's wicked that I don't mind not being with Norah? You were fond of your Mum and Dad, I could tell you were when you talked about them. But her and me, we didn't like each other, never really talked, not proper talk. And my Dad must have been a right swine, that's what she told me.'

'There might have been circumstances we don't know about.'

'Rum sort of conversation, Miss. I bet Matron would be tut-tutting if she could hear what we're saying. Not supposed to talk about things like men and having bastard kids. I'm not the only one in here who doesn't know the name of her father. I think Matron wants us all to believe the fairies left us under the gooseberry bush.' Then, as if she once again realised she was letting herself sound too friendly, the scowl was back in place. 'And you, a spinster lady, I don't expect you know as much about the world as I do, bet your Mum never brought her fancy men home. Learn all you can, that's what all you people tell us. But I could teach you a few things. She loved it. Different men, but always the same game; you wouldn't know.'

The moment was saved by the sound of the brass bell that hung just inside the porch.

'What's that for?' Lydia asked, grateful for a change of subject.

'I gotta go. Teatime. Miss, I've been a bit rude. I get like that. Can we talk again when you come back? You don't have to, I don't care one way or the other, I expect next week you'll have a lot to—'

'I hope we can talk again. I've enjoyed it. And Sybella—oh, I do wish you had a shorter name. May I call you Bella? It suits you—keep practising your drawing. I don't know much about drawing, but I know someone who does. I'd like to take some of your work to be looked at.'

'Don't tell the others about calling me Bella. Just us'll know.'

'Right. Off you run, or you'll be late for tea.'

Cycling home, she went over their conversation in her mind, trying to form a picture of the loveless upbringing the child must have had, trying to conjure up a way of altering her understandable view of her father. By the time she wheeled her bicycle to the shed at Drydens the subject was overtaken by more pressing and more exciting thoughts. This evening Christian would come; she would prepare a meal for them to share, he would linger, that same miracle of love would end their day just as it had started it. Small wonder every other thought was pushed from her mind as she gathered the ingredients for the supper they would share.

But the evening dragged by and he didn't come. She looked for convincing reasons, never going out of earshot of the shrill bell of the telephone on the wall of the hall. But it remained silent. Perhaps he'd been too busy settling into his new accommodation, she told herself; perhaps he would arrive later. Seven o'clock, eight o'clock, nine, so the minutes ticked by until at last she had to face the truth. Christian wasn't coming.

The night seemed long and empty. Had she not been expecting him, she would have taken comfort from memories of those wonderful hours they'd shared. Now, though, she was frightened to let herself remember or to try and relive the miracle. For him, had it been a miracle or just a repetition of other nights he'd shared with other women in the past—and would again in the future? No, no, it wasn't like that—it must have mattered to him too. In the morning she'd hear the roar of his motor cycle and, when he arrived, he'd explain why she'd waited in vain. Yet despite all her resolutions she was frightened to let herself trust. He'd let Norah down, he'd forsaken his own child. Sophie? He couldn't be blamed for that. Or could he? If he'd been gentle with her, if he'd been the lover she'd yearned for, would she have turned to Dulcie Fulbrook? Despite her resolutions, memories of the night pushed themselves to the forefront of Lydia's mind. Had *she* craved gentleness? No, oh no, she'd wanted—needed—demanded—a passion as wild as her own. Yet, in the loneliness of her bed, rather than desire she was filled with humiliation that her unleashed passion had been so obvious. How patently clear it must have been to him just how repressed she had been through the years. Like a starving man given his first meal, she had snatched; greed, excitement, thankfulness, all these had combined and yet none of them had been more than the backdrop for the physical wonder that had spurred her on. What must he have thought? Poor sex-starved Lyddy, perhaps that's how he had seen her as he'd obligingly transported her to unknown realms of ecstasy.

'If it was like that I couldn't bear it,' she whispered, alone in the darkness. 'No, it was the same for both of us. It was, it *was*.' But was it? Make him come in the morning, please make him come in the morning and tell me what kept him from being here with me tonight. Don't let him be laughing at me. Hot tears stung her eyes, tears of shame and misery. Is this my punishment for loving Sophie's husband? I ought to go down on my knees and beg You to bring them back together again and make her realise it's him she loves, not Dulcie. We are as God made us, that's what she said. And how has God made me? If He means me to spend my days helping lame dogs over stiles, why am I plagued—yes, *plagued*—with this longing for physical love. I should say thank You for last night, beyond anything I'd ever dreamed. And yet, it couldn't have meant anything to him or he would have come back this evening. He said he would, well, not actually said, but implied he would. And what did I tell him? Tonight and every night, I told him. Don't let him have been laughing at me, don't let him have been seeing me as 'poor old Lyddy, poor hungry old maid'.

She gave way to the tears she couldn't hold back a second longer.

Night had found her at her lowest ebb; by morning hope had returned. But there was no sign of Christian. Still she let herself imagine that he might have decided to leave his drawing board and stool in the office until the sale of the business was completed. But when she opened the door on Monday morning the first thing she was aware of was the emptiness. She had taken over her father's desk; her own had been pushed back against the wall leaving extra space and light for Christian. But he had cleared everything away, it was as if he'd never worked there.

She slumped into Archibald's swivel chair, twisting it first one way and then the other, hardly aware of what she did. Everything that was Christian's had been taken away…but why? Was it his signal that he wanted to be free of her? Was he telling her that he had obliged her by going to bed with her, but now he wanted freedom? Shame, anger, humiliation, one emotion chased the other through her mind. It took all her willpower to make sure that the lasting one was anger. How dare he use her like that! If he'd behaved like some rampant stud to give her pleasure, then just let him try it again and he'd find that he'd misjudged her! How dare he! Probably Sophie's disenchantment had been deeper rooted than what she called 'the beastliness of marriage', probably she'd understood just the sort of man he was. So Lydia's thoughts raced on. Could this be good, kind, sympathetic Miss Westlake, champion of the underdog, taking such comfort from filling her heart with hate?

How different it used to be in this barren room. If only her father were here, so solid, so sane, so dependable. Would he condemn her for loving Sophie's husband? No, she believed he would have understood. And the business, the sale of it…Dad, if only you were here, not that I could talk to you about Christian, but I wouldn't need to, you always understood things without being told. So do you still understand?

Do you know the way I long to *live*, do you know how that one glorious night with Christian brought me to life? I can't go back to what I was before, dreams can't be enough.

But when the business was gone, what would she have? Good works, fund-raising, empty days, lonely nights. Her heart was filled with the plea: please God bring Christian back. Then there was something else: there was Bella. So another plea mingled with the first: please bring him back so that I can tell him about Bella, about the way Norah has cheated and left his daughter with no one; please make him understand and be glad to have found her.

She sat taller, pulling her thoughts into focus. Bella isn't on her own, she never will be, she has *me*. I can't sit here dreaming, talking to Dad, talking to God, surely they both know how I feel without my telling them. I have work to do. She drew on all her strength of character to concentrate on the day ahead.

When at last it was time to lock the office, the image of a solitary evening at Drydens held less than no appeal. Instead, she hopped on her bicycle and turned towards Meadowlands. Through all their years, until now there had never been bad feeling between Sophie and her. Surely Sophie must be as miserable as she was that they had parted in the way they had. By now Sophie must have had time to realise that selling Westlake's could never be a betrayal, indeed it was because of her determination that nothing should lessen her father's high standards that Lydia knew the business must be run by someone whose heart and soul was in the trade. Having had time to reflect, she would understand. Lydia's thoughts leapt from the business to Sophie, then to herself: 'We are as God made us'…everyone's need for the fulfilment of love and un-

derstanding…the years we've shared when we've kept no secrets from each other and surely will share again in the future. So images rushed through her brain as she pedalled,
never doubting that Sophie would be as thankful as she was
to put their last meeting behind her.

Seeing her prop her bicycle against the fence and walk up
the short path, Sophie opened the door just as Lydia had
hoped she would. But there was no look of relief, no smile
of welcome.

'You! Dulcie, Dulcie, it's Lyddy,' she called as if she
couldn't cope with the situation without support.

'It's all right, love. Don't get yourself upset again. Bring
her inside, we don't want all Meadowlands listening to our
affairs.'

Immediately Lydia was the outsider, but only for a brief
instant.

'There's nothing for the neighbours to interest themselves
in,' she told Dulcie, hearing the ice in her voice. 'You may
leave us.'

'Oh no, that I won't. I thought Sophie made it clear to
you about her and me. And it's no good breathing down
your nose at me like that. You've always professed to be so
fond of her—your little sister—yet the gossip in the village
this morning is spreading like a forest fire in a heatwave.'

The inference was clear. They must be holding her responsible for spreading tales about their relationship!

'You can't think *that*! Sophie, you don't believe I would
have talked outside about anything that you do?'

Sophie shook her head, her already reddened eyes swimming with tears.

'Not about that. That's not what they're saying. It's

you, you and him. You've always wanted him. You may not have said so in so many words, but I knew from the way you used to watch him. Before he asked me to marry him, I shouldn't be surprised if you had hopes it was you he was interested in. Now you've made me a laughing-stock.'

'I don't understand.'

'Then,' Dulcie said, a protective arm around Sophie, 'use your imagination. With the noise a motor cycle makes, it's not to be wondered that he was noticed. Never mind who it was saw him park his noisy contraption in your front garden. That was Friday evening. And there it still was late at night and still there on Saturday morning—and him letting himself out and locking up like master of the house. Nothing goes by unnoticed in Kingshampton, as well you must know. I heard the whispers in Alf Wright's shop when I was buying the meat on Saturday morning. Not just whispers. Came right out with it to me, knowing I was living here amongst it. Then one of the men—never mind which one, I'll not be responsible for getting him into trouble—was in the yard when up he rolls to collect all the clobber he'd been keeping in your office. Got a place of his own in Brackleford, he told the men, rented somewhere where he could live and work from the one address.'

'You didn't want him.' Lydia's good resolutions were being swamped with anger as, ignoring Dulcie, she turned to Sophie. 'You refused to live with him as a wife should and yet you resent it that he's trying to make a fresh start for himself!'

'Don't be horrid,' Sophie wept, 'it's not my fault. I couldn't help it that I hated being married. I never meant it to end like it did. But now that it has, I've found the way to be truly happy. Anyway, he doesn't care about anyone but himself. And if you imagine he gives two hoots about you then you'll find what a fool you are to trust him. Tell me the truth: was he with you Friday night?'

For one glorious moment, pride flooded through Lydia. 'Yes. Yes, he was. Now you can say what you like, the pair of you. Tell the world for all I care.'

'I don't want to tell the world,' Sophie snorted. 'I'm frightened to go out, what will everyone think when they see me? When I got married, wherever I went in the village, people would say what a lovely couple we were, prettiest bride they'd ever seen. Now what am I? I've been deserted. And you, good, sober, hard-working, with never a hint of any man looking twice at you, you must be laughing! Well, don't imagine you'll earn the respect of all the gossiping locals, because you won't. They'll see you as a home-breaker. They probably all recognised how you threw yourself at him, just like we all knew it—Mums, Pops, all of us could see. Anything rather than be left a dried-up old maid.'

'Hush, hush, love,' Dulcie cooed, 'you mustn't say such things to your sister. I'm sure she believes he cares about her or she wouldn't have encouraged him.'

'Not my sister,' Sophie hiccupped, 'she's my cousin. I'm just nobody. Wish Pops was here, nothing's been right since Pops and Mums went.' Then, turning again on Lydia, 'I loved them more than you ever did. Me and Pops, we were closer than you could ever have been with him. You were more like her, sensible, practical. Pops and me, we knew how to laugh and have fun. Anyway, what have you come for? To gloat and tell me that you like all that beastliness in bed with him, is that it? Romance! Is that what you think it is? Of course it isn't. Romance is courtly, heroic; romance should make you feel cherished and beautiful. I hate even to think about how disgusting it was. He's gone and I'm thankful, just remembering makes me feel sick. Yes, I'm thankful—but how can I face anyone in the village? They'll laugh at me, or worse they'll look at me with pity. I can't bear it.'

'Personally I don't give a damn whether they are laughing at me or not,' Lydia kept her voice steady. 'And I doubt if anyone finds what any of us do particularly interesting.'

'You'd be surprised,' Dulcie said. 'I'd like half a crown for each person who stopped me this morning to pass on the whispers they'd heard and to ask what I knew. Of course I told them he's not good, Sophie had seen him for the bounder he is and had turned him out of her house. I said she was happier without him. And so she is. You don't need to concern yourself about her, I give you my word of honour I will see she's happy. Once all this blows over, we'll settle down as comfy as can be. Dry your eyes now, Sophie love. Trouble enough with the way things have broken up without your shedding tears over it. Your Pops wouldn't want you to be miserable, now would he?'

'I bet he knew.' Sophie made a supreme effort as she blotted her face with a wet and wispy handkerchief. 'When he said he'd give this house just to me, I bet Pops knew that Christian would soon be looking around for someone else to amuse himself with.' Then to Lydia, determined to have the last word even though she was no more than repeating what she'd said before, 'And everyone *must* have known you were ready to throw yourself at him, we could all see it.'

'Sophie, do we have to behave like this? I would never have let it happen if I'd thought there was a chance that you and Christian might have made a new start. But you'd told me, we are as God made us. I've thought and thought about it; I have tried to make myself understand. I came today to say it mustn't make any difference to us, to you and me. However things are, surely *we* don't need to fall out.'

'Just hark at her!' Dulcie tightened her hold on Sophie. 'What does she think she knows about anything, one night with someone else's husband and she thinks she can come here talking to us in that condescending voice. Send her away, love. Come on, now, before the daylight is gone. Remember we'd promised ourselves an hour or two tidying the garden. There won't be many chances left to us now the hours of daylight are drawing in.'

'Sophie?' Lydia prompted.

'You'd better go. Nothing's like it used to be, so it's no use pretending. Don't rely on him though, Lyddy. He's rotten through and through. I know him better than you do and if you knew the sort of past he's had you wouldn't be so keen to throw yourself at him.'

'No one is rotten through and through—not you, not me and certainly not him. As for knowing more about him than I do, I doubt that. And I'll tell you how I know: because he told me.' And with that, her head high, her long face unsmiling under the crown of that unflattering hat, Lydia turned and left them.

That was on the Monday. Whether Sophie and Dulcie kept the promise they'd made themselves and spent the hours of fading daylight tidying the garden, Lydia didn't know. Back at Drydens she waited, listened for the sound of the motor cycle, tried to hang on to fast-fading hope. So ended the day, followed by another, Tuesday, and then Wednesday.

Even her evening with the Guides did nothing to raise Lydia's spirits, for she couldn't forget what Bella had said about the unfriendliness they'd shown to her, a stranger with no secure, comfortable home. Had she been wasting her time all these years? The girls worked for their badges, they enjoyed the camaraderie they found in belonging to the movement, and yet faced with someone from an alien background, even after all her training, did they really extend no hand of friendship? The thought added to her depression. She even asked herself for whose benefit she spent these hours of each week: for theirs, in the trusting hope of making them better citizens? Or for her own, trying to boost her belief that what she did served a useful purpose?

Lonely, frightened to look into an empty future and even more frightened to let her imagination follow a road that had small hope of fruition, she saw the last of the girls on their way, then locked the church hall, dropped the heavy key through the letterbox of the caretaker's house, then set out for home. After all these days she had schooled herself into accepting there would be no motor cycle in the front garden. Rounding the corner into Laurel Lane, she pedalled past a group of semi-detached villas. Her mind carried her back to what Dulcie had said about someone watching what time Christian had arrived and left on that one night that seemed to divide her past and her future; whoever had started the gossip on its way to snowball through the village must live in one of these houses. Syd Brown the cobbler? His wife spent most of her time in conversation with anyone prepared to listen. Arnold Smutts, who worked in the butcher's? Daisy Summers, who served in the Copper Kettle during the week and played the organ in the chapel on Sundays? Did it matter who it had been? Did it matter what anyone said about her? What if instead of being looked up to and respected as good Miss Westlake, there were nudges and whispers—and titters too, she had no doubt about that? Nothing anyone could say had any power to hurt her. And yet…and yet…half formed at the back of her mind was the image of Bella, trapped in the orphanage. When the idea had come to her the previous Saturday she had been fool enough to believe that her future and Christian's would be together, and into that picture it had been natural to add Bella, who'd never known the security of a proper home.

No good thinking along those lines, she told herself. Now somehow I have to persuade the authorities that I am of good character; more than that, I have to make them see that an unmarried woman, a spinster, an old maid (she needed to hurt herself) is the right person to have care of a young girl on the brink of becoming an adult.

Unthinkingly, she hopped off her bicycle as she approached the side gate of Drydens, something she had done thousands of times. It was only as she came round to the front of the house that she realised it wasn't in darkness: lights glowed from the hall and from behind the closed curtains of the drawing room too.

'I saw you coming up the path,' Christian greeted her as he opened the front door, his smile as natural and confident as if he'd been away only hours instead of days. If her immediate reaction was relief and thankfulness, it only took seconds for it to turn to anger.

'I didn't expect you.' Her heart thumped so hard she seemed to feel it right through her chest, but there was no hint of welcome in her tone.

'A pleasant surprise, I hope? I've been waiting ages. I ought to have remembered it was your evening for Guides.'

'If you'd had consideration enough to telephone first, I would have reminded you.'

'Oh dear,' he teased, 'is my Lyddy cross with me? Come on now, Lyddy, tell me you're pleased to see me.' Drawing her close, he turned her face up to his.

'Whether or not I'm pleased isn't important. It's days since I heard a word from you, all I knew was that you'd moved out of the office. Now you expect to be welcomed with open arms as if it's your right. I'm no one's plaything to be picked up and put down at will.' What was she saying? How could she speak to him like that, driving him away when all the time she longed just to feel him holding her? Listen to yourself, Lydia Westlake, then remember who you are and what you are. They all saw how willingly you let yourself fall in love with him, Mum and Dad saw it, Sophie saw it, he must have seen it himself and probably the men in the yard saw it. Now they'll all be whispering and sniggering, knowing that he's taken his things away in case I think one night means as much to him as it does to me. And of course it doesn't! He thinks he can use me as he likes!

'Lyddy, darling Lyddy, forgive me. I'm a thoughtless fool. Of course I ought to have telephoned you and explained. At the weekend I moved my things across to my rooms in Brackleford, then on Monday morning I had a letter concerning some work I'd been negotiating in Oxfordshire. It was a commission I was keen to get, the sort of house any architect dreams of. I dropped everything and went there. I only got back at teatime today.' Then, pulling her chin gently towards him so there was no way of avoiding his gaze, 'Forgive me, Lyddy. And you're right. I took you for granted. It was wrong of me. But, somehow, I imagined—if I gave it conscious thought at all—I supposed that you and I had the sort of trust that didn't need explanations. You must have known I'd come back.'

'Didn't see why you should want to.' She sounded like a sulky child.

'Didn't you? Then my blessed Lyddy, I'll have to remind you why I should want to.'

Where were her resolutions that if he came back to her she would be aloof, she would let him see she hadn't been watching, waiting, hoping, praying?

'I didn't expect to be away more than a day,' he told her as he pulled off her navy blue uniform hat and with unerring aim threw it at the hallstand. 'I was given the commission, a fine house to be set in a landscaped garden in the south of the county. It's always better to talk to clients face to face.'

'I wish I'd known,' she started. 'I thought...' but she let the words trail into silence as pride came to her rescue.

'You thought I'd made my escape?' he laughed. 'Oh, Lyddy, why do you always belittle yourself? Come here.'

She came. Resolutions were made to be broken; nothing mattered but this. And so that night rekindled all her fading dreams, nothing could mar her future. It was somewhere in the early hours, lying in his arms, utterly at peace with herself and the world, that she told him about Sybella.

'I pretended the name meant nothing to me. Matron told me she'd been abandoned by her mother and had been brought to the orphanage by the vicar. Your own daughter, Christian, and so much like you it's uncanny. There's nothing of her mother in her. She has inherited your looks—'

'Handsome, is she?' he teased.

'Yes,' Lydia answered seriously, 'she is beautiful. I call her Bella, and that's what she is, really beautiful. And, Christian, she has inherited your talent too. She draws.'

'Lots of youngsters fancy themselves artists. Anyway, Lyddy, don't get ideas. Even if you wanted to, they wouldn't let an unmarried woman take responsibility for an orphan in their care. As for me, a mere male, they would hold up their hands in horror.' She could tell from his tone that he had no real interest.

'But you're her natural father,' she argued. 'If you told them that, they would only have to look at her to know it was the truth.'

'Leave her where she is, Lyddy. We have nothing to offer her and it would be cruel to raise her hopes.'

The last hour had given her confidence more than a boost; with joyous love like theirs, the future had seemed secure and certain.

'Together we could make a home for her, we could be a family.'

Silence. Her words seemed to fill the room, echo and re-echo and still he said nothing. She felt his mouth tugging the lobe of her ear, she felt his hands working their magic. Was this his answer? She hadn't the strength of will to hold him away, to keep the conversation on the road it had been heading. Erotic excitement pushed everything else from her.

It wasn't until breakfast that she broached the subject again.

'When I go to the orphanage on Saturday, I thought I might talk to Matron. Don't worry, I won't say anything about your relationship with Bella, I'll simply say that I have a friend who would be interested in looking at her drawings, assessing whether she might have a future in designing. I thought I'd ask if I could bring her home either for Saturday night, or if that isn't possible, then at least bring her out for a few hours on Sunday. Christian, you ought to meet her, your own daughter. She's had such a rough deal, we could try and make it up to her.'

'And then what? No, Lyddy, it's no use keep harping on about it. She accepts she is in the home until she is old enough to start work. Leave it at that. Taking a hungry man out to a restaurant doesn't do him any favours, and neither would this.'

'A little interest in what she wants to do wouldn't kill you!'

'Leave it, can't you. We have nothing to offer her. I don't know what idyllic picture you have in your mind, but the truth is that you are a single woman—therefore ineligible to adopt—I am a married man whose only hope of freedom is to expose his wife's sexual orientation—'

'You can't think of doing that! Christian, promise me you'll never do that to her.'

'I have no intention. But it leaves me completely unsuitable in the eyes of the authorities. And if, as you seem to believe, I am her natural father, my track record on that score would do me no favours. So forget it, Lyddy. If you and I want a lasting relationship, that's our business. But believe me, no orphan would be allowed to visit a ménage like ours would be.'

Even those two words 'lasting relationship' went almost unnoticed as Lyddy thought of Bella. If only he'd meet her, talk to her, then he wouldn't be able to brush her aside so easily. Or would he? The thought pushed itself to the forefront of her mind before she could stop it. If anyone had the capacity to walk away from situations he found uncomfortable, then it was Christian. She knew it and she condemned him for it, yet it had no power to weaken the hold he had on her.

'To have one uncaring parent is cruel enough, but she has *two*. Imagine growing up with no happy memories to build on.'

He leaned across the kitchen table where, now that Lyddy lived alone, she always ate breakfast for the sake of convenience, taking both her hands in his.

'We make our own memories. And ours? Yours and mine? Tell me, my precious, solemn Lyddy, do you find happiness in remembering all that we share?'

Her throat felt tight, there were no words to tell him of the miracle his love had brought to her. So poor loveless Bella's plight was forgotten.

It was as she put the washed-up dishes away, the last job before getting ready to go to the yard, that she asked him, 'Are you coming this evening? I'll be in time to cook us a proper meal.'

'Don't expect me,' he said, lighting a cigarette and smiling affably. 'If I have a change of plan I'll come across. But

I anticipate being invited to dine with a client I'm meeting later in the day. Just carry on without me, Lyddy. I'll be back soon, but I've a lot of work on hand.'

'Yes, of course, I understand.' But did she? Despite herself she felt rebuffed, a feeling that festered within her as the days passed. Another visit to the orphanage, another lonely weekend, the emptiness of her own future closing in on her as the wheels turned, bringing the sale of the business closer.

It was Monday of the following week when he arrived unexpectedly. He was picking her up and putting her down just as he pleased; she knew it and despised herself that at the sight of him, at the sound of his voice and the nearness of him, her anger evaporated, she had no power and no will to resist.

CHAPTER NINE

Before Lydia made an official application to adopt Sybella Knight she did what she looked on as essential groundwork. Clearly Christian wasn't to be swayed, and if she were honest she had to admit that it was hardly likely the child would be put in the charge of the man who had walked away leaving her mother pregnant. So another way round the problem had to be found.

She obtained a character reference from the Girl Guides' District Commissioner; she was given the backing of the vicar who had found the child and delivered her to the orphanage, of Sir Herbert Dinsdale of Shelton Manor, Kingshampton's squire, of her solicitor and her bank manager. To each of them Miss Lydia Westlake was known as a good woman, sensible, honourable, a fine example of citizenship. It was when she considered their willingness to help her that she thought of Dulcie's tales about the gossip being enjoyed by the locals. She couldn't have made it up, she must have heard the story somewhere…and yet… Nothing could have been designed to make Sophie more resentful and unforgiving of Lydia, so had the story been simply a ploy, knowing the effect it would have?

Lydia cared nothing for gossip; if she were truthful she admitted she would be proud to be seen as Christian's mistress. But she soon realised the scandal was not tarnishing her own good character. A rift between Sophie, everyone's darling, and Christian, such a handsome young man, that in itself was enough to feed the imagination of women with a hunger for romance in their lives. Lydia's role was one for which they saw her as perfectly cast: the shoulder to cry on, the patient listener, and no wonder her brother-in-law's motor cycle was seen at her home some evenings. To the owners of prying eyes, that it was still there in the morning simply meant that in a house the size of Drydens, where he had always been welcomed as one of the family and where poor Miss Westlake must find life very lonely, it must have been comforting for her to have him come and go so naturally.

Knowing his visits were dictated by his work schedule, Lydia accepted without question that he often couldn't get to Kingshampton. By the time the day came to finalise the sale of the business, it was more than a week since she'd seen him.

This is the beginning of the rest of my life, she told herself, as she pedalled home from Brackleford on that day of completion, her talk to the estate agent casting the die on her future, and her visit first to the solicitor and then to the bank tying up the ragged edges of what had gone before. Ahead of her was a new freedom, but more than that, surely, it was the start of a life shared with Christian. Would he agree to what she envisaged for them? As her imagination leapt ahead, some of her confidence faded. Hope turned to prayer. Please, please, I beseech You, even if I can never be married to him, let us live as man and wife like he said—in happy sin, wasn't that what he called it? But how can it be sin if it's based on love? Let us be parents to his children—Bella and others, others that will be his and mine.

Approaching Kingshampton, she turned into the lane that led to Meadowlands. Today was a day of reckoning, of mending rifts, of building a bridge between the past they'd shared and the future in which surely there would be a place for understanding and forgiveness. So, once again, she carried her olive branch of peace to Sophie. Her hopes soared when she found that Dulcie was out.

'If you've come from Brackleford I wonder you didn't see her. Still, you say you've been settling business things. Dulcie was shopping, she tries not to do much in the village these days. People are so nosy. You're thicker-skinned, I dare say it doesn't hurt you. I feel like a prisoner in my own house. I knew what it would be like as soon as they saw what was going on, and Dulcie says it's horrid. She won't let me go there, throwing myself open to questions, whispers, nudges. She knows how sensitive I am. I suppose you don't care about the things they're saying about you.'

'You're wrong, Sophie. They see me as they always did. What man is going to look at an old maid as firmly on the shelf as I am?'

'Don't lie to me. You said yourself—'

'I mean that that's what people think. Anyway, I don't care one way or another. Thick-skinned, you call it. It's no one's business but our own, and there's nothing unwholesome in what's between Christian and me.'

'Now you're being hateful! You think because I'm different from you and all those other women that how I feel is unwholesome, you think—'

'I think no such thing. We are as God made us, you said

that yourself. Listen, Sophie, I didn't come to rake over all that. I want to tell you the thing I'm planning—praying for with all my might. There's a girl in the orphanage, I've applied to be granted custody of her. And doesn't this prove that Dulcie has been imagining the things that she says are being bandied about? I've had references from so many people, people I've known for years. Nothing is settled yet but I *think*, I've been given grounds to believe in fact, that they are going to let me take Bella to live with me even though I'm not married. It's unheard of, to let a child go except to a married couple, but I've had a lot of backing.'

'Bella? Sybella, you mean? The one whose mother discovered where Christian was and tried to get money out of him? I bet you didn't know about that! Or perhaps he came crawling to you with his begging bowl, expecting to be paid for the favours he was granting you. He tried to persuade me to raise money on the house so that he could pay her off; I bet he didn't tell you *that*. But I refused. So I suppose that's why she cleared off and left the child behind. I expect she thought he'd pick up the pieces. But not him! I heard about her being found in the wood, the vicar told me. But of course he didn't know who her father was and I certainly didn't tell him. He's brought gossip enough on us without adding that to it.' The words poured out at a great rate; it was as if she mustn't leave a space for Lydia to fill. 'Does he know what you're trying to do? I bet you won't see him for dust if he thinks his murky past is catching up with him. He's rotten, Lyddy, I told you he was. Why can't you see it?'

'Stop it, Sophie. You saw him as rotten, but I never have. Is there anyone who has never made a mistake? And I said before, he told me all about Norah Knight. You and he might not have been right for each other, but don't let that colour all your thinking.'

'Pure gold, that's what I used to say you were. I thought you had such high principles you'd never let yourself do any- thing but what was right. Yet now, for the sake of getting a man, you take even your brother-in-law to bed with you! Not that I care, he can go to bed with every woman he fancies— and probably does—it makes no difference to me as long as he leaves me alone. You're a fool, Lyddy. Surely you must know that when he gets tired of you he'll walk out on you just like he did that child's mother—and lots more too, you can be sure of that. If you want to hang on to him just see that he doesn't make you pregnant or you won't see him for dust.'

'Let's not talk about it, Sophie. Forget Christian, we shall never agree about him. Nothing can ever be like it was when we were all at home together, too much has happened. But surely it needn't drive you and me apart. Sophie, if Christian and I make a life together we know it can never be in Kings- hampton. I don't know where we shall go, but distance can never come between you and me as these last months have. Can't we just try and be as we used to be?'

'Away from Kingshampton?'

'Yes, of course. For everyone's sake it's the only way. That's something else I wanted to talk to you about. I'm so glad you're on your own, I hate discussing our affairs in front of an outsider.'

'Don't call her that! If it were a man I loved you'd simper around him like you did around Christian. Dulcie means more to me than anyone—yes, *anyone*—and if she were here I'd want her to share whatever it is you say.'

Ignoring the outburst, Lydia went on, 'It's about the house, about Drydens. I talked to the agent this afternoon. Sophie, the past is always with us, it's in our memories and nothing can take it away. But I have to make a new future. Drydens will be sold. They think they know of someone who will be interested. Then I shall leave Kingshampton. Don't know where I shall go—I just pray the orphanage will let me have the care of Bella. And Christian. You don't love him, so won't you please be happy for me?'

'First it's Pops' business, then it's our home! It's as if I don't know you at all, money's all you care about!'

'You know that's not true. Anyway, today is important. Purposely, I came to you on my way home from town because today was completion day for the sale of the business. I've been to the bank and now I want you to take this.' She passed Sophie the cheque she had written in readiness. 'Please, Sophie. It's what Dad would have wanted, and Mum—and me. It makes things the same for both of us; half the business each, you with this house, me with Drydens.'

Not letting her gaze move from Lydia's, Sophie took the slip of paper and tore it in half without so much as glancing at it.

'I know who *would* want me to take it,' she sneered. 'Christian would. And if he thought I had, he'd be crawling back here like a shot. Not that I'd take him. No, Lyddy. And I suppose when he hears that I won't let you buy me off, he'll hang on to you for every pennyworth of comfort. Why can't you see what he's like? Anyway, I don't want your money. I have a good house, I have something of my own that Pops left for me because he loved my father. Dulcie has taken a job; she's helping Dr Dean's wife in the mornings.'

'Dr Dean? But he's in Brackleford, surely. That's a long way to go for a part-time job.'

'I told you, we try to keep away from the village. You say people haven't changed towards you, but she says she is sure they are whispering. I expect she's more sensitive than you are. That's why she was so pleased to get this job in Brackleford. She leaves Mrs Dean at about midday unless she is particularly busy. You know Dulcie, she'll never leave a job half done.' All the anger and bitterness had gone from Sophie's voice as she talked about Dulcie. 'Then she goes into town and collects the shopping. It's working out very well.' There was a new confidence about her, sure of her place in life. 'We mean to be independent. We are truly happy, Lyddy—although at first when Christian stopped putting money into the house each week for food, I think poor Dulcie was worried. It upset her that we were living on just my money. As if that mattered! Now that she works a few hours each morning she insists on paying half; a feeling of independence is important to her. I've got quite good at doing things in the house, she's really pleased with how well I've learned. We want to manage without any outside help. So you see, there's no chance I'll ever change my mind about what you're offering.'

Lydia knew she was beaten. Riding home, she knew an aching sense of loss. Today she and Sophie hadn't quarrelled, there had been no tears, and yet the gap between them had never been wider. Even though she made herself accept the relationship between the two women, she couldn't even begin to understand it. One thing was clear, though: Sophie had found her niche, there was an aura of contentment about her that only went to emphasise Lydia's solitary state. Today had seen the last of her association with Westlake Builders, it had made her aware that she was an outsider in Sophie's life, it had spelled out clearly what in her heart she must always have known: that Christian used her to suit his own convenience and could walk away without a backward glance. As if all that weren't enough, she became aware that the familiar road back to Drydens seemed unusually bumpy. Even before she hopped off the saddle she realised there was a puncture in the back tyre.

Pushing her bicycle the rest of the way home, she told herself that mending a puncture would give her something to do in the morning, the first day of her new and empty life. But that went against her nature. So when she arrived she got out her puncture-mending kit, a bowl of water and a spoon to lever the tyre back on to the wheel, then she set to work. The hole was found and patched, the tube inflated and she was just checking in the bowl of water for tell-tale bubbles that would mean further damage when she heard the sound she'd been longing for, the roar of a motor cycle.

Sophie was wrong, of course he wouldn't cast her off when he was bored with her! Her spirits soared.

'Are there no end to your talents?' he greeted her, laughing.

'Absolutely none. I've only got to put the tyre back on and I'm roadworthy again. You've had a busy week?' A stupid question, for of course he had or she would have seen him days ago.

'So so,' he answered. 'Come on, Lyddy, leave that. You can finish it in the morning when you haven't me to distract you. I suppose you're a free agent now; wasn't it today the final strings were tied up?'

'Yes. I have done right, haven't I, Christian? I must have.

Yet I feel like a ship broken free of its mooring, set adrift in a vast sea.'

'Silly girl,' he laughed. 'It must be all that wealth making you light-headed. Did you manage to persuade Sophie to take her share?'

Lydia lifted her upside-down bicycle and carried it into the shed to complete her job in the morning.

'Good girl,' he said approvingly. 'You were saying…did you have any luck with Sophie?'

'No. She's adamant. And there's a new strength about her. Have you seen her lately? You must go there to collect post, I suppose.'

'Actually, no. Dulcie is working in Brackleford, she drops anything that's for me as she goes by. Come and wash your hands and say hello to me properly. Have we any food in the house or shall I take you out to eat to celebrate your new freedom?'

'We have—but, yes, you can.' Celebrate her freedom, he said. There was that and so much more to celebrate. After days of silence he had come back to her. She was thankful not just for that but for his easy manner, his certainty that they took each other for granted. She felt safe, certain of her place in his life. Yes, this evening they would go to the most expensive restaurant in the district. 'Christian, this evening is special. In a way it's as if Dad's responsible for the celebration. So before we go, I want you to let me give you the money to pay—his money. It's as if he's giving his blessing to you and me being together. Please, Christian, don't argue and be difficult.'

'When have you ever found me difficult? I think it's a lovely idea. Let's look on it as a celebration of the success he made of the business. Go and smarten up—and don't you dare come out in that damned awful hat.'

'This one? You've never said you hated it.'

'Perhaps I felt I didn't know you well enough,' he teased, his words bringing alive memories of just how well he knew her. Anticipation, happiness, thankfulness, all these jostled for place as with inelegant strides she took the stairs two at a time. Smarten up, he'd said. But all her clothes were dull. Into her mind came the image of Bella. If Bella were here she would help her make the best of herself. Even the best would still be plain and dull; Lydia had no illusions. She scrubbed her long, capable hands hard in the cold water, rinsed her face and rubbed it vigorously in the towel, unpinned her hair and brushed it then coiled it high on her head. Her mother had sometimes worn hers like that if she was going anywhere dressy, and after pinning it securely had wound a string of pearls around the top-knot. Could she do that? Would she look overdressed and stupid? Bella would know. This evening she must cast discretion overboard into those unchartered waters that beckoned her. Ten minutes later, her new coiffure adding to her height, and bedecked with pearls, wearing a plain dark green silk dress adorned with a long rope of pearls that also had been Adelaide's, she emerged.

'Well, well. The lady looks like the heiress she is. Let me feast my eyes.'

Her face felt uncomfortably warm. Did it show, could he see she was ill at ease? 'You said I had to smarten up. Do I look silly?'

'Hold your head high. You look like a duchess.'

If only he didn't have such a teasing glint in his eyes. Being the ugly duckling of the family had at least been so familiar that she'd become hardly aware of it. But a duchess! Of course, he couldn't have meant her to take it seriously, but even so it unnerved her. She would have been far more comfortable in that 'damned awful' hat he'd forbidden.

For the rest of her life, that evening would stand out. Perhaps in retrospect she would remember only the aura of romance, the candlelight, the fine food, the headiness of the wine, all that and the echo of his voice telling her she looked like a duchess. Forgotten would be her underlying lack of confidence, the ever-present knowledge that tonight she was the ugly sister pretending to be Cinderella; although it was something she could never quite forget, on that night of magic she tried to give it no chance to rear its head. And Christian didn't fail her. No duchess could have been treated in a more courtly fashion.

'If your father is looking down on us, my Lyddy, he must be proud of the daughter who was so dear to him.'

For a moment her eyes stung with hot tears, making her thankful for the soft light of the candles. She nodded, not trusting her voice. She wanted to say all the things that were in her heart, that he was the beginning and the end of her reason for living, that he'd brought her more joy than she'd known possible. And in those minutes the preceding days of watching, waiting, praying, being disappointed, were forgotten.

And so the minutes ticked away, the evening passed. But the magic still held through the hours of the night.

The next morning as she cooked breakfast and listened to him moving about overhead, she knew she was being fanciful to pretend they were the same as millions of married couples, together today, together for ever. Yet where was the difference? Certainly there could never be a marriage, but did that matter? Not to her, and as for the rest of the world, she cared nothing.

A few minutes later, as she poured their coffee, he surprised her by saying, 'A boat casting off from its mooring, that's what you said, Lyddy. And why not? It's time we thought seriously about our pastures new; it may take ages to sell the house. We've talked about it, but now there's nothing to keep us here.'

'I'm a step ahead of you,' she answered confidently. 'I spoke to the agent yesterday. He believes he has someone looking for a property like this.'

'Well done! Your years in business have seen to it that you're not some shrinking violet afraid to make a decision. So, my Lyddy, the world is ours. Where shall we go? I'm building a reputation, I shan't be short of work whatever district we decide on. And you, my lady, are comfortably cushioned against hardship. We'll move far away from here; you don't want to spend the rest of your life in the shadow of good Miss Westlake who's been led astray by her rogue of a brother-in-law? We can't marry, I've promised you I won't expose Sophie even though it's a humiliation for a man to find his wife turns him down in the way she did, but I've given you my word.' Then, his eyes lighting in silent laughter. 'The word of a gentleman. I'll buy you the necessary gold band, I'll give you permission to use my name. What more can a man say, except those things I told you weeks ago: you and I are partners, lovers, friends, true mates. Lyddy, what is it? Don't cry, Lyddy.' He said it kindly enough, but she was uncomfortably aware of what tears did to her face. She knew her long nose would be red, her eyes immediately puffy and swollen. 'Does marriage mean so much?'

'Doesn't mean anything. Just too happy to bear. Love you so much.' From her pocket she took a larger than ladylike handkerchief and blew her nose, then rubbed her face hard.

'So you agree? For a minute I thought you were turning me down. From now on we are officially engaged, not to be married, but to live in happy sin for the rest of our days.'

She nodded, her momentary loss of control over. 'And Christian, there's Bella too. If only they'll give their permission for me to adopt her. It seems so dreadful that the formalities—and I just pray it will get to that stage—have to be put just in *my* name, when the truth is that we shall be a proper family. But if they knew *that* it would really put me beyond the pale. As long as I'm living here we shall have to be careful there's no cause for gossip—if Bella is here too, I mean. You'll be so proud of her, Christian, there's nothing of Norah Knight about her, she is wholly your daughter. My application is coming up at the next meeting of governors, I'm not sure when that will be. Until that's over I don't want to mention it to Bella in case it gets turned down. But if it isn't— and I've had so much help locally, Christian, people whose names matter have written backing my request—and if they stretch the rules letting me give her a home, then once it's all finished I'll be free. We can move away and start afresh. By then perhaps the house sale will be agreed; they seemed confident it would sell quickly. Once we're somewhere where no one knows us and no malicious busybodies can rock the boat for us, you can join us.'

'You mean because of the kid, I have to wait?' She knew his jocular tone was forced.

'It won't be for long. And in the meantime we can start looking for somewhere else to live. You have commissions to complete, I have a lot of sorting out to do. Apart from everything here in the house, I can't leave the Guides without a new Captain in place to take over and I must find someone (probably the same person) to carry on my Saturdays at the orphanage. The children look forward to it.'

'So the Board at that orphanage have the power to seal our fate. Don't bank on their letting one of their charges go to a home without a married couple to lead her into the paths of righteousness.' And she could tell that his hopes were on her application being turned down. 'I must go, Lyddy my love. I have an appointment near Stockbridge, I've a long ride ahead. I say "near", in truth it's a few miles out so the only way I can get there is on the motor cycle. I would suggest you come with me, but it looks like being a busy day.'

'Will you be home this evening, home here, I mean?'

'Very unlikely. I have a lot of work on at the moment. You give some thought to where we ought to make our home. Mr and Mrs Mellor—oh and their daughter, the unknown Bella. What a ménage!'

'Don't joke about it, Christian. Just keep hoping, keep trusting. I'm almost frightened to imagine how it could be, I'm not strong enough to face the alternative.'

'For us there is no alternative. The child is the only uncertainty. You're absolutely certain you want a constant reminder of my misspent youth?'

She had no doubts.

Even so, she was unprepared for the speed at which things moved. On the following Monday she had a telephone call from the estate agent asking if it would be convenient for a Mr and Mrs Laidlaw to see over the house.

'At any time to suit you,' she was assured. 'They only come from Brackleford and have their own transport.'

'Is that Mr Laidlaw, the tailor? He always made my father's suits.'

'Indeed it is. I did mention to you I had someone in mind I believed would be more than interested.'

Charlie and Alice Laidlaw arrived just after two o'clock that same afternoon, he a portly, smiling man whose suit was an advertisement of his craft, his bald head topped with a high-crowned bowler hat. Alice was small, aged before her years, yet still with a suspicion of the pretty young woman she once had been.

'Well, Mother?' he asked her when Lydia brought them back down the stairs, having completed their tour of inspection.

'Oh Chaw, it's like everything I've ever dreamed. Right down to the last bit of furniture, it's—oh dear, I don't know the words. Will we be able to do it out as lovely as it is?'

He smiled at her indulgently. His patient Alice had waited many years for the day to come when they had the wherewithal to move out of town and he was jiggered if he was going to spoil it by penny-pinching now.

'I don't know your plans, Miss Westlake. I heard you'd sold the business; well of course you did, what choice could a young lady like yourself have had? Building is a man's trade and no mistake. I knew your father, a fine man. It won't be easy for you to pull up your roots. Are you moving locally?'

'No. With the business gone I feel it's time for a new beginning.'

'So now I'll come to what's in my mind. The furniture— it seems my Alice has lost her heart to the place just as it stands. Would you be prepared to leave anything behind? Name a figure, of course; I'm not trying to diddle you.'

Lydia found herself warming to this quaint pair. Although she'd talked about a new beginning, moving out of Drydens and leaving the past behind, she hadn't been able to focus her mind on the moment when it would happen.

'Except for a few personal things, I shan't be taking much. While I make us some tea, why don't the pair of you go back upstairs, up and down too, have a good look around by yourselves. Then we'll talk.'

So it was that by the time the sun went down and the gaslighter came along the village street putting on the streetlights, the wheels were in motion for Drydens, the outward sign of Archie Westlake's worldly success, to pass into the hands of Charlie Laidlaw, who, until then, had lived above his shop and workrooms in Mill Lane. Lydia's future began to take shape. She didn't know where she and Christian would settle, she didn't know whether Bella would be handed into her care; but there was no going back to what had gone before and in typical determination she started to sort drawers and cupboards, to tie 'Sale Room' labels on some items and 'Not to be removed' on others. When she called at Meadowlands to tell Sophie what was happening no one was in, so she wrote a note and put it through the letterbox, asking her to come to Drydens and take anything she wanted. There was no reply.

Off Fore Street in Brackleford was Butchers' Row, at the end of which was the yard of the abattoir, the narrow street deriving its name from a time when it had been the marketing centre for the trade. But times change, and now only two butchers traded there, sharing the small street with a bicycle shop, an ironmonger's and a grocery store. It was outside the ironmonger's that Dulcie hopped off her bicycle and wheeled it along the alley towards the back of the premises. There she leaned it against the wall, then carefully lifted a package from the basket on her handlebars, and, carrying it flat on the palms of her hands, mounted the wooden staircase to the front door of the rooms above the shop. There was nothing unusual in her coming here: often there was post to deliver to Christian. Sometimes he was out and she pushed the envelopes through the letterbox; sometimes he heard her coming and opened the door so that she could hand them to him. In the beginning she'd made her deliveries part of her morning duties, but recently she'd found herself looking forward to their brief contact. She didn't delve into the reason for her disappointment when there was no post to bring, anymore than she asked herself what had prompted her to bring about this particular visit. For today was different. Today she had no letters to bring, she had come purely on her own account, unknown to everyone—even to Sophie, or more truthfully, most of all to Sophie. Rapping on the door, she waited, her heart pounding as she heard his footsteps.

'Dulcie! Something too big to come through the letter-box?'

'It's not post.' She'd been a fool; she shouldn't have come. 'It's just that I was making apple pies and I remembered how you always enjoyed them when you were back at the house. So I made an extra and popped it in my basket.'

'That was very civil of you. Did Sophie suggest it? Surely not!'

'No. I thought it best not to say anything to her. There's

no harm in making you something nice for your meal, but she's easily hurt. If I pass it to you, mind how you hold it. The pastry is light as a feather, I don't want you crushing it.'

'Then why don't you bring it in and put it safely on the larder shelf for me?'

Was this what she'd hoped for? Was this what had prompted her to make more pastry than she needed? The question pushed itself to the forefront of her mind, but she wasn't prepared to find the answer.

'Is that supposed to be your dinner?' The words were spoken before she had time to tell herself it wasn't her place to comment on the plate of bread and cheese by his drawing board.

'It's a hard life,' he laughed. 'Tell you what, Dulcie, while I roll away what I've been working on, what about you making us a pot of tea—or coffee—whichever you prefer.' He turned up the gas-fire and pushed two armchairs closer to the warmth. For all the months he'd lived in the same house as Dulcie, apart from the part she apparently played in Sophie's life, his thoughts of her had gone no further than the food she brought to the table or the unfailingly well ironed clothes she brought to his room. As for entering into a meaningful conversation with her, such a thought hadn't entered his head. So now he felt he was looking at her anew, vaguely and comfortably surprised at the pleasure he found in the sight.

'Take off your coat.'

'I can't be staying above ten minutes. I don't need my coat off.'

'After even ten minutes by the fire, you'll feel the cold when you go outside. Come on, now.' Already he was lifting it from her shoulders, as without further ado she slipped her arms from the sleeves.

'I'll see to the tea,' she said, making sure her voice gave no hint of the strangely unfamiliar excitement that made her feel she was living a dream. But where was the logic? If she'd had dreams they certainly hadn't involved Christian Mellor, darling Sophie's unfaithful husband. Unfaithful… from what Sophie had told her, he would never be faithful to any one woman; like a butterfly he'd flit from flower to flower. Well, he wasn't likely to see her as a flower, even in the village, where the young men had none of his worldly sophistication, she'd never had a sweetheart. And now? What she shared with Sophie was surely what she wanted of life. All those fantasies she used to have about falling in love with some handsome young man, they had been nothing but the empty imaginings of a young girl. She was a woman now, and the love she and Sophie gave to each other was full of the sort of understanding that could never exist between a couple not the same sex. Their thoughts ran along the same rails, they never needed to put up a pretence one to the other. What man could possibly know how to fill a woman with that nameless, consuming longing? For Christian, handsome enough to turn any silly young head though he might be, there was always just one aim—or so Sophie said. Where was the tenderness in that? She knew just what it was Sophie's body yearned for, of course she did, for her own feelings were the same. But a man, how could he know? And yet…and yet…What was the matter with her, letting her thoughts stray like that just because she was alone with Sophie's cast-off husband? He was a bounder, didn't Sophie say so? While her thoughts raced she busied herself making the tea and taking cups and saucers from the shelf in the larder. Poor man, fancy, when he'd been used to a lovely comfortable home like he'd had at Meadowlands, having to live in a miserable place like this without even a nice cabinet to keep his crockery. As if to make up to him for his misfortune she passed him his cup and saucer with a more than warm smile.

Christian was enjoying himself. She really wasn't a bad-looking woman…a bit on the plump side and more at home in the kitchen than the bedroom…but what a waste. She was conscious of his scrutiny; it made her feel unsettled and less than sure of herself. To escape, she leaned forward, holding her hands towards the gas-fire, half wishing he'd stop watching her and half excited by an experience so new. Christian let his imagination run on unchecked. Some women trussed themselves into underwear he thought of as little short of battle armour—and thank God some of them did, they'd have been an unlovely sight if they didn't keep themselves in check. But clearly Dulcie wore nothing restraining under her crocheted jumper. Her large, rounded breasts hung free, not pushed up unnaturally high nor yet flattened almost out of position and yet not drooping as if they were looking for something she'd dropped. He imagined the warm weight of one, filling the palm of his hand, his fingers awakening desire only hinted at by the slight protrusion of her nipples.

'Umph? Pardon?' He pulled his thoughts up smartly like a man suddenly woken from sleep. 'Forgive me, Dulcie, I was thinking of something else. You were saying?'

'Only that I didn't get the sugar; I remembered that you don't like it. I shouldn't be here interrupting you from your work when you've got things on your mind. It was just that, well, when you said about a cup of tea, well, I thought, now if I say yes at least you'd make time to have one for yourself.

It worries me to see you without a good hot meal inside you. Cold as charity it is out there, too.'

'And charity can be extremely cold. Are things all right in Kingshampton? I mean, for you and Sophie? People can be very uncharitable. Although I expect I'm looked on as the villain of the piece.'

'I never heed gossip. But, Mr Mellor, sir—'

'Christian.'

'But, Christian.' There was a strange excitement in saying his name. 'Christian,' she repeated, 'you mustn't let yourself worry about Sophie. It's not an easy thing to talk about but, well, I try to give her the love she needs. She is very dear to me.'

He watched her closely, weighing her words, wondering about the pair of them. Marriage to Sophie had been the biggest mistake of his life. But what about Dulcie? Did trying to give Sophie the love she needs sound like the words of a woman who had found her own fulfilment?

'Life plays strange tricks, Dulcie. And where we find love is the strangest of all. You and Sophie are managing in your all-female household? Is it necessary for you to cycle to Brackleford for a few hours' work each day? If memory serves me right, the dinner you find waiting when you get home must leave much to be desired.'

'That's not kind,' Dulcie said defensively. 'Sophie is turning into a good little cook. And yes, she and I take care of each other very nicely.'

He raised his eyebrows, his dark eyes shining with silent laughter.

'In the house, I mean.' Poor embarrassed Dulcie bent again towards the fire, anything rather than look directly at him. 'I've some shopping to do before I set off home, so I'd better be putting my coat on and leaving you in peace. You won't forget to put your apple pie in the oven for your dinner, will you?'

'I shall think of you and bless you with every mouthful.'

As he helped her into her overcoat he let his hands rest on her shoulders longer than was necessary. What was she thinking? He was amused by the suddenness of her departure, it was hardly the behaviour of a grown woman happy in a loving relationship.

'You'll come again, Dulcie? Don't wait until there are letters for me, just knock on my door on your way home from Mrs Dean. I'm not always here, my work takes me away as you know. But promise me you'll come.'

'If you really want me to, of course I will. But—this sounds unkind—but I don't think I ought to say anything to Sophie. She never goes anywhere without me; that's the way we live, you see. She'd be hurt if she thought I was coming here for a cup of tea on my way home.'

'Then it's our secret.'

'You won't tell Miss Westlake either, promise me.' She made herself say it, and purposely she turned to face him, looking for some sign that would tell her if the rumour she'd heard held any truth.

'I told you, it's our secret.'

From the open doorway he watched her tread firmly down the stone steps, his eyes shining with silent laughter. Then he turned back towards his drawing board, his mouth turning into a smile. Another hour's work and he'd ride over and see Lyddy. Whistling softly and tunelessly, he lit a cigarette, climbed back onto his tall stool and unrolled the large sheet on to his drawing board.

* * *

Despite Lyddy's busy days spent in sorting the accumulation of years at Drydens, nothing was allowed to alter the routine of her Saturdays. And this particular Saturday was like no other, for she knew that it was the morning of the governors' meeting. No one looking at her would have guessed at the excitement, hope, fear, emotions of every variety that filled her as, armed with bundles of remnants she'd bought from the fabric department of McIntyre's Emporium at a greatly reduced price when she'd explained to the manager her reason for wanting them, she arrived at the orphanage. She'd bought a paper pattern earlier in the week and cut replicas, some a little larger, some a little smaller.

On this occasion even Bella showed an interest in the project. Work started as soon as she arrived in the morning. The only place with space enough for each one to lay out her material and pattern was the floor of the large, empty hall. A spectator would have thought it an odd sight, the stone floor covered with girls on their knees, the sound of excited chatter as they clipped and snipped. And perhaps oddest of all, tall unbending Miss Westlake making a crawling progress amongst them as she watched and advised. By the time the bell rang out, telling them it was dinnertime, cutting was done, snippets were tidied up and the afternoon couldn't come soon enough so keen were they to get on.

'Miss Westlake, a word with you if we may, before you join Matron.' It was Howard Marsham, Mayor of Brackleford and Chairman of the Governors. Her heart raced. Let it be, please, please, let it be, she begged silently.

He ushered her into the room where she faced those who had it in their power to mould her future.

'We have given your application our most careful thought. Indeed, I personally have followed up the many letters of support your request has had. As you know, the aim of this orphanage is to find homes for these parentless girls, homes where they will have the care and guidance of two adoptive parents.'

So it was 'No'. Was that what he was telling her? Her mouth felt dry, her jaw stiff, she wanted to scream at them that they had no right to deprive Bella of her own father's love (for he *would* love her, once he knew her, of course he would love her).

'This child you want to give a home to, we realise you probably feel drawn to her because she lived in your own village. But there are other considerations.'

'Of course there are. In any case I didn't know her in Kingshampton.'

'Then, Miss Westlake,' boomed a large woman in a hat not dissimilar to the 'damned awful' one Lydia had relegated to the dustbin after Christian's comment, 'perhaps you are able to explain to us why you are so keen to give a home to this specific child. There are others who have been here waiting adoption for far longer; indeed there are those who can remember nothing outside the orphanage.'

'Why do I feel drawn to Sybella?' Lydia looked at each of them sitting there in judgement. These were all 'good' people, the sort of people she herself had always looked on as friends and allies. 'How can any of us say why we are instinctively drawn to any one person? She knows I am her friend. I don't think she is a child who talks easily to strangers, in the beginning she was hard to approach. Yet there is an affinity between us, I'm sure she is as aware of it as I am.'

'I don't like it,' muttered Ralph Baker, the local pharmacist, chewing at the corners of his drooping moustache. 'I have friends in Kingshampton, and without hinting at any of this to them I have tried to steer them to give me some local colour. You have a sister, or more accurately a cousin who was brought up as your sister, I understand?'

'That's right. Everyone knows Sophie. She lives in one of the new houses my father built in Meadowlands.'

'You must miss her. Her moving out has left a void in your life, I don't doubt.'

'Her moving out left a void in the whole house. But since then so much has altered.'

'Indeed yes, and I know everyone here was touched with sympathy at the dreadful accident that robbed you of your parents. However, it is your so-called sister who has left the gap you must wish to fill. There she is, according to my friends and to the local gossip they saw fit to pass on to me, abandoned by her husband. Perhaps I am speaking out of turn, but we have a young child's future at stake here and none of us round this table takes our responsibility lightly. Gossip is a cruel thing, but seldom without a grain of truth. Word in the village is that your brother-in-law brings his troubles to your door—and why not, my dear Miss Westlake, for if anyone has influence over his young, and I understand beautiful, wife then it must surely be you. Yet even you can't separate her from this woman who lives with her. My dear friends,' he cast his troubled glance around the table where some had followed his innuendos, some were floundering in the dark, 'if I am wrong may my God forgive me, but all of you—even Miss Westlake herself—must see that if I let such a situation go unchallenged I would be failing. Two girls, growing up together, two young women, then one of them breaks free and marries. But marriage is an unhappy mistake, or so I have been told, and her comfort and consolation is to be found in the woman she has taken in to share her home. So we are left with one of those two sisters, unattached and no doubt lonely,' his teeth worked vigorously on the moustache, 'coming here to find an innocent young girl to fill—'

'No! Be still! How dare you make such hateful, venomous suggestions!' Lydia was trembling with rage. Every instinct in her wanted to shout that he was wrong about her, perhaps all of them were wrong in their opinion of her. What if she followed that instinct and screamed at them that she was the mistress of Bella's father, that they were going to live together for the rest of their lives, the three of them making a family? But she knew she mustn't. She would stand more chance of being granted custody of the child on her own than with the man who had forsaken her even before she was born. So she bit back her words, simply stood before them, her head high, her expression defying them to follow where Ralph Baker was trying to lead them.

Howard Marsham rapped on the table, and those seated around it seemed to sit a fraction straighter.

'I believe, ladies and gentlemen, that before we asked Miss Westlake to join us we had discussed the situation most thoroughly. To be sidetracked at this point seems to me to be without justification. Rumour and gossip is rife in any village, yes, even in a town the size of Brackleford we know there is always someone whose character is being maligned for the entertainment it brings. But as for character, surely we can find no fault with Miss Westlake's. Here before me I have not one but more than a dozen letters assuring me that this child, er, let me see, who is it? Ah yes, Sybella Knight, will be in a good home. We have no right, no right at all, to deprive her of the opportunity. From all that I have heard—for in my capacity as Chairman of the Board it behove me to visit the village myself and lend my ear to local gossip—the child's mother was…let me just call her a lady of the night. Before I brought Miss Westlake into the room our decision was made. I propose that despite Mr Baker's comments,' spoken very clearly and with undisguised criticism of what he felt to be the pharmacist's unpleasant and unnecessary aspersions cast at a good young lady such as Miss Westlake, 'yes, casting such ill-mannered and malicious gossip to one side, we let our decision stand. Will someone second me?'

And so it was over. All the weeks of waiting, of building up a relationship with Bella and fighting down her desire to share the truth with the child, were behind her.

It took all Lydia's willpower to make herself concentrate on an afternoon of overseeing the pinning and tacking of the garments under construction. Before she went home she wanted them to have reached the next stage so that she could watch over each girl's initial attempt at a French seam. With that done they would be able to continue unsupervised until the following weekend when Monica Sherwood, her assistant guider, would be there with her. It was almost frightening how well everything was going: a keen helper to take over the Guides and to carry on her work at the orphanage, Bella within hours—almost minutes as the afternoon progressed—coming home with her to start a new life. And over and above all that was Christian, her lover, her reason for existing. Over the last few weeks he had been even busier than previously, his visits less frequent. Yet the wonder of their being together never diminished. Bending over the shoulder of a plump child with bitten nails and an unfortunate habit of sniffing, Lydia recalled his last visit.

'That's good, Millie,' she said encouragingly, 'lovely neat stitches. You're going to make a really good seamstress.' She heard her own voice, marvelling that there was nothing in her tone to hint at the memories that crowded her imagination. Tonight he was sure to come. Ahead of her was an evening of planning the sort of house they would look for, thankfulness that after these weeks he was prepared to look on Bella as his daughter; then a night…thinking of it there in the scrubbed, comfortless surroundings of the orphanage of their own volition the words 'the power and the glory' sprang into her mind. Such power, she had felt consumed by it, her body and his too had had a strength that knew no bounds; and the glory…is there such a thing as heaven on earth? Yes, oh yes, yes, yes, she cried silently. Had there ever been a moment like that one? Or did she think that every time? 'Let me show you a better way to hold your needle, you'll find it easier,' she told the pretty child who would certainly never make a seamstress.

'That's good, Sybella,' and how hard it was to speak to her just as she did to the others. 'Keep your stitches small, the seams will be all the stronger.'

At last she'd seen everyone's work and told them they must all roll it carefully away so that they could carry on if they had an opportunity during the week. 'And next Saturday when I come, I'm bringing someone else with me. Miss

Sherwood. Actually she sews much better than I do, and I know you'll all like her. We've timed the afternoon just right, there's the bell for your tea.' Just for a second she rested her hand on Sybella's shoulder. 'Stay behind a minute if you will, Sybella, I want a word with you. Don't worry, Matron knows.'

Sybella looked anything but pleased as the others jostled for the door, each clutching her sewing. There were calls of 'Bye, Miss' and 'Thank you, Miss', and there were curious glances at the one girl left behind. No one had made a friend of Sybella, something they all considered—rightly—to be more her own fault than theirs. Any approach was always rebuffed.

'You didn't ought to do that.' Her dark eyes looked at Lydia with undisguised hostility. 'We talk by ourselves when the others aren't there, I know that. But you didn't ought to tell me to stay behind.'

Lydia suspected that her bad grammar was an intentional attempt to distance herself from the girl who had sometimes come regrettably close to baring her soul. It was something she could understand.

'I wouldn't have, had there been any other way of our talking by ourselves. What I want us to talk about doesn't concern any of the others. Bella, I couldn't say anything to you until now because I was too frightened that it wouldn't happen. But today I've been given permission.'

'You're making me late for tea. You'll get me into a row.'

Lydia shook her head. 'Please Bella, be glad about what I'm going to tell you.' For, suddenly she was frightened. Taking a breath, straightening her shoulders, she looked Bella squarely in the eyes. 'I believe you and I understand each other pretty well. I have been given permission to adopt you, make you legally my responsibility.'

'You didn't have to do that. I don't want you feeling sorry for me, just cos it was your interfering old vicar who brought me to this place. Just cos his stupid dog sniffed me out in the wood at Kingshampton, that doesn't mean I have to go back there. Don't want you being responsible for me, nor any other interfering busybody. In a few weeks I'm going to be fourteen, they'll let me out of this prison then. What makes you think I want to be put into someone else's charge when I get free of this lot? If you want to know, what I want is to be free, to have a chance to earn a few bob and look after myself. And you needn't worry that I shall get my living the way Norah did, cos I won't. Buggered if I will.' Perhaps they were two of a kind and that's why Lydia was so certain that her belligerent manner was her armour against hurt. Did she honestly believe a home was being offered to her out of sympathy?

'Bella, I thought you and I were friends. Do you mean that all this time you have really seen me as an interfering busybody? Now that permission has been granted I wish I'd talked about it to you ages ago. But I was so frightened that the governors would say I wasn't suitable because I don't have a husband.'

'Don't see what difference having a husband makes. He'd probably only try it on with me like some of the dirty buggers Norah used to bring home.'

This time Lydia laughed. 'Give me credit for better taste than that. Bella, we're going to make a new life. New for you and new for me. I can't talk about it to you here. You see, it's because they know the home I can give you, they know that I do charity work—a local busybody in fact—that they consider me suitable. Remember I said to you weeks ago that both of us, you and me too, were on the brink of making new lives for ourselves. It could be so good, Bella.'

'Don't see why you want to lumber yourself with me. Encumbrance, that's what Norah said I was. Then, here's you with a nice home—and I know you have cos I used to look at it sometimes. First time I saw it I was with Norah. She stood outside, black as thunder she looked, and she said something about—oh well, never mind what she said. Expect it was a load of rubbish anyway, I never took much notice when she used to carry on about him.'

'Him?'

'Him who got her pregnant, then buggered off and left her.'

'Did she tell you his name?'

'Never called him anything except slippery devil, crafty bugger, or sometimes—oh well, I don't want to say it, not to you.'

'No, don't say it, Bella, and don't think it either. I can understand that she felt let down, but it's not fair to paint him jet black. None of us is perfect.'

She could feel a change in Bella, she knew that now she had her full attention.

'How do you know anything about him? Do you know who he is?'

'Yes, I do. I'll tell you everything I know presently, but not here. Is there anything you want to bring with you? If so, I'll wait while you collect your things, then we'll go and say goodbye to Matron.'

'Funny old stick she is,' Bella said, 'but I reckon she tries to do her best for us lot.'

Half an hour later, with Bella's first attempt at sewing and precious drawing pad and pencils in Lydia's basket, they were on the bus trundling back to the village.

'We'll get off a stop early,' Lydia said as they turned off the main road. 'Instead of going right into the village we'll walk from the war memorial, that'll give us time to talk.'

'I thought you told me you lived by yourself. Who's going to hear us talking when we get home? Cor! Home, did you hear what I said, Miss Westlake?'

'I did, and it sounded fine. No, probably no one, but just in case there should be a visitor, my sister or anyone. So we'll talk as we walk.'

'Sounds good.' As Bella's confidence strengthened, so her aggression weakened.

In fact Lydia had suggested they should walk the last part of the journey for two reasons, neither of them the unlikely event of a visit from Sophie.

'Cor,' Bella voiced her favourite expletive as the bus left them standing alone in the winter dusk. 'I haven't 'arf missed the smell of the country. People are funny, most of them. They all herd together in the town where all you can smell is dust. I'm never going to live in a town.'

'That's one decision made, then,' Lydia laughed. 'You see, Bella, what I plan is that we will move away from Kingshampton, go somewhere neither of us know, find a house that we know is right for us.'

'Cor!' Bella breathed. 'Here, pinch me, pinch me hard so I know I'm not dreaming all this. Where are we off to then, Miss Westlake?'

'We'll find somewhere. But Bella, it won't be just the two of us.'

'… won't…?'

Lydia knew from her tone that the child felt her dream receding.

'You asked me back at the orphanage if I knew who your father is. Yes, I do. And that's how I know, absolutely *know*, that he isn't those things you say Norah calls him. When you were conceived he was just a boy. Yes, he ran away from responsibility, I'm not defending him. But he wasn't even sure that he was the father of her child. Can you understand that?'

'You mean, do I know about babies and all that? Course I do. And I know about Norah and the chaps who paid her to let them—I don't know what you call it, but I know about getting babies. She never had no more though, only me. But if he wasn't sure, then how can you know that he's the right person to blame?'

'It wasn't until I saw you that I knew without a doubt—just as she must always have known just from looking at you—that you are Christian's daughter. When you meet him you'll understand what I mean.'

'Christian? Crumbs, what a name!' Her voice was mocking, her expression giving no hint of how she must feel to know that the man responsible for her loveless life was soon to become a reality. Lydia suspected that she was playing for time, not ready to change her preconceived ideas and yet, despite herself, excited by her discovery. 'Anyway, you just said about there not being just you and me. You mean your sister is going to live with us. But she got married. I've seen her—Norah hated her like poison, don't know why. But she pointed her out to me one day, the "little princess" that's what she called her, her voice sort of dripping with hate. She wasn't 'arf pretty—your sister I mean.'

'Yes, she's more than pretty. She's really beautiful. But she won't be coming to live with us. I expect Norah hated her because she knew she was married to your father.'

'Crumbs.' Then, with a sudden laugh that belonged to childhood, 'That means, Miss Westlake, if you're adopting me that means my father is my uncle!'

'A bit of a mix-up, Bella. But I've only told you half of it. The next part isn't so easy.' But it had to be told, so treading firmly, looking straight ahead, Lydia stated her case in a voice void of emotion. 'Christian will be living with us. He and Sophie are separated. He and I would marry if he were free, but he isn't so we plan to move away where none of us is known. His name is Mellor, Christian Mellor. I shall be known as his wife even though it can never be true, and you, Bella, will bear the name that is rightfully yours. You will be Bella Mellor, our daughter.'

'Bella Mellor, 'truth, Miss Westlake, sounds like one of them tongue-twister things, you know like "she sells seashells on the seashore" or "plum bun", that's a hard one, but Bella Mellor's not much better. Does he know about me, Miss? I mean, he may want to call you his wife and all that, but having an encumbrance as old as me come as part of the parcel must put him off a bit. After all, if he didn't want me right from the beginning, why should he change his mind now? And Norah had been chasing him for money for months, she told me she had and never got a penny piece out of him.'

'That's not true. He gave her a lot of money—and he did it for your sake. Of course he wants you.'

'Crumbs!' This time it was hardly audible.

For a while they walked in silence, both of them needing time to get used to their new roles.

'We won't tell anyone here in Kingshampton about what

we're going to do, will we, Miss? They'd all gossip and make it seem dirty and nasty. Let's just keep it a secret, shall we?'

Lydia's long, capable hand took Bella's childlike one in her grasp.

'Bella, oh Bella, there are such wonderful times ahead of us. But, like you say, they shall be our secret until we get on the train and set out for our new life. Christian has looked at some places in Surrey, but he hasn't found anything he thinks absolutely right for us.'

'Norah and I were in Surrey once. Wouldn't it be nice if we could go somewhere none of us had ever been to. Sort of like starting a new drawing book, every page empty and waiting. You know what, Miss? When we get away from here I won't be able to call you Miss Westlake. Will I call you by your name, like I did Norah?'

'Perhaps you could learn to say Mum. Mum and Dad. We'll be a proper family, Bella.'

'Crumbs. Pinch me, go on pinch me.'

Sitting on the edge of the bed, Bella gazed slowly round the room. *Her* room, *her* bed, not just a place where she would be sleeping until they had to move on because the rent hadn't been paid. Miss Westlake had found some winter forsythia and put it in a vase on the dressing-table; she had made up the bed with lovely crisp sheets, so clean that it seemed a sin to lie on them. She'd done all that before she even knew for sure that the busybodies at the orphanage would say 'yes'. Didn't that prove just how much she had wanted to get their permission? It was all so sudden and unexpected, no wonder Bella was frightened to believe. Just think, she told herself silently, only this morning I got up just like every other day, never knowing that back here Miss Westlake must have been out there in the garden cutting those yellow flowers. Supposing those busybodies who make all the stupid rules at the orphanage had said she couldn't bring me, I reckon she would have been quite sad coming into the room, seeing it all nice and knowing they didn't think her a fit person. But wouldn't that have been wicked! I bet there isn't one of them fit to clean the mud off her boots. Mum…not while we live here in this gossipy place, but once we get away and start being a proper family. And Dad. Crumbs! That won't even be a lie. Miss Westlake says he's all right, well, she must think so or she wouldn't be chucking away all this to live with him without so much as being married. So who's right, her or Norah? He was a rotten sod to Norah, don't matter how many excuses Miss Westlake makes for him, he got her up the spout and washed his hands of the pair of us. No one's perfect, isn't that what she said? Well, course we're not. I know I've told plenty of lies—and we shall be telling plenty more once we get away from the village—Mum, Dad and me, Bella Mellor. Pity he has to be called Mellor, it sounds all wrong. But it won't be wrong, it'll be *right*. My proper name—just like this is my real room. I wonder if everyone's life has a plan it has to follow? Who decides on a bit of luck like this is? Is it my sort of payment for being good? But then, I don't reckon I've ever been up to much. Given half a chance I used to slope off going to school—think of the wallopings I've had when the beadle's come calling and Norah's found out what I've been up to. Will I have to go back to that rotten school in the village?

Remembering it and the way the girls used to whisper and snigger because her elbow was poking through the sleeve of her jumper, or because when they knelt for prayers in the morning they could see the newspaper she'd folded into a thick wodge and put inside her shoe to cover the hole in the sole, some of her newfound happiness evaporated. Perhaps Miss Westlake would say she needn't go any more. The beadle wouldn't come looking for her here, after all no one would be expecting her at the village school.

She was still pondering the point when she heard the peal of the front door bell. He must have come! Christian Mellor, her father! She wanted a chance to look at him without his knowing, she wanted these first seconds to make an impression that would last a lifetime and wipe away all her preconceived ideas. Creeping out of the bedroom she moved stealthily along the landing then stood in the shadows near the top of the stairs. In the hall a light was burning, but on the upstairs landing it was dark, so she felt safe from being seen.

Crumbs, I can feel my heart going bang, bang, bang. Suppose he doesn't like the look of me, suppose he is keen to go away with Miss Westlake (Funny really, she isn't a bit the sort of lady you'd expect a man to fancy, not like they used to Norah, all smarmy with their hands everywhere. Wouldn't think she'd fancy it either), but going off with his fancy lady isn't the same as getting a nearly grown-up daughter planted on him. I might make him think of Norah, and I bet he'd rather just forget her. Anyway, same goes for me. I might think he looks a right sod, just like Norah said he was. Gave her money, that's what Miss Westlake said, gave it to her so that she could start off fresh with a home for me. Not bloody likely, took it and went. And I don't blame her. She put up with me all those years; like she said, no chance of any fun with a kid always in tow. But likely as not he never even gave her the money at all, that was probably just something he told Miss Westlake. It depends who's right about him, her or Norah.

All those thoughts tumbled through her mind in the seconds it took for Lydia to come out of the kitchen where she was starting to prepare a celebratory supper and cross to the front door.

'Sophie! Sophie, whatever is it? What's happened?'

From her vantage point at the top of the stairs Bella couldn't see on to the dark porch, it was only as the visitor came into the hall that she understood Lydia's alarm. No trauma, no tears or tantrums could make Sophie less than lovely, not even as she stood in front of Lydia, tears falling unchecked, her face a mask of despair.

'He's no good! I told you he was rotten, but you, oh no, you could hear no bad of him.'

'Hush, Sophie,' Lydia moved to draw the younger woman close, only to be thrown off.

'You encouraged him, I knew you were asking for trouble, now you've got what you deserve. You wouldn't even see that he was using you to hit at me. Oh no, you flattered yourself he'd fallen for you. I knew you were making a fool of yourself, but I didn't feel sorry for you, not after the way we'd all known you'd been begging him.'

'Stop it! You don't know anything about Christian and me.'

'Doesn't matter now anyway,' Sophie snorted, wiping her palms across her wet face. 'I suppose he could see I didn't care if he went to bed with *you*. So he tried another way to punish me for not wanting him.'

'Calm down, Sophie. I don't know what you've been hearing, but it's time I told you what we're going to do. I've been granted permission to adopt Bella, Christian's daughter, today I brought her home. The three of us are going away, a new beginning, a proper family. The three of us, Sophie, but soon I'm almost certain it will be four. Too soon to see a doctor to have it confirmed, but I'm *sure* I'm expecting a child.'

Opening her purse, Sophie took out a single sheet of paper and thrust it into Lydia's hand.

'Read it and see for yourself. You wouldn't listen to me, now see for yourself.' But the crumpled letter wasn't written in Christian's hand.

CHAPTER TEN

The bedroom was cold. *Her* room where, not half an hour before, she had been aware of welcome and warmth that had nothing to do with temperature. But how would Miss Westlake feel about her now? We will be a family, that's what she'd said. Mum, *him* and her. Now none of that would happen. Would she be sent back to the orphanage? Well, if that's what they thought, they could think again! She wouldn't go! But even driven by fear and insecurity, she couldn't believe that Lydia would make a decision like that without discussing it with her. Perhaps she'd be able to stay here until she was old enough to find a job and pay for a room somewhere. That was the hope she must hang on to. She ought to have waited outside on the landing where she could hear what was being said; yet, somehow, once she saw that look on Miss Westlake's face, she had wanted to crawl away.

Norah had been right about him all the time; he was a rotten bugger just like she said. The pretty sister—Sophie, didn't Miss Westlake call her?—said more or less the same and she was his wife so she ought to know. But Miss Westlake had looked so…so sort of horror-struck, as if her world had tumbled. He must be a rotten devil or he couldn't have done it to her. Yes, Bella's thoughts raced on, but where does that leave me? If he's treated Miss Westlake the same way as he did Norah, she'll not want me around the place. I'm not just *any-oldbody*, I'm the rotten sod's daughter, that's why she fetched me out of the orphanage. Every time she looks at me she'll be reminded of how he's made a monkey of her.

So deep in her own miserable thoughts was she that it was a wonder she heard the final exchange between Lydia and Sophie. The front door must have been open. She moved to the window and looked down into the garden where she could see the shadows cast by the two of them in the open doorway. As quietly as she could she opened her window an inch or two so that she could listen.

'Don't go back there on your own. Stay here. Please, Sophie, don't let's say goodnight like this. Let's all make a new start together, you, me and Bella. I don't know where we're going,' then forcing herself to say it, 'I'd expected we would talk about it this evening when Christian was here too. Stay here, Sophie, let's work it out together. I have to be out of here in a fortnight, but we don't need to wait as long as that. Everything's sorted up and labelled, there's so much the Laidlaws want to keep. Handing over to people who appreciate everything makes it so much easier. Say something, Sophie, say you'll make a fresh start with Bella and me.'

'I don't want to stay here. As if I'd go away with you and the daughter of that—that—hateful sex-driven beast. I hate him, I hate all of you.' Oh but what a rasping cruel way to shout at Miss Westlake. 'This isn't my home any more, it's not a proper home at all since Mums and Pops have gone. It's just a house, *your* house, the place where you behaved so disgustingly with your own brother-in-law, flattering yourself that he was as besotted as you. Well, now you know. He wasn't. Not with you, not even with me—although that was different, at least he wanted to marry me—probably not even with Dulcie once he's amused himself with her for a while. I used to think you were such a good person, I used to want to be like you. Not now, though. You'd sell your soul if anyone wanted it. You threw yourself at my husband—well, don't imagine he would have looked at you even for a minute if you hadn't had money to pay off that woman. You were going to find somewhere to live together, you say. And who was going to pay for it? *You* of course.'

'Hush, Sophie. You don't mean these things. Please, Sophie, stay here with us, don't be on your own. Forget all these last months, we'll make a new beginning, no Dulcie, no Christian—'

'You think that's what I want? If you want to lumber yourself with his illegitimate brat, that's your funeral.'

'What will you do?' Lydia said, just as if she hadn't heard Sophie's cruel words. 'You can't go on living there on your own.'

'I'll do what I like. You hear me? What *I* like, not what other people think is good for me. Pity a train doesn't come and get me like it did Mums and Pops. That's what I wish.'

'Perhaps she'll come back.'

Bella frowned, puzzled. Perhaps who would come back? Miss Westlake's mother? But that was silly. So who?

'And if she did, if she finds him as revolting as I did and leaves him, I suppose that's what you hope, so that he could come crawling back to you, I expect you'd welcome him with open arms until the next time. You know what, Lydia Westlake? You are worse than that whore whose child you say you've adopted. At least she was honest, she charged for her favours. But you feed him, house him—and beg him to share your empty bed.'

'Stop it, Sophie. I expect you're right, I expect I let him see how much I wanted him, I expect I'd welcome him back. But then, you see, I love him. That's something you never did.'

'Then you're a fool. Never love anyone. If you do, you get hurt. You know what? I used to think I loved you—oh, not like I love Dulcie, not that sort of love. I used to look up to you as being so good. But I've learned. Everyone in the village used to think you were such a fine person, such an example of good living. Now you have to sell Drydens and run away before anyone realises you're pregnant. You'll be a rich woman, Lydia. But money won't buy you happiness. I'm surprised it didn't buy *him*, though, he must have got *really* bored with you to give up all that comfort.'

'Go home, Sophie. We can't talk tonight. I'm truly sorry about Dulcie.'

'Liar! You're sorry he's gone off with someone else, but I bet you're glad to see the back of Dulcie. If you think she made me fall in love with her, if you think she was the one to lead the way, then you're wrong.' Her voice broke on a croak; she turned away so that her back was towards Lydia. 'I wish it had been. But it was *me*. With him I hated it all, then suddenly I understood why. Don't know—never did know—if it meant the same to her as it did to me or if she was just being kind. I prayed for her to love me like I did her. Thought of her all the time, wanted to be with her, to make her as happy as she made me. Go on, tell me I disgust you!'

'You know you don't. Sophie, please don't let's part like this.'

'Doesn't matter,' Sophie snorted, while from upstairs Bella watched her, not understanding but feeling angry and impotent that her dear Miss Westlake could be spoken to like that and she could do nothing but stand by and listen. 'I don't care what you think. And when he gets tired of Dulcie and comes crawling back to you, don't imagine it's because he cares. There's only one person he loves and that's himself. Wish he'd been killed like Pops and Mums.' And with that she pushed her bicycle into the lane, leaving the gate swinging on its hinges. As she rode away they could still hear the wrenching sound of her sobbing. Then there was nothing but silence.

Coming back into the house, Lydia closed the front door, leaning against it. As if the crumpled letter were still in front of her, in her mind's eye she could see Dulcie's carefully penned writing: '... telling you I worked longer hours so that I could go to Christian's rooms...'; '... no man had ever touched me, I tried to believe what you and I had was what I wanted. But now I can't put the thought of him out of my mind. Dear, sweet Sophie, I am so sorry'; 'He will be away on business for a few days—and he must have purposely told me where he's staying, knowing that I would be there for him. I'm frightened, I'm excited, and yet I feel like a traitor knowing that what I am doing will hurt you. I believe I would go to the end of the earth with him, yet it hurts to think of you and know that I'm failing you. Forgive me.'

Lydia's mind raced. What if Sophie hadn't come here this evening? I would have waited, expecting him, trusting him. I ought to be grateful. Dear God, help me, help me to be strong, help me to see ahead and build a life where he can have no place. But no, that's not possible. Bella…and not just Bella…tonight I planned to tell him about being a month overdue. Now I can tell no one. Miss Westlake is pregnant with her lover's bastard child; that good, clean-living spinster with an illegitimate offspring. Help me to think straight, to see what has to be done and to have the courage to do it.

Whether she'd stood leaning against the closed door for seconds or minutes she had no idea; her eyes had been closed, time had lost its meaning. It wasn't until she heard a movement on the stairs that she became aware of her surroundings.

'I heard what she told you, Miss.' All Bella's recently acquired confidence had forsaken her; once more she was the unloved waif who'd been taken to the orphanage for shelter. 'You haven't got to worry about me, Miss, honest. Course you won't want to keep me now, now that the slippery sod's done it again. Honest, I understand.'

'What? Not keep you? Bella, I thought we were friends.' Forgetting her own misery, in that moment Lydia thought just of the child. 'You heard what Sophie said, so yes, he's done it again. More like last time than he knows, too.'

'Why? Cos of me, you mean? Cos those people at the orphanage said I could come home with you?'

Lydia shook her head. There was a feeling of unreality about the situation, about this conversation with a girl young enough to be her daughter.

'He ran out on Norah when he heard she was pregnant. I hadn't told him, I hardly know myself, but I'm sure it must be true.' She held out her hand to the girl, who still stood halfway down the stairs. 'We have to make plans, Bella, you and me. It looks as though, even without him, we are going to be a family after all.'

'A baby! 'struth! And him gone off just like he did last time. People won't half get their tongues around a bit of gossip like that when you begin to show and there's you, still "Miss Westlake". Won't you mind, Miss?'

'To be truthful, I don't know how much I'll mind. At the moment I truly believe I wouldn't give a jot what people said. But when the time comes, that may not be true. My parents were always regarded highly, somehow I'd feel I was failing them if I gave rise to gossip. But we shan't be in Kingshampton, Bella. If only poor Sophie would come with us…'

'Poor Sophie be blowed. She don't deserve sympathy, talking to you like I just heard. But, Miss, you said about making plans. Do you mean I can stay?'

'I thought we were going to be a family. Of course you stay.'

'I thought…when I heard what she told you about him scarpering…I thought I'd get sent packing…'cos of being his daughter, I mean. I wouldn't blame you, Miss, honest, I don't want you to take me in cos you've told them back at the home that you will—and not cos you know how I wanted to get away from being like in prison there either. I told you before, I don't want pity. I just want a chance to do things for myself. I may be not quite fourteen yet but I seen more of life than most kids have, I know the sort you can trust and the sort you have to give a wide berth to. What I thought was that you might let me stay with you until my birthday in a few weeks, then I'll be old enough to get a job and look after myself. But of course with a baby on the way I expect you got more to worry about than me.' Her words poured out as if she had no power to stop them.

'Bella, Bella,' Lydia raised her hand, 'didn't I say we had

plans to make?—plans that involve you and me, and later on, unless I'm much mistaken, a baby too. But for the moment it'll be just the two of us. We needn't think about a third for months—and by that time we shall be settled. I was just starting to get a meal ready, come down and help and we'll talk as we work.' How it tore at her heart to make her voice ring with eagerness. Why had he done it? He must have been bored with her—friends, partners, lovers, mates…the words echoed and re-echoed. Surely he'd meant it when he'd said it, and surely if the flame had dimmed she would have been aware. Or would she? Was she so besotted with him, did she live so utterly for the hours he was with her, that she'd let herself believe what she wanted to believe? Don't think about him, don't let yourself remember. Just look at Bella, poor neglected Bella; see that look of hope in her eyes, eyes so like his. Mum always said that the surest way to find happiness was to give it to others. Mum, do you know what's happened to us all? How can you find eternal peace when Sophie and I are so divided, when for both of us the world has fallen apart? In giving happiness to someone else you find it for yourself. But wanting to give it to Bella goes much deeper than that. I want to protect her, I want her to know security and love, not for my own sake and, if I'm honest, not even entirely for hers, but for his too. His daughter, his genes alive in her. And this other life, one that is no more than a shadowy hope, his child, flesh of his flesh, a legacy of those glorious weeks. I should go down on my knees and thank God for giving me this new beginning. With no hint of where her thoughts had carried her in those few seconds, she took Bella's hand in her own. 'I'll show you how to prepare the sprouts—or do you know?' to which Bella shook her head, 'and I'll finish the bread sauce. All right?'

It was so 'all right' that Bella was lost for words.

The evening was to have been a celebratory affair. When Lydia had prepared the roasting hen for the oven she had been uncertain whether the meal would have been shared just with Christian or whether Bella might be there too. Whatever the Board of Governors' decision, she and Christian would have had cause for celebration, for she'd promised herself that this evening she would tell him about her belief that they were to have a child. Now, though, she turned her back firmly on what might have been and concentrated on making the evening something special, to leave a lasting impact on Bella.

'Have I got to go back to that rotten school, Miss?' Somehow in Bella's ears just 'Miss' sounded more personal than 'Miss Westlake'. Never in her life had she tasted a meal so wonderful, and it was hard to keep her eyes from wandering to the trifle that stood waiting on a small occasional table in the drawing room where they had put up the gate-leg table near the fire. Everything was so perfect that she could almost make herself believe Lydia would say she needn't wait until her birthday before she gave up going to classes.

'You'll have to go to school, Bella.' Lydia saw some of the wonder fade from Bella's expression. 'In fact, it's not up to me to say you can or you can't; it's the law. But it won't be a school in Kingshampton.'

'It's only a few weeks till I'll be fourteen.' Hope refused to be banished.

'And where shall we be by that time? Plans, that's what we promised ourselves. But first, can you eat some more chicken? There's lots of everything left.' But of course there was, her heart cried, as the image refused to be ignored of how this evening might have been.

'Crumbs, I'm really stuffed. If I don't, will we have it again tomorrow? It was better than I ever thought food could be. Do you reckon, Miss, that while we're stuffing ourselves till we hardly got room to fill the cracks with some of that lovely-looking pudding, do you reckon there are people—probably lots of kids too—with their tummies rumbling away and nothing to put in them?'

'Yes, Bella, I'm sure there are. It wouldn't do any of them any good for you to say you mustn't enjoy your food because they haven't enough; all we can any of us do is try and help them when we can—give to those poor men playing their instruments in the streets or trying to earn some pennies cleaning your shoes in town, there are so many of them, poor souls. Probably they have children at home, like you say. Mum—my Mum—used to say that if each one of us did what we could in our own small corner then the world would turn more smoothly.'

'She sounds like a nice Mum.'

'The best. Let's carry these dishes out to the kitchen and bring the plates for the trifle. And while we're eating it we can start to think about where we go from here.' Did she hear a scarcely audible 'Cor, crumbs,' as Bella followed her with the remains of the chicken.

They sat up late on that first night. It was an evening so different from the one that had filled Lydia's dreams and yet there was truth in what Adelaide had taught her. As the hands of the clock slowly turned, the tinkling bell-like tone of its chime drawing their attention to each passing quarter of an hour, she was aware of a growing ease in Bella's manner. Not once did she correct the child's frequent grammatical lapses anymore than she did the language that might have passed unnoticed in a public bar and was a constant reminder of the sort of company Norah Knight had kept. Time and environment would be Bella's teacher and Lydia was sure she was bright enough to be a quick learner.

'The new owners of this house are moving in the week after next,' Lydia said. 'Things are pretty well in order for them, I've been sorting and labelling up for weeks. There's nothing to keep us here, the sooner we move on, the better. We'll leave here tomorrow.' There! She said it! She wouldn't wait here day after day, looking out of the window, listening for the sound of his motor cycle, imagining him with Dulcie. What could he possibly have in common with Dulcie Fulbrook? Friends, partners, colleagues, lovers, true mates…she mustn't let herself think of it, she must make herself deaf to the sound of his voice in her head. She wasn't a fool, she knew there had been plenty of women in his life in the past and probably always would be; but to take Dulcie away with him was something quite different. Had he done it to spite Sophie? 'Tomorrow's Sunday,' she pulled her thoughts up sharply and managed to instil something akin to eagerness into her tone, 'there are fewer trains on a Sunday. But we'll telephone to the station and ask for a taxi-cab to collect us from here. We'll not make any firm plan until after that, we'll just go as far as London. We can stay a night or two there, do some shopping, both of us get some new clothes, then we'll be ready for our fresh start.'

'Phew!' At least it was a change from the usual 'Crumbs'. 'Tell you what we'll be like, Miss, we'll be like chrysalises when they shed their skins and find they're butterflies.' Lydia laughed, almost forgetting her own problems at the sight of

Bella's face. 'And then what, Miss? You said we'd be off to somewhere different.'

'Oh yes, so we will, Bella. But sufficient unto the day. We'll decide on the next step when we've turned into butterflies—although I somehow think I shall find I'm more of a humble moth.'

'Oh no you won't be, Miss. Honest, you could get some nice things to wear. You know what I think? I think being tall is *grand*. You could look like a duchess.'

Was it only in Lydia's imagination that she felt a shock at the unexpectedness of the description? 'You look like a duchess.' Even then had he been spending his daytime hours with Dulcie? All the times when she'd watched for him, listened for the sound of his motor cycle, had he been with Dulcie? But what could they have in common? Yet compare the two of us, Lydia's honesty prompted, what normal, sex-driven man wouldn't rather be in bed with her than me? There's nothing feminine about me, no soft warm flesh. I'm as strong as an ox, I'm like that 'damned awful hat' I used to wear and never knew he hated till that night he told me. I'm functional, hard-wearing. I was hungry, starving, for all the joy he brought to me. I never tried to hide it from him, I wanted us to share every act, every thought, every second of wild joyous abandon. And all the time he was just obliging the poor sex-starved old maid that I was? Was? And will be again? No, it can never be the same again, now even that is taken from me, always I'll remember how it was for us, always I'll be reminded that he preferred someone else.

'Oh Miss, don't you want us to do it? Please, don't look like that. You're crying.'

Happiness comes to you if you give it to others. And

wasn't this evidence of the truth of it? Her hot tears seemed to have killed Bella's new-found certainty; again she was lost and floundering.

'It's not that. Yes, I want us to go away together and make a new life. It's not because of that.' Lydia took out her man-size handkerchief and rubbed it hard across her eyes, then blew her nose. 'Better now, Bella, I'm so sorry, don't know what came over me. Not really a crying type.'

'I know you aren't. You can tell the sort who blub easy, can't you? No, you cry cos it's something important. First you have a row with your sister, then we talk about going off from the place where you've always lived, not just the excitement of having a new beginning but you got me to be—well, I know you say I'm not, but to have to worry about me and school and all that, well, course I'm a sort of encumbrance, like Norah said.' At some stage while she talked she'd come around the small table and was kneeling at Lydia's side.

'Without you there would be no purpose in any of it,' Lydia told her, 'and no fun or excitement either.'

'Then I know what it is. It's *him*, that's what's upsetting you, isn't it? Rotten sod, he is. Trouble is, you can't put him out of your mind while you're lumbered with me, you say I even look like him. Don't know why you want to be both ered with me at all. We talk about making a new start, but me, I'm just a leftover from what you'd be much better to forget.'

'No, Bella. That isn't true. I don't want to forget him, I never want to forget any of it. You call him a rotten sod, but you wouldn't if you knew him. He let Norah down, I know he did, he was young and probably frightened.'

'You know what? It's not that that gets my back up about him. It's because he's treated you rotten. Fact is, he's buggered up your life and mine too cos he doesn't care tuppence about anyone but himself.'

'Try not to hate him, Bella. Perhaps now you'll never have a chance to know him, so try and believe and trust what I say. I thought he and I would be together for always—and now I know we shan't. But he gave me more happiness in these last few months than I knew possible. If it had been the same for him, then he would still have been here. So it couldn't have been; it must have been me who failed. And he won't find real happiness with Dulcie Fulbrook, of that I'm certain. I just pray—yes, I mean that, I honestly do pray that someday, somewhere he'll know the sort of joy he gave to me.'

'Well,' Bella knelt back on her heels, her shoulders very straight, 'if I been wrong and he's not all bad, then he must be soft in the head. I don't know this Dulcie What's 'ername, she may be as pretty as Mary Pickford or clever as—as—crumbs, I don't know any clever names, but you know what I mean—whatever she's like he's plain daft to choose her when he could have had you.'

Even though her eyes still stung with tears, this time Lydia laughed.

'Bless you, Bella. I truly wish things could have worked out the way he and I were planning. You would have been so proud to know he was your father.'

'Huh! Dunno about that. If you like, Miss, I can wash up the supper things. You stay in here by the fire.'

'No, we'll do them together. Then bed. We have a busy day ahead of us tomorrow.'

'Cor! Can't believe I'm not going to wake up and find I'm

back in that prison of a place. A new start, a new life.' Determined to do her bit, Bella loaded the tray and led the way to the kitchen. 'We can't pretend he doesn't exist, though, can we? Not with you thinking you might be having his kid. So what can we do?'

What indeed, Lydia thought, trying to make some sort of a shape of a future when she would make them outcasts of society by giving birth to an illegitimate child. But Bella's mind was moving more constructively. 'I'll tell you how we gotta make ourselves think. We gotta look on him as a part of what's gone, gone and got lost, I mean (easy for me, cos I never even clapped eyes on him).'

'You're so like him. And nothing will stop me feeling the way I do about him. When we used to talk about going away and making a fresh start we knew there was no chance that we could ever marry.'

'Don't know much about divorces, but some people do get rid of their marriages like that, don't they? If he really meant the things he said, then why couldn't he have done that? Doesn't that pretty sister of yours have a sweetheart?'

'No. But somehow none of that mattered. He was going to buy me a gold ring, and even though he couldn't marry me he would give me his name and we would,' her voice broke on what Bella wasn't sure was a laugh or a battle against more tears, 'would live happily in sin together for the rest of our days. I thought he meant it. I'm *sure* he meant it at the time.'

Bella dumped the tray on the kitchen table and turned to look at Lydia, the movement and the serious expression in her dark eyes adding weight to what she said.

'Then you know what we gotta do, Miss—first thing when

we get up to London we got to go to a jewellery shop—or even Woolworths, cos I seen plain gold-coloured rings in Woollies—and buy you a pretend wedding ring like what he'd said. We're going to be a family—and if he doesn't want to be part of it then that's his loss. You'll be Mrs Mellor and, like we said when you got me from the orphanage, I'll be Bella Mellor (crumbs, don't half sound a mouthful). And when we have our baby, it'll be Mellor like it should be with him for a father. We'll have to say he's gone. Got himself killed in an accident just a week or so ago? Would that do?'

'No! Oh no, Bella. I couldn't say that about him. It's like tempting fate.'

'Then we'll have to say he's sloped off with someone else.'

'Yes, we'll say that. No good comes out of making up lies, we'll tell the truth—at least as near the truth as we can. He left me before he knew about the baby.'

The future began to take shape.

Once the meal was cleared away, more than willingly Bella went up to bed. She could hardly wait to put on the long-sleeved pure silk nightdress that used to be Sophie's and to climb into a bed such as she'd never slept in before. Already she'd pushed her hand between the crisp, white sheets and let it sink into the comfort of the feather mattress. She longed to lie there, wide awake, absorbing the atmosphere; but for all her eagerness not to waste a precious second, she was soon lulled into sleep.

Downstairs, out of sheer habit Lydia banked up the kitchen range for the night, the action bringing home to her that this was the last time it would burn through until morning and, this time, smoulder on until there was nothing but cold ash and cinders. With both hands gripping the wooden mantelpiece above the range, she rested her face against her arm. All her bravado vanished. Misery was a physical thing, it ached in her arms and legs, it felt like a leaden weight in her chest, it took away all power of logical thought.

Always practical, always dependable, yet in those moments she felt she was throwing away everything that had been her world. Mum…Dad…Sophie…Ethel…that's how it used to be. And me…what was I? Frumpy, reliable Miss Westlake, a future as certain as the changing seasons as I moved through the years in the easy rut that was my life. If he hadn't come to Kingshampton, none of that would have changed. Sophie would have married one of her many admirers, all of them as malleable as putty in her hands, not one who would have expected more of her than she was prepared to give…but for Sophie could there ever have been happiness in marriage to anyone? I don't understand, I don't want to think about it. Not about her and all the bitter things we have said. What a way for Sophie and me to end up. No, for us this can't be the end, I won't let it be. Tomorrow I'll get the taxicab to come early so that I can go and see her just once more. We can't part like this. And Mum and Dad, what peace, what everlasting peace can they find if they know that we can't mend the rift?

She raised her head and looked round the room, a room so familiar that normally she didn't consciously see it. Ghosts from the past, moments of laughter, moments of tears, some as far back as her memory carried her, all of them jostled in her mind. Now she was walking away from it, looking for a new life as if it was waiting out there to be discovered. Nothing comes from nothing, there had to be a goal. She knew what she'd believed it to be, with *him* she'd known just what she was looking for. Yes, and she would have found it too. I'm sure—her thoughts ran out of control—yes, I'm *positive* he meant the things he said, and those glorious hours of love, not just the final moments that were out of our control and which were almost too much to bear, but before that, him knowing every inch of my body just as I did his (even if he was spending his time with Dulcie Fulbrook, even if he was going to bed with her while I waited here for him), I *know* that what we shared meant the same to him as it did to me. Or am I being a fool? I'm inexperienced and naive, no man had ever so much as given me a second glance. Lydia Mellor, that's what Bella says I should call myself. And so I will. I will make myself a mother to his first child and I will bear his second (Second? Yes, second. I won't let myself even imagine there might be others), and that way he will always be a part of my life.

With the decision came a new strength. If they were to set out in the morning she had things to do.

The bedrooms were cold, but once started on her task nothing deterred her. Moving as quietly as she could, she lifted the first empty portmanteau on to her parents' bed and started to pack the things she meant to take. Each ornament held a memory, each picture brought back the visit to the photographer's studio. Adelaide's jewellery box was laid carefully on top of her Persian lamb coat. It was as Lydia was putting the little key into her pocket that temptation got the better of her and she remembered the last time she had unlocked the box. 'You look like a duchess.' Again came the echo from that magic evening. But when she lifted the lid, it wasn't the pearls her hand reached out to. Another memory: the three of them in the hospital, Sophie, Christian and her, the Sister carefully putting Adelaide's brooch and wedding ring into a packet, sealing it and passing it to her. Her mother's wedding ring. Mum, is that what I should do? Would you see it as wrong to use your ring to base my life on a lie? No, you'd know it's not like that. You'd understand. Surely it's better than doing what Bella suggested and going to Woolworths—or even a proper jeweller and pretending I'd lost my original one. No, this must be the right thing to do. Is it silly, over-emotional and stupid, for me to feel like this, as if wearing Mum's ring is a sign that this new life I'm making for Bella and myself isn't cut off from the past? She slipped the ring on her long finger, grateful that her mother's hands had been much the same as her own. Yes, it fitted reasonably well. Wasn't that a sign?

In the silence of the night she heard the tinkling chime of the drawing-room clock and then the strokes of the hour. Two o'clock. There was still packing to do and letters to write: one to the estate agent, instructing him to collect her rents—with the exception of the house occupied by Ethel and her sister—and to hold the money until he had details of her new bank, and one to Ethel, enclosing a spare key in the envelope, asking her to come to Drydens to make sure everything was in readiness for the Laidlaws. After that there was no excuse; she had to face what was left of a lonely night full of aching misery.

Bella's worldly goods had gone no further than the clothes she had left the orphanage wearing, and her drawing things. Clearly it would have been useless for Lydia to lend her anything of hers to wear, but fortunately when Sophie had married she had left behind anything she had seen as functionally boring. Some of her cast-offs had been given to the church jumble sale, but there were still items of nightwear and undergarments she hadn't considered pretty enough to be part of her trousseau. Thrifty and practical, Adelaide had left them in her drawers in case the time ever came when she might need them; and when Adelaide had gone, Lydia let them remain; to do anything less would have seemed like playing into the hands of an already unkind fate. So Bella had slept in the silk nightgown that made her feel like a princess.

First thing in the morning she packed Sophie's left-behind underwear into the case Lydia had brought to her room. Ready for 'the new life', Bella looked in wonder at her reflection.

'Phew,' she breathed, barely audibly as, alone in her room, she paraded in front of the pier glass, turning first one way, then the other. The dark brown velvet dress with its Puritan-like coffee-coloured lace collar hung too loosely on her thin frame, but the shorter length Sophie had so delighted in made the dress a perfect length for her. Never in her life had she worn anything so luxurious; she ran her hands down the material, marvelling at its richness, its softness. Soft as a kitten, she mouthed silently. Just look at me, *me*, *Sybella Knight*, who'd have thought I could be living all this? New life, that's what Miss Westlake says, and so it is, it's a new everything. Crumbs, I wish Norah could have a look at how I am now. Bet she thinks I'm working in a kitchen somewhere—no, bet she doesn't think about it at all. And why should she? How often do I wonder how she's getting on? Course I hope she's fallen on her feet, and without me tagging along I expect some chap'll see she's set up comfy enough. That's what she always told me, except for being lumbered with me things would have been different for her. And now that I'm making myself think about her, I honestly do hope things are going all right; but if I'm honest, most of the time she doesn't come into my thoughts at all. Just imagine now—now, this minute—there was a knock at the door and there she was, come to get me. I wish I knew how to pray, properly I mean, like the vicar did in the church where I had to go with the other kids from the home. All those long words and Thees and Thous. If I just asked God straight out, same as if I would if He were a proper person, I wonder whether it would be any good at all. Perhaps He only listens if you talk posh like the vicar did and keep curtseying and all that. Well, look, no one can see me, I'll just have a go. Can't do no harm.

'How are you getting on, Bella?' came Lydia's voice from downstairs. 'The taxi will be about ten minutes.'

'Just getting my coat on, Miss.' Cor, but it's like a wonderful dream. Well, for me it is. Miss Westlake's been let down really rotten, but we'll be all right, it's got to be up to us to look after things. I've gotta—I've *got to*, in her mind she remembered to make the correction—got to see things go right for her, for us both. And I *will*, just see if I don't.

She put on a dark green coat trimmed with fur, with a matching hat. Right from the start Sophie had disliked it, so there it had hung in the wardrobe, unloved and unworn. On that Sunday morning, it came into its own.

'You look very smart, Bella.' Lydia smiled at her as she came down the stairs. 'And the dress, did that fit?'

'Cor, Miss, I never touched anything so soft. Won't your Sophie mind if I borrow it? We don't know when I'll be able to give it back to her.'

'She won't want it back, she told me to get rid of the things she'd left here. But I never did, it seemed so final. Providence must have made me keep them. And the hat and coat, they've had almost no wear; Mum and I bought them in the January sales in Brackleford before Sophie was married, knowing they were her size. But she said she didn't like the colour.'

Already Bella's opinion of Sophie had been far from high, looking down at the coat, it plummeted further.

'It's bea-u-ti-ful.' Each syllable pronounced separately as if such beauty demanded special attention to detail, Bella couldn't resist another glance in the mirror of the hallstand. The usual 'Crumbs' or even 'Phew' were silenced; somehow they weren't in keeping with the young lady whose bright-eyed reflection looked back at her.

Lydia and the driver carried the portmanteau to be strapped on the back of the taxi-cab while Bella struggled manfully with two heavy leather suitcases.

'The London train comes through at ten minutes to midday,' the driver said as he climbed behind the wheel, 'you've plenty of time and to spare.'

'Good. Thank you. I want you to stop for a minute or two in Meadowlands on the way,' Lydia heard herself answer, trying to focus on what lay before her. But her mind seemed numb. 'Wait, wait just a moment,' and already she was reaching to open the door, 'I think I've forgotten something. Wait here, Bella.' Her heart was racing, she felt the breath was being forced out of her as she blundered back up the path to the front door and let herself into the silent house, shutting the front door behind her and leaning against it, her eyes closed. The very air she breathed here in the hall conjured up ghosts. A new life, a fresh start, that's what she and Bella were making. And Bella depended on her. So what was she doing, running back as if she could recapture all her yesterdays? Mum, Dad, Sophie, Ethel, the house seemed full of their spirits. Suddenly and uncharacteristically she was frightened. She had no end goal; ahead of her was a wall of fog, she had no idea where she was heading.

'Christian,' she murmured, 'it wasn't going to be like this.'

If he'd been with her, if instead of just Bella and her there had been the three of them, would the old house with all its memories have been so hard to leave? It took all her willpower to stand tall, to cast one quick glance around her then, pulling her hat more firmly on to her head (yet another hat that Christian might well have considered 'damned awful'), chin up, she hurried back to the waiting taxi-cab.

'You all right, Miss?' Bella whispered.

'Yes. I forgot a letter I'd written, I want to post it in the post box at the station.'

First, though, she had to see Sophie.

But when they arrived at the house in Meadowlands, its garden tidy and weed-free (thanks largely to Dulcie), there was no reply to her knock. In desperation, she tore first one page and then a second out of the little notebook she always carried in her handbag, then, using the front door as a firm base, started to write.

Sophie, please, please try and understand. Selling the house doesn't mean memories don't matter. They do. You do. Soon I'll write. When I know where we shall be living I'll write and you'll come to stay. It'll be like old

times. Nothing between us can ever really change. I
loved—still do love—him, but you didn't want him so I
didn't steal what was yours. He didn't love either of us.
Soon it will be over with Dulcie. If that's where your
happiness lies, then I pray she comes home to you.
God bless you and make you happy again. Lyddy.

She pushed both small pages through the letterbox and hurried back to the waiting cab. At the railway station she posted her other letter, this time addressed to Ethel, asking her to take anything she and Sophie wanted from Drydens marked in readiness for the auctioneers.

They spent two days in London, living in a small hotel in Bayswater, each of them rehearsing for their new roles. There was no logic in the comfort Lydia found in wearing Adelaide's wedding ring, just as she did in hearing Bella become more at ease in calling her 'Mum'; but logic wasn't at the forefront of their minds as they shopped, looked at timetables, sat in the reference rooms of public libraries dipping into books describing various districts of the country. When something caught the eye of either of them, she would nudge the other and point to the sentence or paragraph, obeying the stark notice over the door: STRICT SILENCE AT ALL TIMES. With so much to say, silence was frustrating so, once out in the cold air, they found double the pleasure in hunting for their new wardrobes.

'Tell you what, Mis—Mum,' Bella corrected herself, 'tell you what you ought to do. I reckon you'd feel like a different person if you went to the barber and had your hair done. You got real nice hair, thick and shiny. The barber would know the way you ought to wear it. Then we could go to the hat shop and kit you out with some new stuff. But…well, here's me telling you what you ought to be splashing out on, but I don't know if you've got that sort of money. When you know you haven't got a chance of doing things, it's a sort of game you get used to playing, deciding what would be a good sensible thing to do. And it would, honest it would. If you looked in the looking glass and saw yourself looking changed, then you'd find it easier to leave Miss Westlake behind and be Mrs Mellor.'

'I know you're right, Bella. But…well, I've never been inside a hairdresser's, I've just let my hair grow long and once in a while cut an inch or so off the bottom. But a hairstyle…you mean have it cut short, or waved or something? I don't know.'

'I don't know either, not about what they'd say you ought to have done. But they know much more about it than we do. And I tell you one thing, one thing I know to be true. When I put on that lovely dress what used to be Sophie's, I looked in the glass and I didn't see the old me at all. I saw someone smart, the sort of person people speak to as if they matter. It would be the same for you. I don't mean you don't matter in any case, of course people speak to you with that sort of respect, doesn't matter what you wear. But *you'd* feel different inside. Let's do it, Mum.' Purposely Bella put emphasis on the name, 'Let's go to that place over the road and see what they think you ought to have done. It'll make you feel you're the new *you*.'

A surge of excitement swept through Lydia as they crossed the busy road where horses pulling delivery wagons or hansom cabs were outnumbered by motor vehicles. Today overtaking yesterday, Lydia thought, and so it would be for them.

* * *

It was two days later, in the small but busy seaside town of Deremouth in south Devon.

'I see there are new people in Nellie Turnbull's place. I just happened to be looking out of my window when that estate agent drew up in his motor car and they all got out.' Annie Wiffin had a local reputation of having eyes in the back of her head and an ear never far from the ground.

'Good, I'm glad Nellie's got someone straightaway, she'll be glad of the rent,' Nellie's neighbour answered. There was no need to ask for details, Annie liked nothing better than being the harbinger of news.

'A very well set up woman, or so I should imagine. Just her and a young girl, her daughter, I dare say. Both of them smart as paint.' Then, with a knowing nod of the head, 'Only a woman and child, no man. Probably a war widow, I shouldn't be surprised. Not easy for a woman to find herself a second man when she's lumbered with a family even if she was left well provided for—and, just between ourselves, she didn't look the sort of person the men would go flocking after. Tall, austere, you might say.'

'You've not spoken to her?' Meggie Wells egged her on.

'Not with the agent there. Later in the day I shall step across and offer her a hand of friendship. I dare say the poor soul could do with it. She can't have any friends around here or surely by now someone would have given her door a knock.'

'I dare say you've missed any callers there might have been. I've certainly seen nothing.' But then Meggie Wells hadn't Annie's natural aptitude for 'happening to glance across…'

'No, no one's been. I've been busy cleaning my front windows, then I changed the curtains in the bedroom. No, no one's come calling. Well, I'll not let the day end with no one to wish them well. And I dare say she'd like to know a bit about the owner of the place. When you live in someone else's house, use their furniture, you must wonder about them.'

Well intentioned or merely an interfering busybody, her hand of friendship did nothing to endear Lydia to her new and temporary surroundings in Station Hill.

'It's kind of you to call,' Lydia told her, 'but we don't intend to make a permanent home here. Tomorrow we shall start our search. Mr Davies from the agency is calling for us in the morning to take us to view various properties in the district.'

'The rent'll be high here, I dare say.' A hint might be enough to bring forth a confidence about the husbandless woman's situation. 'I dare say your husband is working away somewhere?' she ventured, when the first bait wasn't taken.

'No.'

'No husband. Oh dear, oh dear, that wicked war had a lot to answer for.'

'Indeed it did,' Lydia agreed. 'But thankfully we lost no one.' She heard herself being aloof to the point of rudeness, but the knowledge did nothing to soften her manner.

'Dear me. Lost him in illness, how hard that must be with a child to bring up. If you stay here Mrs—dear me, I don't think I caught your name?'

'Mellor. And this is my daughter, Bella.' Thick-skinned though Annie was, she couldn't pretend to herself that the information was given in friendship.

Taking Lydia's hand firmly in hers, Bella stood squarely in front of their uninvited visitor.

'My Dad's pushed off. But Mum and me are fine, so you don't need to go feeling sorry for us.'

'Oh dear, oh dear, the breadwinner deserted you. What a cruel world this has become. I blame the war, you know. Up until then everything was stable, we all knew where we were—our allotted place and we stayed in it. But four years of war tore up all the old roots. Look, my dear, the last thing I want to do is poke my nose, you'll find I'm never one for that, but there must be times when you want another woman to talk to and I'm only just over the way. Number fourteen. If we can't try and give a lift to each other in a time of trouble, then it's a wicked world indeed.'

'Indeed yes.' There was something almost regal in the way Lydia bowed her elegant head, her straight, dark hair trimmed to just below her shoulders then coiled into what the hairdresser called a French roll down the back of her head. Gone was the hard line around her forehead, the hair was no longer pulled tight; rather it was lifted into the coil, the appearance much more feminine. Left alone, it's doubtful if she would have had either the patience or the talent to effect such a transformation; but Lydia was no longer alone. Bella was a true artist: not only had she the eye to see beauty but also the skill to produce it. And the hairstyle was only part of the transformation. Buying clothes had always been a necessary evil for poor, plain Lyddy Westlake, but all that was changed. Unquestioningly she had followed Bella's guidance—just as she had in the purchase of garments for her new 'daughter', the first brand-new clothes the child had ever possessed. No wonder those days in London had had a headiness which seemed unrelated to reality.

'We're all right, Mum and me.' Bella eyed the visitor jealously. A woman to talk to! As if *she* wasn't the one to be important to Miss Westlake! Why couldn't the nosy old creep bugger off home and leave them alone? We don't need her, not her nor no one, we're all right, just the two of us. But did you hear what you said to her? You said 'Mum and me' and it came out easy as wink. I'm glad my rotten father pushed off, now I shan't have to try and call him Dad; when you say Dad you ought to feel sort of warm towards him. And I don't. I suppose it's wicked of me to be glad he's not here. I know that even when we laugh together, deep down inside she's crying. But it won't always be like that; I'll make her see that we don't need him or anyone else. Well, we'll need the baby when it comes. Phew, won't that be just grand. Mum, me and a baby.

'Now then, Mrs Mellor, what about you popping across to number fourteen tomorrow for a cup of tea? I could introduce you to some of the neighbours.'

'You're very kind,' Lydia answered, still as stiff as a ramrod, 'but we have no idea how long we shall be out viewing properties. And really, there is no point in the neighbours offering us friendship when our stay here will be so transitory. I believe tomorrow we may find what we're looking for.'

'Hoping for a rent are you? Not easy these days. You were lucky to fall on your feet with this place.'

'Indeed we were. It couldn't be more convenient.' She gave not an inch.

'Ah well, I can see you have plenty to do without having me take up your time. I'm sorry if I came at a bad moment.' Clearly the only thing she was sorry about was her lack of progress. 'A good house is up for rent in Thackeray Street, on the large side but with plenty of scope of lettings.' Hope died hard; still fishing for information, she put out one last feeler.

'I have details of various properties. We are going to sort them through this evening, aren't we, Bella.'

'We were just looking forward to getting on with it when you knocked at the door.' Bella left their visitor no alternative but to move towards the door.

'You see to the door, Bella, will you. Goodbye Mrs Wiffin, it was good of you to call to welcome us.'

They listened for the click of the front gate.

'Crumbs! D'you know what? You didn't sound a bit like the Miss Westlake from Kingshampton.'

'But I am, Bella. I am the same.'

'Course you are. You know that and I know it, but I bet that nosy parker thought you were real hoity-toity. It must be that posh hair-do and the new dress!'

Like naughty children who'd wriggled out of some misdemeanour, they started to laugh. Bella felt no guilt for the inhospitable way they'd treated their unwanted visitor: she saw the incident as proof of how easily they were slipping into their new situation. Lydia's sentiments were more complex: what was it her mother used to say? People who spend their time trying to mind other people's business have lives empty of interest. But in laughing with Bella, Lydia was building a protective barrier around her aching heart. In Bella's happiness she must find her own—and these last few days had been like a rebirth for both of them.

They spent the evening looking at the details the agent had left with them, imagining what the next day would bring. Lydia envied Bella her open excitement, she tried to match it and to pretend to herself that the aching loss wasn't there.

Where were they now? Was Dulcie with Christian, was he
making her his friend…lover…partner? No, no, Dulcie was
good-natured, hard-working, kind, but she could never be
those things to him. Lydia pulled her imagination away from
them. Think just of Sophie, unhappy, lonely Sophie. As soon
as they found the house they were looking for—and surely
they would recognise what was right for them—she would
write to her, make her understand what surely she really
knew: being sisters went much deeper than having the same
parents, being sisters stemmed from the sort of closeness she
and Sophie had always shared. And was it any different for
a natural mother and daughter? Surely the bond was more
than an accident of birth. When Bella had said, 'We're all
right, Mum and me,' she had known a deep sense of rightness. So the evening passed, followed by long and wakeful
hours of night for Lydia while every conceivable hurdle
teased her mind as she tried to envisage where they were
heading. In the next room, Bella's childlike trust never wa-
vered. Tomorrow, she thought as she drifted towards sleep,
Miss Westl—Mum—and me will see all around the countryside; of course we can't say what it is we're looking for,
cos we neither of us been here before. But we shall know, just
as soon as we clap eyes on the right place we shall know.

Next day Mr Davies, the agent, drove them from one disappointment to the next. By mid-afternoon even Bella's confidence was dented.

'There's just one more place I could show you. We've
only just received instructions, my secretary typed the details
before I came out this morning. But I don't want to raise your
hopes. Too big, too sprawling, and not in the sort of condition I know you would want.'

'We'll see it, anyway,' Lydia told him. A run-down house, probably the sort of place where once there had been servants, a luxury harder to come by since women had found there was more to life than domesticity.

'Some way out of town,' he warned her. 'Beyond Otterton St Giles and a mile or so inland, across the estuary. It won't interest you. I fear I am wasting your time.' Yours and mine too, he added silently. Now, if there'd been a sensible man with them, their accommodation would have been sorted out before midday. What more could they want than that good, sound, well-built house on the hill above Newton Abbot? But no, madam hardly gave it a glance. Well, if this one got the thumbs down, then he'd done. Let them try Masters and Clark and see if they could show them what they were after. All the hours of this day wasted, and not a brass farthing to show for it.

The none-too-well-sprung motor car bumped and jolted down the lane through Downing Wood, the winter-bare branches of the trees almost meeting in an arch above them. Then, just as they came to the edge of Otterton St Giles, they turned to the right on to what was little more than a track. A minute or two more and they saw the house.

'It's not what you're looking for,' he told them, by this time making no attempt to hide his irritation for his wasted day.

Climbing out of the motor car, Lydia and Bella looked at the house, then at each other. They needed no words. Hadn't Bella said that as soon as they saw it they would know?

CHAPTER ELEVEN

The trouble with women like this Mrs Mellor, Eric Davies the agent grumbled silently, was that they weren't prepared to make any compromise; they built up a picture in their minds of what they wanted, and expected him to be not only a thought-reader but a magician too. And that child, she was no better. 'We shall recognise it as soon as you take us there,' she'd told him, just as if he had nothing better to do with his day than drive them from one place to another while they hardly bothered to get beyond the front gardens. This was about the last thing he had to show them, Badgers' Holt, on a steep rise above the hamlet of Combydere—and what woman in her right mind would consider coming to such an isolated spot? Looking southward they could see the silver shimmer of the sea, some two or three miles away at Otter ton St Giles, but between Combydere and there, except for the leafless trees of Downing Woods, there was little except rolling hills populated by sheep. Oh well, he gave a mental sigh of resignation, best to get on with it. The sooner they told him it wasn't what they wanted, the sooner he could take them back to Deremouth and recommend they try Masters and Clark, his local rivals.

'Yes?' The pretty child was looking expectantly at her mother.

'I believe "yes".' The haughty-looking woman surprised him by turning to him with a smile that seemed to transform her long face.

There was no accounting for taste! In his opinion the house had little to commend it, it seemed to be held in a previous century. No doubt when it was built those attic rooms would have housed maids to carry coals and boil water on the kitchen range. But if this scrawny beanpole of a woman imagined she'd get girls to come and work out here, she had another think coming. In the days before the war girls from working backgrounds went into domestic service as a matter of course. Unless they came from families who could afford for them to live at home until some fellow married them, there were few opportunities, and for many of them getting a position in a good household was looked on as success. But times were different now; if a girl attended to her schoolwork, kept herself neat and tidy and was prepared to work hard, the field had widened. Yes, the war had opened their eyes and broadened their horizons. These days many clerks were women—as if there weren't more than enough men looking for work without having things made harder by employers liking the look of a pretty girl in his office, especially when he could get away with paying her less than he would have done a lad. Like the troubles that flew out of Pandora's box, once out there was no stuffing them back in again. So it was no use Mrs Mellor looking so set on what she saw on the outside of the house; give her a few minutes indoors and she'd come out looking as hang-dog as she had with all the others, for Badgers' Holt needed work done to it—and plenty more

work to keep it up to scratch. Mrs Mellor was hard to please
and, to be honest, he'd be glad to see the back of her; but he
recognised that she was no fool and she'd soon see the pit-
falls at Badgers' Holt.

'I've brought you here because it's the last thing I have to
show you. But you won't like it, of that I'm certain. It's stood
empty for over six months.'

'Empty, you say? Even the furniture gone?'

'Not a stick left. Some houses show themselves up well
without furniture. This one's in a bad state, nothing done for
years. Is it worth you wasting your time even going in?'

Bella laughed. 'You are funny, Mr Davies, talking like that
when you're supposed to be selling it.' She caught her bottom lip between her teeth as if she was holding back the
mirth that bubbled up within her.

'I'm a realist, Missie. I've shown you some good, sound
houses and they've not been right. So how can this one be
what you're looking for?'

'If it's empty you have no need to show us around—'
Lydia told him.

'There! I knew it'd be no use to you. Too large, too isolated.'

'You keep warm waiting in the motor car; just give me the
key. Bella and I will browse on our own.'

He watched them go, turning up the velvet collar on his
overcoat and settling his bowler hat more firmly on his head
as he prepared to wait. Not that it would take long for them
to see the uselessness of their inspection. He'd give them five
minutes at the most.

But he was wrong. They went into each room, looked out
of each window.

'Crumbs, Miss—Mum—phew, crumbs! A great big house like this must cost a mint of money.'

'It's been hard to sell. I don't think they'll refuse an offer. We said when we found it we'd know. Forget what my feelings are, Bella; just tell me yours.'

'Mine? It's you what's got to pay for it, you've got to be the one to say.'

'We both have to live in it. Mr Davies thinks we're mad, you can tell he does. But to me it feels *right*.'

'You know what I reckon? I reckon that's why no one has bought it and it's been empty and waiting like this for months. Cos it was waiting for us. Today is cold and miserable as anything, yet we both knew it was what we'd been looking for and couldn't find in all those smart places he'd shown us. Just think what it'll look like when it's springtime. Look across the hills, just lots of sheep. By about March there'll be little lambs too. Cor, pinch me. Go on, pinch me hard. It don't seem real that here I am, dressed in these posh things, all brand new. Cor, Mi—Mum, I wish some of the kids from the home could have a chance like you've given me.'

'What's right for you—for us—might not be right for them. Their lives will have a pattern too, Bella.'

'Hope so. Shall we go and have a look at the kitchen. All that nice cooking you do, I reckon it won't be posh like your kitchen at Drydens.'

In that she was right. The range was not only ancient, it was rusty and appeared never to have been introduced to black lead. The sink was grey stone. The only promising feature was the waste pipe. Where the water drained to, Lydia didn't like to imagine, but at least it gave her hope. The house was partly Georgian and partly Victorian, the original coach house large enough to hint that the household had kept two or three coaches, probably a carriage, a trap and a governess cart, sufficient for family use. The greenhouses had been erected in the kitchen garden some time later, but had weathered less well. Another outbuilding, part brick and part timber, was less easy to identify; Lydia believed that at one time it might have been some sort of workshop. They could have it demolished, for what would they want with a workshop? Approached from the yard outside the back door was a lavatory, presumably for the servants. On the ground floor was the stone-flagged kitchen and scullery, a panelled dining room, a large drawing room, a housekeeper's sitting room and a breakfast room; on the first floor, five bedrooms, leading from one of which was a smaller room. Perhaps long ago it had been the nursery section—or perhaps it had been the main bedroom and dressing room. There was one lavatory on that floor but no sign of a bathroom; then up again to three attic rooms under sloping ceilings.

'You know what I wish?' Bella said, gazing around her as Lydia relocked the front door with a large and heavy key.

'I'd guess that you wish we could jump ahead, say, three months and be living here. Am I right?'

'Cor, yes, that would be best of all. But what I was wishing was that we didn't have to wait all that time in Deremouth with Mrs Nosy-Parker keeping an eye on us. Wouldn't it be good,' and this time remembering in time and seeming to emphasise the name, 'Mum, if we could get somewhere in that place down the hill. Comb-something-or-other he called it. Then we could keep walking up here and looking at it, planning how it's going to be.'

Bella knew all about dreams, they had been her constant

companions. Now as she put her thoughts into words (an experience that was new to her) she had no realistic expectation that such a thing might be possible. But she underestimated Lydia.

'We'll make an offer on the house—and if I have to pay the price that's being asked then I will, but it needs a lot spent on it and I think they ought to accept a fair offer. Next we have to find people to undertake the work. I want a new range, one that will heat hot water like Dad had put in at Drydens. One of those bedrooms must be turned into a bathroom. And that sink is quite disgusting, we'll have a porcelain sink in the kitchen. Lighting? There'll be no chance of gas out here. At home Dad had electricity brought into the house, perhaps we can and perhaps we can't out here.'

'Tell you what, though, Mum. I wouldn't care if we never had nothing but lamps like they must have used before. Just being here, that's what matters.'

Lydia felt a tug of affection for the starry-eyed girl. There was nothing new in that, she had been drawn to her from the first, but she was honest enough to admit that was because in caring for Bella she felt she still had part of Christian in her life. In that moment, though, the love that tugged her had nothing to do with him, nothing to do with anyone except themselves. A wave of joy washed over her, joy in this new chance to make something worthwhile of her life. In giving happiness, so you find it. If only her mother had been here with them, and seen for herself the road she was taking. Could she see? Did she know and understand? *Me*, sober Lydia Westlake, look at me now! Pregnant with one illegitimate child, mothering another, and both of them because no matter what he does, no matter how much of a womanising roué he is, I love him.

'Wake up, Mum, you were daydreaming same as I do.' Bella tugged her hand.

An hour later they were back in Mr Davies's office, and his typist was writing a letter to the inheritor of Badgers' Holt.

The next morning Lydia and Bella took a taxi-cab from outside Deremouth Station and were driven the five miles or so to Combydere.

'Can you come over and collect us later on?' she asked the driver as she paid him, making sure the tip was sufficient to make him agree. 'Let's say, from this spot at four o'clock this afternoon.' It wasn't quite eleven and she was committing them to five winter hours in a hamlet that could be viewed in not much more than so many minutes.

Combydere nestled at the foot of a long and steep hill at the top of which, beyond the view of the cluster of houses that made up the community, poor neglected Badgers' Holt stood in solitary splendour. Dotted across the hill a flock of sheep nibbled half-heartedly at the grass, unaware of the interest taken in them by the newcomers.

'Funny-looking sheep,' Bella observed. 'Look at their coats. Did you ever see a sheep with a coat like that? I never,' then, correcting her grammatical lapse, 'I never did.'

Lydia hid a smile. Bella was showing herself to be quick to learn.

'Such long fleece, not tight and woolly like they usually are.'

'People have sheepskin rugs, don't they? Don't reckon I'd fancy that long, hairy stuff on the floor.' Then, catching hold of Lydia's hand, 'What we gonna do now we're here—Mum? I wish Mr Davies had given you that key to keep, we could have gone inside and got on with making plans.'

'We've got all day. And we'll have to keep moving or we'll freeze. Let's walk around the village—if you can call it a village, there doesn't seem to be much of it. Perhaps it used to have more people than it does now; the church looks too big for a community this size.'

'It's got two public houses so there must be enough people to keep them going. Once a church is built it'll go on standing there even if no one goes to it, but a pub is different. That has to sell enough or it would close down.' Then, with a giggle that showed just how much she was enjoying their outing, 'Perhaps they're a lot of what Norah used to call "boozed-up sots".'

'Christian always said that the best place to find all the local gossip was the inn. So, Bella, that's where we shall go.'

'What, inside you mean? Cor! I never been right in before. When I was little, too little to stay back at home by myself, Norah used to leave me in the porch. Didn't half sound jolly in there, all the laughing and that. You say I can come in?'

'The publican can but turn you out. There's nothing quieter than a public house in the morning, especially in a sleepy place like this looks to be.'

The Bottle and Glass proved her right. Last night's ashes lay in the grate, the chairs were stacked on the tables and a rotund, rosy-faced man wearing a rubber apron was busy sweeping the stone-flagged floor.

'Morning to you, ma'am. Blow me, I didn't expect any custom at this time o'day. Give me half a jiff and I'll put a table and chairs to rights. Oh but, the young lassie, is she old enough to come in? Be more than my licence is worth for me to have her in the bar if she's under age, you understand.'

'I know. But we haven't come to order drinks, much as we

could do with something to warm us. It's a bitter morning. No, I just hoped that you might be able to give me some advice. Unless I'm mistaken, this will be the hub of the village.'

Wiping his hand on his apron, he held it out to her.

'Cyril Godwin, at your service, ma'am. If I can help, then be sure I will.'

'My daughter and I are hoping to move into Badgers' Holt. We aren't from around here and have taken a temporary let in Deremouth. House-buying can be such a protracted business and we're anxious to settle into the community. Bella, my daughter, needs to attend the local school; I don't want to start her in Deremouth and then, within a month or two, have to move her again. So what we're hoping is that we can find something here for a temporary let, either for us to board, or to rent rooms or a house, anything that's possible.'

'Well, jigger me! Badgers' Holt, eh? I mind well when that was a well-run establishment, back in the days when I was a nipper.' Then, grinning broadly and slapping his bow-shaped stomach, 'Scrawny little brat, so I recall, but who'd guess it, eh? My old lady cooks too well, and I never did learn to say "no". Plenty enough on the breadline, it seems to me it's nothing short of a crime to throw away good food. Ah, feeds me too well, docs Maggie, bless her. But never mind about me. You say you've come to ask for a bit of local knowledge, eh. Now let me see, Mary Gibbons takes a lodger every now and again, but I think there's no more than the one small room, not good for the pair of you. Just hang on a couple of shakes, I'll have a word with Maggie. She'll rustle you up a good hot drink, I dare say you can do with a bit of a warmer on a morning like this. Best we talk through in the parlour, on account of the youngster not being allowed in the bar, you understand. Our local bobby lives just across the road with his mother, as nosy a body as I ever had the misfortune to stumble on. He was on the prowl just before you walked in, and you may bet your last shilling that he didn't miss out on seeing you. Just come along through to the parlour and I'll have a word with Maggie.' He ushered them into a small room leading off from behind the bar and then left them, moving with surprising alacrity for one of his size.

'Nice,' Bella whispered, tugging Lydia's sleeve. 'Fat and jolly. You know what I reckon? I reckon we been sort of guided to come here first, like a sign that this place, Combydere (what a funny name) is gonna be right for us.'

Lydia nodded. She had the strangest feeling as if none of this was real, as if she would wake up to find herself at Drydens. The builder's yard, the sound of the men collecting their tools, her father, home and her mother, Sophie, Ethel. Those were the people who'd made up her world—then Christian. But Christian was part of all this, knowing him, loving him, being loved by him.

'Mum,' Bella tugged her hand, 'Mum, isn't it the most exciting day you've ever known?'

Lydia pulled herself back into the present. Nothing must dim the wonder in Bella's eyes. The best day she'd ever known…the words brought alive a picture of what her childhood must have been: left waiting in the porches of public houses, learning to avoid the gropings of those she called 'dirty old buggers', a life devoid of the warmth of love. An encumbrance. In that moment Lydia was again aware of that new emotion as she smiled back at her 'daughter': the tug of love she felt was for Bella—and Bella alone.

'I hope his wife can recommend somewhere for us. I feel sure that, if she can, we can depend on it being suitable.'

'I reckon anywhere round these parts would be suitable. You know what? Cor, but I wish I'd done more learning so that I could find the words I want. But it's just this funny sort of feeling I have, like as if we've been chucked in the air and come down to the ground right side up. Is it like that for you, Mum?'

'That about sums it up, Bella.' Oh, but was it true? Tossed up in the air, yes. But landed back right side up? How could she be when there was such a cloud of bitterness between Sophie and her? How could there be when Christian had grown tired of her? There was no comfort in telling herself that he had always been thus, that perhaps he wasn't capable of keeping faith with a lifelong love. So, don't think of him. Push him to the back of your mind, to the back of it and beyond. Be thankful that you have his daughter and that with every new day you become more certain that you will soon have living proof of those glorious weeks you shared with him.

'Hush,' Bella cut across her thoughts even though she wasn't speaking. 'He's coming back.'

The parlour door opened and they were confronted by his wife, Maggie, her girth as much evidence of her culinary expertise as his own.

'Fancy now, new people coming to that place on the hill. Pleased to meet you, I'm sure and I hope you'll be happy amongst us.'

'I'm sure we shall be,' Lydia said, holding out her hand in greeting. 'I'm Lydia Mellor and this is my daughter Bella.'

'Pleased to meet you, Mrs Mellor, and you too, Bella m'dear. Is it just the two of you?' She wasn't as openly inquisitive as Annie Wiffin, but her remark brought it home to Lydia that a woman with no husband—excluding the many who had been widowed in the war, she added silently—didn't fit easily into society.

'Yes, just the two of us,' she answered, meeting Maggie Godwin's eyes, her chin high. 'My husband and I are separated.'

'He walked out on us,' Bella said, defying anyone to criticise her new-found mother, 'found himself someone else. But we'll be all right, Mum and me.'

'Dear oh dear, what a way to behave. Now then, my dears, it's cold as charity in here, I only light the fire in the "best" at the weekend—and not always then, if I'm truthful—but it's toasty enough out in the kitchen. Come along out there with me and while I try and think who best I can put you on to, we'll have a nice pot of tea and a slice of cake.'

A quick glance from Bella seemed to say to Lydia, 'Didn't I tell you we've come down right side up?'

Maggie showed herself to be remarkably incurious; she didn't put out any feelers into what had led them to Combydere, simply gave them useful tips about life in the small village. 'Most of the girls of your age go into Otterton St Giles to school, Bella, I dare say that's what you will do. Summer days, it's a nice ride on your bicycle and when the weather's bad there's just the one bus goes through Combydere in the morning taking people in to Deremouth. It picks up in Ottercombe just up the valley before coming here, then on to Otterton St Giles before it crosses the bridge and on into town. I believe one or two children take the bus of a morning, you'll soon find your way into things.'

If Maggie Godwin expected Bella to show some sign of

pleasure or even relief, she was wrong. School wasn't part of her plan for a new beginning.

'I'm almost old enough to give up school,' she glowered, 'it'll be hardly worth me even starting.'

Lydia put an arm around her shoulder, a silent sign of understanding.

'We mustn't break the law, Bella. And you may well make friends with girls from Combydere and be happy to stay on for another term or two.' Then to Maggie, 'At this age, so much depends on what she means to do with her future. Whatever it is, and perhaps it's selfish of me, but I hope ambition won't take her away from home for a long time yet. Will she need to wear a school uniform?'

The slight inclination of Bella's head told her that the message had gone home and brought back to her their early conversation about the treatment she'd received from the girls the child had so scathingly called 'your Guides' in Kingshampton. A school uniform would lay so many ghosts.

'If it's only for such a wee while I don't expect they'd insist on it. Any road, at the national school down in Otterley they don't go in for uniforms. Muriel Handley—her father is some sort of a big-wig down at the boat-builder's in Deremouth and they live out here in the village—Muriel Handley must be about your Bella's age and she goes to a private school. Now, for pupils there I dare say they insist on putting them all in the same clothes. But, like I say, at the national school just their ordinary clothes are all they go in for.'

'I'm so glad we came in here,' Lydia said. 'Both of us are grateful, aren't we, Bella?'

She'd known Bella was a quick learner, and there was evidence of it as she recovered from her sulky scowl and gave the innkeeper's wife her sweetest smile.

'We don't feel like strangers anymore,' she said, with a charm that must surely have come to her in genes from her father. 'It's as if a kind Fate made us come into the Bottle and Glass and, like Mum says, we really are grateful.'

Lydia looked at her with pride.

Their day was one of exploration, all of it based on information gleaned from Maggie Godwin. Taking their leave of the Bottle and Glass, they wandered on through the small village, noting the bow-windowed cake shop, over the door of which was a painted sign saying 'Café and Home-Made Cakes'. What could be better? Probably the lunch they were served could have been better, but neither was in a mood to complain. On a damp winter morning, their choice wouldn't have been for a plate of cold, very rare beef, with mashed potatoes and Brussels. If the pastry of the apple pie that followed was any indication of the standard of cooking, Lydia decided the cake shop wouldn't get custom from Badgers' Holt.

It was evident that having two strangers in the café was no ordinary occurrence. Wondering how it was possible to eke a living out of such a place, Lydia forgave the overalled owner her culinary weakness and her curiosity too, telling her that they hoped to move into Badgers' Holt, although it would be some time before the sale could go through and then the necessary work be completed.

'We're in a rented house in Deremouth, but I wish I could find something here in the village. We'd like to be on hand when work starts. I suppose you don't know of anywhere?'

'Fancy that! Now I'll tell you, it's not a house to rent, mind you. But I've heard it on good authority that Clarissa Yelland from Winkley Farm is on the look-out for a lodger. Farmers have a hard time of it these days. All the promises that things would be better for them, disgraceful that's what it is, repaying them like this government does after the way they kept us fed all through the days of war. Fancy having to open their homes to strangers just for the sake of making ends meet! Same with so many of the poor chaps who fought—yes, and for us who were left without our young husbands.' Lydia's heart softened towards her. 'Still, we're better off than some. At least we have good sound roofs over our heads. And so will you, Mrs…?'

'Mellor.'

'And this'll be your daughter?'

'Bella,' the girl answered. 'There's just Mum and me. But we're lucky too, aren't we, Mum? We knew we would be when we came looking for where we'd live.'

'You're like me, I dare say, your husband taken from you in the war. And your Bella must have been small, poor little mite, growing up with no father.'

Before Bella could have her say that they were all right and that her father had just abandoned them for another woman, Lydia replied, 'My husband and I are separated, but Bella and I are determined the future will be good. Isn't that so, Bella?'

'This is our new beginning. It's gonna,' in her excitement her diction momentarily lapsed, 'going to be splendid.'

'Dear me, oh fancy that, separated. There's nothing harder to bear than loneliness. I just hope you never come to regret striking out on your own.'

'That's something I shall never regret,' Lydia said with

conviction—and with truth too, for one thing she hadn't done was strike out on her own. That was a far cry from picking up what was left of her life and determining to make something worthwhile of it. Changing the subject, she asked where they would find Winkley Farm.

'You can see it from Badgers' Holt. You'll remember the dip to your right as you stand with your back to the house? Then up a rise on the other side of it there stands the farmhouse at the top of the hill.'

'Isn't that where those funny-looking sheep were, Mum? Like we saw after the cab dropped us off this morning here in the village. Never seen such shaggy-looking sheep.'

'Wensleydale, that's the breed they are. Winkley Farm used to be arable back in the days of the war—no, I tell a lie, I suppose you would call it mixed. Most of it was arable, given over to fields of potatoes, greens, all the things needed to keep folk together body and soul. No living in that these days, growing tatties wasn't worth the space it took up nor the labour they had to pay out looking after veg. So Edward—that's the farmer—he put it down to grazing. Lucky for them, I expect, he had a cousin who farmed sheep on the hills up-country and he gave them a bit of a start in stocking the place. That was five years or more back and the flock's grown. He sells the wool of course and Wensleydales make good eating. It's a hard life, though. Even down here in Devon the winters are no picnic if you're out on those open hills. When lambing time comes around there's poor Edward out there at all hours, and, near the moor like we are here, we may be only a few miles from the coast but we're a deal higher up and snow's no stranger, ah, snow and drifts too. Tell them at the farm it was me who told you to enquire. There now, have you done with these plates? What about a cup of tea before you set out?'

'No, we'll settle up and start walking,' Lydia said, 'it'll take some time and I have ordered the cab to pick us up where he put us down, by the memorial, at four o'clock.'

'Tell you what I'll do, I keep an eye out for him. If I walk out into the street I can see the memorial. So if you're late I'll bring him in for a cup of tea and one of my rock cakes. How would that be? Is that what you'd like me to do?' She wiped her hands down the front of her floral overall in readiness for taking the money.

Lydia knew without being told that the offer was made for more reason than one: for one thing the owner of the little café-cum-cake shop needed all the trade she could get, for another she hoped to be kept up to date with developments and, thirdly, something that on their first day in Combydere was most important of all, the offer was made out of genuine kindness. Thinking of what a hard, lonely life the poor war widow's must be, Lydia took two half-crowns from her purse.

'You've been very kind, I'm sure he'll be grateful for some tea on a day like this. And, in case we don't get back in time for us to come in again, could you put that cherry cake in a bag and give it to him for us.'

'The big cherry, oh yes, that I will.' Flushed with delight the woman looked at the two coins. 'I'll see if I can find you your change if you wait just a tick.'

'No, don't bother. You might find he has a bigger appetite than you thought. If he's hungry he'll get through more than one of your nice-looking cakes.'

'I'll see to it that he does. Come again, won't you.' Clearly, her unexpected diners had made this a red letter day. 'Just down the street a bit and you'll see a stile. Go over that and stick to the track round the edge of the field and you'll soon find your way up to the farmhouse.'

Once out of earshot, Bella turned to Lydia with a puzzled expression.

'What made you buy that cake?'

'Just a whim, I expect,' Lydia laughed. 'The difference between our lives and hers suddenly struck me. We have hope, Bella, we have the challenge to make something of what we have. But what chance has she?'

Bella didn't answer. But, with the stile behind them, as they set out along the track bordering the hedged field, she slipped her hand into Lydia's. At one time Sophie would have understood the affection that prompted her action. Lydia, Miss Westlake, Mum, what's in a name? She was pure gold.

Another stile faced them at the top of the first field where the sheep had gazed at them in a disinterested manner. The next field appeared to be empty but they still kept religiously to the track around the edge as they came nearer to the farm buildings. Winkley farmhouse had little beauty to commend it: a gaunt red sandstone building probably about a hundred years old. Going towards the front door, Lydia noticed there was rot in the wood of the window-frames; in fact there was an air of neglect about the place. She tugged the bell-pull and almost immediately heard footsteps. For a second she panicked. This wasn't a bit suitable: one thing she hated was inefficiency and seeing the lack of care given to the flaking paintwork and decaying wood, she could see it had a prime example in Winkley farmhouse.

Then the door was opened and she was face to face with

a woman probably four or five years her senior, one who bore no resemblance to her expectation of a farmer's wife. She was as tall as Lydia was herself, but with an hour-glass figure that seemed to belong to an age of Edwardian corsetry. Her mouse-brown hair was plaited and pinned around her head like a coronet, her round face was pallid, her eyes so pale they were hardly blue at all and yet if they weren't blue they certainly weren't any other colour. Her heavy bosom was held well in check and yet still low-slung, her waist was small—thanks again to the tight lacing of yesteryear. Her broad hips weren't flattered by the straight cut of her mid-calf length skirt, below which protruded two large feet attired in black lace-up boots.

'Yes?'

'Good afternoon.' While every instinct told Lydia she and Bella ought to apologise for coming to the wrong house so that they could turn and run, convention prevailed. 'We have just had lunch at the café in the village, where I heard that you might be prepared to give us temporary lodgings.'

'When the good Lord shuts a door, to be sure He opens a window. Come inside.'

Like a fly trapped in a spider's web, Lydia had no choice. She was relieved that Bella accepted the invitation eagerly.

'The only warm room is the kitchen. Do you mind if we discuss it in there?'

'Of course not. We'll follow you.' She dreaded to see the state the kitchen would be in if the outside of the house was anything to judge by. Yet the flagstone floor of the hall was clean and the hallstand positively gleamed.

'Phew! Crumbs, Mum, look at all those funny pots! Cor,

aren't you glad we got brought in here instead of some posh room?'

'It's a lovely kitchen. I expect you use it all the time, don't you, Mrs Yelland.'

'My husband works outside, mud, dirt, you've no idea. It's bad enough that he treads farm muck in here, I will *not* have him treading it beyond here on to my good clean floors.'

Instinctively both the visitors looked at the shining linoleum just as both of them imagined some poor hen-pecked farmer having to leave his shoes outside the door before he was allowed in. The room was enormous; the fire in the range only warmed one end of it. Outside the window, the yard looked desolate and depressing.

'I'll draw the kettle forward to keep it on the boil and take you upstairs. We have little enough here, but the one thing we don't lack is space. If you decide to take the rooms you must give me a few days to air them. I do run the old warming pan across the mattresses once a week, but it's not the same as having them brought down to stand overnight by the fireside. Now then, this is a double room and next door to it there's a single.'

A fresh smell of wax polish assailed them when she opened the doors. The inside of the house was in sharp contrast to the neglected exterior.

'We are going to be your new neighbours,' Lydia explained to the farmer's wife. 'We're taking Badgers' Holt, but it'll take a while for the sale to be completed and then there's essential work to be done before we can move in. Look, Bella, you can see the house clearly from this window.'

Bella's answer was a vigorous nod of her head which might be translated as 'Cor,' 'Phew' or 'Crumbs' but seemed to Lydia to convey that what she saw defied words.

'In the meantime I want Bella to get settled into school.' Another silent message from her new daughter prompted her to add, 'She's so near to coming to the end of her schooling I don't want her to miss more than she needs.'

'The motorbus can take her in, she only needs to cut down the edge of the field to where she can get on. Are you meaning you'll take the rooms? We haven't even named my price yet.'

'I'm sure it'll be fair, Mrs Yelland.' And in that Lydia spoke the truth. The farmer's wife had little to commend her by way of manner: she was unbending, unsmiling, yet her honesty couldn't be doubled.

So that's how they came to Winkley Farm, a decision that set them on a hitherto unimagined path.

Any social butterfly of the era might have looked on Lydia's life as having been narrow, dull and empty. Perhaps it had to do with her home background that it had never been idle. Now, with the business gone, all her local social work nothing but a memory, she was resolved to fill her days with some sort of productive activity. During their first week in Devon she made great strides: she visited a local solicitor; she opened a bank account in Deremouth and arranged for the closure of her existing one in Brackleford. She wrote a long letter to Sophie telling her about Badgers' Holt, begging her to be part of this new beginning and giving her address as Winkley Farm. And interwoven into all this was her attention to Bella.

Bella Mellor, the new and expensively uniformed pupil at Perbeck House, was far removed from the ragged child who had been a figure of scorn as she'd drifted from one school to another in the wake of her rent-evading mother. In those days each morning she had woken with a sick feeling of dread, uncertain whether there would be enough bread—or anything to spread on it—to take to eat at midday when her classmates tumbled out of the schoolroom to go home to a hot meal. Her dream had been of the day when she could leave school and find work, earn enough shillings to rent a room for herself somewhere. But right from the time she put on her first brand-new gymslip and velour hat, her first brand-new reefer overcoat and shiny shoes, a new Bella was born. This was what Lydia had hoped for. The child was quick and intelligent; despite the lack of continuity as she'd moved from school to school, openly regarded as a misfit, or perhaps in part because of it, she had always found solace in reading.

Her affairs attended to and her offer on Badgers' Holt accepted, she wasted no time in finding a reputable firm of builders to carry out the work she wanted done to the house. That done, she decided there was no point in their staying any longer in Deremouth. It was on Monday of the following week that she commissioned a taxi-cab to collect her, together with her portmanteaux, from the house that had had no feeling of home. In the window opposite, the net curtains were unashamedly pulled to one side.

'Not off so soon, Mrs Mellor?' Annie Wiffin could contain her curiosity no longer. 'You've sorted out your differences with that husband of yours, is that it?'

'Staying here was always to be temporary,' Lydia answered, giving nothing away. She heard her voice as cold and unfriendly. Perhaps that was another reason she would be glad to be gone. In giving happiness you find happiness time again, she remembered; she couldn't feed her neighbour's curiosity, but the anger it aroused in her made her feel miserable and mean. Soon though it would be over, the front door shut and the key returned to Mr Davies. Another big stride would be taken on the road to the life she and Bella would make.

Anyway, she thought, a quarter of an hour later as the taxi-cab chugged up the long slope out of Deremouth to join the main road that crossed the bridge over the Dere, when I get to the farm I feel sure there will be a letter from Sophie waiting for me. To fall out when we were both in Kingshampton was bad enough, but when she reads my letter from so far away I *know* it will make her see the most important thing is that we can't part like we did.

Whilst she couldn't pretend that Clarissa Yelland's welcome might be described as warm, neither was it unfriendly.

'If your driver will help us get your luggage into the hall, Edward will carry it upstairs for you. He's coming back to the house for his dinner.' She stood back while the portmanteaux were unstrapped from the luggage grid and carried through the wide front door, and Lydia had paid the driver. Then, in that same cool tone, 'Your rooms are all ready. Bella will need to put a hand torch in her pocket of a day if she means to walk back from the bus along the field path. It's a good short cut, but today I expect she'll come round the lane. I expect you want to get on with your unpacking. There's a letter waiting for you.'

'I thought there would be something.'

Sophie had answered her! Relief flooded over her. And then she saw the envelope, the address on it typed. It was from the bank manager she and her father had known well for years, confirming her account was transferred, wishing her well in her new surroundings and telling her that owing to his wife's sadly failing health he, too, was leaving the bank.

'Edward won't be here for a while, he's got the vet with him. I've put a match to the fire in the sitting room and laid your table. I'll bring your meal in there in five minutes. Would you like to go up to your room while you're waiting?'

Lydia had the strangest feeling, rather as she might have as a child when she'd been taken to visit some elderly and starchy relative.

'You're very kind,' she answered, hearing her own voice as equally stiff and stilted. It flashed through her mind just how much she had changed during those weeks with Christian. Until then surely she'd been as unbending as Clarissa, a hard worker and always willing to help the deserving, yet how few had ever seen beyond the facade she'd chosen to hide behind. Fast on the heels of that thought, in fact crowding into her mind at the same time, was the relief and the joy when that protective wall had crumbled and for the first time she had become at ease with herself.

'I'll ring this bell to call you down when your meal's ready,' Clarissa announced unsmilingly.

'I'll come straight down.'

It was a relief to get away, to shut the door of the bedroom she saw as a sanctuary. Walking to the window she looked across the valley to Badgers' Holt, needing reassurance and finding none. Involuntarily she shivered. What was she doing here, making herself mother to a child who a few months ago she hadn't known existed, exchanging the haven that had been home to her all her life for that rambling edifice which, on this grey and overcast winter day, looked ugly and foreboding? Moving her hands across her flat stomach, she could feel her hip bones. Was it possible that somewhere in there Christian's child was developing? That must be the foundation stone for her future, that new life, and Bella. There was triumph rather than humour in the smile that tugged at her mouth; Christian might be looking to pastures new, but nothing, *nothing* could take from her the legacy of their love. She thought of those parentless children at the orphanage and wondered whether in similar homes there might be others who were the outcomes of his philandering. Perhaps what she ought to do with Badgers' Holt was make a home for children he'd fathered and abandoned. Thinking of plain, honest, good-living, respectable Miss Westlake, she marvelled that she could have given herself so utterly, body, soul and all that she was, to the sort of man she'd always held in contempt.

From downstairs came the tinkling sound of the bell calling her to her meal.

Edward Yelland was a man of few words, or few words aimed in her direction. While she was eating her meal, sitting alone in the antiseptically clean sitting room, he carried both the portmanteaux upstairs. On her previous visit her only sight of him had been at a distance. Now, hearing him coming back down the linoleum-covered stairs, she went out into the hall to thank him.

'We haven't met, Mr Yelland. I'm Lydia W—' it was so nearly an error, 'Mellor. Thank you so much for taking my luggage up for me.'

'No bother. I happened to meet Mrs Phillips the other day, from the café you know, she said she sent you over to see the rooms here. Spoke very highly of you, she did.' He nodded his head as if to emphasise the words, making Lydia aware what an accolade it was to have Sarah Phillips' approval.

Clarissa came out of the kitchen, throwing an irritated look in his direction. That was the moment when Lydia had the first hint that all wasn't well at Winkley Farm. She hardly knew either of them, yet she surprised herself by instinctively feeling in sympathy with her unsmiling landlady. Yet was that fair, she asked herself? Certainly it wasn't simply that she gave backing to one of her own sex. Rather it had to do with the way Edward spoke of the war widow who made a meagre living from her unappetising baking.

'I'm going down to the village,' he said, his voice casual. 'There are one or two things I want a word about with Fred Hobbs.'

'Waste your afternoon any way you like,' Clarissa said, as he put on his worn tweed overcoat and picked up his cap, 'but just bear in mind, Wellington boots or your tidy shoes, you take them off in the lobby before you walk on my kitchen floor. The same goes for Bella when she gets back from school, Mrs Mellor, if she's walking that muddy path skirting the field I don't want it all trodden inside. Best the child gets to know my rules right from the word "go". And you too, Mrs Mellor, but I can see you're a tidy sort. Today you came in the taxi-cab, you'd not been treading across the field so I said nothing. But I'll thank you in future if you'll remember outdoor footwear stays in the porch. That's where the polish is kept—I don't want shoe-cleaning up in my bedrooms. I dare say Edward will see to it your shoes get done at night. Isn't that so, Edward?' Was it a question or an order? He didn't answer, but his silence spoke volumes.

Lydia had noticed his stockinged feet and now she understood. There was no doubt who ruled in Winkley farmhouse, yet to look at him there was nothing of the hen-pecked creature she had expected to find Clarissa's husband to be. He was a big man, tall, broad, his lost waistline disguised by his overall stature. He was clean-shaven and his iron grey hair was neither straight nor wavy, but despite being in need of a visit to the barber and despite the fact he paid it no attention once it had had a comb run through it first thing in the morning, it managed to fall into place.

'Huh!' Clarissa muttered as the door closed behind him. 'Men! You count your blessings, Mrs Mellor. Going to have a talk with the blacksmith indeed, as if he hasn't better things to do with his afternoon than spending it jawing with Fred Hobbs. Drinking tea together, yarning away as if there wasn't work to be done up here.'

'He meets this Fred Hobbs at the café, you mean?'

'Not likely. What would he want with poor Sarah Phillips' rock cakes—Rock of Ages, that's what folk call them—when he gets good home cooking for free? In any case, that café of hers is shut on Mondays; that's the day she does her baking. Poor Sarah, even her best friends couldn't call her a cook, but there you are, needs must. Before the war it was her husband who used to be the baker; I remember when I first came here thinking I'd never seen prettier fancies. He had a real talent. Pretty fancies or good sticky lardy cakes, Jimmy Phillips' would take some beating. Still, poor little Sarah, she does her best. As I said, she shuts on Mondays and gets her baking done. If you need to buy a cake, then Tuesdays is the day. What's left towards the end of the week would be an insult to your digestion. Poor Sarah,' she said again. 'She pushes the bolt along on the shop door and comes up here to the farm sometimes. Not that she and I have anything in common, but she's lonely, I dare say.' All the time she talked she busied herself washing up from the meal and, automatically, Lydia took a tea towel and started to dry the china. 'Men!' Clarissa went off at a tangent. 'Men! Not one of them worth the time of day, if you want my opinion. And that'll be yours too, I don't doubt, or you wouldn't have left him.' She waited, giving Lydia her full attention and clearly waiting to hear what had driven the Mellors apart.

'I wouldn't say that,' was the disappointing reply. 'I shall leave most of the unpacking until Bella is here, she'll like us to do it together.'

'Poor child, I expect she misses her father.'

'Bella is wonderful, she is so full of hope for our future.' Lydia felt they were playing cat and mouse with each other, neither asking direct questions nor yet giving full answers. As she anticipated living here until Badgers' Holt was ready for occupation, it was important that she and Clarissa were comfortably companionable, so she made an effort. 'What are you making?' she asked, touching the unbleached wool of a half-made garment rolled around the knitting needles on the dresser.

'It's a cardigan for Edward. Out there in all weathers, he needs all the wrapping he can get,' Clarissa answered, surely not the attitude of one with such a low opinion of all men— and seemingly her own in particular. As if her own thoughts had been following the same route, she added, 'Not that he kills himself with labours, but the elements take the same toll on the industrious and idle alike. The wool comes from the flock here on the farm. Wensleydales, you may have noticed them when you walked up from the village the other day. Are you a knitter?'

'Yes and no. I can knit, but I'm no expert.' Only just in

time did she stop herself from saying that until recently she had been busy in a building business. Not the way a married woman would spend her time. She twisted the plain gold ring on her finger, a reminder of the role that had to become second nature to her. 'Do you spin the yarn yourself? I noticed there was a spinning wheel in the sitting room.'

'That's where I keep it when it's not in use. I can't have it cluttering the place out here in the kitchen.'

'Isn't that wonderful, Mrs Yelland, your own sheep, preparing the wool, making your own garments. Do you ever dye it?'

'It wouldn't keep him any warmer if it was coloured. Same colour as the flock, nothing wrong with that. Same colour, but a good deal cleaner. The hardest job is washing the skeins when I've got it spun. Now then, Mrs Mellor, how about a cup of tea?'

It seemed Lydia's advances of friendship had been well received.

An hour later, dusk already falling, armed with a pocket torch, she set out for a walk before daylight quite faded. On Bella's first day at the farm Lydia decided she would meet her from the bus and they'd walk together along the path that edged the steeply sloping hill. Recalling Clarissa's carping tones as she protected the well-scrubbed flagstones of the kitchen floor, she wanted to make sure Bella's initial introduction to life at Winkley Farm held no word of criticism. There was plenty of time before the bus was due so instead of taking the short cut around the field she explored the neighbouring lanes, coming to Barrows Lane, as the street was called where Combydere's few shops were to be found, just beyond Sarah Phillips' café and cake shop.

Today the window was empty; she supposed the remains of last Monday's batch of baking must have been fed to the birds. 'Poor Sarah', came the echo of Clarissa's voice. From the opposite side of the street she raised her eyes to the window of the room above the shop. The lamp had been lit and there, pulling the curtains to shut out the damp and unfriendly dusk, was Edward Yelland. If that hadn't been the exact moment that the bus drew up by the war memorial she might have given what she'd seen more thought. Just for a fleeting second she felt surprised, and then put it out of her mind, remembering that Sarah was a friend of the Yellands.

The sale of Badgers' Holt moved at its own slow pace. By the time it was completed and the property was assigned to Lydia Mellor the snowdrops had bloomed and faded, the first daffodil bulbs were opening. Twice more Lydia wrote to Sophie, finally writing her address on the back of the envelope; twice more her letters were ignored, the last one being delivered back at the farmhouse marked 'Return to sender'.

It was the first week in March; workmen from Otterton St Giles had begun the transformation of Badgers' Holt. The smallest bedroom on the first floor was to be turned into a bathroom, a new plumbing system installed and a range in the kitchen where the fire would heat water for the house. The garden was being excavated and a septic tank put in. Each room in the house was to be repapered and repainted. The future was beginning to take shape. Another big stride towards that future was that Bella no longer talked of leaving school. So much of her happiness could be laid at the door of that school uniform: it made her the same as everyone else. No longer did she shrink away, eating her midday meal alone, a meal that on a good day had been a sandwich and on a bad day plain bread or even nothing at all. Now she sat at the long table with other girls who lived too far away to go home at lunchtime and ate a cooked meal. The second thing that set her life apart from the years that had gone before was that for the first time she had found a companion of her own age. To start with she had gone on the bus alone in the morning, getting off just before reaching Deremouth; at teatime she and Muriel Handley would come back to Combydere together; after a week or two the routine changed and Mr Handley picked her up by the stile and took the two girls to school together. Perhaps if life had always been easy for Bella, she would have taken her present lifestyle for granted. But even after these few winter months she woke each morning filled with wonder. It was largely for her sake that Lydia fought down her own aching misery. Not long ago she too had had a dream, she too had been sure of her future. Now all she was sure of was the challenge, the knowledge that it had to be up to her to make something good out of what was ahead—for her own sake, because she wouldn't accept failure, for Bella's and for the sake of her unborn child.

Each day she looked for a letter from Sophie. None came. That's when she made her decision: she would go back to Kingshampton. She intended to try and do the return journey in a day, but both Clarissa and Bella assured her that she needn't rush.

'Go all that way and back in a day! That's a waste of good money. When you get to see your sister, you'll have a lot to say to each other. She's sure to want to keep you for the night and, Bella, you'll be all right with me, won't you, if your mother goes.'

So it was agreed and two days later Lydia was on the train to Reading. There she would change to the other line and make her way to Brackleford, where the station taxi-cab would take her to Meadowlands.

It seemed so simple. Even after all that had happened to her over the last months, she still fell into the trap of believing one could know what lies in waiting.

CHAPTER TWELVE

At Reading station, Lydia took her overnight case from the hammock-like luggage rack and climbed down to the platform. For more than three months she'd been in Combydere, time enough for her to have become used to wearing her 'wedding' ring; it wasn't until, at the exit from the platform, the inspector held out his hand that she became aware of it. As she pulled her gloves off to feel in her handbag for the ticket, she was suddenly and uncomfortably aware of the glint of gold. Instinctively she turned her hand so that her third finger was hidden from view.

'The Brackleford train leaves on the southern line in seven minutes,' the inspector told her, punching a hole in the ticket and returning it. 'Platform one.'

She thanked him and hurried out to Station Approach. It was as if the last months had never been; the transformation of Badgers' Holt where, now that it was hers, an army of builders and decorators were already turning her ideas into reality, might have been on another planet; Reading drew her back into the past. This was where, usually on their own, she and Adelaide had come on shopping expeditions, this had been where they'd delighted in finding a surprise to take home for Sophie, who rarely chose to come with them. She remembered the day they had been so delighted with the coat which, scorned by Sophie, had given such pleasure to Bella. But Bella was as removed from her now as everything that had happened since she'd left Kingshampton. Miss Westlake was reborn. Before she crossed to the entrance of the adjoining station she stopped to put her gloves back on. She felt furtive, guilty. But that's ridiculous, she told herself, I'm not some child playing make-believe. It's for Bella's sake and for my own baby's that I'm Mrs Mellor. They may never have a chance to know him, but they have the right to bear his name, to hear about him as their father. Once again wearing her leather gloves she showed her ticket and went through the barrier to where the stopping train to Waterloo waited. A ladies only compartment was empty and thankfully she got in and slammed the door shut behind her. Then, unobserved, she removed the evidence of her lie and put it carefully into the inner pocket of her handbag. Miss Westlake had come home to her roots.

As if to reassure herself, she stood up and surveyed her reflection in the speckled mirror above the empty seat opposite. But, wedding ring or no, this wasn't the Lydia Westlake who had left Kingshampton. It was warm in the compartment, and she unbuttoned her smart, up-to-the-minute overcoat; still looking at the woman in the mirror, she set her tall-crowned and stylish hat a little higher on her head, making sure it didn't spoil the line of her coiled hairstyle. In imagination she saw herself as she had been not so long ago: angular, plain, her flat hair crushed under some 'damned awful' hat; then, her shoes were always low-heeled and sensible, careful not to add anything to her height. But Bella had taught her to stand tall and be proud of it; even her stylish footwear was evidence of the transformation. Transformation? Nothing can alter me, no one but a magician could make me better than plain. Angular? Just as she so often did when she was unobserved, she cradled her stomach in her long hands. A stranger might not immediately recognise that she was pregnant, but then a stranger wouldn't have known the young woman who more than one in the village had considered to have 'less meat on her bones than a bit of scrag-end'. *She* was aware of the changes, the new roundness where in the past every bone had been apparent; just as she knew the changes she felt when she moved her hands to cup her still-small breasts. Small, but not flat as they had been. I was so ashamed, silently she told the woman who looked back at her. Every time he touched me I was ashamed of my body, there was nothing womanly about me, nothing except…with a hiss of steam and a trembling jolt the train started, taking her by surprise and throwing her back on to the seat…except, her mind raced on, except for the way I loved him, wanted him. Now look at me: am I any different? When I'm with Bella I try and build my world around her. But now, just *me* here on my own, now can I say anything has changed? If he could see me now, if he could hold his hands on me like this, like *this*, our child growing inside me, surely he wouldn't turn from me for Dulcie or any other woman. Stop it, she shook her head as if to drive away thoughts and images she couldn't bear, this isn't why I've come back. He's not in Brackleford; he and Dulcie were going away. In any case, it's Sophie I've come to see. This evening we'll sit together by her fire, we'll talk, I'll make her understand. She is part of my future, she *must* be. Please God, this time help me to make her understand. Poor Sophie, just think how miserable she must have been. Losing Mum and Dad was the same for her as it was for me—remember the day it happened, she was like a frightened child. Then she lost her marriage. She lost me—because that's how she must have thought of it. Was there any wonder her hurt made her bitter?

There was no anger or bitterness in Lydia's heart for her young sister. Resolutely, she kept her thoughts on the years they'd shared, clinging to the belief that coming all this way would surely make Sophie realise how much she mattered. When the nearness of home brought thoughts of Christian and the love she had felt for him, even before those magical weeks they'd shared, she crushed them before they had a chance to take hold. This journey was about Sophie; think just of *her*, the little girl she'd adored, the adolescent sister who had turned many a local heart and who had gone into marriage with confidence and hope. Poor Sophie. Today they would talk, not quarrel but simply talk, understand each other, move forward.

At Brackleford she hurried outside the station to be sure that no one would reach the taxi-cab rank before her, then, seconds later, she was on her way to Meadowlands. It was as if she'd never been away. She knew every bend in the road out of the market town, every cottage and farm on the way towards Kingshampton. By the time they came towards the outskirts of the village and the development of houses that had turned the course of all their lives, it was her stylish attire that seemed out of place.

Arriving in Meadowlands, she paid the driver and turned towards the house. Walking up the familiar path to the front door, she was uncomfortably aware of her changed appearance and felt as self-conscious as she might have some six months earlier. The sound of the doorbell seemed to echo through the house, then the clip of heels as she waited for Sophie to answer the door. Help me, please, make things be right for us. We've lost so much else, please don't let us lose each other.

Then she was face to face with a stranger, a woman a few years her senior, rosy-cheeked, a look of enquiry on her face.

'Good afternoon?' Her words brought home to Lydia that it was indeed afternoon and she hadn't eaten since an early breakfast.

'I'm Sophie's sister. Is she in?' Disappointment threatened.

'Sophie? You must have the wrong house.'

'Of course I haven't. Why, this house was…' Her sentence drifted into silence.

On the main road in Brackleford, two doors from the pickle factory and too close to it to avoid the smell of hot vinegar, were the premises of Edgar and Hunt, the local estate agents. Bill Edgar and Cyril Hunt had served together in France, in the war, always promising that if they were both lucky enough to see a return to peace they would go into business together. The most crying need after the war would be homes for the returning men so, to them, it seemed obvious there would be a fortune waiting to be made in selling houses.

Reality had proved them wrong. But they'd scraped a better living than many and boosted their income by taking over the management of lettings. When Archibald Westlake had developed Meadowlands they had taken the houses on to their books; when Lydia had sold the business it was Edgar and Hunt who had found the buyer just as they had so soon afterwards for Drydens, and, since she'd been gone from the area, they had been responsible for collecting rents from her houses.

'There's a lady to see you, Mr Hunt.' Kathleen Richards, the firm's inexperienced and unconfident young office worker, put her head around the door following a timid knock.

'I told you, I'm busy with my books for the auditor. Take her to Bradley, surely he can deal with it.' Bradley was older, wiser and the public's first contact.

'I'm really sorry, sir, but it was Mr Bradley who said to tell you. She's not the sort to be turned away—if you see her you'll understand. He did try. She just ignored what he said about you being too busy and not wanting to be disturbed. He said to tell you it's Miss Westlake.'

'Ah.' Cyril Hunt sighed in resignation, placing a large sheet of blotting paper between the pages of his ledger as he closed it.

'You'd better show her in, Miss Richards,' he told the nervous sixteen-year-old with resignation. He'd dealt with Lydia Westlake often enough to know that if she had a goal she would sweep everything out of her path to reach it. However, bearing in mind that he'd made a more than tidy profit out of Westlakes in the past year, he stood up in preparation to greet his visitor.

His first impression was surprise; who would have imagined that that gawky and unattractive creature could have been so transformed by the trappings of fashion? In that moment of greeting he realised that she was probably younger than he was himself, something he'd never considered in his previous business meetings with her.

CONNIE MONK 367

'It's good of you to see me.' Lydia held her hand to be taken in his. 'There's nothing worse than an unexpected interruption when you're busy.'

'On the contrary.' He smiled, surprised to find that in his curiosity there was truth in the statement. 'I'm delighted to find you're back in the district.'

'Mr Hunt, I've come to you hoping you can help me. You must have sold my sister's house…can you tell me where she's living now?' Then, seeing his hesitancy, 'There were reasons why I went away—there was difficulty between her and me—I don't intend to go into details and I'm sure you don't want me to. I came back to Kingshampton certain that by now we must both realise that nothing is worth putting a rift between us.'

Holding a chair for her, he indicated for her to sit down, and then went back around his desk so that they sat facing each other. It was no more than a ploy to give him time to think. He remembered his surprise that the house in Meadowlands had been in the sole ownership of Sophie Mellor; he recalled the rumour that she and her husband had parted. So where was the rift? Another and less believable tale had filtered back into the office, something picked up by Jack Hibbard the rent collector on his round in Kingshampton. At the time both Cyril and his partner had discounted it, even laughed at anything so unlikely as they made a mental comparison between the two women.

'If I could help you, I promise you I would be only too pleased. But I'm afraid I can't. I've not seen her since I took her house on to our books. A first-rate property, furnished to a high standard, that is something I remember from when your late father entrusted me with the development. Not surprisingly, it sold as soon as it went on to the market. To be honest I imagined that after the tragedy that befell your parents, the two of you had decided to pull up roots in the old district and were moving somewhere else close to each other.'

Neither of them mentioned Christian, and if Cyril Hunt was curious he gave no sign of it.

'I wish that were the truth. I suppose she used the same solicitor as we always had?'

'In fact she didn't. She went to James Minton; you'll remember he set up practice in the Market Square. He may well have her present address. And you, Miss Westlake? Are you established in your new surroundings? Are you able to give me an address where I can contact you direct instead of through your bank should the need arise?'

'No. I'll let the present arrangement continue; it works very well.' She felt as if her face were nothing but an animated mask as she forced her mouth into a smile. 'I'm going to leave you to get on with better things than wasting your time on me, and thank you for seeing me.' What a web of lies I weave, she thought, panic suddenly gripping her. At Combydere she had begun to believe in her new identity. She shouldn't have come back...no, that was nonsense, she *had* to come back, how else could she find where Sophie had gone?

Any hope that her visit to James Minton might guide her to Sophie proved short-lived. When the legal side of the sale of her house was completed, Sophie had left no forwarding address.

There was more than an hour's cold wait for the train back to Reading. When there was a problem to overcome she had always met it with determination, but on that March day, when the wind cut along the empty platform as if it had been sent direct from Siberia, she felt lost, empty, hopeless. All her will to build a brave new life seemed to have deserted her, how could she build a future when the roots of her past had been destroyed?

I'm hungry, she told herself, clutching at fast-fading willpower. When did I last eat? This morning at the farm and even then I was too eager for the day to bother too much with breakfast. That's why I feel so—so—so what? Yes, I feel empty, but worse than that, I ache. Misery makes you ache, misery and hopelessness. My legs feel like lead—why do people say that, when the truth is that lead doesn't have any feeling? Sophie said that to me once, years ago. Poor little Sophie, she had so much pain with her periods; remember how she used to creep into my bed for warmth and comfort, sometimes she'd be crying with the pain. She used to say she felt as if there was something inside her wringing the life out of her. Her mind baulked at the sudden image that tried to push into her mind. Where has Sophie gone? How could she go away without answering my letters and telling me where I could write to her? People can't just disappear…or can they? There was no escaping from the image of the river…the echo of Sophie's voice telling her she wished she'd gone with Mums and Pops. Oh no, not that. I failed her. She felt she had nothing, nothing and no one. Wherever she is, make her know how much I care about her. Make her still be alive, I beg, I *beg* and make her come back to me. Make her know she is loved. I'm lucky, I have Christian's baby, I have Bella. But what has she? Nothing but memories of those she's loved and lost. Dad who left things looking as though he didn't love her as much as he loved me—but he did, he *did*. Christian, who left her; Dulcie, whose 'love' wasn't what she believed;

me, the one who she must see as coming first with Dad, first with Christian (at least until he tired of me). Here comes the train. I must have sat here too long, how can I find the strength to stand up? Can misery make you feel like this?

Somehow, she wrenched open the carriage door and climbed in. She seemed to be living through some sort of nightmare. She couldn't bear to remember how she had dreamed this day would end, she and Sophie together by her hearth, the warmth of the fire, the warmth of knowing they were together.

At Reading she walked across Station Approach to the main line station, thankful her train was almost due. On the platform was a refreshment room, the windows running with condensation. The thought of railway tea in its thick cup, stale buns or rock cakes no better than those produced in Comby-dere in Sarah Phillips' Monday bake, made hunger turn into nausea. She wanted just to get away, away from everything the day had brought, away from herself.

She was more than four months into pregnancy without once feeling less than well, yet as the train rushed westwards she was aware first of aching tiredness and then, of pain that frightened her, just as it does those who are habitually fit. It's been such a dreadful day, I'm tired, I'm hungry, I feel sick, my back hurts as if it's going to break in two, my legs ache. With her hands thrust deep into her pockets she cradled her new roundness, looking for comfort, finding only fear. Opposite her an elderly couple slept, their books open on their laps. Don't let the pain be the start of losing my baby…please don't let it be that. But why do I hurt so? Let me get home…home? The farm isn't my home, Combydere isn't my home, even Badgers' Holt isn't where I belong. Don't belong anywhere. Is that how Sophie felt? Please take care of Sophie. We've all made such a mess of things. What must Dad and Mum think if they can see us? What sort of happiness and peace can they have if they know how we've destroyed the world they made for us? Is it all my fault? If I'd not sold the business, if I'd turned Christian away…yes, what I can't make myself say is, if I'd lived up to the standards they had set for us…then would we be in this dreadful tangle of misery now?

Without warning something happened to make her mind jump in another direction. What was that I felt? A sort of trembling flutter inside me…don't let it mean that something is wrong…I know I've done wrong, I've betrayed Sophie, is that what You think? But don't punish me through my baby. It's happening again as if hundreds of bubbles are bursting inside me. My back hurts dreadfully, my groin, my legs; if You want to punish me for snatching my own happiness and not thinking about Sophie, then give me pain, but don't let anything be wrong with my baby. There it is again. Please, please, if you're a God of Love like we were taught, then I beg You, don't let me be starting to lose my baby. A baby conceived from my sister's husband. But I truly *loved* him, I love him still, I always will. Even though I know what he's like, that he makes women fall in love with him, then he drops them, that he's shallow and pleasure-seeking, I know all that, yet it makes no difference. Let me have his baby, our baby, let it be well and strong, let it love me…despite her pain and hunger, despite her fear, Lydia like the couple opposite was rocked to sleep by the rhythm of the train.

It was another three hours before the taxi-cab from Deremouth Station put her down outside the door of the farmhouse.

'We weren't expecting you before tomorrow,' Clarissa greeted her, looking up from her knitting. Lydia found a strange comfort in the sight of the spotlessly clean kitchen. Bella had carried the spinning wheel through from the parlour, her pride in her mastery of this new skill plain to be seen in her beaming smile.

'Look, Mum. Mrs Yelland taught me, she says I'm doing it well, didn't you, Mrs Yelland?'

'Sharp as a needle, the child is, I only had to tell her the once and she seemed to have a natural knack. Now then, Mrs Mellor my dear, I'll just finish this row while you take your hat and coat up to your room and then I'll find you something to eat. I dare say you can do with it after that train ride. How did your day go?'

Lydia's control left her, here in the kindly warmth of the old farmhouse she had no power to save it. Dragging a wooden chair towards her, she flopped on to it, bending forward, her head bent.

'You're about done in, I can see it. Never mind the knitting. I'll get you a cup of tea to drink while I find some food.'

'Don't think I can. I don't feel very well.' Not very well! She heard herself say it, while silently she shrieked in terror. She'd never felt like this, she'd taken her well-being for granted as surely as she had the days of the week. Through the months of her pregnancy not once had she felt less than well; the developing child had been part of her—was surely still part of her. Please don't let it be what I'm frightened even to think. I ache, from head to foot I ache, and now it's as if the child is becoming separate from me. What else can it mean except that I'm going to miscarry? Please, no, not that. It's all I have of him, don't take his baby from me.

Slumped in her chair she wanted to say what terrified her, that she was terrified the strange unnatural feeling must be the start of a miscarriage. But to put it into words would be like tempting fate.

'When did you last eat? Not since midday, I'll be bound. You just sit there quietly. Something inside you and you'll feel better. It's been a long day—and you in your condition. What made you decide to come back tonight?'

And so the story came out, the telling of it bringing some sort of relief. Or did the relief come from the flow of words she couldn't hold back, as she described her terror at the unfamiliar pain and at the strange bubbly feeling inside her.

Clarissa listened with a puzzled expression.

'You don't need me or anyone else to tell you what you're starting to feel. Isn't that how it was when life began to stir in Bella?'

Even the excitement of learning to use the spinning wheel couldn't compete. Bella left her job and almost leaped across the space that divided them and then fell on her knees at Lydia's side.

'Mum, it's started to be alive! Our baby!'

Lydia felt hot tears on her cheeks. What an ignorant fool she was. How could she have thought God was punishing her when all the time He'd been giving her a sign that the baby was well and strong? What did an aching back matter, that or aching legs, either? Drawing Bella close with her right arm, with her left hand she picked up the cup of steaming tea Clarissa put on the table within easy reach.

'Not like me, behaving like this.' She needed a hand to find her handkerchief, but rather than release her hold on Bella she put the cup back on its saucer. 'Not the crying sort.'

'You'd pinned a lot on talking to your sister, what with that and not stopping for a meal, it's enough to bring anyone down. I'll scramble you a nice bowl of new-laid eggs and Bella can take the fork and see to the toast, the fire's just right for it. That won't take us but five minutes and it'll put the spirit back in you. Then up to bed, you'll feel better when you're rested.'

Half an hour later Lydia was in bed, where she found two stone hot-water bottles wrapped in old towels, waiting for her. Her back still ached, and her legs too; her mind was heavy with such anxiety for Sophie that even the slight flutter she felt again inside her hadn't the power to banish it. Despite all that, within minutes she was asleep.

Next morning she penned a notice to put into *The Times*, asking Sophie Mellor to contact Lydia Westlake and giving her address care of the bank where the Brackleford estate agents paid the rents into her account, and where she was still known by her official name.

Days turned to weeks; no words came from Sophie.

By the end of May the work on Badgers' Holt was almost completed. She and Bella had seen their dreams unfold: a small bedroom was converted into a bathroom with hot water on tap, heated by the new range in the renovated kitchen. They'd chosen wallpaper and watched the transformation of each room; they'd gone to Deremouth to find furniture, and when the small town had fallen short of what they wanted, they had taken the train to Exeter.

'This time next week we'll be *there*, Mum,' Bella said when Lydia looked into her bedroom to say goodnight—an unnecessary attention for a girl old enough to have left school, but Bella was no ordinary girl. Lydia believed she did it to make up for a childhood so void of affection; but in truth she did it, too, because of the need within herself. 'These weeks have been lovely, I really like it here on the farm, don't you? But getting to Badgers' Holt will be the real start of our new beginning.' It was as if she hugged herself in a shudder of suppressed excitement. 'Our proper home.' Then, as Lydia stooped over the bed to kiss her goodnight, 'Nothing can go wrong, can it? Nothing can stop it actually happening?'

'Of course not. We saw for ourselves, everything is just as we wanted.'

'It's so perfect it's quite scary.' And for her, that was true. Only Lydia knew the misery of loss, of being cut off from those she loved. No harsh words between herself and Sophie could have led to a separation like this. So where was she? There were only two explanations: one was that Sophie and Christian had 'found' each other again, had made a fresh start, both of them more experienced and wiser, both of them realising their need of each other. That was one explanation; the other was too dreadful to give a chance to form in her mind. Yet, always it was there, waiting to catch her unawares with the echo of Sophie's heartbroken cry that she wished she'd gone with Mums and Pops. So where was she? Why didn't she write? Keeping her innermost feeling hidden had become second nature to Lydia, and her assurance that nothing could prevent Bella's dreams from becoming reality gave no hint that for her, the future was less full of the same promise.

Later, lying awake, the ghosts were all too ready to haunt her. What was that? Had she been nearer to sleep than she'd believed? Could it have been part of a dream? She lay still and listened. No, there it was again…someone hammering on the front door. Who could want the Yellands at this time of night? Not thinking beyond a sense of foreboding, Lydia climbed out of bed, expecting to hear Edward go down to answer the door. It was more than curiosity that prompted her to cross to the window and open the bottom sash to lean out. The night was cloudy, no moon, no stars; it was impossible to put shape to the figure stamping his feet and beating his hands against his side more from impatience than cold.

At the sound of the window being pushed open he looked up.

'Is that you, Clarry? You'd better get some clothes on quick as you can and come.'

'I'll go and wake her for you. Who is it?'

'Tell her it's Jim Reynolds, she'll know.'

Lighting her bedside candle, Lydia didn't even wait to put on her dressing gown. Clarissa slept alone in a small room along the corridor, looking on to the farm buildings at the back of the house, her door opposite that to the main bedroom occupied by Edward. She had never referred to their sleeping arrangements.

'Mrs Yelland!' Lydia shook her shoulder. 'Mrs Yelland! Wake up!' Another shake. No wonder the hammering on the front door hadn't disturbed her.

'Oh dear, is something wrong?' With the sudden movement of a jack-in-the-box, Clarissa sat bolt upright.

'There's someone called Jim Reynolds at the front door. He said you must get your clothes on as quickly as you can. I think he wants you to go with him. I don't know why.'

'Jim Reynolds? He's from next door to Sarah. It must be Edward. He hadn't come home when I came up to bed.' Even before she got the words out she had her feet on the ground and was pulling her nightly plait of hair to pin it around her head. Then, moving faster than Lydia had ever seen, she rushed across the corridor and opened Edward's door. By the dim and flickering light from the candle they both saw the unslept-in bed. 'Let Jim in, Mrs Mellor. Tell him I'm putting on my things. Leave your candle—no, take it, you'll need it. Can't think straight. Edward…something wrong with Edward…You'll need your dressing gown,' she added as if to prove that she was still in charge of her reason.

So it was that Lydia was first to hear.

'They're both so good to poor Sarah Phillips,' the visitor told her as they waited. 'He's been smartening the place up for her, wallpapering and a coat of paint. It's a hard life for Sarah there on her own. She gets very down in the dumps; he thought it would cheer her up, I dare say they'd mentioned it to you. He'd done out the bedroom and the sitting room and was well on with the stairs when he overreached himself and fell. Trying to whiten the ceiling, and that's a fair drop, he had the ladder extended right out and even then Sarah said he could barely reach.'

'I didn't know.' He was so seldom home in the evening that his recent absence hadn't registered with her. 'Is he badly hurt? She'll be down in just a minute.'

'Best wait till she comes, her ears ought to be the first to hear.' If his tone was anything to go on, his news was something no one would want to hear. 'Ah, here she is now,' he said as Clarissa clumped down the stairs with more speed than elegance. 'Sorry to have to come like this, Clarry. You'll need a thick coat, it's cold as charity out there tonight, more like January than May. Edward's had a nasty fall, down there at Sarah's. He's been taken off to Deremouth to the Infirmary and I've said I'll get you there. It'll mean your bike, but I'll ride in with you.'

With some of her usual composure back in place, Clarissa's expression gave nothing away as she heard how the accident had happened.

'They fetched him in the ambulance?'

'Not more than half an hour ago. I can't give you any more details than that, just that he had a fall, had to be taken in to the Infirmary and they let Sarah drive in with them. They'll not be much more than there yet. If we get a move on you'll catch up pretty well as soon as a doctor's had a chance to check him over. Things look worse at night, Clarry.'

'I'll put my coat on. You get home to bed, Jim. I shall be perfectly safe on my own. But thank you for turning out at this time of night.'

'We'll argue that one out as we ride.'

Lydia was forgotten. Once she'd watched the flickering lights from their bicycles disappear, she retraced her steps upstairs, where she found Bella waiting to hear what the disturbance had been. She listened to the account of the accident, her frown deepening.

'He's always down there at the café, I've seen them when I get off the bus after school. He goes to do the decorating, you say. Huh! One thing he doesn't go for is her cakes, that's for sure. You know what, Mum? I really like strait-laced Mrs Yelland, but he's a lazy bu—' Habit died hard; after all these months the old expression nearly escaped. The two of them looked at each other, both recognising the unfinished description—and Lydia secretly thinking it wasn't far from the truth—then laughing in spite of the sudden tragedy that had befallen the farm.

For, by the next day they were all facing the fact that it was, indeed, a tragedy.

'There will have to be changes,' Clarissa told Lydia the following morning when she at last returned from Deremouth. 'There can be no more outdoor working for Edward—no more working of any kind. It's hard to muster my thoughts, that's the trouble.'

'It's early days, Mrs Yelland.'

'It's time you and I did away with surnames. Call me Clarissa.'

'I'd like that, Clarissa, and I'm Lydia, and quite time too. It's early days,' she repeated. 'Whatever damage he's done, he's a strong, healthy man.'

'It would take more than normal good health to put him on his feet. It's his back, oh not just that he'll have backache, no nothing like that. If the spinal cord is broken, then there's nothing that time or the best medical care in the world can alter. I'll have to buckle to and see to things on the farm while we sort out what to do next. Old Jake Hawkins is a good man, but he won't see seventy-five again. Edward has imposed on him for years, leaving him to carry the work of this place. I've always known that I could run this place a deal more efficiently than Eddie ever did, I could have *then*, but now I shall have other calls on my time. For better or for worse, that was the promise I made. I suppose I have to tell myself that what's gone was the better part of the bargain, now I've got the worse. He won't be able to do anything for himself. So there'll be no chance of me being out there tending the flock. I shall take on another man, someone young and keen, someone tough and not work-shy. Another week and you'll be in your own place, he can take over both the rooms you and Bella use. A wage and his board, his own bed-room and the little one Bella uses can be somewhere of his own if he wants to get away from us. That ought to get me someone. If he's not had all the experience we could wish for, I'll know well enough if he's to be trusted and willing to learn. Jake will put him on the right lines. That way the old lad will still know he's useful but he won't be burdened as he has been with Edward making a pretence of looking after things. No, for the first time in all the years we've been here, someone will really be in charge—and that someone will be *me*.' Her tone held something akin to relief.

'It's a dreadful shock—for both of you.'

'Shock, yes of course it is. But it's more than that; it's a challenge. Don't misunderstand me, I have sympathy enough for the poor man—and for myself too, for I have no illusions in that respect. Looking after him will take more than the physical help he'll have to depend on me for. No, the hard-est part will be giving my time to seeing he doesn't let him-self fall into depression. But that's only half the challenge, it's the other half I want to grapple with—the making of something of this run-down place. Yet even hearing myself say it makes me ashamed. There he lies, poor Edward, and all I can think of is how he's let the place go to rack and ruin.'

'You'll have your hands full, Clarissa.' Lydia wanted to stop her saying things that she might come to regret.

'It might be worth spending out on putting an advertise-ment in the national farming magazine; that might bring someone with experience of Wensleydales. Give this place a man with a bit of spunk and time to do the jobs that have been crying out to be done for longer than I care to say, that's what I want. I'll see it's smartened up. When did Edward even so much as put a coat of creosote on the sheds? And as for the guttering, he'd let it fall apart with rust before he stirred himself. No, give me a young man with a bit of energy and I'll knock this farm into shape.'

Ignoring the criticism, Lydia said, 'Clarissa, even if he can't do anything himself, Mr Yelland will probably want to be the one to give the orders, to oversee what's done.'

'Huh!' came the reply, 'Not him! Of course he'll make a song and dance about the arrangement, he'll tell me I don't know what I'm talking about. But all the decision-making will be mine, and he'd better be grateful he has a wife with two pen'orth of gumption or he'd have found himself in Queer Street.' Then her expression softened as she went on, 'Poor Sarah. She was at the hospital with me today. Some women cry easily, I've never been one of them. Nor you, I'll be bound. But Sarah, she's different. As we came out into the street, she was snivelling away. She's going to miss him, miss the pair of us except for the days she decides to slip the bolt along and come up here to the farm. For once I have the outside to keep an eye on, Edward to care for like a baby—for that's what it's going to mean—even *I* won't have spare time to go visiting in the village. And there she is, tied with her cake shop and that café—or ought to be tied to it if she means it to bring in anything of a living. No, I've never been the crying sort, it seems to me that if there's a job to be done, then best get on with it. How many people get all they want out of life? Precious few— as you know all too well. For self-preservation, a bit of spunk is more important than all the beauty and fine ways.'

'You'll never be found short of spunk,' Lydia laughed, 'and I hope I won't either. You know I'd like to help if I can—for what I'd be worth.'

'I know you would. You and I are two of a kind. Oh, you're younger, and I dare say you've had a more comfortable life, more money behind you, all that sort of thing; but none of that matters when there's a problem to be overcome. We're fighters, we're survivors. When that husband of yours walked out on you, did you sit and weep? No, you wasted no time in picking up the scattered pieces and fitting them together to make a new picture—no time at all, that baby not much more than half way to getting itself born is fair evidence of that. And I'll not sit back and let time slip by either. The future of the farm depends on *me*.'

'Clarissa, he's broken his back, not his head. When you discuss things with him you may find he intends to take a manager; learn to oversee things for himself.'

'I told you, you don't know him as well as I do. The last thing he'll want is to be stuck up here away from the village with only me for company. That's what worries me. He and idleness are good friends, but he won't like being a prisoner with no one to chatter with.'

Some changes are planned and anticipated, others come like a bolt from the blue, drawing a line under the past and leaving no alternative. Either way, by the time another month was over, in the farmhouse and at Badgers' Holt too, new patterns were evolving. Lydia and Bella had been in their own home for about ten days when Edward was deemed fit to be discharged. Fate had been on Clarissa's side at least over the hiring of a strong and willing man and, for a bonus, had sent her one with experience of shepherding Wensleydales. A week or so before Edward came home Sam Pritchard arrived on her doorstep. One look at him and she sent up a silent word of gratitude, whether to God, Providence or some guiding star she didn't question. Immediately she saw him she knew he was to be trusted and, more than that, he was well-built and strong, everything she could have hoped. Her instinct was to offer him the job straightaway, but reason whispered in her ear that she would make a fool of herself in Edward's eyes if she didn't go through the formalities. So she read his references, she heard his reason for moving south from his previous post in North Wales: he had a sweetheart in Otterton St Giles. So it was that by the time the ambulance from Deremouth Infirmary delivered Edward home, it was Sam who wheeled the chair down the ramp and pushed him like a visitor into his own home.

About a week later, having given Edward and Clarissa time to start to adjust to their new relationship, Lydia walked across the valley to visit them. In her imagination she had built a picture of Edward looking pale, feeble, unkempt in his helplessness. She ought to have known better; coming under Clarissa's care meant that his appearance was the human counterpart of the well-polished accommodation.

He was sitting in his wheelchair outside the front door.

'How kind of you to call to enquire after me,' he greeted her, with something bordering on the regal in the way he inclined his head.

She had never seen him so well turned out, his starched collar a gleaming white, his polka-dot bow-tie neatly tied, his shoes highly polished and his nails manicured. He was a new man! And clearly he was pleased with the transformation.

'It was a dreadful thing to happen, for you and for Clarissa too. But you're looking so much better than I'd feared. Are you in pain now?'

'Try spending your days sitting in one position and you'd know the discomfort that I must get used to. It's a sad thing to happen to a man who has been used to working hard in the outdoors.'

Lydia bit back the retort that nearly escaped her. There was something about his manner that made him far removed from the dour, often surly and invariably untidy man she'd come to accept. If he'd been irritable, bitter, even resentful of her sympathy she could have understood it. But the truth was, he seemed to be enjoying his new role.

'I'm glad you've come,' he told her. 'Just move my chair over there in the sunshine, will you. She's gone off somewhere and left me here with no way of calling her. When you've shifted the chair, just go into the hall and get me the gong, you know where it is. I expect she purposely forgot to leave it with me. If I bang that hard enough she hears me. I need attention, you know. Can't do anything for myself.' Then, from the narrowing of his eyes as he fixed his gaze on her, she saw plainly that he was hoping to shock her. 'Can't even have a piddle without being helped.'

If he was trying to embarrass her, Lydia made sure he was disappointed.

'That's rotten for you, for both of you. She must have her hands more than full. But knowing Clarissa, she'll cope. I can see by looking at you that she is taking good care of you. Can you reach to take the brake off your chair for me?' He fell into the trap and reached down to pull the lever. 'Well done,' she praised. 'Now then you can turn the wheels and move your chair independently. You know where it is you fancy sitting.' He could do no less. She read in his expression that independence wasn't as important to him as having someone always at his beck and call.

'I'm going to find Clarissa.'

'I'll have that gong where I can reach it first. Can't think how she can have forgotten to give it to me.'

Indoors, she found Clarissa working at her spinning wheel. As they talked, the speed and unvarying rhythm never faltered. Lydia watched her, fascinated.

'I can see why Bella was so keen on learning. What are you going to do with the wool?'

'Wash the skeins, get them into balls, those are the first things. Then I'm going to make Sarah a cardigan for her birthday in September. I've never done any dyeing before, but I thought I'd try to get it a nice creamy yellow. Not very practical, I dare say, but poor Sarah, she deserves something more pretty than practical.'

'Can you buy that colour dye?'

'I dare say I could, but I want this to be something completely home-made. I'm told that onion skins make a good yellow dye. I thought if I make the solution really weak it would be no more than a hint of yellow. With that bought rubbish, you have to accept the shade it gives. I thought I'd get some really pretty buttons to fancy it up. She walks up here every evening once she's closed the shop—and sometimes she'll throw the bolt across the door in the afternoon too, if I'm truthful. Combydere hasn't much call for anyone fancying a pot of tea in the afternoon, well, why should they? Better to go home and make it for yourself. So since Eddie has been so restricted she comes up and keeps him company for an hour or two in the afternoon sometimes. At this time of year the evenings stay light, but she won't fancy cutting across the field when the days start to get short. I worry about her. Before Eddie's fall either he or I used to make a point of popping in for a few minutes whenever we could; but now, well, you can see for yourself, what chance is there for either of us? She hasn't got enough fight, that's Sarah's trouble. She feels crushed by life and it's no use trying to tell her the only way to climb out of her depression is to fight her way up, she can't do it, she really *can't*.'

'Onion skins for yellow, you say.' Lydia's mind had moved away from Sarah Phillips' depression. 'Clarissa, will you sell me some wool, just plain undyed? For months I seem to have been working on things for the baby, soft white on thin needles. What I'd like to do is make something pretty for Bella. Don't expect—' she swallowed what she'd started to say, that she didn't expect anyone had ever made anything for her before. 'Don't expect I can keep it a secret from her, but she'd enjoy helping to dye the wool. I suppose you have to take it out of the tub when it gets as bright as you want.' The prospect was exciting.

'Sam has been clipping the flock. Edward always sold it straight to a buyer up country; I used to just about manage to get my hands on enough to knock up a sweater for him. But from what Sam tells me, there are better prices going than Eddie got bamboozled with, so I'm going to put my price up. Not to you, I don't mean that. I only said it to show you that running this place isn't going to be beyond me. *He* thinks it is, he thinks that if you're born a woman and haven't the brawn of a man it follows that you haven't the brain either. Well, he'll see he's wrong.'

'Bravo!' Lydia laughed, looking affectionately at the woman who had become her friend. 'But Clarissa, while you're looking for a buyer, can you rob your stock and let me have what you think I'll need to make a jumper for Bella—at the new price, of course.'

'Better than that, I have a plan. Send the child up to me and let her spin it for herself. I'll show her how it has to be washed. Then when it's done she can bring it back to you for the dyeing. I'll charge the price Edward charged, that and no more. It ought to be less, really, if she's doing her own spinning.'

So it was agreed.

Bella loved designing clothes, partly because she was a gifted artist, partly because in her imagination she saw them as finished articles. So it was with spinning. As she worked the treadle and as she rolled the fleece between thumb and fingers, feeding it steadily on to the wheel, what she saw in her mind's eye was the finished article. Then back at home, she took an old jumper and counted the stitches on a row, counted the rows, transferred her sums on to a sheet of clean white paper. It was Lydia who suggested the pattern, a combination of deep yellow, pale yellow and green, made from nettles they would gather in the lane.

'It's so exciting, Mum!' Bella's dark eyes shone with the wonder of it all. There were sudden and unexpected moments—and this was one of them—when the past seemed to come alive in her mind with terrifying clarity. Involuntarily, she shivered, dropping the pencil as she gripped Lydia's hand. 'Mum...don't know really, just...I never thought anything could be like it is here. You like it too, don't you? Just the same as I do?'

Lydia laughed, tightening her fingers around Bella's.

'Yes, Bella, just the same.' And it had to be true, she told herself. Yet what right had she to happiness that was based on a lie, a lie that cut her off from her past? With each day that went by she became more used to her new identity, and did it really matter that she was deceiving the people in the village, deceiving Clarissa? No, it wasn't *that* that was important. But cutting out the past, living as if it had never happened, there could be no real happiness based on deceit like that. Dad, Mum, do they understand? Do they watch over those they loved—still *do* love, surely, surely, not still being alive can't change that—so can they understand that the *me* people know in Combydere is just the same as the me I've always been? That's what I want to believe, what I *have* to believe if I'm ever to find peace within myself. And Christian? To me it's the same now as it was when we were together: he is the only man I could ever love. Is that the hurdle? Is that what gives me this feeling of betraying the standards they brought me up to believe? He is a compulsive womaniser, he flits from one to another like a butterfly in a garden of flowers. Well, I'm no flower, I never was. Lovers, friends, partners, true mates—it was true, we both of us knew it, and yet he cast me aside because he lusted after Dulcie Fulbrook. If it hadn't been for the baby, if I hadn't run away from Kingshampton, when he tired of Dulcie he would have come back, knowing I would welcome him just as I had before. I have no guilt about deceiving him, stealing his name, making him part of the web of lies I weave; it needn't have been like this. Where is he now? Are he and Sophie together again? Sophie…and here her mind baulked. Thinking was too painful; with every week that went by, surely it became more certain that Sophie had gone from her life, whether by design or accident. Painful or not, the images crowded in on her: the sunny, happy little girl they'd all adored, the beautiful young woman it had been everyone's delight to please, the certainty through the years that the very differences in their characters and personalities held them together, neither was complete without the other.

All these thoughts rushed pell-mell through her mind, but still her fingers gripped Bella's; her expression was the answer the girl looked for.

They gathered their nettles, they bought their onions in Deremouth market and, on the same shopping trip, brought home two huge fish kettles. But before the spun skeins could be dyed they had to be washed, which Bella did at the farm under Clarissa's watchful guidance. Then, after they had been hung until they were thoroughly dried, they were brought back to Badgers' Holt for the exciting experiment of bringing about the shades they wanted.

'He doesn't bother a jot about what she does, you know, Mum.'

'Who? Edward Yelland?'

'Lazy bu—' she checked herself just in time, adding, 'Well, that's what he is.'

'He hasn't much choice, Bella,' Lydia answered, speaking out of loyalty to Clarissa. In truth she too had felt uneasy about the way he accepted his helplessness.

'Course he has a choice.' Bella had no finer feelings about him. 'There's lots he could do. When I was there collecting the wool that had been drying, there he sat in the sunshine while she was shelling peas for their dinner. I told him, I said why didn't he offer to do them.' Her voice took on a plaintive note as she mimicked his, '"You don't understand how hard it is for me to be so helpless. She rushes about as if she's so important and I'm nothing. That's what I've come to." But I went back to what I said about helping by shelling the peas, "I've never been used to that sort of work. I'm a farmer, that's man's work." Huh! Precious little of it he ever did. The place looks a thousand times better without him. But it's not fair on her. He saw us go into the barn to check if the wool was ready, so what did he do? He banged that gong so that she had to go rushing and push him indoors. He could manage for himself if he wanted to. He won't budge that wheelchair and as for taking himself for a pee, even a two-year-old can manage with a pot. He's got no pride. That's what I hate.'

'I know. So do I. But for Clarissa's sake I don't want her to know we are critical of him.'

'I'll tell you what: you'll never find me tying myself up to a man, not *any* man. If you ask me, they're all the same, they only think about themselves.'

'Oh, come on,' Lydia laughed. 'One of these days you'll fall hook, line and sinker.'

'Like you did with my father. And look where it got you. No, Mum, I won't let it happen. I saw enough of it with Norah to put me off—smarmy lot of buggers—sorry, but that's what they are, the rotten lot of them. There's only one thing they're after. And if they get married they think they can have it for the asking—that and get their washing done and their meals cooked too. Well, you won't catch me falling for it.'

'Put like that, we must be better off as we are.' Lydia didn't argue with her; she sensed the outburst was the result of past hurts which even now still left their mark.

'Goodness, yes. Just you, me and soon our baby too.' As

if to emphasise that it was 'our baby', not Lydia's alone, she rested both her hands on the fast increasing bump. 'I can feel it. A proper squirmer, isn't it,' she chuckled.

'Never still. Let's get our nettles and skins on to boil, Bella, and see what we can make of our experiment.'

Wool from local sheep, dye from local vegetables and nettles from the hedgerows, a pattern devised by Bella with endless patience as she counted numbers of stitches and rows of knitting and, on to that, drew out a pattern that blended their home-produced colours, then hours of knitting as the garment took shape. The day a back, a front and two arms finally became a jumper, they were justifiably proud.

'I want to go and show it to Mrs Yelland.' Then, seeing the way Lydia suddenly leaned forward, the flat of her hands pressed hard on the table, her eyes closed, she said, 'Mum? Mum, are you all right?'

'Yes…no…yes, but Bella, I think the baby must be starting. I've felt a bit odd for a few hours but this is different. I've never had a pain like this.' It seemed to take her breath away.

'Crumbs…what have we gotta do? You better go to bed, hadn't you? I'll ride my bike to fetch the midwife. You be all right while I go?'

'Yes…babies take hours…yes, go now, Bella. Ohhhh,' the breath seemed to be being forced out of her as she fought the contraction. Lydia had gone through adolescence with none of the pains suffered by so many in her class at school, by Sophie too. For many women the early weeks of pregnancy bring sickness or worse; in Lydia's early weeks she had never been less than well. And apart from the day she'd gone to Reading, when hunger and tiredness had been the root cause of her trouble, she had sailed through the months with nothing worse than the inconvenience of a cumbersome body as time had gone on. So the sudden onslaught of her contractions caught her unprepared.

Of course it's going to be the same for me as anyone else; of course it will hurt. I'm not afraid of pain. My baby's coming, by this time tomorrow it'll be here, part of him and part of me.

She saw Bella cycle past the window, pedalling hard as she set off down the hill to the village. Here it comes again, press the table, clench your teeth, please God help me. It ought not to be here yet, not for a fortnight. Panting as if she'd been running, she bent forward, her head on the table that she beat with clenched fists, hardly aware of what she did. Her legs seemed to be folding under her. Somehow she was kneeling, rocking backwards and forward. She heard herself whimpering. Time ceased to have any meaning. Had Bella been gone minutes or hours? All she knew was searing agony as if her body were being torn asunder. How was it that she was lying on the floor, not lying in a quest for comfort, but because something she couldn't control had forced her there just as it forced her to draw up her knees? She heard herself gasping for breath; instinct was her only guide. As one contraction eased so another gripped her. Her exploring hand told her she was lying in a pool of—of what? It looked like blood and water. Help me, help me, my baby's being born and there's no one here.

Then through the haze she heard Bella.

'Mum, Mum, she's not there. She's been with someone else all day.'

'Get Clarissa. Hurry,' her words were lost in a cry, what she felt now was like nothing that had gone before.

Bella saw the stains on the stone-flagged floor. Out of her depth, more frightened than she'd ever been, she knew there was no time to fetch Clarissa, it had to be up to her. In a second she was on her knees, tearing off Lydia's blood-sodden underwear.

'Hurry, Bella, hurry.'

Instead, Bella rushed up the stairs, coming back with her arms full of covers she'd torn from her bed.

'Too late to get her,' she said as once again she fell to her knees. 'I can see the baby's head, it's nearly out. Push, push hard. Take my hand, grip it, Mum. Push, push, it's coming…' What should she do? There must be things you had to do when a baby was born. She couldn't see clearly, her eyes swam with tears of joy, of love and, perhaps most of all, of fright. Suppose Mum died. Some women died having babies, even when they had doctors and nurses looking after them.

'Our baby, Mum. It's nearly here. It's head's come right out. Push again, Mum, harder, harder. We gotta get its shoulders through.' But shoulders were much wider. Suppose it got stuck like it was now, suppose the shoulders didn't have room to come. 'Push, huge push, Mum, it's gonna hurt like anything, but you gotta do it. Help us, please please help us.'

Then, from Lydia an unearthly sound as with every ounce of her strength she pushed, tearing her body in her effort to give her baby life. A quarter of an hour before she had been frightened, desperate for the midwife to arrive. But these last moments had cleared her mind of everything except agony and the will to force the child into the world. That there was no one to take care of her except Bella hardly registered and, if it did, it wasn't important. This battle was her own.

Then the pain was over, the room was silent, she drifted

somewhere between consciousness and oblivion, unaware of Bella as the girl cut the umbilical cord then lifted her tiny, blooded sister. Make her cry, make her start breathing, please, don't let anything be wrong; in the sudden silence of the room she did what she'd once seen a picture of a midwife doing: she turned the baby upside down as if it were a doll.

CHAPTER THIRTEEN

That day, the first of September 1926, saw more than the birth: it saw a great stride in the relationship between Lydia and Bella. To be mother to Bella because she was Christian's child had been Lydia's choice, to become fond of her for herself had followed naturally, and being 'Mum' was something nothing would alter; but they moved on to a new plane in those moments as they shared the baby's impatient entry into the world.

'We did it all by ourselves, Mum,' Bella said that same evening when she sat on the edge of the bed where, by that time, Lydia had been settled comfortably. The doctor had been brought to examine her, Clarissa had left Sarah at the farmhouse keeping Edward company and being on hand to do his bidding. Now, though, even Clarissa had gone home. Once again Bella saw herself as being in charge. 'Our baby, we didn't need no—any—doctors and nurses, was just you, me and her. Afterwards, that was different, but we got her born all by ourselves.' Such pride in the young voice!

Lydia suspected that for the first time in her life Bella was experiencing possessive and protective love. What memories it brought back: herself, certainly much younger than Bella,

Sophie, not a tiny babe but a bewitchingly lovely toddler. But that protective love had been the same. Keep darling Sophie safe, silently she begged, make her happy, *please* take care of her; hold her in Your loving hand. Where was it I heard that expression? The thought nudged her mind at a different level from the deep-felt emotions made all the more profound after the birth of her baby. Somehow, I don't know how, but somehow, help me to find her and bring her home to me. Despite her aching love and anxiety for Sophie, her body was exhausted; she seemed not to have the strength to hold her mind in one direction; somehow the image of Sophie faded, in its place she saw Christian. His baby, the God-given legacy of loving him…so why is it I can't pray that he'll come back? It's not because I don't want him, he's there in my heart every hour. He'll never be faithful to any woman. Perhaps there are other men like that. I don't know anything about men, I don't want to know—except him. I've stolen his name, but my baby is his gift to me, to love and cherish all my days. And Bella, today has brought us closer than years of ordinary living could have; today we shared the greatest miracle there is. A family…Christian's family…he'll never know…gone… gone… Her eyes closed, she slept. So how was it that Bella, holding vigil over her and the 'miracle', saw a tear escape the closed lid and roll unheeded on to the pillow?

Next morning Mrs Hibbard, the unqualified but experienced 'midwife' who had seen most of Combydere's children into the world, arrived.

'I got no message, it wasn't till I was getting my milk in this morning that Sarah called out to me and told me. It wasn't a bairn I was seeing to yesterday, it was old Granny Cummings from Glebe Lane—very likely you don't know her—she had a nasty fall yesterday morning. Only badly bruised, mind you, but it shook the poor old dear up. I was called out before I'd even made my morning cup of tea and I was with her until I saw she was over the shock of it and I'd got her comfy in bed for the night. And here were you, getting on with having this beautiful baby without me.'

'We managed jolly well, didn't we, Mum?' Bella was on the defensive.

'Thanks to you, we did. She was wonderful, Mrs Hibbard.'

'So Sarah tells me. Now then, if you want to go on being useful, bring me up a bowl of nice warm water and fetch a towel. Then, I tell you what wouldn't come amiss, and that's a nice cup of tea. Your mother needs to drink plenty, see if we can't help things along to give the bairn something to nourish her.'

Kathleen Hibbard was more than overweight, she was obese. She didn't so much walk as waddle on her swollen legs, puffing as if she'd conquered a mountain. Lying in bed, feeling fully recovered from the previous day's trauma, Lydia felt their positions ought to have been reversed; *she* ought to have been the one to be doing the caring. Later on, when the midwife had gone, she'd get out of bed and perhaps even go downstairs. She wasn't an invalid. Nine months of pregnancy hadn't slowed her up; surely now that her body was her own again she ought to be back to normal instead of lying here like some sort of invalid.

But she was thwarted. Before Mrs Hibbard went home, saying she'd return in the evening, Bella was back in charge.

'I'm glad she's gone, Mum. Now we gotta talk about our baby's name.' Her lapse into the old 'gotta', especially letting it pass uncorrected, was a sure sign of her excitement. 'Funny the way we both thought it was going to be a boy. Christopher, that's what you said. Better than Christian, anyway. Not that he deserves to have even a boy named after him. Expect you'll want to call her Sophie, won't you Mum?'

'No! And yet, yes! If only Sophie were here, then of course I'd want to name my baby after her. But to speak to her as "Sophie"…' Her words trailed into silence, to speak her fear might give cruel fate a crack to work on. 'But, Bella, I know what we'll do. We'll have her christened Sophie Adelaide— Adelaide was my mother. Sophie Adelaide Mellor, SAM. We shall call her Sam.'

'Cor, Mum, I reckon you must read my thoughts. I knew your mother was an Adelaide and I thought you'd be sure to want it to be Sophie Adelaide. I've been telling her that to me she was going to be Sam. But now that's what she'll really be, to us and to everyone. It suits her, Mum. Isn't she just as pretty as a picture?'

Beauty is in the eye of the beholder, Lydia reminded herself. Her only disappointment was that there seemed to be nothing of Christian in the tiny creature. But at one day old, who could tell? All she was certain of was the tug of love she felt for Bella, remembering how often over the last hours she'd seen her leaning over the crib that stood in the corner of her room. So that's what she'd been doing, making the acquaintance of her new sister, silently telling her things.

'That's settled then, Sam she shall be. Now for the next step. If anyone thinks I'm going to lie here feeling useless for days, they're mistaken. Pass me my dressing gown, Bella, and my slippers.'

'Oh Mum, you gotta stay in bed. That's what the nurse said.'

'When I'm ill I'll stay in bed. But today I am anything but ill. Gracious, I've plodded about for weeks carrying that great hump, now that I'm myself again I want to stand on my own feet.'

'You didn't ought—you ought not to get up till she says you can.'

'Bella, there must have been hundreds of women who gave birth yesterday. Some will be in a position to be waited on, some will have families waiting to be fed. What about the sheep up at the farm, do you see them lying about after they've lambed? Of course you don't. And anything a sheep can do, I can do too.'

'Oh Mum, I don't know…'

'Yesterday you and I managed beautifully, without anyone's help and advice. And so we shall now. I'm healthy, I'm as strong as an ox—or a sheep if you prefer.' Already she had her feet on the ground. Bella knew when it was useless to argue.

So began their next phase, Lydia and Bella enjoying their first autumn in their new home, Sam thriving. Although Bella's fourteenth birthday had long gone, she said nothing about wanting to leave school. She had made friends of her own age, but Lydia recognised there was nothing of the herd instinct in Bella: during the weekends or holiday times she had never brought other girls to the house. For her, they were friendly acquaintances, but unlike most of them, she was content with her own company—and most content of all simply being part of a family. Sam's early weeks went by; she was doted on by the pair of them. Throughout the months of her pregnancy Lydia had never doubted that her baby would inherit Christian's looks, just as Bella had. It soon became clear that she was wrong. Too young to have definite features, even her colouring had nothing in common with her father's. Her hair was fair, her blue eyes showed no sign of changing; she was a long child, with slender feet, slender hands. In fact there was much of Lydia in her, although her colouring must have been a throwback to some family gene shared by Sophie. Always she looked for any slight resemblance to Christian, but she found none.

Through the dark days of Sam's first winter Clarissa often came to Badgers' Holt in the afternoon. In the beginning she had said that as long as Sarah was with Edward she knew he wouldn't feel neglected. But surely Sarah had a cake shop to run, and a café too.

'It barely brings her in enough to cover her living, poor Sarah. You know what Edward and I are suggesting? That she should give up the struggle and move in with us. He's going to talk to her about it this afternoon. He's a good deal better at that sort of thing than I would be. She has to be made to see that she wouldn't be taking charity. Three can live as cheaply as two and if she wants to bring her own things and take over the whole of the attic rooms for herself, she'd be welcome to do that. And as Eddie says, if she's there to keep him company that would give me a clear mind to spend more time seeing to how things are going outside.' Then, as an afterthought and with a twinkle that might even have been seen as mischievous, 'I'll still see to cooking the meals.'

Something prodded uncomfortably at the back of Lydia's mind, something Bella had said when they'd been living at the farm, that when she came home from school she so often saw him at the teashop. Whatever suspicions were forcing their way into her mind, clearly Clarissa had none.

'I wonder she made anything at all,' Lydia said, probably with more spite than the occasion demanded. 'My Girl Guides made better cakes.' It was a thoughtless slip into the past.

'Girl Guides? You hadn't told me you were anything to do with the Guide movement.'

'A long time ago. Until that moment I hadn't given it a thought for years,' came the nonchalant reply. With her whole existence based on a lie, what difference could one more make? 'So you think he'll persuade her to sell up? And you won't mind—having her under foot all day and every day?'

Clarissa held out her arms to take freshly fed Sam.

'She only rents the place, and the shop can barely bring in enough to pay the landlord. This way at least she'll have her few shillings' war widow pension to herself. And she won't be under my feet, if she's under anyone's it'll be his and there's nothing Eddie likes better than having someone ready and waiting to run around for him. Not that I spend hours of my day on the farm, but I attend to the wool. With the higher prices we should have a good year. And let's hope it'll be a successful lambing season too. I've had enquiries from another source.'

Looking back afterwards, Lydia was never sure how it happened, what prompted her to speak the words she did. Yet, even on that first day, she knew no regret, no fear that she was riding for a fall, only a sense of unspeakable excitement. She'd sold her father's company because she couldn't walk in his footsteps; she'd been sure that at some stage she would see a pointer to her future. She'd even tried to believe that she could make a contented life being mother to Christian's children.

Then, on that afternoon in early December, while Clarissa dandled a chortling Sam on her knee, the words seemed to speak of their own volition.

'Clarissa, listen, Clarissa! Suddenly, I know just what I mean to do.' It must have been why she'd known immediately she saw it that Badgers' Holt with its outbuildings was right for them. 'Whatever quotation you are giving to these people who have approached you, will you give the same to me?'

'Quotation indeed. The few ounces of wool you could knit hardly needs a quotation. When you want to make anything you know I could always find you sufficient.'

'It's not things for ourselves I'm thinking about. Listen, Clarissa!' Proof of the importance of what she was about to say was in that repeated 'Listen, Clarissa!' 'I can't think why I haven't seen it before. Bella and I have collected plants for boiling to make dyes; we've experimented with colours; we've enjoyed what we did; and you know how we worked out the pattern with different-coloured stitches for her jumper. Yet until this minute I didn't see what is so obvious.'

'You've lost me. Stop talking in riddles that may be obvious to you but are clear as mud to me.'

'I expect it was that until Sam arrived my mind wasn't free to look ahead.' She wished she could have told her whole story to her practical, hard-working friend, explained about selling her father's business and being certain that somewhere, if only she could find it, was the right road for her to tread, making her own footprints and following no one else's. But she couldn't. To share the years when she'd been her father's assistant would lead her to ground too dangerous to trust. Instead, she went on earnestly, 'I can't be content with having nothing else in my life, no challenge, nothing to strive for.'

'That bounder of a husband of yours ought to be ashamed.'

'It has nothing to do with Christian. It's the need to have a challenge. Look at the way you organise the work on the farm. You say yourself it's never been better run. And who do you do it for? For yourself of course, because you aren't going to be beaten by doing something that is new to you; I'd be just the same if I were in your shoes. Suddenly what I have to do is so clear to me. Give me a quotation for all the wool you can supply—unwashed, Bella and I will do the washing. I shall dye it, and I must find knitters. There must be local women glad to make up the garments I intend to sell. What do you think? All the months I've lived at Badgers' Holt and only now I can see what brought me here. The outbuildings are perfect, just crying out for me to find a use for them.'

'Sell the garments? Here in Combydere?'

'No. I'll find outlets in the retail trade. Don't you see, that's all part of the challenge.'

Clarissa looked worried. She saw it as a hare-brained scheme, especially when Lydia had a house to run and a baby to look after. She said as much. But Lydia wasn't prepared to listen to the voice of caution. That afternoon had given her a shaft of light to pierce the blanket of fog that had made her future so uncertain.

'It seems all wrong.' Clarissa still shook her head, uncertain whether she ought to sell her wool for a scheme that must surely lead Lydia into disappointment, apart from the money she could easily lose in paying knitters without the certainty the garments they made would find homes. 'The way lives change is hard to understand. There's you, never been used to working for your bread and butter; there's Edward, sitting there hour after hour, day after day, helpless and useless when it comes to adding a penny to the coffers; there's poor Sarah—how would she have felt when she saw her man go off to war if she could have looked ahead and seen herself being offered a home at the farm? Whatever dreams she'd had for the days after the war, they weren't like the hand life dealt her. And there's me—well, looking around at the others, I dare say I'm the lucky one.'

But luck changes, good and bad too. And that afternoon saw the beginning of a new way of life for all of them—even Bella, who on hearing Lydia's half-formed schemes, was determined to leave school at the end of that term and be part of the project from its inception.

Before her 'cottage industry' could see daylight, Lydia called in the workmen who had so transformed the house. The out-buildings had to be adapted, the electricity which had been brought to the house had to be extended so that whatever the season there would be light and warmth. Great vats were installed for dying. And through the weeks, while the work progressed, Lydia read everything she could lay her hands on about the old country ways of life, when and where to collect the right hedgerows and vegetation used for natural dyes, the methods used by generations long forgotten. By the latter part of the 1920s England, like the rest of the western world, was striving to find new innovations, modern and labour-saving methods. Not so for Lydia. She looked back to previous years, believing that nothing devised by man could improve on the miraculous gifts of nature. Had her father felt like this when he'd left the company where he'd served his apprenticeship and set up to employ his first staff? Lydia had heard him talk about it, she'd known that ring of pride in his voice as he'd reminisced about the early days of Westlake Builders. Just himself and two men, the three of them skilled and keen, but it was he who had put his meagre savings into paying the wages and buying the materials they needed for the first house, he whose dream it was that this was the start of a business to be reckoned with. Lydia smiled to herself as she remembered him, sure that if he knew what she was attempting he would applaud her for it.

On a February afternoon she was striding home from Melrose Cottages, a terrace of Victorian villas on the outskirts of Combydere. On that afternoon, hope was riding high. In answer to an advertisement for outworkers she'd put in the *Deremouth News* she had received more than enough applications to start her business, and on that afternoon she had been to take wool and a pattern to one of them in Melrose Cottages, only to find when she arrived that the next-door neighbour was keen to take work as well. A knitted suit in a deep lavender blue was to be the end product and it had been agreed that one would knit the skirt and the other the jacket. Mentally, Lydia totted up the number of garments in the process of construction: fourteen. Not enough to start on her round to try and interest retailers, but it was a start. By Easter and the turn of the season, she would have a day in Exeter taking a case of samples.

At home she found Bella busy winding a batch of newly washed, dried, dyed and redried dusky pink into neat skeins, while Sam protested loudly from her crib, every now and then stopping yelling long enough to stuff her small fist into her mouth and suck furiously.

'Jolly glad you've come, Mum,' Bella said as Lydia came in, 'me and Sam too. You'd think she was starved the way she's been carrying on. I picked her up and cuddled her, but it wasn't cuddles she wanted. I changed her to see if she'd settle, but I think she wants her tea. Did Mrs Morton like the pattern we'd done?'

'I'll tell you while she feeds.'

'I'll make us some tea too.' Bella never ceased to be conscious of the wonder of being part of a family, sharing moments of easy companionship with the first woman she'd ever called Mum, helping look after 'their baby'. 'Kettle's nearly boiling, so I'll run upstairs with your hat and coat while you see to her.'

Unbuttoning her blouse, Lydia automatically felt her breasts, still so small that she marvelled at her ability to sustain fast-growing Sam. They felt hard and overfull, reminding her how long she'd been out. She picked Sam up, then pulled the low, nursing chair nearer to the kitchen range. Even before she sat down, instinct had guided the tiny mouth to its goal. Lydia clenched her teeth, feeling the pull on her stretched nipple, aching for something yet she knew not what. Knew not? Or wouldn't let herself admit.

'Just hark at her, Mum,' Bella laughed, coming back into the room. 'Didn't I tell you she was starving?' Lydia laughed too, giving no hint of the yearning ache that gripped her. 'Good, the kettle's boiling. I'll make the tea, then you can tell me all about your afternoon.'

It was an easy, companionable relationship, rooted in their early acquaintance at the orphanage, nurtured in the first months together then brought on to a new plane by their experience on that September day when Sam had made her impatient entry into the world. Now there was an extra bond: the business they were starting to build.

So the months went by. Sam proved to be a joy to both of them, the helplessness of early infancy giving way to the making of a personality. Still there was nothing of Christian in her, but time and again Lydia looked at her and seemed to see Sophie in some nuance of expression or manner. She'd never have Sophie's dainty build; even as a baby, Sam's long body, her slender hands and feet, were inherited from her mother. But surely it was from genes she shared with Sophie that she knew just the way to hold her head when an admirer looked into the perambulator, just the way to smile showing her new teeth, just the way to chortle.

Pushing the perambulator back down the bumpy lane from Winkley Farm, Bella frowned as she thought of the scene she'd left behind. How different the atmosphere was now from what it had been when she'd been living there. Was that because Edward Yelland was so changed? Or was it more to do with Sarah Phillips always being there fawning round him? Of course, he lapped it up, he would, smarmy bugger. And that was nothing new, he always had been too fond of himself by half, taking it for granted that his wife waited on him. It probably suited him down to the ground just sitting there all day long. And look at him this afternoon with his lecherous leers in Mrs Phillips' direction; and you can't tell me she didn't notice and love every second of it. Not that he could get up to anything, but then being stuck in that wheel-chair probably helps him to believe he could be no end of a Cassanova if he hadn't had the accident. And where was his wife while simpering Sarah was making sheep's eyes at him and he was trying to give the impression that if he'd had two good legs he would have given her what she was asking for? On her own in the sitting room, spinning the wool. It wouldn't hurt Mrs Phillips to learn to spin. But, oh no not her, she prefers to sit knitting, keeping him company. Then Mum pays her for the work she does! Things can be beastly unfair. Still, like Mum says, simpering Sarah may not have been any good making cakes, but her knitting is good, so I suppose we have to look on her as one of our best workers. Mrs Yelland doesn't seem upset by how things are and that's the most important.

Bella would like them to have spun their own wool, really *made* the things themselves. But Mum wouldn't hear of that; she said that would mean they paid less than they did for the huge skeins they bought all ready to be washed. Mrs Yelland based her profit from the farm on selling the fleeces already spun; it was more important to her to have the money than the time.

'And what do you think, then, my darling precious little angel?' she asked the baby, who concentrated on banging the side of her pram with her rattle as she sat bolt upright and safely strapped. Only alone and with a baby too young to repeat her words would she let the love that welled in her find voice. Then, making Sam the recipient of her opinion and voicing her thoughts aloud, 'Tell you what I think—I think the last thing I'd want is to hang around him all day long like that Mrs Phillips does. "Poor Sarah, been starved of love for so long," that's what I heard Mrs Yelland say to Mum the other day. Tell you one thing, if she is it's not for the want of trying. Not that he'd be much use to her. Too fond of himself, just look at the way he preens himself when she makes a fuss of him. No wonder Mrs Yelland likes to escape to her spinning wheel. But it's not right, Sammy. He does *nothing*, nothing at all. If he were half a man, I bet he could sit in that low chair in front of the wheel and spin as easy as she can. But him! He'd rather lap up the goggle-eyed looks simpering Sarah chucks at him. One thing, he can't do much harm stuck in his wheelchair. Tell you what, though, you and Mum and me, we're better off as we are.' Down the hill they went, Bella steering the pram to avoid the worst of the ruts even though Sam seemed to enjoy what was something of a switchback ride. Once in the valley that divided the two houses, the land levelled. But not for long. Soon they were on their way up the other side. Bella bent forward: a pram on a steep hill needed all her strength. But of course Sam was too young to understand; to her it seemed natural that a face coming closer meant some form of fun. So she chortled her pleasure, until she realised that Bella wasn't smiling back at her.

'Men! Selfish lot, they are. Just think of that Christian, our father. We're better without him. But Sam, Mum isn't daft and she thinks the sun shines out of his arse. That's what Norah would have said. And over some things Norah wasn't daft either. When you get big like me, what will you think about him? Of course we'll never be able to tell you the whole truth, we'll have to stick to the story that Mum's husband ran off with someone else before he knew she was expecting you. The real truth is something only Mum and me share—and him, I suppose, although he didn't know about *you* either.' She sighed and stopped walking, partly because she was out of breath (the result of all this talking and pushing at the same time). 'I'll tell you something funny, Sam—I can say it to you because you won't be able to tell Mum. When I was with Norah—cor, but that seems like looking back at someone else's life—back then, I honestly hoped I'd never set eyes on the rotten sod who could walk out when he knew I was expected. But since then, living with Mum who'd never hear a bad word against him, you know what I wish? I wish I could have a peep at him. I just want to make up my own mind. Not that it would make any difference: he doesn't want us, not her, not me and even though he doesn't know about you, not you either. Norah must have been right. But Mum isn't daft. Oh yes, and of course there was Sophie too, he left her. But from what I heard that night—not that Mum ever talks about it— I reckon she wasn't the same as most women. If she'd been made the same as other people, you know—well, you don't, but you will when you get bigger—stayed in love with him instead of falling for that woman they call Dulcie someone-or-other, then all our lives might have been different. You wouldn't be here, I'd be—dunno where I'd be, free of that orphanage dump by now, trying to earn a few bob to keep myself. And Mum? I reckon she's happier as she is, even though he did do the dirty on her. We're going to make a really good go of what we're doing. You just see if we don't.'

With new strength she plodded on, stopping when they rounded the bend in the lane and Badgers' Holt came into view.

'Phew!' A sound that combined breathlessness with wonder. Work had started on extending the outbuildings where, more than a year ago, electricity had been carried from the house and dyeing vats installed. So far all their garments had been made by hand, but as soon as the building work was complete knitting machines were to be installed and full-time workers engaged. In the beginning there would only be three machines, but often she and Lydia looked ahead to the day they neither of them doubted, a time when the garments produced under their Naturally Beautiful label would find a place in high-class retail outlets across the country. Dreams cost nothing, they bolster many a monotonous life; but combine them with determination and they can become reality. Other people made the garments, but no one other than they themselves created the shades of colour, prepared the wool, worked out the patterns the outworkers used. And so it would be when the new buildings hummed with the sound of machines. There were some things that would have to be done by hand: the machines only made flat pieces of knitted material which then had to be hand-finished.

'Here we are, home again, Sammy,' she told the adored baby as she pushed the pram through the gate.

Lydia had been working in the old carriage house, keeping a watchful eye out for them.

'Bella, I've been experimenting,' she called through the open door. 'We may think of a better way of doing it, but this is a trial run. I'm making rainbow wool. Just think how good it would look in sets of berets, scarves and gloves. Hand-made of course, they would have to be. Come and see.'

She had re-skeined the undyed wool into something about three feet in diameter so that it could be hung over each dyeing vat and a portion lowered into the liquid. Section by section, the colour would be taken up until the whole skein had been dyed, the colours blending. When the wool was re-washed and dried, the skeins would be wound into balls and sent to the outworkers, who would turn them into the beret, scarf and glove sets. Lydia believed that to break into the mar-

ket they needed something individual, something that soon
would be recognised as coming from the house of Naturally
Beautiful.

In that she was proved right.

Nothing happens overnight, at least not when it has to
grow from a small beginning. It was in 1928 she had the
inspiration to produce her rainbow sets. Certainly they
were in the country stockists in the West Country by the
following winter, but it took far longer for her to achieve
her goal and send her first batch to London. And in the
wake of the rainbow sets came acceptance of Naturally
Beautiful machine-knitted garments, their colours and their
style setting them apart from the factory-produced
knitwear of the high street department stores. The county
magazines carried their advertisement: 'The gifts of nature,
skills learned over centuries, the style and artistry of
today's world, combining to produce garments unmistak-
ably from the house of Naturally Beautiful.' On the first
day of each month, when the copy of the glossy magazine
was delivered to Badgers' Holt, the first thing Bella did was
flick through the pages to find it. The wonder of it never
ceased to thrill her. The same advertisement was carried
each week in the *Deremouth News*, but that couldn't compare with the quarter page in the glossy monthly, backed
by a picture of the Wensleydale sheep on the hills of Winkley Farm.

With each month their orders increased. Naturally Beautiful had become established, the label a symbol of quality
and style. It would never be a household name: the prices
were as high as their quality demanded, but in those first few
years its roots became solidly established.

* * *

'The boy's brought the local paper, Mum,' Bella called as she heard it drop through the letterbox on an August Friday morning in 1930.

'See if our advert is in. I hope we get some applicants, I'd like us to be able to put those three new machines into use as soon as they are delivered.'

Turning to the Situations Vacant column on the back page, Bella saw what she was looking for. Set out from the rest by its heavy print, it would be sure to attract attention. Being five or six miles out of town, labour was always a problem. Women wanted work, home knitters were keen to earn, home assemblers—skilled and talented needlewomen who made up the separate knitted pieces and sewed in the 'Produced by Naturally Beautiful' labels—could be found too, although in both cases it usually meant that Lydia had to put her newly acquired skill of driving into practice to deliver, collect and pay the wages. She and Bella were perfect partners: they shared everything they did, from looking after Sam (a labour of love) to dyeing and washing wool, to delivering and collecting from outworkers, Bella from those close by and Lydia from further afield. In every respect Bella was quick to learn, and even though until she had come to Lydia she had been a stranger to home cooking, right from the outset she had watched Lydia, missing nothing, eager to help. So before long they were able to share the cooking and shopping, although Molly and Malcolm Lawley, a husband and wife from the village, toiled up the hill three times a week, she to take care of house-cleaning and he to tend the garden. By that summer of 1930 another link was binding them: under Lydia's instruction Bella was learning to drive the Morris Oxford. By that time she was as strikingly lovely as one might expect a daughter of Christian's to be.

'I'll take the grocery order down to Mr Hopkins if you like. Sam can come with me. Then you'll be on hand in case anyone is keen enough to telephone you as soon as she reads the advert.'

'Small hope, I fear,' Lydia answered. 'But I'll stay in earshot of the bell just in case.'

'I's bringing Bunty,' Sam announced. 'Wait for me, Bella, I's going to put her bonnet on.' Bunty was Sam's constant companion, a lifelike china doll with real hair, her third birthday present from Clarissa, together with various hand-knitted outfits. The doll's pram had been from Lydia and the pillow and crocheted pram cover from Bella (although the making of it had been Clarissa's handiwork). Taller than most children of not yet four, Sam had much of Lydia in her build, but there all resemblance ceased. Her fairish hair curled prettily, her smile was enchanting (and, as if already she was aware of the power she held, she used that smile to her advantage). Certainly as child or woman, perhaps even until that day, Lydia hadn't the confidence of her young daughter.

While Lydia was writing their weekly grocery order and Sam was busying herself preparing Bunty for the outing, Bella flicked through the pages of the *Deremouth News*. There was nothing to interest her in the item about the new town hall to be built; the site had been cleared weeks ago on the junction of Exeter Road and Merchant Street. Just two words stood out. She felt that what she read must be apparent in her expression as, consciously, she made herself turn the page as if there was nothing there worth reading. Later, when she was alone, she'd read it properly. But for the moment the best she could do was casually carry the paper with her to her own room, hiding it in the drawer of her dressing table before she brushed her hair and painted her lips. Then, putting on her hat of fine Italian straw, with its turned-up brim, she ran back down the stairs.

'Me and Bunty's ready,' Sam announced. 'Mum's outside. A lady's come.'

Half past nine on the morning of publication of the advertisement and already someone had pedalled up the hill in answer. In a small community such as Combydere, word spread from one housewife to the next: working for the Mellors was a steady job, Mrs Mellor treated her workers well. In fact those employed by Naturally Beautiful were looked on with respect and not a little envy.

All that was to Bella's advantage. It meant that Lydia intended to be on hand throughout the weekend so that if any other applicants materialised she would be able to show them the knitting machines and tell them something of what was needed. That's exactly what she was doing as Bella and Sam set off for the village. Having discussed hours and wages with Dolly Hiscock, that morning's eager applicant, she had handed her over to one of the machinists to be introduced to a knitting machine.

'It looks more awesome than it is,' she assured the recruit. 'And, don't worry, you won't be pushed straight into making goods for sale; to start with you have to have time to feel thoroughly at home on the machine—and there are always others on hand to help you.' Her early doubts had melted; wasn't her prompt caller proof that she would be able to get the staff she wanted? Her mood of confidence was further boosted by the sight of the two girls setting off for the village, Bella bending towards Sam as the little girl proudly pushed her doll, both of them deep in conversation. There were moments, and this was one of them, when she felt a flood of gratitude for what her life had become. Yet, even after more than four years, those same thoughts never failed to be followed by others: Christian…Sophie…the void that nothing could fill. On that Friday, though, even though it was still before ten o'clock in the morning, the silence was shattered by the shrill sound of the telephone bell. Applicant number two and an interview on the following afternoon. By the time the additional knitting machines were delivered it looked as though there would be enough workers to use them.

'This one is coming out from Deremouth,' she told Bella as they sat at the lunch table. 'She sounded very keen, but I can't see her cycling all those miles each morning in the winter.'

'She wouldn't have applied without considering how far out we are,' Bella said blithely. 'If she's young she won't mind.'

'She sounded very keen to be employed.' Lydia looked and sounded anxious. There was still much of Kingshampton's Miss Westlake in her despite her more flattering hairstyle and changed style of dress. 'Imagine, Bella, needing so desperately to earn the sort of money we pay that you commit yourself to a good forty-minute cycle ride in all weathers.'

'Mum,' Bella laughed, cutting her jacket potato and dropping a wide slice of butter into the crack, 'you make worries for yourself, honestly you do. I bet you, when you talk to her you'll find that her husband comes this way and has a motor cycle.' Then, to Sam, 'Here are you Sam, half for you and half for me. Shall I mash it up for you?'

'She's coming at three o'clock. I shall see then whether

she has to bring herself on her bicycle. I'm sorry it's on a Saturday, I was tempted to put her off but she sounded so desperate. Your afternoon for driving; we'll have to go on Sunday instead.'

'I was going to say about that, Mum. You haven't had to tell me what to do for ages, surely I'm safe as houses on my own. Can I? Can I take the car out by myself? Or with Sam?'

Lydia hesitated for a moment. Suppose she let Bella out alone and there was more traffic than she'd been used to, or suppose someone else did something stupid and she hadn't had experience enough to think quickly and keep out of trouble?

'Please, Mum. It's only when you drive on your own that you feel you are really in charge. And I'm ready, honestly, I feel safe as anything.'

'If I say yes and let you take Sam, she might distract you. With two of us there we can hold on to her and stop her fidgeting. If I say yes, but don't let you take her, it looks as though I don't thoroughly trust you.'

'I only suggested taking her because I thought you would rather have your full attention for this interview. If you let me take the car, by myself or with her, either way I shall know you think I'm ready. And I am. Honestly, Mum. Please. I know we could go on Sunday instead, but by then the shops would be shut in Deremouth and I really wanted to look in Stebbings to see if I could buy some really thin stockings.'

'Promise you'll be careful. And Bella, if you want a proper drive, don't spend the afternoon in Deremouth. Why don't you drive out over Picton Heath? The roads are empty once you get into the countryside. You can practise your turns and reversing.'

Fate was playing right into Bella's hands.

'Good idea. As long as I know you aren't watching the clock and panicking that I'm in trouble, I'll not hurry. And I won't stay longer than I need in town, I promise.'

On the Saturday afternoon, the lunch dishes washed and Sam happily occupied parading her doll's pram and keeping up a more or less non-stop conversation with its occupant, Lydia watched Bella crank the engine into life, jump back into the car and, with a vigorous squeeze of the horn, set off on her maiden journey.

Once in Deremouth and the car parked by the kerbside in Waterloo Street—parked very neatly too, Bella told herself proudly—she made her purchase in Stebbings, then, just as Lydia had told her, drove on towards the Exeter Road. Merchant Street was a long and gradual incline, and her expertise in changing down through the gears, from fourth to third, then finally to second, gave her grounds to be proud. Then, as the road levelled out at its junction with Exeter Road, she came to the site where already the foundations were laid for the new town hall. Her one doubt had been whether on a Saturday afternoon there would be anyone there. She need have had no fear, the workmen were due to lay down their tools at four o'clock; until then the site was a scene of activity. But would any of these labourers be able to tell her what she wanted to know? Driving through the opening from the road, she turned off the engine and got out of the car. She would have had to be blind and stupid not to have been aware of the interest her arrival was causing, not a scrap of work was being done as some dozen pairs of eyes looked on her with appreciation.

'Is there anyone here in charge?' she called, trying to sound more confident than she felt.

'Him in the shed there. He's the foreman—or site manager

as some call him. Mr Griffith, that's his name.' That was the one nearest to the car, a fatherly, good-humoured looking man who had a daughter at home much Bella's age and didn't like the looks some of the 'lads' were throwing in her direction.

'Thanks very much, I'll go and see him.'

'I don't know, missie. There's a gentleman with him. Perhaps it's best if you wait.'

But Bella didn't intend to waste her afternoon waiting. What she wanted to know would only take a second.

Even in her early years, when she'd been the butt of sniggers and sarcastic remarks, when she'd been dressed in little better than rags, Bella had never been shy. Now her assurance didn't come entirely from knowing how good she looked in her Judy dress and straw hat, although she was much too honest to pretend that her well-stocked wardrobe wasn't an asset to her. So she walked, head high, to the wooden shed and rapped smartly on the door.

'I told you, I'm busy,' came a gruff voice from inside.

Undeterred, Bella opened the door.

'Yes, Mr Griffith, they did warn me I ought not to interrupt you. But my question will only take half a minute.' Then, before he had a chance to interrupt her, she rushed straight into her reason for coming. 'I read in the paper that Mr Mellor is the architect for the new hall. I need to get in touch with him. Do you have his address?'

Ted Griffith's visitor had been standing with his back to the door, looking out of the window. At her words he turned.

'You want to get in touch with me? I am Christian Mellor.'

For a moment Bella was lost for words, a most unusual

occurrence. Then, drawing herself to her full five foot four inches, she inclined her head in something like regal acknowledgement of his statement. Only silently, and springing straight from the past, did an inner voice say 'Cor, 'struth, it's *him*! I'm daft, coming here. Suppose I muck things up for us all. Mum's all right as she is. We're all of us all right. I ought to have let well alone. I'm not the only kid who's grown up not knowing her father. Just plain selfish of me, coming chasing after him. Slippery, cheating bugger. Was Norah right? My Dad—and just look at him, smart and dandy as can be.' Even as those sentiments chased each other through her mind, she answered him in a voice of cool politeness, nothing more and nothing less. 'I'd like to speak to you privately, Mr Mellor, but I can see that you and Mr Griffith are busy. I have my car parked off the road here, I'll sit in it and wait until you're free.' How grand it sounded: '… my car parked…' The statement did much to restore her flagging certainty.

'I'll be with you in just a minute, Miss…?'

She pretended not to hear the question. When she dropped her bombshell she didn't need the site manager to be there to hear. So she walked back to the waiting car, glancing neither left nor right. All her life she had wondered about him, the image of him in her early years based on Norah's 'slippery bugger'. Then she had heard Lydia's opinion, one so different. Lydia had been so emphatic that he was no such thing and that having him as her father should be a matter for pride. Pride that he'd thrown them all aside and gone off with some floozy called Dulcie? But it was ages since he'd been mentioned at all at home. Mum was engrossed in Naturally Beautiful—that and being a family. And that's what they were—a complete family. Now she was risking all that contentment just because she had—yes, that was the truth, she simply *had*—to meet him and form her own opinion. As for needing him to care about her, or her about him, that didn't come into the picture; she was meeting him so that she could lay a ghost to rest.

'Here I am.' Christian's voice cut into her thoughts. 'May I get in and sit while we talk?' Oh yes, he had charm as well as good looks. Poor Mum, living such a narrow life in Kingshampton, no wonder she fell in love with him; so too, most probably, had every other woman he'd decided to have fun with. The thought helped her to whip up the anger she needed.

'Yes, get in and close the door. We don't need to entertain the workmen.' In her tone she heard the asperity of a prudish schoolmarm. A pause while he did as she said, a pause long enough for her confidence to grow at the same pace as her anger: 'You asked me my name. It's Mellor. Naturally it's the same as yours.' As she spoke she turned in her seat so that her gaze held his, two pairs of eyes so alike.

From the moment Lydia had seen her she had known her to be Christian's child. Now, as they silently sized each other up, they were drawn as if by some invisible cord. Had he known from the moment she'd walked into the foreman's site office? No, it wasn't possible. And yet he felt no sense of shock. In truth he wasn't sure what he felt. For the first years of her life he'd given her no thought at all. Then had come Lyddy, Lyddy with her plan that they could be a family. That's how it could have been if he hadn't been such a fool. So had someone else adopted her? Hardly likely, adoptive parents look for babies, not girls old enough to earn their own living. So what had she been doing since she left the orphanage, how was it she looked so prosperous?

'When I read in the paper that you were the architect they'd used for the new town hall, I knew it was my chance to see you. You don't know, do you—and you have never cared either—what it's like not to be able to see for yourself what sort of a man your father is. Mum said I ought to be proud—'

'Norah said *that*?'

'Norah? Not likely, she didn't. A slippery bugger, that's what she said.'

'Mum? Who…?' His mouth felt dry. After all these years, after every road he'd followed in his search had lead to the same dead end, at last dare he hope? 'You mean Lyddy? Sybella—isn't that what you were called?—are you saying that the orphanage let her adopt you, that even when she believed I'd gone she still went ahead?'

'Don't know why I came here. I oughtn't to have come. Mum, Sam and me, we're fine as we are. She never even mentions you, hasn't done for years. Then I have to go and mess everything up. She told me in the beginning that if I knew you I'd know that Norah had been wrong. Well, now I've met you. And I'm no better off. I'm supposed to be out having a drive in the country. You see what you've made me do? You've made me tell lies to her. Still,' what a joy it was to speak to him in that sneering voice, a joy and yet a pain, 'lies don't mean anything to you, do they? You use them any time it suits you. You lied to her, made her believe that you were going to be family with her and me. Tell you one thing, for a bit I expect she felt let down, but as far as I'm concerned I'm glad you left us alone. We're doing fine, her and Sam and me.'

'Sybella—'

'Don't call me that stupid name. I'm Bella. When Mum fetched me out of the home she gave me a proper new beginning. Bella Mellor, that's what I'm called.'

'Why not Bella Westlake?'

She'd fallen into a trap of her own making. Until that moment she had never queried why Lydia hadn't chosen to be Mrs Westlake with her daughters.

'You say you're fine. So tell me about yourselves. What are you doing in Deremouth? I knew she'd left Kingshampton.' His manner changed, he spoke so earnestly that she found it difficult to harden her heart to him. 'Bella, I've followed so many false roads looking for her. After that weekend I went back to Kingshampton. I had no right to expect her to be there waiting. It doesn't make it any better to say that she always had been. But this time the house was shut. I went to Sophie—oh yes, I'd walked out on her, I'd played games with Dulcie—'

'But who *was* Dulcie? Sophie was in a dreadful state because Dulcie had gone off with you.'

'Dulcie lived with Sophie.' He didn't elaborate. 'When she went, Sophie was alone.'

'Well, she needn't have been. Mum tried to persuade her to come away with us, but she carried on as if she was the only one to be hard done by, made a dreadful scene when she brought the letter to show Mum what Dulcie had written about you and her running off together. She said hateful things to Mum. And now look at me, sitting here talking about it to you, to *you* of all people. It's like Norah said, you are a rotten sod, you use people just for your own amusement. You even ran out on this Dulcie woman. Norah, Sophie, Mum, Dulcie—and lots more, I expect. You know what I think? I think you're all the things Norah said.' So why did she feel so churned up with misery and disappointment? She'd known what he was before she came; she hadn't expected him to be the man to be proud of that Lydia had tried to make her believe.

'I expect you're right.' His voice sounded flat and tired and when he turned to look at her she felt uncomfortably moved by the desolation she read in his eyes. 'But, hear just one thing that I swear is the truth. Just once in my life I have known—' for a second he floundered, searching for a way to make her understand, 'I have known the *rightness* of what I did. Don't ask me why. Throw all the abuse you like at me for the Dulcie incident, although it was hardly worthy of the name, and for all the other affairs I suppose I've amused myself with. Norah was right in a lot she said about me.' Silence fell between them, both following their own thoughts. Bella, sitting there by her father's side, talking not as parent and child but as two adult human beings; she wanted to hate him, surely that would free her of the dream that had always been deep in her heart. Christian, strangely touched by this girl he'd scarcely given a thought to; now in those few moments of honesty he was aware of a tie that had nothing to do with time. 'I have only ever loved one woman. I call her Lyddy, you call her Mum.'

'Then what the hell did you do it for?' It seemed the years with Norah hadn't been shed as thoroughly as it had seemed. 'What did you have to bugger everything up for? Mum brought me home from that hell-hole of a dump, we got a lovely supper ready, then Sophie turned up with a letter she'd got from this Dulcie saying she was going off with you. That's why I hate you, that's why I don't want you for my father.' It would have been so easy to burst into self-indulgent tears; then she pictured Lydia and the image helped her to overcome her momentary weakness. 'Mum's a million times too good for you.'

'I know that. Tell me, why did you come here today, Bella?'

'Because I'm stupid, that's why,' she answered belligerently. But by now she was in control, her voice was strong again. 'I never felt I belonged to Norah, that's the truth. So I suppose that's why I've sort of made a picture in my mind of a father, even though she told me you were rotten and didn't care about what happened to me. Oh, don't worry, my dream father wasn't like you. Anyway, like I told you, me and Mum and Sam, we're enough for each other. And you needn't worry that I'm chasing after you for anything, like I know Norah did before she miked off and left me. We're doing really well. You won't have heard of us, we don't do men's things, but we make the most heavenly woollen fashions, real top notch.' Such pride shone in her dark brown eyes.

'You mean you knit?'

'We don't, not Mum and me. We run the company and it's getting bigger and better all the time.' Then, as if she realised how near she was coming to relaxing with him, she pulled herself in check. 'Still, I'm not going to discuss our business affairs, they don't concern you,' she said, making herself as rude as possible. A little wiser and more experienced, she might have known a better way of handling him.

'And you trade as Westlake—or Mellor?'

'Nothing so boring. Our label is Naturally Beautiful; that's because we make all our own dyes from natural sources.'

'And this business is in Deremouth?'

'No. Anyway, I told you, I'm not discussing Mum's affairs with you. You treated her badly and I didn't come here to make friends with you, I came to tell you that what Norah said was right, you've always been a rotten sod. And I came because it's so hard to know that somewhere you have a father you've never seen—a bit like taking a cutting from one bush and grafting it on to another. I feel rotten about this afternoon, cheating on what I told Mum I was going to do. Still, it's done now and I'd better get going or I'll be late and she'll start to worry. Tell you what, though: I feel mean having to lie to her about where I've been. Mum isn't the sort you can tell lies to—at least, most people can't. Still, you wouldn't know about that.'

'I've asked for a lot of the things you've said and I'm not making any excuses. How I could have been such a fool as I was with Dulcie, God knows.'

'Sophie said something about you doing it to spite her and that it was to spite her that you used Mum, too.'

'That was never true! You can think as badly of me as you like, and I probably deserve it, but what I said just now is the solemn truth: only with Lyddy have I ever known—oh hell, what is it I'm trying to say?—and why am I saying it at all to you, a child?'

'I'm not a child. And you may be saying it to me because I love Mum.'

He reached out his hand to take hers, hardly aware of what he did and yet aware just as he had been when their eyes had first met that the moment was important.

'What I'm saying, and saying badly, is that I'm not good enough for her, I never have been and I'm honest enough to know I never shall be, but she and I were right for each other.

With her I knew the true meaning of friendship, understanding, love—'

'But not faithfulness.' To her own ears her voice sounded prim.

'My heart was faithful, then and always. Bella, you are my daughter, this is an odd way for a father and daughter to get to know each other.'

'Ours is hardly a normal relationship. Most fathers don't disappear in a trail of dust like you did when you were frightened of being lumbered with *me*. Anyway, it can't matter. We're not likely to see each other again. I think you had better get out. If I hurry I'll have time to drive out over Picton Heath and into the country for an hour before I go home, then at least I shall have something truthful to tell her of where I've been.'

'I'll crank the engine,' he said as he got out and at the first swing of the starting handle the engine sprang to life. 'Bella,' he said as she slipped into gear, 'if it's not Deremouth, where is it you live?'

'Isn't it bad enough that I've deceived her coming to talk to you? Leave us alone. I told you, she never talks about you anymore, her and Sam and me are fine.'

'Sam—you didn't tell me—who is he?'

With inexperienced haste, Bella took her foot off the clutch and the car leaped forward before she had a chance to pull herself into control and remember her lost dignity. Looking over her shoulder, again with that regal inclination of her head, she left him.

At Badgers' Holt, Mary Giles, the applicant for the job of machinist, arrived exactly on time. Punctuality was always important to her, but never more so than on that Saturday afternoon, the day after her husband had brought home the news that he was one of three carpenters at the local furniture maker's who had been given one week's notice. Deremouth was no different from the rest of the country: unemployment was every worker's biggest dread. As if Fate was playing a hand, Mary had seen the advertisement in the *Deremouth News* and was determined that she would find a way to keep the rent paid and food on the table.

If she was nervous, one look at the woman she hoped would be her employer was enough to relax her. After the interview Lydia intended to spend the rest of the afternoon in the shed used for dyeing and, as she always did when she was handling dyes, she was dressed in a pair of dark grey slacks ('A woman in trousers! She looks more like a workman than the owner of a business like Naturally Beautiful'—the thought was reassuring), and a stained smock that might have belonged to a shepherd who'd cared for the Wensleydales whose wool she transformed.

The interview followed the usual pattern: questions, answers, each forming a silent opinion of the other and, in Mary's case, she finding herself telling Lydia of how her husband had lost his job.

'Are there just the two of you?'

'Oh no, there's Meggie and Peter, they're twins coming up to eight. But Mrs Mellor, I'll be as reliable as if there was no one to consider except myself. I know I've never seen one of these lovely up-to-date machines before, and I can see you must be thinking all I care about is the money. But if you give me the chance I promise you won't regret it. I'll ride up here on time, you needn't worry that I'll jib when the rain's chucking it down; that's not my way, honest it isn't.'

Lydia's smile was warm and spontaneous, transforming her long thin face. 'I wasn't doubting you. I was just thinking how difficult it will be for the family. For the first few weeks it will be essential for you to cycle up here every day, but once you've got used to the work and are thoroughly at home on the machine, how would it be if I let you have it at home so that you can work the hours to suit yourself?'

Surprise, relief, gratefulness: all these were plain to see in Mary's face.

'But why should you do that for me?' Then, as the suggestion sunk in, her gratitude touched an emotion she'd been trying to fight down ever since her husband had come home the previous day. Her eyes welled with tears, tears that overspilled before she had time to dig in her pocket for a handkerchief.

'I have had problems too, and like you I have two children—only one of them is grown up now and works in the business with me. We have to stick together, we women,' she smiled. 'And perhaps it's not the altruistic suggestion you think. As long as you have somewhere safe to keep the machine at home I have a feeling you will find more time to work at home than you would if you slogged all the way out here each morning. Those who come here each day to the workshop all live either in Combydere or Otterton St Giles. From further afield I have a number of outworkers, all paid piece rates. If you can give the time to it, it could be to your advantage—and mine too. I find it hard to keep up with the orders that are coming in these days. Things are going remarkably well.'

Mary Giles looked at her with something not far short of adoration. How could she have seen her as plain? Beauty was more than having a pretty face, hers was the sort of beauty that came from kindness and understanding.

The interview over, Lydia checked that Sam was safely organising her family of dolls under the weeping willow tree, then went into the shed where dyeing the wool in autumnal shades was already in progress. The system had been of her invention, although the blacksmith had been responsible for turning her brainchild into reality. The natural wool was wound on to something resembling steel bicycle wheels which, in turn, were attached to a beam which could be raised or lowered on a pulley. A section at a time, each wheel was immersed in one of the row of vats each containing different dyes, then, when it had taken sufficient colour, it was dried; then the wheel turned and moved into position over the next vat, where it was lowered far enough for the whole procedure to be repeated. It was a messy job and time-consuming, but something Lydia found satisfying. At the end of the row, the last wheel in place lowered to dip into the final vat, she rinsed her hands and rubbed them dry on the roller towel that hung on the back of the door. Often Sam would come in to keep her company, but today she must have been too busy in her make-believe world. Lydia glanced out through the window, surprised to find no sign of her in her usual shelter of the willow tree. Sam would never wander away from the sloping garden, but even so Lydia went outside to reassure herself that all was well. Yes, there she was, right at the bottom of the incline where the ground levelled out. The dolls were being treated to an inelegant performance of cartwheels and handstands, Sam's latest achievement. Satisfied, Lydia looked around her at the rambling house, the outbuildings, then back to Sam. She ought to be utterly content: alone, she'd made a place for herself, for herself, for Bella, for Sam. Of course she was content. So why couldn't she forget, why couldn't she be like Norah and learn to hate him for the way he'd treated her? Hark! She raised her head as she listened. There's a car. Bella must be home. She moved towards the open gate, looking forward to seeing the expression of pride on Bella's face as she drove in. Disappointed, she saw that it was a dark green coupé drawing up in the lane, then someone getting out.

It couldn't be! After all these years, why should he come now? It is…it is…help me, please help me to be strong. Don't let me forget what he is, don't let him guess what it's doing to me just to see him again. We're safe here, we're independent, I'd made myself forget. But she knew it wasn't true, she knew she could never forget, until the day she died he would be the centre of her world. Don't let him guess, please God help me to be strong, help me let him see he hasn't the right to come here upsetting everything.

He was walking towards her, both hands outstretched.

'No!' Instinctively she drew back, feeling out of control as she thrust her own hands behind her back.

'Lyddy, hear me.'

'Listen to you like I used to?' Don't listen to him, she cried silently. You've fought to forget. Don't let him know that even after all this (and in her mind 'this' encompassed Badgers' Holt, her business, the barrier she'd tried so hard to build between herself and the past), yes, even now all I want is to believe him, to be like we were. But she gave no hint of the battle that raged in her as she met his gaze and answered stonily, 'Believe you like I used to? Is that what you expect? All these years and you think I'm still waiting to be picked up and dropped just as you like. How did you find me?'

'Later. That can wait, Lyddy, I beg you, just hear me. All these years, you say. If you only knew how I followed every lead I could find that might take me to you. On that first Monday I went to Drydens, but you hadn't waited. I'd taken you for granted, you and I understood each other. That's what I believed. You'd always been there for me—

'Oh yes, good old Lyddy. Pick her up, put her down, see who else is available for your amuse—'

'Stop it! You know none of that's true.' Letting go of her hands he gripped her shoulders, willing her not to lower her gaze from his. Then, just as suddenly, the fight seemed to go out of him. 'Sam, she said you and her and Sam…Lyddy, you can't have married someone else. You belong to me, you always will.'

'She?' Lyddy was playing for time, the beating of her heart seeming to throb through her body. 'Bella? Is that it, did Bella tell you where I was?'

'No, she didn't. Yes, I've seen her. I enquired in the town where I'd find Naturally Beautiful. Bella told me to go away, leave you and Sam and her in peace. Damn him, Lyddy. You belong to me—I belong to you. How can there be anyone else?' But he felt the gold band on her tightly held finger. In all her life she'd never felt like this, frightened to look at him, almost frightened to breathe. Perhaps this was just a dream, one like all the other hundreds she'd had over the years. In a second she'd wake and find him gone. 'Forgive me, Lyddy. I'm probably all Bella says, but you know—you *know*— you're the only woman I've ever loved—I married Sophie knowing it was *you* I loved—'

'Sophie!' She cut in on his words, for a moment the thought of Sophie overriding everything. 'Did you go back to Sophie? Where is she? I've searched everywhere I knew, always it was the same blank.'

'So you know how it was with me—searching for you. It seems you Westlakes know how to cover your tracks. No, I don't know where she went. I told you years ago that I had no intention of divorcing her, exposing—well, we've been through all that. Lyddy, this man, Sam…you're laughing…'

Yes, she was laughing even though her eyes brimmed with unshed tears. There were no words for the joy that swamped all coherent thought. Yes, she was laughing as she leaned close against him and felt herself taken in his arms. She couldn't fight, she didn't even want to. Anger, misery, loneliness, fear too, all these were gone; all she knew now was joy and thankfulness.

Glancing up from a far from successful cartwheel and hoping her failure hadn't been noticed, Sam saw the couple at the top of the slope. Who was that man? And what was he doing squeezing Mum tight like that? She swallowed a dry lump in her throat, suddenly uncertain. Neither Lydia nor Christian noticed as the little girl climbed up the incline.

'Mum…?' She tugged at Lydia's apron, her face telling her disquiet even more than the one word. But it was a word that rocked the very foundation of Christian's new-found hope. Lyddy, *his* Lyddy, not only married to some other man but with a child. In the same second came another thought: with a child as old as this, she could have waited no time at all before rushing into someone else's arms.

'It's all right, Sam,' Lydia took the child's hand in hers, at least partially restoring her.

'Sam?' the man said, said it as if it were a question.

The little girl nodded. 'I'm Sophie Adelaide, that's really me. But we like Sam, don't we, Mum?'

Why was he smiling like that, a smile that looked as though it wanted to be a proper laugh, not the polite sort that you put on your face when you meet someone you didn't know?

'Who's he, Mum?'

Only for a second did Lydia hesitate, that's all it took for a thousand misunderstandings to be swept aside. There was only one truth: it echoed through her memory as it had time and again: friends, partners, true mates, lovers. How could she have lived through these years, how could she have made herself believe that she had a life where he had no place?

'Mum?' Again Sam pulled her sleeve.

'Who is he, Sam? He's your father, your father and Bella's. Your Daddy's come home.'

CHAPTER FOURTEEN

'You've taken the bounder back, then.' Never a woman to mince her words, Clarissa let her opinion be plain as she walked into the yard of Badgers' Holt just as Lydia came out of the workroom the following Monday afternoon. 'Nothing is secret in a place like Combydere,' she explained when she saw the surprise her comment evoked.

'Even so, unless the rooks carry messages, how did anyone know? And Clarissa, you'll soon know him yourself and understand. He isn't the bounder you believe.'

'That's as may be. He may be no worse than any of them, given half a chance. Just be sure what you're doing, Lyddy, my dear. You and your girls have a good life; you can see your business flourishing month by month. Has he come crawling to you expecting to live off the back of your earnings? And little Sam, she's never known a man about the place, how will she take it?'

'How did word get up to the farm that Christian and I are together?' Certainly Bella had taken a hand in it, but it was unlikely that she would have been chattering either in the village or at the farm.

'Word spreads around the village like a heathland fire. The

Lawleys were up here working for you this morning. You mustn't blame them for spreading the news when they got back down the hill. Your plight hadn't gone unnoticed, Lyddy my dear, you pregnant with the rascal's child and coming here to make a life for your family. There's a lot of respect for you in Combydere—and not much for him, I'll tell you that. Anyway, this morning I was busy doing my cleaning—trying to clean round Edward and moving the chair from place to place. Tutting and sighing at the inconvenience, I wouldn't wonder. Sarah suggested she might give him a treat and push him out. It worried me a bit, she's but a slip of a woman and Eddie's no lightweight. But the look on his face was a joy to see. I know he's sick and tired of being a prisoner at the farm. I'd take him walking myself if I had the time. I watched them go, like a pair of children let out to play, they were. Fancy, though, Lyddy, she managed to hold the chair back as they went down that steep hill and, even more, she got him back home again.'

'If he wanted to he could assist by turning the wheels himself.'

'Well, I dare say. But who are we to criticise, strong as a pair of oxen like we are? Anyway, it was as they started back towards the upward climb home that they found a little group of people chattering, and what more natural than for them to stop for a word. Such pleasure there was, Sarah says, when they saw poor Eddie. A fine-looking man, he never was anything less. And I take pride in the way he's turned out, shoes gleaming, a nice white hankie in his breast pocket, a flower in his buttonhole. To be honest, he was never one to care about those little extras, but I'll not have it thought that just because he can't walk and do things for himself things are allowed to slide. Still, I was saying…the Lawleys had just finished the hours they give to you up here and were telling the tale of this husband of yours seeming to be living here with his family again. Christian Mellor. Well, I could have told them that was his name, not that it meant anything to me. But it rang a bell with Emily Vickers and quick as a flash she put two and two together. Her son is working on the building of this smart town hall Deremouth is to have and he'd talked to them about the architect, Christian Mellor, being there on Saturday. Was Bella the young woman who came visiting him there? From the excitement the sight of her caused the workmen I put two and two together and decided that's who it must have been. With looks like hers, she'll create a stir wherever she goes.'

'I didn't know she was going there. I didn't know he was anything to do with the new hall. She read it in the paper and went to see him without telling me anything about it.'

'Poor lassie,' Clarissa said, thinking affectionately of the child who'd come to live at the farm, poor little soul, always ready to champion her mother yet deep down how her heart must have been breaking for the father she'd lost. 'Doesn't that just show how much she must have been missing him these last few years? I thought it must have been Bella. Paul Vickers told his folk about it, she caused a real flutter amongst the men, it seems. Not many girls have Bella's looks and manner. So she brought him home, did she?'

'No. She just wanted to talk to him. He came here by himself.'

'And you did right, do you think, taking him back easy as that?'

'I've never been so sure of anything, Clarissa. It's going

to take a little while for Sam to get used to having him around, and he'll have to adjust to having a grown-up daughter in Bella. It's been a long time. This morning he's taken them both out to Deremouth. When you meet him you'll see for yourself, there's a magnetism about him. Bella wants to hang on to her anger, Sam is uncertain—and a bit sulky—but she follows Bella's lead. And Christian will soon dispel any doubts.' She smiled confidently as she said it, certain that even after one trip to Deremouth the ice would be melting. Clarissa wasn't to be so easily persuaded.

'And you? Can you slip back into what you were five years or more ago, before you came here, before you tried your hand at business? Men expect their wives to be there at every beck and call, will he be agreeable to let you go on making your woollens? You're not a free agent like you were this time last week.'

Lydia laughed. She wanted to hug her dear friend, to tell her that five years or fifty could make no difference. She was her own person, she was no one's doormat and that's the last thing Christian would want her to be. Friends, partners, colleagues, true mates, lovers with a love that transcended every earthly bliss…they were all those things now, just as they had been in the past; what bound them couldn't be altered by years of separation. It wasn't in her nature to bare her soul anymore than it would have been to show physical affection and, if she had, Clarissa would have drawn back and been embarrassed. She and Clarissa were two of a kind in so many ways, presenting an unemotional front to the world. Only in the privacy of memory did she recall the hours of Saturday night, the miracle of the love she and Christian shared, and afterwards, lying close in each other's arms, how they had talked softly like conspirators in the silent house, talked of that weekend when she'd brought Bella home, talked of his brief and mistaken escapade with Dulcie, even touched on his wayward affairs over the last years. Listening, she had realised how unimportant any of them had been to him: they were no more than a game he hadn't enough power to resist. Hadn't she known right from the start that women would always fawn round him and that he would enjoy their flattery, repay like with like? He had no more power to resist than an alcoholic could resist drink. Lying in the darkness, she had smiled, certain in her acceptance that his superficial flirtations were no more to him than a game, a game in which she could never take part. The *real* Christian was hers and hers alone—friend, partner; sharing a love that went far beyond that quirk in his nature which lapped up the female admiration so generously showered on him. She was the only woman who knew and loved the man he really was. Those nocturnal thoughts flashed into her memory as she looked affectionately at Clarissa, but rather than put them into words she took the conversation back to where it had started.

'Why don't you share some of the chores with Sarah?' she suggested. 'Why should you slave away while she does nothing but fuss around after Edward? He's *your* husband, for goodness sake.'

'It's not easy to find words to make you understand. You lived in the house with us long enough to know the way things always were with Eddie and me. He never was a lovey-dovey sort of man. You know, Lyddy, in a way this accident of his has brought us nearer than we had been for years—perhaps ever. It's me he looks to for—well, for all the personal help and care he needs, if you understand what

I'm saying. I'm the one he relies on, the one he can take for granted. If I'm out he'll suffer in silence till I get home rather than ask Sarah to help him relieve himself. Poor Eddie, such a fine strong man he always was; now I look after him like I would a tiny child. And I thank my God every day of my life for the closeness it's brought to us. I doubt if he thinks of me as a separate being, if you can understand my meaning, it's as if I'm a necessary part of himself. Men! Puffed up with vanity more than half the time, yet when the chips are down none of that counts for anything.'

'I'm not suggesting Sarah should share looking after Edward, but what's to stop her polishing the floor sometimes or getting in the coal?'

Clarissa frowned, anxious to make Lydia understand something that on the face of it seemed to have no logic.

'It has to do with what I said just now about men being as vain as peacocks. Not being able to walk or work—not that Eddie ever killed himself with labours and I'd be a liar if I said otherwise—but he had the strength and ability. Now all that's lost to him. Now, me, can you see me fussing around him like Sarah does? No, of course you can't. But it's what he needs, it gives him a boost, it's a sop to his male pride. Oh, I'm not blind—and neither am I stupid. I see the way she looks at him, I see the way she bends over him so that he can rest his head against the softness of her bosom. Well, what's the harm? It was never the way he behaved with me, not even in the days when we were first together, so it's not likely that either of us would want it now. He needs to be made to feel that he's still man enough to be seen as attractive; and poor Sarah, if fussing around him gives her something to fill her empty life, well, what harm can it do anyone? I've put my bed in his room now, you know. We haven't shared a bedroom for pretty well fifteen years. Between ourselves, Lyddy, I knew from almost as soon as we wed that he had no use for a wife—not in the married way, I mean. I could tell poor Sarah a thing or two about Eddie if I wanted, but I see no point in upsetting her dreams. Eddie thrives on the amorous looks she gives him, he returns them measure for measure; from the safety of his wheelchair that's easy. He might even persuade himself that if he were a whole man instead of being paralysed from the waist down, he'd be able to give her what the poor soul is begging for. There! Now I've told you! I've never breathed a word of that to anyone. In the first year or two, even before he said he thought we'd sleep better apart, I remember how I used to butter up to him, something like Sarah does now. He liked it, oh yes, he used to encourage me and lap up all my advances. But, oh dear, poor Eddie, the sex bit, that just wasn't in him. Still, they play along with it together, and like I say, they do no harm. Anyway I was telling you, after all these years, he asked me to come back into his room and I'm glad to be there and take care of him. There are times where he has a job to get comfy, needs turning in his bed, sometimes four or five times in the night; then most nights he wakes me needing a pee. It's not Sarah he looks to for taking care of him; it's me. I've thought a lot about it, about him, about me and Sarah, poor Sarah. And not a day passes when I don't thank my God for letting me be the one to care for him. They say the Lord works in mysterious ways his wonders to perform, and I'd say that's about the truth. But what's got into me, talking like this?' She seemed to stand a little straighter, pull back a few inches, as if to distance herself from her sudden burst of confidence. In all the years Lydia had known her she'd never heard her speak so freely. Then, as if to draw a line under what had gone before and turn Lydia on to another path, she went on, 'And if you can tell me that one of His wonders was to bring your Christian back to you, then I'll be happy for you.'

'Then be happy for me, Clarry. I've tried, honestly I've tried with all my power, to put the past behind me. Misunderstandings, lack of trust, perhaps pride too, none of them count for anything compared with honesty. I left him knowing I could never be whole without him.'

'I thought he went off with some other woman?'

Lydia shrugged. 'Perhaps. But it wasn't serious. I ought to have had more trust. Some men drink, some men gamble.' She looked her friend squarely in the eyes. 'Christian has a weakness for women, he enjoys making them feel attractive—and I dare say he enjoys the way they make a beeline for him. But they mean nothing to him, they don't come near to the person he really is. Perhaps you're right, Clarry, perhaps there's something of the peacock in all men. We are as we are. You say a day never passes when you don't thank God for letting you be there for Edward; I can understand that. My own thankfulness isn't so very different. Women are a game that amuses him; he and I are united by something I can't put into words.' That wasn't true, of course, but the words were too precious and personal: friends, partners, colleagues, true mates, and more than that, they were lovers.

It was towards the end of September in the following year when an agitated Molly Lawley bustled across the yard to the dyeing shed. If there was one thing she dreaded when she was alone, working in the house, it was 'that ruddy telephone bell disturbing the peace'. Anyone in the house with her might have thought 'peace' an odd way of describing it, for as Molly worked—which she *did* with great energy—she sang lustily. One hymn tune after another proclaimed her whereabouts.

'Mrs Mellor, you there, Mrs Mellor?' Standing in the middle of the stable yard, she yelled with all the might of her lusty lungs. 'It's a man on the telephone for you.' Then, as rubber-aproned Lydia appeared, 'He did say who he was, but I couldn't catch it, so I just told him to wait where he was while I ran out to the sheds to get you in.'

So it was that Edgar Rumbold's introduction to Naturally Beautiful was anything but professional. However, once Lydia put the receiver to her ear and spoke clearly into the mouthpiece, his optimism returned. He knew it was a business based on the bounty of nature, but surely to have achieved even as much success as it had in a few years was an indication that someone must have a business brain.

It took all Lydia's resolve to remain calm and not give a hint of her excitement when she heard the reason for his call. As soon as he said his name she realised who he was, for *Rustic Life* was delivered each month to Badgers' Holt and regularly she read his articles. Now he wanted to bring a photographer with him and carry out an interview with her and with her daughter, whom he believed played an important role in the business. To Lydia the suggestion was evidence that Naturally Beautiful had risen from the cottage industry of its early days to a business fit to take its place in the fashion world, or at any rate the rural fashion world.

A date was fixed for the following Monday and that

evening there was plenty to celebrate at Badgers' Holt. Christian returned home, having been in Gloucestershire, where he had been given the commission of designing a concert hall; add to that the prospect of an article in *Rustic Life*.

'This evening deserves nothing less than champagne.' Christian viewed his family with such possessive pride that anyone looking in on them might have been forgiven for thinking that he was responsible for their success. Even Sam, a tall five-year-old who'd been allowed to stay up beyond her usual bedtime so that she could see him safely home, was carried along by the atmosphere.

'For me too?' she enquired hopefully, tugging at his jacket. 'If it's special it's got to be for me too.'

'Indeed it has,' he agreed, rumpling her light brown curls while she threw back her head and laughed in delight. Lydia watched them and thought what a lot they had in common. He treated the child in much the same way as he might a grown lady of promise. And as for Sam, charm was inbuilt into her nature.

They waited while he went to the dining room to fetch the celebratory bottle, brought it back and uncorked it with a pop that sent a shiver of pleasure down Sam's spine as she watched him adoringly, then poured four half glasses. A year ago she'd seen him as an interloper in the family, but soon his never failing magnetism had cast its spell on her. They understood each other perfectly, each responding to the other. So now, her milk teeth exposed into a wide smile of anticipation, she watched as into one of the half-filled glasses he added lemonade, into the other three more champagne. Her quick scowl told them that she hadn't been fooled, but she thought better of it than to push her luck. She knew that as it was she was more than an hour past her bedtime, so better a half measure of festivity than none at all. Anyway, something very exciting was afoot and on Monday a real photographer was coming. She'd smile her very best smile at him and perhaps he might put a picture of her in his magazine.

Three days later, a warm afternoon of Indian summer when the air was heavy with the scent of autumn fruitfulness and a haze hung across the valley, Edgar Rumbold arrived promptly at two o'clock as arranged, his black Humber car adding dignity to his untidy, middle-aged appearance. With him came Harold Bailey, by contrast a smart young man probably no more than twenty two or three and yet already making his mark in the world of commercial photography. Just as at that age Christian had dreamed of designing a cathedral or a palace, something that would still be standing long after he and his generation had gone, so Harold nurtured dreams of professional acclaim. Pictures for a magazine were a means of earning his keep, but his ambition lay in portrait photography. It would be in his power to make plain women appear attractive, and attractive ones breathtakingly beautiful.

He was thinking along those lines as he watched Edgar greeting Lydia and silently telling himself that he would be hard pushed to make her worth a second glance if she were to be judged by looks alone. And then he saw Bella crossing the lawn towards them. Was it just her looks that made him unable to take his eyes from her? Introductions over, the interview proceeded and, while they were talking, Harold watched from under the camera hood, occasionally taking pictures.

'While you make everyone some tea, Mum,' Bella said with easy hospitality, 'suppose I drive down and pick Sam up from school?' Then to their visitors, 'She's my five-year-old sister and she's over the moon with excitement about your visit. Promise you won't go before we get back.'

'May I drive down with you?' Harold suggested. 'I could take the camera and perhaps get a shot of the village, a sort of backdrop to the Naturally Beautiful enterprise.' The other three all thought a picture of the village would be a good idea; only he heard it as a feeble excuse to have a chance to talk alone to surely the loveliest girl he'd ever known. But then beauty is so often in the eye of the beholder.

That was late in September 1931. The article appeared in the November issue of *Rustic Life* on sale at the end of October. For a long time the delivery of the magazine had been important, Lydia and Bella flicking through the pages to make sure their advertisement—put in at considerable expense—was there. When the November issue was delivered all four of them gathered round to see the result of the interview, even Sam caught up in the atmosphere of anticipation.

That article, their first in a national paper, set them on the road they'd dreamed of. From local stockists of high-class country wear, in one mammoth leap they reached some of the most exalted outlets in London. Never would they produce enough to flood the market and so their label was held in exclusive high esteem.

If their new success stemmed from that Monday afternoon in September, even more so for Bella: it was the dividing line between 'before Harold' and the rest of her life. Not that she was eager to forsake Lydia's empire, but through that autumn and winter Harold arrived in his noisy sports car at every opportunity, more than ready to sweep her off her feet and away with him. It took a little longer than that. They married in the autumn of 1932, the wedding of Combydere's year, never before had there been such a gorgeous bride; never before had a national magazine sent a journalist and photographer to cover the event. As she posed outside the church porch, Lydia's mind took a backward leap to another wedding more than nine years before, and another bride, just as beautiful but so different. Sophie…closing her eyes, she felt herself carried back, she could see the trust and happiness on Sophie's face, the pride in Adelaide and Archie's, and surely the adoration in Christian's. Adoration is what she had believed at the time, she could almost feel her own pain of isolation as she'd looked at the bridal pair. Less than a decade ago and yet worlds away from life as it was now.

Memories were overtaken by another thought: what if Norah Knight read *Rustic Life*? It wasn't likely that she would, but Lydia liked to imagine it, she wanted Norah to see for herself how Bella had overcome her poor beginning. Would she be glad, relieved? Or had she never given a thought to the girl she'd so cruelly abandoned? Most of all, Lydia wanted her to see for herself that Christian had taken his rightful place, and father and daughter were together. At that point most women would have considered their own role. But Lydia wasn't like most women. Pure gold, Sophie had called her…long ago. Sophie…as the autumn sun shone on the bridal party Lydia was haunted by the memory of her. In all these years there had been no word; letters with 'Please forward' on the front of the envelope and 'Mellor, Badgers'

Holt, Combydere, near Deremouth, Devon' neatly on the back had been returned marked 'Unknown'. How could anyone simply vanish? It took all her willpower to pull her mind back from where it was trying to carry her. Today belonged to Bella and Harold; no cloud must cast a shadow.

The reception was held at Badgers' Holt, where more photographs were taken outside on the sloping lawn as the hazy sun shone on the bridal party, which included Sam, full of self-importance as the only bridesmaid. Christian was the perfect host, moving from one guest to another, collecting admiring glances. He was as handsome at forty as he had been at that other wedding. Watching how the guests were drawn to him, seeing his look of appreciation as he was introduced to Harold's pretty cousin, there was nothing of indignation in her feelings: simply pride, pride, adoration, never-failing thankfulness and a silent indulgent laugh.

'Mum.' She felt Sam tug her skirt. 'Mum, aren't we gorgeous! Will my picture be in the paper?' Indeed, she was gorgeous in her bridesmaid's outfit.

'I don't know about the paper, Sam. But, yes, we are very smart in all our finery and Bella looks beautiful.'

'And me, Mum. Harold's Mum said I look beautiful too.'

'So does she, Sam, she's really elegant in that lovely hat. Today, Sam, we're all at our best.' So often when Sam spoke it was like hearing an echo of Sophie. And why shouldn't they want to hear they were beautiful when it was but the truth?

'I'm going to talk to Dad,' Sam announced, disappointed at her mother's response. Usually she saw Lydia as the most comfortable person, especially if you were tired or if you'd fallen over, always the same, always taking care of her if anything was wrong. But Dad was more exciting to be with; he looked at her as if she was a grown-up lady, a proper person he was pleased to be with. Skipping happily to Christian, she slipped her hand into his, looking up at him with a laugh she couldn't contain. This was the most magic day she'd ever known. Lydia watched them as he excused himself from Harold's pretty cousin and moved off hand in hand with the little girl.

All that was a year after the interview for *Rustic Life*. The excitement of the article had long since faded into history, or so they must have thought as they settled down for another winter.

It was seldom that the postman had to cycle up the hill to Badgers' Holt with a midday delivery. He would have been tempted to leave the letter in his canvas bag until next morning but for the fact that it had 'URGENT' printed across the top of the envelope and it bore an American stamp. Turning the envelope over, he saw that it must be from one of the family, someone called Mellor like the rest of them. Hardly any distance up the hill, he got off his bicycle knowing he'd have to push it the rest of the way. All very well for them up there at Badgers' Holt, fit and fine they were he didn't doubt; but him, varicose veins standing out like walnuts and here he was trudging up with one wretched envelope, even now he was in two minds whether to turn round and freewheel back to the village. Had he been a man of lesser conscience, Lydia's afternoon might have been very different.

'Christian! Christian! Look what's come!'

As she threw the door wide open, one look at her was

enough to tell him that the letter she was waving at him was important. Nothing less would put that colour on her usually pallid face, or light lamps behind her eyes. His first reaction was to speculate what had sent her bounding up the stairs (he'd heard her coming, two at a time). An order from someone important, perhaps even someone with royal connections? A special order from one of their important outlets? His second thought was an awareness of how right they were for each other. He'd known it right from those early days when, clumsy and bashful, she had first been his friend. He had known it then and with each day, each month (and please God each year that lay ahead of them too), their need of each other grew. Nothing of the duchess about her appearance as she stood there in the doorway, clad in far from smart flannel trousers and the rubber apron over a sloppy smock that told him she'd been working in the dyeing shed; yet no beauty queen could stir him as she did. With no conscious effort on his part he was suddenly aware of all that she was, the generosity of her love, the passion that he alone unleashed, the intelligent interest she took in her business and his too. Those thoughts crowded in on him even while half his mind speculated curiously about the latter.

'Read it. Christian, after all these years, Sophie's written to me. Read it.'

He took the neatly written sheets from the envelope, realising as he did so that, except for when they'd signed the register in the church vestry on their wedding day, this was probably the first time he'd seen Sophie's handwriting. Pretty writing, but then what else ought he to expect?

Silently, he read.

'… At last I can write to you. In a minute I'll explain how I found out where you are, but I'm going to be very sensible and start at the beginning. When Christian enticed Dulcie away from me and when you, even though you knew what a scoundrel he was, never condemned him, I wanted to hate you as much as I did him. But somehow I couldn't; all I felt was misery. Then, so quickly, she came back to me. She'd hated the way he used her. Anyway, for us none of that matters, we are together and so we shall be for the rest of our lives. And Lyddy, I am utterly content. That's funny, isn't it? When we were young, I was forever wanting something I hadn't got, and you and Mums and Pops spoiled me as if I were a little princess. I can see that now.

'We came out here to make a new life and, Lyddy, I love it. It's so good to be able to tell you all about it. We are on the main highway and run a house where people can take an overnight stop. Dulcie is in her element: she loves keeping house and feeding them; my side of it is making sure everyone is comfortable, welcoming them into our home. And people like me, I know they do. It works well and we are making a living at the same time as enjoying what we do.

'Today I had to go to town to the dentist and that's where I saw an old copy of an English magazine. I'll never want to live anywhere but here in America, but I automatically picked up this copy of *Rustic Life* and that's where I read about you and knew what you have done with your years. It was just as if all my prayers had been answered. No, that's not quite true. I've prayed that I'd find out where I could write and tell you about us, but I never prayed that you would have been fool enough to get mixed up with Christian again. Mrs Mellor, they called you in the magazine, and they said your husband was a successful architect. I knew you had some wild idea about being responsible for his illegitimate daughter, but pretending to be married to him has somehow spoiled my pleasure in finding you. It's a crime to commit bigamy, surely he hasn't done that?

'I am his proper wife, so I am entitled to say what I know to be the truth about him. You used to talk down to me about him, as if you knew it all. Open your eyes, Lyddy, see him for what he is. He'll get tired of you and move on to the next. Don't imagine he'll be faithful to you just because you've always let the world see that you're besotted with him. Women (all of us) are nothing but a game to him. He's no good, he never has been. I know you're years older than me, but you were so naive when you got that crush on him and, I suppose, you were afraid you'd end up like every other spinster in the village. Well, surely that would have been better than the lie you are living now. The article said that he wasn't at home, he was away on business. I bet he was! And what female had he found to amuse him and pander to his vanity? You're too good for him; why can't you see it? One day news is going to get around in the village where you live that you aren't his wife, that your name isn't Mellor, even the business is based on a lie.

'Dulcie and I have talked about it and this is what we suggest—you ought to join us out here. Of course I would love it, and Dulcie is perfectly agreeable—in fact it was her idea. That bastard child of Christian's must be grown up now and can't need you. We three could get on happily. Break free of him, Lyddy. Think how Mums and Pops must feel if they know you are living like you are.

'Lyddy, I have missed you an awful lot. If it's just that

you're frightened of having no one to love, you needn't be. Think how happy we used to be. And just because Dulcie and I are—well, you know what I mean—you mustn't think I don't love you just like I always have. You and I were such good friends, but we knew that was just something to base the rest of our lives on. For me, life is truly good. You may think you and Christian intend to stay together, I don't know. But if—or when—he packs his bags and leaves you, you aren't his wife and you will have no legal claim on him.

'Write to me, Lyddy, tell me we're friends and sisters still. And tell me you're happy for me that Dulcie and I have found in each other everything we need, and promise me you'll think seriously about what I've said. Secrets always come out in the end and you'd hate the gossip and beastliness.

'Congratulations on Naturally Beautiful. I never thought of you as liking pretty clothes. You might send me (and Dulcie too) a sample, it gets mighty cold here in winter.

'Don't worry about me, I'm truly happy and the guests who stop over really like me. And Dulcie, too, she is in her element. So you mustn't worry on my account—but I am truly worried on yours.

'Write back to me soon, so that I know nothing has changed for us.'

Only when he'd finished reading did he look at Lydia, who had stood with her back to him, apparently concentrating on something outside the window. The letter was so utterly Sophie: it seemed to bring her into the room with them—beautiful, selfish, emotionally childish, confident that those she loved were put on this earth to make her happy. How different was Lyddy. 'Pure gold,' Sophie had called her, and so she was, that and so much more.

'Lyddy?' Then, hearing the unladylike snort she could no longer contain, he came to stand behind her, turning her to face him. 'Lyddy, darling Lyddy, has it meant so much to you that we can't be married? I never even think about it—'

'Not that,' she croaked. 'I've been so frightened…all this time I've thought about her…that last night she seemed demented…when I couldn't trace her, I was too frightened to imagine what she'd done.' Taking her characteristically unfeminine hanky she mopped face and nose, then looked him straight in the eye, 'I thought she was dead. There! Now I can say it, now I know it isn't true.'

'Why didn't you talk to me about it?'

'Couldn't talk to anyone. It was like a cancer inside me, growing bigger with every month, every year.' The luxury of tears couldn't be suppressed. 'She's well, Christian, she's happy.' The floodgates open, she felt herself drawn into his arms.

'And us, Lyddy? She has a right to say those things about me. I'm everything she says—except where you're concerned. You know that, don't you?'

Against his shoulder, he felt the nod of her head.

She looked at him with bloodshot eyes, their lids swollen, her nose unattractively red as she answered him earnestly, 'Marriage is a sacred promise, and I make that promise every day of my life. I always have, Christian, even when I thought we'd never be together again.'

He drew her head back towards him; he could feel her wet cheek against his neck. Moving his fingers into her loosened coil of hair, he was conscious of his deep love for her.

'My hair's falling down,' she said, sniffing in an attempt to regain control. 'Must look such a mess…'

'Yes, a complete mess,' he said, and she knew without looking at him that he was smiling. 'Nothing of the duchess about my Lyddy at the moment.' As he spoke, he was taking the restraining pins out of her hair, letting it fall about her shoulders.

'Better now?' he asked her, taking his freshly laundered handkerchief and wiping her face. It was a gentle act, in contrast to the teasing expression in his eyes.

'So much better.' More than better: often and often she had been overwhelmed by the intensity of her love for him, but today there was a difference. She didn't question why it should be, but she knew a sudden and glorious freedom. Sophie hadn't gone from her, miles could never divide them; all the anguish was wiped away as if it had never been.

From the drawing room they heard the clock on the mantelpiece chime, then strike. Two o'clock.

'I must wash my face and brush my hair.' There was nothing of the seductress in Lydia. Did he read the silent message in her eyes or was it there simply in answer to something she saw in his?

'Never mind your face,' he whispered, rubbing his cheek against her ruffled hair. 'I'll come with you.'

She nodded, her heart too full for words. She noticed how he took the telephone receiver off its stand on his desktop, the action speaking volumes, volumes in tune with the longing and joy that coursed through her veins. Now that Bella had left Badgers' Holt and Sam was at school until four o'clock each day, this wouldn't be the first time they had spent the afternoon this way. But today was different: for her it was as if she'd come out of a long dark tunnel into the sunlight. For her, loving Christian, following every erotic path with him, was always a joy beyond words, but on that afternoon it was that and more. The letter from Sophie had dispelled the one lingering shadow. As for what the letter had said about Christian, *that* counted for nothing.

Later, still lying close in each other's arm, she whispered, 'Listen to the silence.' They both lay still, the sun streaming through the window on to their nakedness. 'It's as if the world is standing still. Some people have so little; I have so much, it's quite frightening.'

'So much? That's not what Sophie thinks. And a good deal that she says about the way I behave is true; we both know it is. Now, at this minute, I feel certain I shall never encourage another woman to flutter her eyelashes at me, never play that game that has been so much part of the way I've lived. But I'm deluding myself. There's one thing I know to be the truth: that's all it is, just a game, it means *nothing*. Remember what I told you years ago; that we belong together, friends, partners, soul mates, all that and lovers too. Then, now and always, Lyddy. But I don't deserve it.' For a minute they lay there not talking, content in the moment. Then, taking her by surprise, he asked, 'How much do you care that we aren't married? If it's important I could petition for divorce on the grounds of Sophie refusing to live with me. And I will, Lyddy, if that's what you want. For me, it would make no difference.'

She felt warmth of the late summer sun on her body, a body just as scrawny, with no hint of the softness of feminine curves. She looked beyond him to the hazy blue of the sky while from across the valley came the sound of a sheepdog barking on the farm. That's when she remembered what Clarissa had said about men being as vain as peacocks, lapping up admiration and flattery. Smiling, taking Christian's hand in hers, she knew a sense of deep peace. Women would always be drawn to him—and he to them—but none of them would ever be more than part of that game he enjoyed playing.

'Well?' he asked.

'A piece of paper doesn't make a marriage,' she said softly. 'The things we have and share, the understanding, the trust, those are the things that matter. For the girls' sake I called myself Mellor. Anyway, if news got around that you were divorcing Sophie, even though after all this time you could get your freedom without using how she and Dulcie are living, it would cause a scandal, it wouldn't be fair on Sam.' Then, smiling, as she remembered, 'I think poor Bella wished your name had been different, Bella Mellor was a tongue-twister. No, don't dig up the past just for the sake of getting your freedom. The vows of marriage are between two people.'

She expected he would accept her answer and let the idea of marriage drop. Instead, he turned on his side, facing her and took both her hands in his.

'And this I vow, Lyddy: as long as we live I will love you as the partner of my body and soul.'

'And I,' she said, surprised that her voice could sound so normal when her body ached with emotion as her fingers clung to his. 'I swear before God that I will love you with all that I am for as long as I live.'

'No bridal gown for my darling Lyddy,' he said softly as he drew her naked body to hold her tightly against him. Then, laughing softly, 'No gown at all.'

With her heart so full of thankfulness, perhaps it was in her imagination that this was as sacred as any giving and taking of vows at a wedding ceremony. Their union was blessed in a moment of holiness. Those words would stay with her as long as she lived: '… the partner of my body and soul…'

'We are as we are,' she seemed to hear Sophie's voice. Revelling in the flattery of one pretty woman after another, taking pleasure in encouraging them, always the peacock in Christian would play that game. Lydia smiled at the thought. Not one of them would come near to knowing the real man; he was hers alone.

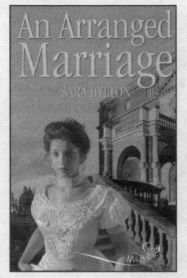

The bonds of friendship and family are tested in this emotional war-time story set in the Worcestershire countryside.

When war breaks out, the idyllic village life of good friends Sally Kennedy and Tessa Kilbride is over. By 1940 both their husbands have volunteered for the armed forces and Sally lands a job translating foreign radio broadcasts at a nearby listening station. None of them imagines how anything other than war could shape their destiny, but the advent of peace brings with it undreamed-of changes. Then a terrible accident shatters them all…

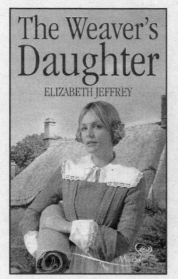

The Weaver's Daughter

ELIZABETH JEFFREY

**A sweeping
romantic saga
set against a
background of
Colchester and
Holland in
the 1580s**

When Anna hears her father's plans to marry
her off to an old widower, she is determined to
escape. Gathering together everything they own,
Anna and her childhood sweetheart Jan board
a boat from Holland to England. Heading for
Colchester, life is not easy for the young lovers.
With no money and nowhere to live, a perilous
future for Jan and Anna is certain…

www.millsandboon.co.uk

M&B™

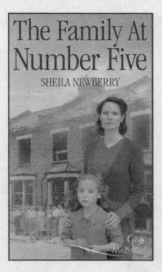

LONDON, 1932

Moving into Number Five, Kitchener Avenue, heralds the start of a new life for the Hope family...

Pregnant with her first child, Miriam knows it's a safe environment to bring up her family. For her fourteen-year-old sister Barbara, it means independence, boys and ballroom dancing. For Fred Hope, it's his chance to prove he can be a good husband and father. And with the birth of baby Glory, the Hope household is filled with joy.

But World War II is just around the corner and soon Number Five is more than a home – it becomes a life-line. Can they survive the war and be reunited as a family once again?